The Complete Tales of the Mongoose and Meerkat

The Complete Tales of the Mongoose and Meerkat

By Jim Breyfogle

Cirsova Publishing

2025

First printing: 2025

ISBN:
Paperback: 978-1-960381-39-2
eBook: 978-1-960381-40-8

Hardcover Cover: OSHRED
Paperback Cover: Chelsea "DarkFilly" Hopper, Colors by Raven Monroe
Interior Illustrations: Chelsea "DarkFilly" Hopper, Raven Monroe
Layout, Design: Cirsova Publishing

Table of Contents

The Battlefield of Keres

Two months after the fall of Alness (not that Mangos cares.)

It was, Mangos thought, the stupidest bet he had ever made. Not that it should surprise him; he had been winning all evening. Arm wrestling, bar bending, handstands, and a dozen other tests of strength and agility had seen him victorious—each victory bringing another tankard of ale. Small wonder his pride was high and judgment low.

Now he sat, head down, the morning sun angling through the inn's window to illuminate the table before him. His head hurt, his stomach wouldn't sit quietly, and worst of all—"I don't even know who Gorman is," he muttered to himself.

"He fought for the Duke of Endgras."

Mangos lifted his head. A young woman sat across and further down the long table, her back to the fire. Mangos savaged his memory, trying to remember her. Dark hair, torn clothes, yes, she had been playing dice last night – and winning.

"He's dead then?" he asked.

"It's hard to say anything for certain, where Keres is concerned, but I think it safe to assume he's dead." Her tone was dry, lightly mocking, as though this should be common knowledge.

Keres—that name *did* have meaning. The Duke of Endgras, Keres—he mulled the names and came up blank. He wasn't in the mood for ignorance. Glaring at the woman, he wondered if she was setting him up. What could a ragged, dirty, bruised little bit of a girl know?

The woman laughed softly, as if his frustration amused her. "What do you know of Gorman?" he challenged.

"You don't care about Gorman," she said. "You just need his helm."

"So tell me of his helm."

"A tough find," she said. "It would be easier if you just admitted defeat and paid for the tankard of ale."

"No," Mangos answered, not even needing to think about it. He would not give Thierry the satisfaction.

"Then listen," she said. "Gorman served the Duke of Endgras. He was

7

stationed near the center during the battle of Keres, but sometime during the battle he was lost. Had his body been plundered, news of his helm would be known, but it's not." She leaned forward, her green eyes clear and piercing. "Gorman's helm remains in Keres."

"Keres, battlefield," Mangos said. "I can go there." Life, since he had left Arnelon, had been less adventurous than he expected. This might be fun.

The woman cocked her head, "I don't think you have a proper appreciation of Keres."

The door opened, and the adventurer Thierry came in, all scars and swagger. Spying Mangos, he shouted, "Mangos! My friend! Do you have the helm? No?" He shook his head in mock sorrow. "The way you spoke last night, I felt sure you would have it already."

Mangos winced as Thierry's shout knifed through his head. "I'll get it," he growled.

"How long? I'm thirsty now!" Thierry roared with laughter. "Maybe you want a drink, too?"

The thought made Mangos queasy. "No."

"Good! Because there's no ale for you until you bring the helm of Gorman." He towered over Mangos as he said, more seriously, "Your tricks didn't impress me last night, and I'm not impressed now. You want to make a name for yourself—pfah!" He sauntered across the room and shouted for the barmaid.

Mangos ground his teeth, knowing Thierry shouted on purpose. Mangos knew he was stronger and faster, and Thierry chose this bet to embarrass him. He wished he had realized it last night. "I will not lose that easily."

He leaned toward the woman; he spoke low so Thierry couldn't hear, "Do you know where Keres is?"

She nodded.

He'd be damned if he let Thierry get the better of him, even if it meant asking this woman for help. "Will you help me?"

She didn't answer, just looked at him, sizing him up. Perhaps she was stupid or indecisive, but watching her face, he got the feeling she saw deeper into his question than he did. If she thought to rob him in the wilds, she would get a nasty surprise.

"Yes," she said finally. "I will help you."

"Good. What's your name?"

MONGOOSE & MEERKAT

"Kat."

"How soon can you be ready to leave?"

"Gorman's helm hasn't moved in sixty years," Kat said. "I'll take a few minutes to clean up. One should look one's best when beginning a project."

Mangos sighed. "I'll wait outside."

He blinked when Kat joined him a short time later. She had washed her body and hair. He looked at her closely for the first time and realized she was pretty. No, he corrected himself, if you ignored the bruises and torn clothes, she was *beautiful*. It was like turning around and finding your sister all grown up.

His headache had subsided, and he felt foolish standing in the middle of the road, ready to drag this woman on his quest to find the helm of a fallen hero. Perhaps it was the ridiculously small stakes involved.

"If you give me directions, I can find it," he said.

Kat rearranged the small pack she carried. "If it were that easy, somebody else would have found it. We'll need to stop in Endgras. I want to search their archives." She started down the road.

With two long strides, Mangos caught up with her. "I'll make it up to you. I'll—"

"Give me half your winnings?"

Mangos felt his face turn red. "No, that wasn't what I meant. I'll..." he fumbled for words because he didn't know what would be fair payment. He gathered his dignity and said, "I am a great adventurer."

"If you were, you wouldn't need to say it," Kat said. "Although," she added before he could protest, "you showed good skill, if not judgment, last night."

Who was she to judge his skill? Mangos wondered. He had thought she might be an escaped slave, but she sounded too confident. A gladiatrix maybe?

He kept wondering as they travelled in easy silence. Kat looked completely comfortable. She kept a good pace and didn't stop or complain. She seemed content in her knowledge of him—which made him wonder if he had said things last night he couldn't remember. Maybe she was a good judge of character. Maybe she didn't care.

But he liked her company, and he was glad she was there, even if he knew so little about her.

After passing through a couple of small towns, Kat looked completely different than when he first met her. She bought new clothes, plain and sturdy, and other gear she lacked. He was surprised, given her apparent poverty, but she reminded him while he wagered ale, she only took money.

She bought a sword, as well—small, to suit her size, but the best available. Mangos prided himself on knowing his steel, and she clearly did too. But when he asked her where she learned it, where she came from, or who she was, Kat answered with long silences. Since he didn't want to risk his bet or her company, he didn't press. Instead, he asked of Keres, and she told him what she knew.

"You said Keres was big," Mangos said as he chewed on a duck leg. If it didn't have wings, Mangos might have thought this tavern served rats. He had entered Endgras hungry, and waiting while Kat stopped at the archives only made it worse. "But really, how big can a battlefield be?"

"You could ride two days east to west and not cross it," said Kat. "And it stretched from the Karris Mountains in the north to the Balmis swamp in the south." She looked up from her scroll. "That's fifty miles." More scrolls curled on the table beside her. An extra candle sat next to her, illuminating her face, the scroll, and the plate of fried duck that sat between them.

Mangos grunted, reluctantly impressed. "I'm surprised they let you take the scrolls."

Kat returned to reading. "They don't know I have them."

"Ah, that explains it." Mangos picked up his cup as he thought of the crumbling city surrounding them. At one time it was one of the largest cities on the eastern continent. Its lands had stretched far in every direction—rich, prosperous, and powerful.

Now it was a shell, its strength destroyed in the Keres, ruled by others while its eastern lands lay cursed by the battle. Of the tens of thousands who once lived here, only a few thousand remained; bone pickers, scavengers mostly, who sifted through the ruins of the city for old caches of wealth.

Mangos leaned over the table trying to see what she read. "What have you found?"

"Not much I didn't know," Kat admitted. "By the end of the first week of battle, things were so confused that nobody knew what was happening. The battle lines had long since broken down. Messengers disappeared."

She shrugged.

"But it is known that Gorman was near the center."

"That's where he was when the battle started," Kat said.

Mangos didn't feel reassured. If they couldn't find Gorman, he would lose his bet. "We have time to look," he said.

"The Keres still claims victims."

The voice came right beside them, and Mangos jumped. Wine sloshed out of his cup. Without looking up, Kat swept her scrolls away just before the wine splashed them.

Mangos glared at the man who seemed to have appeared next to them. He looked…worn, if a person can look so. He had a long face, his mouth turning down in the corners. His skin and hair were pale. His clothes looked to be of better quality but faded. For a brief second, his lips turned up in what Mangos took to be an apology.

"Why do you say that?" Mangos asked.

"Adventurers go to the old battlefield looking for weapons, or armor, or magic. Often, all they find is death. They told me you visited the archives." He flicked his gaze around the table. "I see you took some of it with you. You're from the north," he said to Kat. "You're not," he told Mangos.

"Arnelon, I'm from Arnelon," Mangos said. He glanced at Kat. From the north? Maybe, she did have a little of the look.

Kat neither hid nor apologized for the documents. "Why did you seek us?"

The man bobbed his head around. "Boredom, maybe. Normally I take some small pleasure in the thought of grave robbers dying amongst those old perils. But you, my dear, are too pretty, and it sorrows me that you should perish."

She smiled. "Life is full of sorrow."

"True. Sadly true." He pressed his palms together and bowed his head. "But what do you seek on the field of Keres?"

"Gorman's helm," said Mangos wincing as Kat kicked him under the table, "would be nice to find," he added hastily. "But we're after Alazar's Crystal of Sight." Kat might have mentioned it sometime as they travelled. It sounded familiar.

"You won't find both together," said the man. "Alazar fought for Balmis at the north end of the field. Gorman, of course, held the center for Endgras, a dangerous position.

11

"Do you know," said the man, "artifact hunting is a very dangerous pursuit?" A kind of mad glitter came into his eyes as if the idea excited him, though otherwise his expression did not change.

Mangos did not answer, and neither did Kat.

The man stood motionless. After a long silence, he said, "I buy antiquities and artifacts from Keres. I buy them all."

Kat lifted her head from her scroll. "All of them? Nobody else buys any?"

"Nobody else employs street urchins with sharp knives and stealthy ways."

Mangos set down his duck leg. He frowned, but before he could do more Kat said, "I'm not sure if we're being warned, threatened, or just talking."

"Words are words," said the man, "and not to be confused with knives in the dark."

Mangos tried to puzzle this out. "Who are you?" he asked.

"Forgive me. I am Karl, dealer of historic artifacts." He stopped talking, it seemed he had no more to say, but he stood looking at them.

Mangos waited for him to leave, but he remained standing. Finally, Mangos said, "Why don't you hunt artifacts for yourself?"

"We all hunt them in different ways."

Mangos had no answer and fell silent. Karl stood, watching.

Kat returned to reading.

Mangos picked up a piece of duck, toyed with it, held it up for Karl to see. "Want some?"

"Thank you, no."

"Well then, off you go." He made a shooing motion with his hands.

"Karl. Dealer of artifacts and curiosities. Do not forget." He seemed to glide from the room. "Anything I said," drifted back to them.

"An odd man," Mangos said.

Kat stared at the door. "Odd," she agreed after a moment.

"How far is it to Keres?" he asked.

"If we leave in the morning, we'll arrive early the next day. It would be best to spend as few nights on Keres as possible."

Mangos picked up the cold, greasy duck. "I'm not afraid." His gaze drifted to the door of the tavern. "And I'm not afraid of Karl."

"No," Kat said. "You shouldn't be afraid of Karl." Whether or not he should fear Keres, she left unsaid.

The road passed out of silent, crumbling Endgras city into the silent, desolate country. The fields were a jumble of brambles and stunted trees. Here and there, a homestead anchored a small farm. Grey clouds cast an ominous pall over the land, but it did not rain.

Stone pillars that rose waist-high marked their way. At first, Mangos thought them marking stones, but closer inspection revealed some still had rusted mountings and occasionally the remains of gears and chains attached to the top.

"A polybolos," said Kat, "protecting the supply lines and big enough to handle a dragon."

Mangos shook his head. "How do you know this?" He had never been one to worry about what he didn't know, but he couldn't help wondering again about her. Her knowledge was starting to scare him.

"It helps to know things."

He couldn't argue that.

"The Duke's command fortress is at the western edge of Keres," Kat said.

When they reached it the next morning, the fortress was unlike any Mangos had ever seen. It didn't look like a fortress, in spite of straddling the road. It had doors large enough to drive a cart through and windows to light the interior.

"Customs house," said Kat, and once she said it, he could tell. The road passed through a half-barrel tunnel, heavy gates rusting to nothing at either end. Rooms for confiscated goods crumbled to either side of the main building. "They used it as an administrative post when the war started."

Mangos walked to the nearest door and stuck his head inside. Night's cold still lingered within the building, and a bit of its darkness too. Once his eyes grew accustomed to the gloom, he could see it was empty except for rubble and a thick layer of dust.

Just as he turned to leave, some words caught his eye. Scratched into the wall by a manacle above a jumble of bones was "Madness saved me." Whether written by or written to mock the prisoner, Mangos could not tell.

Wind whispered through the building, stirring the cold air and raising bumps on Mangos's arms.

"This says what I've been trying to tell you," Kat called. Mangos found her in the tunnel, pointing to the wall. Graffiti covered the walls, words of men long dead. Time wore away the scratching, so little could be read from the soldiers who only once passed this way.

Kat pointed at some doggerel that survived:

Should you venture past this gate,
Gird your weapon and hope forsake.
For Keres demands blood and gore,
And death shall feed it evermore.

"Keres sounds like a beast, not a battle," said Mangos.

"Now," Kat said, "you're beginning to understand."

Walking to the end of the tunnel, Mangos looked out over Keres, trying to imagine what it must have been like during the battle. A seething mass of soldiers, fighting as far as you could see, punctuated by fire and magic, so different from the quiet, undulating land before him. It would have been mud and stone instead of grass and scrub brush.

"'Death shall feed it evermore.'" Mangos snorted. "Superstition."

"Which is undoubtedly what is still killing people."

"What do you think is killing people?"

"Traps, stray magic, restless spirits, unbanished demons," Kat said, "and artifact hunters."

"A carnival of death," Mangos said. He tried to laugh, but a shiver ran up his spine. "What happened to the Duke of Endgras?"

"He took the last of his men and rode into Keres."

"What? He didn't come back? Balmis didn't send his head home?"

Kat didn't answer, and Mangos didn't need one. Together they walked out of the tunnel and into Keres.

In spite of the sun, Mangos sometimes shivered, as if passing through pockets of cold air. The feelings came and went, and trying to discover the cause proved pointless.

They travelled east, searching amongst the quiet, grassy fields and ravines. Artifacts—helms, shields, and rotting timbers of war engines— littered their path. Sometimes, rarely, they passed a cairn, something that said in the midst of all the death somebody remembered their humanity and honored a fallen comrade. But these were invariably pulled apart, their contents plundered.

Noon came and went without any clue to Gorman's helm. They probed deeper, sometimes stopping to scrape the thin soil away from an oddity only to move on when it wasn't what they sought.

Later, Mangos saw the sun atop the rim of the ravine they climbed and noticed night gathered in the shadows below them. It would not be long before it crept out to cover the entire land. They should find a safe place to spend the night.

Movement caught his eye. "By the gods of Eastwarn, look at the size of that beast." A wolf, tall as a deer, stood on an outcropping.

"The wolves grew large on the dead," Kat said.

Mangos drew his sword. "We are not dinner." It may have been the wolf understood him, for it gave a growling bark. Another wolf appeared, slightly smaller than the first. More followed until seven huge wolves faced them.

"I'm not sure you should have mentioned dinner," Kat said.

Mangos swung his sword one-handed as he pulled out his dagger. "Come, beast, we'll see who's dinner."

One of the smaller wolves darted in, head down, and snapped at his leg. Mangos slashed its head, but its thick skull turned his blade. The wolf retreated, bone visible atop its grey head and blood pouring through its fur.

Two more dashed in, one from each side. Mangos thrust at one, while Kat lunged forward to stab the other. The rest of the pack swarmed over them, snarling and biting. Mangos buried his dagger hilt deep into one, but its body still knocked him over and tore the weapon from his hand. He gripped his sword with both hands and rolled back and forth, trying to avoid snapping teeth.

Next to him Kat curled, the wolf on her back all grey fur and gnashing teeth. He caught intermittent glimpses of her as she shook off the wolf and thrust, driving her sword straight into the wolf's mouth and out the back of its neck. She slashed another wolf's hind legs, making it collapse with a yelp.

Teeth and tongue filled his vision. He raised his sword—the wolf was too close to thrust or swing; he turned his weapon so the wolf bit down on the edges. It worried the blade, tearing itself badly before releasing the sword and backing away.

Mangos stood, glanced around. Kat stood next to him, resolute. Two wolves lay dead.

Four others bled. The pack leader stood on the outcropping, watching. "Care to go again?" Mangos asked.

The pack leader lowered its ears and bared its teeth, but gave a sharp bark. One of the wounded wolves barked back, and the leader growled. The wounded wolf gave a little whine.

A chorus of tiny yips and howls burst from the cluster of rocks where the wolf had first appeared. A litter of pups followed, tumbling over each other. The wounded gathered around them, guided them up the ravine, nipping and growling to keep the pups moving. The pack leader snarled, pacing until the rest were gone, then vanished after them.

"How's your back?" Mangos asked.

"Fine," said Kat. "I think it just tore my jacket." Mangos looked, nodded.

"That went—surprisingly well," he said. "You—" He stopped himself from saying, "didn't do anything stupid," and substituted, "fought very well." They *had* fought well together.

"Thank you," she said.

"Let's find someplace to rest that doesn't have wolves," he said. "And we can look for Gorman's helm in the morning."

By the time Mangos reached the ridge, the sun had just dropped below the horizon. It lit the western sky, but to the north, another glow, previously drowned by the sunlight, backlit a higher ridge.

Mangos pointed it out to Kat. "Maybe it's a conference of spooks."

She snorted her disbelief. "I wonder what it is."

He grinned. "Let's find out."

Except for the strange glow, it was fully dark when Kat led the way to the top of the ridge.

"What is it?" Mangos said as he hurried to catch up.

"Not spooks," she said.

Several miles away, a column of fire rose to the sky. Flames spiraled up to where the clouds took an orange glow.

"A tornado of fire," Mangos said. "A firenado, but it isn't moving."

"Unbelievable." Awe tinged Kat's voice. She shook her head slowly. "The records didn't mention *that*."

Mangos nodded. "Most magic is tricks and sleight of hand. This is incredible."

"Dicing is sleight of hand," Kat corrected him. "Magic is something else entirely."

"That should keep the wolves away," he said. "Let's go warm our hands."

It took longer than Mangos expected to climb the series of ridges and trudge through the valleys. Finally, the firenado glowed above the last ridge, and he heard its crackling roar. The air grew dry.

Mangos wiped his brow, drew a deep breath. Kat caught his eye, smiled and pressed ahead.

"It'll keep the wolves away, I'll grant you that," she said.

The heat hit Mangos as he climbed onto the ridge, making it difficult to breathe. Wind rushed past him, drying his sweat, but not cooling him.

The firenado roared on the opposite ridge and bathed the whole valley in orange light. The ground reflected the glow back. Hundreds, maybe thousands of bodies still lay where they fell, mummified. Their armor had been burnished by the heat and wind. Nothing grew, for the firenado carried away all the dust, leaving only stone and hard, baked earth.

Mangos licked his lips. "If the helm is down there, I'll for sure need a drink."

Kat drew her hair back. "I don't—" her voice cracked. She swallowed. "I don't think it is. The center is further south."

Mangos shaded his eyes. "What does it burn?"

"Nothing, it's magic."

"It must burn something."

"That is a major magical disaster," she said, still staring at the firenado. "An accident." She paused. "Maybe not an accident, but magic done beyond the boundary of control."

"It must burn something," Mangos insisted. "Ah! It must draw its fire from another dimension. Somewhere in another universe is a whirling vortex of cold."

Kat looked at him, something like surprise on her face. He couldn't tell if she thought him brilliant or ridiculous. "Perhaps," she said thoughtfully. She turned to leave, but Mangos stayed.

"There!" said Mangos, the word scratching his dry throat as it came out. A pile of bodies lay near the bottom of the valley. Men had died by the dozen there, and that meant a hero. "That mound of bodies—who is that?"

Kat came back beside him. "We're too far north," she said. "It can't be Gorman."

"How can you be sure? I'm going to look."

Kat did not answer, nor did she follow. She stood, her face orange from the firenado as he turned to investigate the bodies.

The wind pushed him forward. The heat radiated so strongly he thought he could feel his skin redden. He stepped, with exaggerated care, over desiccated corpses. Everything he did slowly, deliberately.

He thought he heard words, but over the wind and the dull roar of the firenado, he couldn't be certain. It didn't matter anyway, he told himself, for the mound of bodies was … still far away. He didn't know if he should trust his eyes, for the hot air might distort distances.

He stumbled, and a few steps later stumbled again. The body in front of him grinned through shriveled lips. Its eyes had been vaporized. Mangos wondered if enemies had killed the man. Or had the firenado?

He blinked, and his eyelids scraped across his eyes like sandpaper. He couldn't think clearly. Why was he here? How had he come to be kneeling next to a dead man? What was Kat saying?

Kat's hair whipped past her, and she held up a fold of her cloak as protection against the heat. Mangos wanted to say something, but as he opened his mouth she lifted her other hand and squirted water from her flask. It went into his mouth and over his face, stinging his eyes.

She yanked him up, dragging him toward the ridge, only pausing to give him more water. He stumbled often, his legs weak, but she did not let him fall. Once at the top, she threw herself down the other side, protected from the heat and wind.

Mangos collapsed next to her and drank deeply of both cooler air and water.

"That's," said Kat, her words spaced by deep breaths, "not Gorman."

Mangos nodded and closed his eyes. He could almost feel them absorbing moisture. "Good."

For two days they worked their way south and east. Mangos complained of troubled dreams, the feeling of other beings crowding into his head at night. Kat admitted having the same feeling.

During the day, Mangos often saw things at the edge of his vision, but they vanished when he turned his head. He did not mention them because he didn't want Kat to think him foolish. They saw and avoided many hazards but did not find Gorman's helm.

"Here," said Mangos. "We must be near the center. This is where

Gorman would be."

The ground was flat but riven with cracks. At places they could see hints of the old road, at one point even the foundations of a bridge, but only grass grew for miles around.

In spite of being flat, the ground was lumpy and uneven, treacherous to walk on. When Mangos rubbed his foot across the grass, it pulled away. The soil was thin over a rusted breastplate. He took a step and felt something crunch as he put his weight down. Armor or bones, he could not tell.

"Heroes do not die common deaths," said Kat. "Look for something more than this."

Mangos nodded, walking forward, sometimes slipping when the grass slid off an old skull, sometimes crunching through rusted armor or weakened ribs.

He stepped on someone everywhere he placed his feet.

"Who's that?" Kat said.

Mangos looked up in time to see two men, unnoticed earlier, disappear in a crevasse.

"Thierry!" said Mangos. "He wants to claim the helm before us! The scoundrel! He's too cheap to buy drinks, so he has to steal our treasure!" Mangos began to run, not minding his footing. He heard Kat's light footsteps behind him.

Mangos reached a valley, somewhat deep, rather short, but well lit by the overhead sun. Thierry picked his way down the wall, his face obscured by a large shield strapped to his back. He was half way down, his companion followed.

"Stop, you thief!" shouted Mangos, only to be answered by laughter.

"Look!" said Kat. She pointed to the far side of the valley. "Gorman!"

A body in white armor lay under an overhang. It lay as though placed there, on its back, gauntleted hands folded over its chest, helm placed carefully next to its head.

"You thief!" shouted Mangos as he threw himself down the wall, scrambling to catch up with his former drinking companion. He took chances and moved quickly, but it was apparent Thierry had too much of a lead.

Thierry reached the valley floor. "You should be buying the drinks for me!" he called up.

"That wasn't the bet! We bet whether *I* could return with Gorman's

Helm!"

"Well, you can't because the helm is mine," Thierry shouted.

"A cheater and a thief!" Mangos barely noticed the small cuts on his hands from the rocks as he hurried to catch up.

Thierry reached Gorman's body just as his henchman and Mangos both reached the valley floor. Only then did they all notice the creature, an imp really, who sat behind Gorman.

It had dark red, mottled skin, short but wicked horns curling from its head, and claws that shone ivory on one hand. As it climbed over the body they noticed the other arm was truncated above the wrist, and scars crisscrossed its muscular body. It stood less than waist high.

Thierry laughed, and his thoughts were clear. It might have been threatening if it weren't so...*small*. The imp regarded Thierry warily as he approached, but did not run. Suddenly, Thierry swung his fist, catching the imp squarely and lifting it, slamming it into a boulder. It landed, lifted itself on its hand and stump, and shook its head slowly.

Thierry reached for the helm.

"No!" shouted Mangos. He leapt over a stone and charged Thierry. Thierry spun, shrugged his shield over his shoulder and drew his sword. He swung as Mangos neared.

Mangos drew in his breath, felt the sword tear the air in front of him. He drew his own sword.

Thierry attacked again, shouting for his companion. Mangos parried.

Mangos swung, but Thierry lifted his shield in time. "You're a fool," said Thierry. "Lucky to get this far."

"I," said Mangos, "will be the greatest swordsman the world has ever known."

"Oh, stop boasting," said Thierry as he turned aside another slash.

Steel clashed on steel behind him, but Mangos didn't turn. The sound did not stop, but continued rhythmically, with Mangos's attacks adding dissonant sounds.

Thierry sucked in his breath. "You'll never even be as good as *she* is."

With a twist of his wrist, Mangos caught Thierry's sword with his own and slid it down to bind in his cross-guard. He yanked, pulling Thierry forward. With another twist he bent Thierry's sword and freed his own, swung up, catching Thierry's shield and throwing it upwards. He swung under the upraised shield, cutting through Thierry's side, cleaving his gut, and out near his far hip.

Thierry straightened, but his torso kept falling back while his legs stayed in place. His guts cascaded out onto the ground before he fell over entirely.

Mangos turned to check on Kat. She sat on one of the rocks, legs crossed, elbow on one knee, head on her hand, looking bored. Thierry's henchman lay face down and clearly dead.

"That dratted thief!" Mangos said. "Now there's no one to buy my drinks."

The imp had crept back in front of Gorman. It hissed and stood a little straighter as Mangos approached.

"Step aside, little beast," Mangos said.

"He's guarding it," Kat said.

"Surely he is, and he can guard all but the helm when we leave."

"Suit yourself, but I'd leave it there."

Mangos laughed. "After coming all this way? Who would believe us if we didn't have the helm?" He stretched out his hand.

The little imp hissed, sounding like a cat, and took a deep breath. It expanded, kept expanding, growing taller and wider; skin stretched taut over massive muscles. It had teeth like knives, claws like scimitars. Sparks crackled between its horns, and a tongue of fire licked from its mouth. No longer an imp, a demon towered above them. Now it sounded like the roaring of a lion.

"Hey!" Mangos shouted as he jumped back.

With its one hand, the demon picked up a large rock. It held up the rock and crumbled it like a piece of dry cheese.

"I can take strong," Mangos said.

The demon blew fire just far enough to make Mangos move back.

"Hey, that's not fair!" he exclaimed. The heat reminded him of the firenado, and his mouth went suddenly dry.

"That," said Kat, "is a good reason to leave the helm behind." The demon rumbled agreement. "It's guarding Gorman," Kat continued. "It won't bother you if you don't touch the helm."

"Not the helm," Mangos said. "Maybe the gauntlets?"

The demon held up its hand and snapped his claws together.

"Not the gauntlets either." He sighed. He brightened up with a thought. "Well, Thierry wasn't going to buy drinks anyway." He sheathed his sword and backed further away.

As Mangos backed away, the demon seemed to relax. It tore off

23

Thierry's head, tossed it into the air and caught it in its mouth on the way down.

Mangos turned away and started to climb out of the valley, trying to ignore the rending and crunching sounds. He felt very good about not taking the helm.

"You knew it could transform," he said.

"I would stay to ask how the demon got here," Kat said, not admitting anything as she climbed next to him, "but I don't want to disturb its lunch." The crunching sounds began again. She smiled. "You can't win every bet."

"No point going back now. Thierry is dead, and I didn't get the helm."

"There's always treasure," Kat said. "Always adventure."

"We didn't even get the helm," he repeated.

"Our first time," she said. "We'll get better."

He paused, thought of the travel, the danger, and the lure of treasure. "Did you have anything in mind?"

"A jewel that was lost?" She laughed, shook her head. "Why ruin the pursuit with the goal? Sooner or later, we all come to the treasure we most covet."

Mangos grinned. "Then let us pursue without asking what we chase, and when we catch it, let us chase again!"

MONGOOSE & MEERKAT

Brandy and Dye

Four months after the fall of Alness.

Mangos watched the birds fly below him, their rich, dark red feathers in contrast to the white tops of the clouds. The sun shone through the hole in the mountain, illuminating birds and clouds even as it left the rest of Talhorn Mountain in shadow.

The hole couldn't possibly be natural, but there was no reason for god or man to carve a perfect circle five hundred feet across clear through the mountain. It existed as a mystery, sitting at the valley's head, but because it was on the edges of the world, nobody cared.

The plank deck of the rope bridge swayed as Kat came up behind Mangos. She paused to look over the edge. "Minix bird," she said. "That's what it's all about."

The clouds gave the illusion that the valley was only a hundred yards deep and dusted in cotton. In truth, only the makeshift bridge deck and rope handrails kept them from falling seven thousand feet to the valley floor.

"You'll not want to fall," a man said. He stood on the edge of a *holmen,* one of the spires of rock that rose from the valley floor. The network of rope bridges connected the numerous *holmen* with each other and the ridge that divided the valley in two.

"I didn't think I did," Mangos muttered as he finished crossing. "Are you Harlin?"

"If you're the two adventurers I'm expecting, then I'm Harlin." He snorted loudly, dragging phlegm from his throat and spitting it over the edge of the *holmen.*

"Mangos," Mangos said. "My partner Kat." He half turned so Harlin could see past him as Kat crossed the bridge.

Harlin scratched white dust from his hair as he peered at Kat. "You're pretty. You remind me of my sister. Except she wasn't pretty."

Mangos wasn't sure of the compliment, but Kat acted as though she expected it. She should, Mangos thought, for men always acknowledged her beauty but never showed any desire. He didn't ask why, though he sometimes wondered.

"You sent out a call?" Mangos asked. A call for adventurers with an offer of a royal reward. He liked the sound of that.

"You know what we do here?" Harlin asked.

"You mine Minix guano and process it to make dye," Kat said.

Harlin nodded. "Exactly. The birds eat the ridge berries." He pointed to the ridge dividing the valley, which was green with bushes. More bushes grew atop the *holmen*. Mangos could see red berries on the nearest ones.

"They eat the berries, and they," he looked at Kat and clearly changed the word he was going to say, "poop. We make the poop into dye."

"People want bird *poop* dye?" Mangos asked.

"The dye never fades," Harlin said. "It smooths the fibers of the cloth, making wool feel like cotton, cotton feel like silk, and silk feel like heaven."

"No accounting for what people will do," Mangos said.

"The color is absolutely unique, and the dye very rare," Kat said. "Only kings and emperors were allowed to wear it during the Age of Empires. That's why it's called Royal Dye."

"We make so little that we can't even fill the demand of the kings and princes of today," said Harlin.

"So what's the trouble?" Mangos asked.

"Distillers. They harvest too many ridge berries to make their brandy. The birds don't have enough. The birds eat less, we have less—" he hesitated as he substituted again, "guano."

"Can they eat anything else?" Kat asked.

"No. If the Minix birds eat anything except ridge berries, their guano won't make good dye."

"Huh," mused Mangos, glancing at the green ridge, down at the carpet of clouds hiding the valley floor, and at the spidery network of bridges the workers must cross.

"They've hired thugs to intimidate my workers," Harlin continued. He stuck a grimy finger up his nose and fished around until he was satisfied. He inspected the result and flipped it over the rail. "The guano dust gets into you," he explained. "Into your eyes and nose, and folds of your skin."

"Lovely," Kat murmured.

"You need to stop the distillers. Dyers have been harvesting guano from these *holmen* for generations. Now these distillers are destroying our trade. I don't care what you do," he raised his eyebrows, clearly conveying any option, no matter how gruesome, was acceptable, "but get it done."

The next morning, the sun crested the eastern horizon, flooding the valley with light and making the clouds glow gold. The Minix birds flitted around the ridge, dots of motion rising from and settling back into the green bushes. Smaller flocks ate from the bushes growing on the *holmen*.

The scrapers were already up, putting on their harnesses and tying to the safety pins. They tied their buckets to their belts and held their tools through loops of cord.

The clouds parted enough to see down to the valley floor. Mangos then realized how ridiculously thin the *holmen* were, and wondered that they did not snap from the wind and their own weight.

"Don't drop your shovel," remarked Mangos to a nearby scraper. "That's a long way down."

The scraper shook his head. "Can't get it. Wind'll kill you," he pointed to the hole in the mountain. "The Devil's Arse funnels the wind coming through it down into the valley. We're above it, but below the clouds, it'll take the flesh off your bones."

"Devil's Arse?" Mangos chuckled at the thought, looking at the hole more closely. With the sun lighting the face of the mountain, he could see the difference between the mountain rock and a massive ice ledge above the tunnel.

"You should see the snow swirl around in the winter," the man said. "The wind through the hole blows it back up until it catches on the mountain above or gets pushed to the side." He tugged on his rope, nodded to Mangos, and began to lower himself off the side of the *holmen*.

"That explains why they work up here," said Kat, "and not down below."

Mangos nodded, looking down at the barren valley until the clouds closed back up. "The wind must be terrible indeed.

"Do you think the distillers will intimidate easily?" Mangos inquired as he ducked back into the small hut where they had spent the night.

"No." Kat started to gather her things.

Mangos shrugged. It didn't seem hard to run off some distillers. Just drop one over the edge and the others would see reason. "Where are they?"

"Over by the edge of the valley. There's a small grouping of *holmen* close to the north wall off to the east."

"We can just cut the bridges."

"You do that and I'll not pay you a thing," said Harlin. Mangos started and spun, only relaxing as he recognized the head dyer. "You've no idea how hard it is to string the first lines of a new bridge."

"Might be worth giving up a few *holmen*," Kat said.

"No. I want every square inch of ridgetop and *holmen* for growing ridge berries. I'm not giving up a thing. Those are the terms. If you don't like them, that's too bad."

His tone bothered Mangos. "It'd be easier—"

"I can cut the bridges myself," Harlin snapped. "I'm hiring you because I don't want to."

Mangos nodded, not trusting himself to speak. He grabbed his pack, knocking over a pile of supplies at the same time.

"Ha," Harlin gave a short barking laugh. He kicked a small keg that had been hidden by the pile. "Alcohol. Not supposed to be up here."

"Brandy?" Kat asked.

"No. Just raw alcohol we use in dye making."

Mangos eyed the keg. It would fit in his pack.

Kat smirked. "Seems like a drunk man would be susceptible to flying lessons."

Harlin laughed. "It happens. That's why I don't allow alcohol up here." He shrugged. "Glad to see you're getting on with the job."

"I guess he didn't mean he doesn't care what we do," Mangos said once Harlin left.

"He doesn't care what we do to the vintners." Kat said, "as long as it doesn't affect him."

When Kat looked the other way, Mangos pushed the keg into his pack. Harlin would assume whoever hid it came back, and the person who did hide it couldn't complain because it shouldn't have been there in the first place.

He braced himself and swung his pack over his shoulder, trying to make it look no heavier than usual. "Ready."

The distillers and dyers were essentially a small group of men sharing the same dangers so it didn't surprise Mangos they were expected. Two men stood at the far end of the bridge to the distillers' *holmen*.

"You've no business here!" one called.

Mangos slipped off his pack and walked onto the bridge. He felt it bounce as he crossed. "We do." A small stone slipped between the planks and dwindled to invisible as it fell.

The man who spoke stepped onto the bridge, unhooking a heavy club from his belt. "No, you don't. I'll drive it into your head so you'll remember." The second man carried an iron-tipped spear. A third appeared from a small tent on the *holmen*. He carried a crossbow and immediately fitted a bolt into it then began to work the crank.

"Not afraid of heights, are you?" asked the first man.

"No," replied Mangos, unconcerned by the swaying bridge or the long fall beneath him. He drew his sword. If this was how things were done here, that was fine, though the crossbowman worried him.

The man swung the club back and forth as he walked forward, timing his swing and steps so Mangos had to parry or give ground.

"Keep running," the man taunted. "It's the smartest thing you can do." The second man peered around the first, not interfering with his attack.

"You boys need to stop messing with the dye makers," Mangos said, stopping his retreat.

"Not your business," the man said then attacked.

Mangos spun, lay back onto the rope handrail, and let the club swing in front of him. The rope creaked with his weight, and he knew if it broke or his feet slipped he had a very, very long fall, and the last thing that would go through his mind would be his ankles.

His weight shifted the bridge, pushing it away from him and tipping it sideways. The handrail now supported his weight while his body forced the bridge deck to a steep angle.

Kat cried out but grabbed the other rail and leaned into the tilt, somehow keeping her feet.

The man with the club cursed as his feet slipped, he fell, then slid over the edge. The clouds, which looked so thick, did not stop his fall. He plunged inside and was lost from sight.

The spear wielder fell, grabbing the planks as his legs swung toward the abyss.

Mangos's feet slipped from the bridge. He clutched the rail, felt it dip again. The bridge swung back and struck him in the stomach, knocking the wind from him. His right hand slipped; he wrapped his arm around the rope and gripped it tight. Now he hung from the rope handrail, dangling past the deck of the bridge, gasping for air.

Kat advanced past him, not heeding the bridge's movement. The last

guard scrambled to his feet, trying to free his spear, which had stuck between two planks. He yanked it up just in time to fend off Kat.

"Get up," Kat ordered.

Mangos rolled his eyes, afraid to let go of the rope to grab the bridge. His heart pounded, and he found it hard to breathe.

"You killed Jarin!" the guard yelled, his eyes wide.

"It's a long way down," Kat said. "He's not dead yet." She turned her head so Mangos could see her profile. "Get up!"

Mangos heaved his legs up, doing no more than kicking the underside of the bridge. He tried again, managing to get one leg onto the bridge. He lay, mostly over air, one arm entangled on the railing, looking down.

The bridge rocked and swayed as Kat and the guard fought.

Letting go with his left hand, Mangos grabbed the bridge and pulled himself over, the railing rope rising as the bridge took more of his weight. As he stood nearly upright, he unwrapped his other arm.

"I dropped my sword," he said.

Kat glanced back. "Now we can kill this guy." She lunged, knocking aside the guard's spear and laying open his arm. She dropped her blade low, drew it across his leg, and stepped forward to shoulder him off the bridge.

He threw his spear so he could grab the railing. Kat plucked the spear from the air and threw it to Mangos. Then she cut the guard's hands from the rail, sending him screaming down to the valley.

"Well, doesn't this make all kinds of problems," the man with the crossbow said. He pointed the crossbow at Mangos. "I can kill you," he assured them.

"But you can't crank that thing fast enough to prevent me from killing you," Kat said.

"I could kill you instead."

"And face the same fate from me," Mangos added.

"The moment you pull that trigger you're a dead man," Kat said.

"Who joins me?"

"You don't have to die," Mangos said. "Stop harvesting berries, and there isn't a problem."

The man sneered. "Except how I would make a living. Besides, the problem really isn't my picking berries."

"Truce?" asked Kat.

"For how long?"

Kat brushed her hair back. "Until we can get close enough to kill you?"

The man snorted. "Two hours."

"Fine."

The man lowered the crossbow. Kat sheathed her sword. After a moment Mangos grounded his spear. "I'm not giving up on this job," he whispered.

"Of course not," whispered Kat. "But he thinks he's safe from us in two hours. I want to know why." She crossed over to the *holmen* and said, "If your picking the berries isn't the problem, what is?"

"Lijas," the man introduced himself. He didn't answer Kat's question, instead saying, "I started in the dye business. I made the grain alcohol that's added to the dye to keep it liquid. They don't need much, three gallons or so a year. The lads drink a lot, but not enough to keep me busy."

"And what does this have to do with our problem?" Mangos asked.

"I began experimenting with the ridge berries. I fermented them, which made a fair wine. Then I distilled it, which made a better brandy. Then I accidentally allowed the brandy to freeze, which serves to distill it again, and something happened. Fire in the first distillation, ice in the second, and the result is incredible. I cut it with meltwater from Talhorn and call it Imperial Brandy. I can set my price."

"And you're making too much," Mangos said. "The birds don't have enough berries to eat."

Lijas shook his head. "Here's the thing. Harlin's dye can only be made from Minix bird guano after the bird has eaten ridge berries. No berries, no guano. But, the berries only grow in soil fertilized by the guano. No guano, no berries. They have taken so much guano from the ridge and *holmen* that the bushes are sickly and don't produce much fruit."

"So you're saying it's not your fault."

"It's not. When Harlin took over from his father several years ago, he almost doubled his dye production. Now the bushes won't even grow on half the *holmen* anymore because the soil is too thin."

It made sense, and Mangos believed him. It meant stopping Lijas wouldn't solve Harlin's problem, but sometimes the world worked that way. There were no right or wrong sides of issues, only the side you were on.

"That doesn't change the fact that your making brandy means fewer berries for thc birds to eat," Kat said.

Lijas nodded. "Essentially, yes. But in another five years, there won't be any Ridge Berry bushes, so I don't see how it matters."

Thousands of Minix birds rose squawking from the ridge as workers crossed the bridges to begin scraping guano.

Lijas shook his head. "Stupid. They scare the birds off the ridge and *holmen,* so the guano falls into the valley. They should wait until afternoon, when the birds are done feeding."

Mangos ran his hand through his hair. "Doesn't some of the guano always fall in the valley?"

"Of course, but do you know how much guano it takes to make even one flask of dye? No, you obviously don't. I use in a season fewer berries than it takes to make the guano they waste by harvesting in the morning."

Mangos struggled to sort this out.

Kat shuffled her feet a little, moving the soil as if to see how thin it was. "Haven't you talked to Harlin?"

"Haven't *you* talked to Harlin?" Lijas countered. "You know how productive that is. It got me nothing, and I had to hire Jarin and Charl when somebody set fire to my still."

Mangos knew exactly who the "somebody" was.

"Huh," Kat said, clearly thinking. "It's our job to shut you down."

"Walk away," Lijas said. "You can kill me once the truce is up, but it'll kill you. Walk away now, and you might live."

"Ha! You think you can kill us?" Mangos thumped the spear on the ground.

Lijas set down his crossbow. "I don't need to. Those lads you killed were kin to half the workers up here, and friends to most of the rest. You'll have a dozen men after you as soon as word gets out. Stay around until our truce ends and you'll never make it off the *holmen.*"

"Their kin must work for Harlin then," said Mangos. Why would family members work for bitter rivals, especially ones fighting each other?

"'Course. That's the reason I hired them. They'd not kill their kin, and their kin wouldn't kill them. Everybody makes the right noises and nothing changes. That suits me even if it doesn't suit Harlin."

"But they tried to kill us," Mangos pointed out.

Lijas smiled, looking a little sad. "I didn't say they were smart."

"And that's why Harlin hired people from outside the valley," Kat said. "Because he wanted change."

Lijas pointed to the other *holmen*. "Looks like word is getting out. The mob might be here before the truce ends. I'll warn you Jarin's brother is rash enough to cut bridges and Harlin be damned."

Mangos took a step toward the bridge. "I'd rather not be trapped on a *holmen*."

Kat nodded. She stepped close to Lijas. "I'll not break the truce, but neither will I walk away from a job. We're not done here." She spun and led the way across the bridge.

Mangos followed, watching the men gathering on other *holmen*, mapping ways along the network of bridges, trying to figure a path to the valley's side.

There were two bridges to the valley side, one to the west, closer to Talhorn mountain, the other further east. They wanted the eastern one.

"We can take them," Mangos said as he picked up his pack.

Kat glanced over her shoulder. "Unless they cut the bridges."

"There is that," Mangos frowned.

"Or they have bows."

"That too."

The sound of pounding footsteps and creaking ropes surrounded Mangos as he and Kat raced from *holmen* to *holmen*. Workers shouted the news to other workers, who pulled themselves up like insects to the tops of the *holmen*.

The men gathered in twos and threes before moving together to form larger groups. They brandished pickaxes and iron bars, and a couple had small bird bows.

"Go east," Mangos said. Any fight would slow them until they could be overwhelmed. He began to run.

"Cut them off!" Four men ran toward the eastern bridge. "Stop them from escaping!"

"West!" called Mangos, as their escape east was blocked. They veered off, seeking a way around, but other groups converged.

Mangos led them further west, from *holmen* to *holmen*, the pursuit getting closer and more numerous.

"Not that way!" Kat shouted.

Mangos stopped at the beginning of a long bridge. There was no other way off the opposite *holmen*.

An arrow buzzed past, glancing off the rock at his feet. A bowman stood on the only other bridge, drawing another arrow.

There were three ways off the *holmen*: one blocked by a bowman, one led to a dead end, and a mob of angry men closed from the way they had come.

Mangos rushed the bowman, shouting wildly. The man shrank away, his eyes wide, as he loosed his arrow.

"Give way." Mangos swung his spear like a stave, knocking the man aside and jarring the bow from his hands. He rushed past, only pausing to ensure Kat followed. The way to the western bridge was clear.

The long bridge bounced under their feet. The arm of the valley neared.

Mangos's foot shot through a board, he lurched, hitting the bridge hard, knocking the air from his lungs and wrenching his leg. He pulled himself forward, jerking his leg out of the hole. "By the gods of Eastwarn!" he swore. He tried to bend his leg, but pain shot through his thigh. He reached up to grab the hand rope. Kat grabbed him under his shoulder and yanked him up.

"Run!" she urged him.

Using his spear as a crutch, Mangos ran as well as he could. The pursuing men slowed to cross the gap he had made, so Kat and he reached the end of the bridge well ahead of them.

The only path along the valley arm was a narrow, rocky trail; the fall off into the valley was harrowing, the slope to the top of the valley's arm unclimbable.

A half-dozen men crossed the eastern bridge and turned toward them, blocking the path.

"Left!" Kat called. "Go left!"

There didn't seem to be much choice. Mangos turned toward Talhorn Mountain.

The trail narrowed as they approached the face of Talhorn. The sound of the wind ripping through the Devil's Arse grew louder.

Muscles aching, breath laboring, Mangos followed Kat up the trail. Shouts and footsteps grew closer, and he didn't want to look back. He wished he knew where the trail led, besides up.

The air felt cooler as the wind eddied around the ice ledge. They were beside it now, a dirty white projection, impossibly large, like a giant growth.

They reached the ledge proper. It wasn't a solid sheet, as Mangos had supposed, but was riddled with cracks and fissures from the summer heat. "You're not thinking of crossing this."

"You want to stop and die?" Kat tested the ice.

A thin layer of meltwater made the surface slick. Mangos's feet slid, and he found himself leaning on the spear, going too slowly, he thought, and a glance back confirmed that their pursuers were only a dozen yards behind.

Mangos could almost feel the ice shake from the force of the wind passing beneath it. The ledge sloped down, just a little, and it didn't take much imagination to envision sliding off into space to ride the wind until dropping seven thousand feet. The sharp edge looked too much like a knife.

Somebody screamed. Mangos snapped his head sideways and watched one of their pursuers slide down the ledge, scrambling to catch hold. The man gathered speed as he neared the edge and launched into the air where he and his screams were lost in the howling wind.

Mangos swallowed hard.

They neared the highest point on the ledge, and he realized the tremors were not his imagination. The fissures here ran deep. While the far side was only sixty yards away, he could not see a trail.

"Give me your keg," Kat shouted over the wind.

"What?"

"Give me the keg!"

Mangos shrugged off his pack and opened it. "How did you know I had one?"

"How could I not? It weighs your pack like a lead bar and gurgles when you run."

She took the keg of alcohol, fumbling a little from its weight, to a fissure near the mountain's face.

The men were nearer, jeering and threatening, but walking carefully on the slick ice. They did not need to hurry.

Kat lifted the keg and smashed it in the fissure.

"Hey!" shouted Mangos, but she ignored him. She tore the end from her shirt and took a fire starter from her pack. She squeezed the handles, making sparks fly. After several tries, she caught the rag on fire and tossed it into the fissure. She jumped back as flames and heat roared out after her.

"You're burning—"

"Time to go," Kat said. "If this works, we don't want to be here."

Mangos took the hint. He reversed his spear, took two steps and drove it into the ice, pushing himself forward. He threw himself down, sliding by their pursuers who, taken by surprise, could only flail wildly and curse as he shot past.

He pulled himself off the ice the same time as Kat. He didn't need to be told to run.

A crack, like the crack of an angry god's whip, ripped through the air. Mangos turned in time to see the ice ledge slide down the face of the mountain. There was a grumbling, a rumbling, as it twisted and began to crumble.

The men grabbed whatever they could, but it all fell with them. If they screamed, the fall of the ice covered it.

"By the gods of Eastwarn," Mangos whispered, though that, too, was drowned out.

When the last rocks and chunks of ice settled, it was silent.

Silent.

No shouts. No screams. No wind.

Mangos looked down at the mass now plugging the Devil's Arse. "There are a dozen men in there." He looked at Kat, shocked that they could have been so quickly wiped away.

It seemed the ice fall had sucked all the sound from the valley and it was only slowly coming back. The remaining men on the *holmen* murmured to each other, casting black looks at Mangos and Kat, but nothing more.

"You killed my men," Harlin said, his face full of fury.

"We're here to get paid," Kat said.

Mangos spun to look at her in surprise. "What?"

"Paid? For killing my men?" Harlin growled like an angry dog.

"For solving your problem," Kat said. "You said you didn't care how we did it."

"I didn't expect you to kill *my* men."

"You shouldn't be surprised," Kat retorted. "Bring our pay. I'll explain."

Mangos couldn't figure what might have changed other than a dozen men dying in an avalanche. That hadn't affected Lijas at all.

Harlin grumbled as he followed them over the bridges until they reached Lijas' *holmen*.

"You're here to kill me," Lijas said, holding up his crossbow. "You're right, though, the one I'd choose to kill is Harlin."

"What? You treacherous scum!" Harlin ducked behind Mangos.

"I didn't bring him for you to kill," Kat said. "You are to agree not to gather ridge berries from the ridge or any *holmen*."

"In return for my life?" Lijas curled his lip.

Kat turned, shielding her hands from Harlin, and pointed down. Lijas furrowed his brow. Kat pointed down again, then toward Talhorn. Lijas half-turned to look at the mountain.

With a sudden smile, Lijas cleared his throat. "Ah, yes, I'll not gather any berries from the ridge, or the *holmen*."

Mangos blinked. He opened his mouth in surprise and snapped it shut. He wanted to ask why, but didn't trust himself to speak.

"You mean that?" Harlin stepped out from behind Mangos. "Of course. You're not stupid. Good." He scratched his head. "Very good." He glared at Lijas. "Don't think of changing your mind."

Lijas lifted a hand and shook his head. "It's all yours."

Harlin sniffed. "Make sure you remember it." A sly smile crossed his face as he regarded Kat and Mangos. "I can get new men. Well done." He reached into his tunic and drew out a small flask. "Here you are—a royal reward."

Mangos took it. "What is this?"

But Harlin had already turned away and crossed to the next *holmen*.

"What is this?" Mangos repeated.

"A royal reward," Lijas said. "A quart of Royal Dye."

"*Dye?* We risked our lives for a quart of dye?" He drew back his hand to fling it off the *holmen*, but Kat gently took it from him.

"We may as well keep it," she said. "It is rare, after all."

Mangos rolled his eyes and turned to Lijas. The vintner stood with his crossbow pointed down, staring after Harlin.

Lijas laughed, softly. There was no chance Harlin could hear. "Ah, Harlin, you poor fool!" He laughed again, dropping his crossbow. "Come!" He beckoned to Mangos and Kat. He clapped each on the back as they stepped from the bridge. "You two may as well have worked for me!"

"What will you do now?" Mangos asked.

"Do? I have the whole valley!" Lijas threw out his arms and smiled broadly. "Think of it! Hundreds of years of guano building up! And now that there is no wind, I can plant Ridge Berry bushes. I will have the entire valley, while Harlin is stuck on these tiny little *holmen*!"

Incredulous, Mangos started to laugh as well. The sun was setting, silhouetting the solid bulk of Talhorn, the mysterious hole plugged by the avalanche.

"It will take a few years before the bushes are old enough to produce berries, and I'll want to hire guards in case Harlin dislikes our arrangement," Lijas said. He shrugged. "But come, my friends. Harlin has given you a royal reward, let me give you an Imperial one."

Mangos grinned. "I'll drink to that."

MONGOOSE & MEERKAT

The Sword of the Mongoose

Six months after the fall of Alness.

Mangos moved his Mage forward. "The black Monarch has been defeated." He leaned back and grinned. "That's everybody, gentlemen. Pay up." He enjoyed the disgruntled muttering and the chink of silver from the losers.

He swept four small piles of coins into his pouch. It was good to win. Regum had *style,* sophistication. He winked at his partner, Kat, sure she would be impressed, before turning to the fifth player.

"I, ah," the merchant licked his lips, his eyes darted around the common room, obviously aware of everybody's interest, before settling back on Mangos, "don't have the money."

An appreciative murmur seemed to curl through the room like smoke from the fire. Men looked up from their ales, some nudged neighbors who hadn't heard. Regum was an entertaining game, but it became better when it led to a blood feud. The immediate consensus was that Mangos could crush the welshing merchant, but opinion was divided on whether he could get the value of the bet.

"You must have been sure you'd win," Kat purred as she circled the table, drawing the merchant's gaze until his head turned so far he had to snap it back the other way like an owl. But in this case he looked more like a mouse than an owl.

"My debt's not to you," the merchant said. "*You* didn't even play."

"*I* did," Mangos said, nodding to the Regum board. "And I won." It surprised him this scrawny little man would risk cheating. "Do you have silver teeth? I can take those." By custom, he was within his rights to kill the man.

The merchant licked his lips. "Better. I didn't want to do this, but I'll pay you with a story. A story and a Marin sword."

Mangos narrowed his eyes. "Stories don't buy ale." But a Marin

sword… that was something else altogether.

"Listen and decide." The merchant's eyes flickered around. Kat stood between him and the door. "Let me tell you of a man in trouble," he began, and the crowd leaned forward to hear his words.

"And so," he concluded a few minutes later, "the Earl of Riverside decided to hide his sword so the Priests of An Lorum couldn't demand it as his penance."

"As tales go, that's not a very good one," Mangos said.

"Just before crossing into An Lorum, he found a rock overlooking the river—"

"Stop!" Mangos said, slapping his palm on the table, making the coins and Regum pieces jump. He glared around the common room. All the other men hastily looked away, but Mangos wasn't fooled. "The story I will share, the sword I will not. Its location is for me alone!"

The merchant nodded. "Very well." He leaned forward and began to whisper in Mangos's ear, all about markers, locations, and keys.

"Why should we believe you?" Kat said bluntly.

"Here," the merchant passed Mangos a small bronze coin. "A *noblis* of Riverside. Not worth five silvers, but a token of my veracity." He glanced at the Regum board and sighed. "I had thought it would bring me luck."

Kat snorted. "It proves nothing."

The merchant spread his hands, palms up. He raised his voice, "Is there a soothsayer here?"

A young man cleared his throat. "I have a touch of the sight." His friends pushed him forward, no doubt hoping to know the truth as well.

The merchant spoke slowly and clearly. "After making myself familiar with the details in the story, I believe there to be a sword hidden where I described, and that it surely is a Marin blade."

Mangos looked at the soothsayer. "He is telling the truth," the young man said.

"You believe him?" Kat demanded as the tavern door slammed behind the merchant. She curled her lip, making her opinion clear.

"It's not impossible, and you heard the soothsayer," Mangos said. He idly played with the bronze *noblis* as he thought of the merchant's story. The Earl of Riverside had died in the Priests' dungeon where he scratched his secret on the wall.

"It's not likely," Kat said, still standing. "He writes in code, and a hundred years later *this* merchant buys the information from another prisoner who broke the code?"

"Still," Mangos said, "a Marin sword. Do you have any idea what one is worth?"

"More than a five-silver tavern bet," Kat retorted.

"I could have killed him," Mangos said, tapping a coin on the tabletop. "It's worth his life."

"You still can kill him. If you want to go after the sword, you should catch him to keep as guide and hostage."

"Either the sword is there or it isn't," Mangos said. "Unless I want to kill him if it isn't, it makes no sense to take him hostage." He saw Kat's expression and laughed. "Isn't the lure of adventure worth five silvers? Besides, I have no wish to be knifed as I sleep.

"Marin made the first silvecite-alloyed swords," Mangos continued. How could he explain what that meant to a collector? He prided himself on knowing his steel. "Not only are Marin swords strong, well edged, and perfectly balanced, they're works of art."

"Which means you won't find them hidden alongside the road."

Mangos shook his head slowly. Owning a Marin sword would mark him as a dangerous man, a man of success and refinement. It was everything he wanted when they went to Alomar, for it would smooth his way in the city. "It doesn't hurt to check," he mused.

Kat snorted and flipped her hair back as if to say, *It's your call*. "The soothsayer did verify his words." She contemplated the Regum board. "He must have really believed he could win."

Mangos laughed. "But he didn't, and now I have his secret."

Kat lowered her voice. "The others heard the tale, and that the sword lies under a rock just this side of An Lorum. That's a very small area to look."

Mangos stood up. Only he knew the markers, but Kat was right, it was a small enough area that others would try their luck. "Let's hurry," he said.

"I'd expect a dozen men, plus whatever friends and cousins they can enlist," Mangos said. He could see two ahead of them, local youths of the sort who might go off adventuring to avoid farm work. They started to run when they saw Mangos and Kat. He wasn't worried. The boys couldn't run for three days.

He knew of others behind, men who hung back but would pass them at first opportunity. Pass them, or, when the stakes were as high as a Marin sword, kill them.

"Shall we step up the pace?" Kat asked, her tone light.

To answer, Mangos lengthened his stride. They started to gain on the boys who, when they noticed, began to run again. It became almost a game. The boys would run until they tired, then Mangos and Kat would close the gap, and the boys would run again. Each run was shorter, each time the gap closed more until Mangos and Kat passed them. The boys, red-faced and panting, shook their heads and turned for home.

"The others won't give up so easily," Kat said.

They might not, Mangos thought, but he was confident once he had a Marin sword he could best any living man.

The land rolled ahead of them, green grass cropped short by sheep and spotted with grey boulders. There were few trees and they could see for miles.

The sun outstripped them and retired for the night, but they kept moving by moonlight. Only when the moon set did they take shelter behind a large rock.

Early morning light woke Mangos. Some silent sense made him nervous, and he nudged Kat awake with his foot. Her eyes flew open, and she sat up and looked around.

A hawk cried.

"Just a hawk," Mangos said, feeling relieved.

"A white merlin? That's a noble bird. It doesn't belong to some local youth. Somebody else has gotten word of your Marin sword. I'd guess they're late to the chase, but probably mounted."

"That's *my* sword," Mangos said with righteous indignation. "I won the Regum game."

Kat didn't answer. Mangos dug in his pack for food as they started walking again.

The white merlin disappeared, but hours later it was back, circling. Kat stopped, breathing heavily, and looked back. "Look behind us."

A man and his dog stalked them several miles back, a couple miles behind him a group of four men walked, and another three beyond them. But far, far back, just visible at the top of the furthest ridge, rode a dozen horsemen.

The group of three had disappeared, and the four fallen further back. The man and his dog were now two valleys back, but the horsemen were only three ridges back, and Mangos was tired. He leaned over, hands on his knees as he tried to catch his breath.

"We're going to have to rest," he said. Kat nodded, too winded to speak.

Clouds were gathering and he wondered where they came from. He had not noticed them blowing in. In spite of his words, he started down into the next valley, pushed by the images of the horsemen.

Another road ran along the valley floor and intersected their road. A wagon sat at the crossroads. The horse, a dun mare, drank at a stone trough while a man rubbed it down. Battered pots and worn tools hung from the wagon's sides. Mangos could see other goods, all used, inside the canvas cover.

When the man saw them he dropped his rag and drew a curved sword. He called to somebody out of sight and a woman's voice answered.

"She's Alnessi," murmured Kat as she glanced up at the clouds and raised her hood.

Refugees. The fall of Alness had scattered her citizens across the world. That was why they were selling junk. Likely they scavenged their goods as they fled their country.

"Merchants," Mangos said as a man moved between them and the wagon.

"Barely merchants," Kat said, "and they're worried about us being bandits."

"We've nothing you want," called out the man, his voice accented.

That's pretty clear, Mangos thought. "We weren't planning on taking any of it." *How do they sell anything if they don't have anything people want?*

Kat turned so she faced Mangos but had her back to the others. "He's Hafizi," she murmured, but Mangos didn't know who the Hafizi were or why one would be travelling with an Alnessi merchant. "Dangerous."

"Wait," Mangos said. "Maybe we do want something. Which way are you going?"

"South," said a woman, stepping out from behind the wagon. She was barely a woman, a girl really, and looked thin and worn.

"We'll pay you to take us west," Mangos said.

"No," the man said.

"Celzez," the woman said with a wave for him to keep quiet. "How far, and how much?"

"Twenty, twenty-five miles," Mangos said. "We'll pay five silvers." There was a certain symmetry in five silvers, the value of the tale.

"Take us two days out of our way for five silvers?" The girl snorted.

"One day," Mangos protested.

"Two, we have to come back."

Overhead, the merlin cried.

"Ten silvers," Mangos shrugged.

"Twenty."

A few heavy drops of rain fell, raising puffs of dust on the road. Mangos glanced behind them. "But we travel quickly, no lagging."

The girl nodded. "I'm Jalani. This is Celzez. Climb on."

Mangos settled in the back, trying to find space among the junk. The wagon might travel slowly, but at least they could rest as it moved.

"You're Alnessi?" Mangos asked, more to fill the silence than anything else.

"I am," Jalani said. "Celzez was my father's Hafizi guard. My father was a merchant." She said the last with a note of defiance.

"You're a long way from Alness."

"Celzez saved me from the fighting, and we escaped the city," Jalani said. "We found this wagon. I suppose we stole it, though the owners were dead. The best we could do was bury them."

She snapped the reins.

"We caught the horse running wild, no idea who owned it, gathered such goods as hadn't been broken or burned and headed south. We've been living as tinkers and petty merchants ever since."

Looking around the sorry merchandise, Jalani shook her head. "A poor start to rebuilding my father's business."

Nodding absently, Mangos stared out the back. He laughed to see the first men start to run when they saw the wagon. They might gain for a bit, but the last two days travel had been brutal, they had to be as exhausted as he was. They could never keep the pace.

But further back, dust rose from the hooves of a dozen horses. They could not outrun this pursuit; they could only hope to reach the sword's hiding place first.

"That hill there," Mangos said, pointing to a low hill rising up from the valley floor below them. The rain had grown heavier the closer they came to the valley, and now it fell like a lace curtain, making everything grey and hazy.

A river meandered along the broad valley floor, passing on the far side of the hill. Dead trees dotted its banks.

A bridge, long, old, and solid, spanned the river, the top of its arch visible above the hill. Just upstream a tower perched on a rocky island; the flood line of discolored stone was higher than the first floor.

Mangos studied the bridge and tower. "No doubt at all." He turned his attention back to the hill, searching for signs of the sword's hiding place.

"They're close," Kat said, pointing to the horsemen behind.

"Faster!" Mangos urged Jalani.

"No faster," Jalani answered. "Speed downhill will ruin a horse."

Mangos jumped from the wagon. "We can go faster on foot." He began to run.

"Hey!" shouted Jalani. "You still have to pay us!"

"Meet us on that small hill!" Mangos shouted back. He slipped in the mud but kept running.

At the top of the hill, Kat looked around. "You said there should be a marker stone..." She trailed away as she searched the tall grass and short bushes along the side of the road.

The tower stood closer now, three levels of dark stone with slate shutters and roof. The shutters of the first level were closed, but an unnatural glow came from the open windows of the top floor.

The rain had found the seam between Mangos's hood and his cape. He could feel the wetness seeping down his back. Mangos shuddered, not sure if it were the blue glow or the cold rain that sent shivers down his spine. He reminded himself that a Marin sword equaled respect. By owning one he would command better jobs and higher pay. The drinks and pleasurable company would come easy. *Alomar will swoon at my feet*, he thought.

"Over here," Kat called.

Mangos hurried over. Wet grass obscured the overturned road marker. "Now to find the first stone. Ten paces east," he said, starting to walk the distance, "two paces south." He stopped beside a large stone. "Roll the stone." He dried his hands on the front of his tunic where it was still dry and took a grip on the stone. With a heave, he rolled it over.

There was a small cavity underneath with a largish piece of stone inside. At first glance it looked like whatever was hidden there had been taken and the side collapsed, but Mangos knew he needed the stone. He picked it up and grinned at Kat. "Just like we were told."

Kat nodded. "Hurry."

The horsemen were halfway down the valley—close enough to see the riders' armor and weapons.

Mangos carried the stone to the other side of the road, closer to where the tower brooded over the river, the blue light even more ominous in the heavy rain.

"It should be over here somewhere," he said, looking over the stones on the top of the hill. He paced around one, examining it from every side.

"It can't be this easy," Kat said.

Mangos pushed the stone. It wouldn't move. He moved to another spot and took a better grip. He couldn't budge the stone. "I *should* be able to move that," he said. He brushed some water from a small depression, an action that had no discernable effect.

He set the stone from under the first rock on the second stone, wiggling it until it settled snugly into the depression. He couldn't repress a grin.

The stone rolled easily with his next effort. He held his breath as a cavity came into view.

There *was* a sword.

And it was beautiful. The blade was straight and true, without the least sign of rust. The guard was skillfully fashioned to look spare and elegant but still protect his hand. The pommel looked to be a work of art. He reached down to pick up the sword and examined it more closely.

"It looks like a Marin sword," he breathed as he lifted the sword from the ground.

A thunderous crack exploded overhead, and the sky opened up. Rain fell in torrents, so hard it weighed on his head and shoulders. He couldn't see the bridge, the tower, or the wagon. He could barely see Kat standing beside him.

Nonetheless he swung the sword, cutting through the rain and marveling at its balance. He squinted at the pommel and ran his hand along the flat of the blade.

"It's real!" he exulted. "A true Marin blade!"

Wealth, respect, power—Mangos held it all in his hand. Even in corrupt Alomar, a Marin sword would turn heads.

"Too easy," Kat muttered. She paced away but returned to look at the sword. "Still too easy." She shook her head.

Mangos laughed and swung the sword again.

The rain slackened.

Kat froze. "You'll want to look at this."

Mangos lowered the sword and followed her gaze. The river had jumped its banks and was flooding around the approach to the bridge. It rose as he watched, climbing further. The rain dripping down his back felt unusually cold. "That's not natural," he said.

The water already rushed over the roadway. The dead trees stuck from the water like claws with white ribbon cuffs of whitewater trailing downstream.

Mangos shuddered at the mere thought of swimming that flood. "We can't go that way."

"Or back."

Mangos turned. The flood had flanked the hill and was rioting across the valley, turning the boulder-strewn ground into a treacherous mass of swirling white water.

Caught at the far edge of the flood, the horsemen scrambled back up the valley side. On the near side, Jalani and Celzez coaxed and prodded their tired horse to climb faster.

As one, Mangos and Kat turned to look at the tower. The blue light pierced the still heavy rain.

"I'd like to be a little further away from that," Mangos said.

"Cut the horse free!" Kat yelled to Jalani. The flood already lapped at the wagon's back wheels.

Jalani shook her head, but Celzez drew his curved sword and cut the traces. The wagon rolled back and freed the horse from the shafts. The flood lifted the back end of the wagon and pulled it completely into the water. It turned as it moved downstream, briefly hanging up on a tree before breaking free and rushing away.

"So," said Celzez. "We are here. Are we to just wait to drown?"

Mangos turned completely around. It seemed likely. The water raged over the abutments of the bridge, it swirled above the door on the tower, and it climbed the slopes of the hill where he stood.

"What's that?" He pointed to the tower where something moved.

The door opened, a glowing portal under the flood.

"Magic," hissed Jalani.

The water before them swirled. A hole opened in the center, and the water spun outward, revealing a tunnel stretching out toward the tower.

Far down the tunnel, shadows moved, shuffling forward to resolve into the forms of men.

The men's faces were pale and waxy, blemished by scrapes, bites, and gouges. Black and bloated hands hung like blood sausages from the ends of their arms.

Kat hissed, a sound of surprise and revulsion. "Revenants!"

Undead servants of a necromancer. Mangos felt a chill in his guts.

A dozen revenants issued from the tunnel and circled the hill. Their complete indifference to the rain, the mud, and anything the living could do, was harrowing. The final revenant, a man who must have been a smith in life, judging from his leather trousers and apron, lifted a black hand and pointed to the tunnel.

The merchant gulped. "Maybe the necromancer is offering us sanctuary."

"That's a sanctuary I don't want to take," Kat said.

"We may not have a choice," Mangos replied.

Jalani jerked her head up and down, sending drops of water flying. "I think we should risk it. The upper levels of that tower should be safe."

"Not safe," Mangos and Kat said at the same time.

The revenants took a step forward, and the dead smith pointed again.

"Celzez?" Jalani asked.

"We should not go down that tunnel," Celzez said. He swung his sword through the rain. "We should kill them here."

"They're already dead," Jalani said. Her voice cracked as the revenants took another step closer.

Mangos stabbed the one nearest him. His Marin sword slid in easily, a blow that would have killed a man. The revenant pawed at the sword like it wanted to push it away.

"Don't make them angry!" the merchant moaned.

The revenants took another step, and the smell of rot and mold washed over them. With a whimper, Jalani broke away and slipped and slithered through the mud to the tunnel.

"Jalani!" called Celzez. "Jalani!" He hurried after her.

"Damn," muttered Kat.

"It's Hell and high water here," Mangos said. He jerked his sword free. "Maybe the Necromancer does offer safety," he said, though he didn't believe it.

"No. He doesn't. They never do." Kat twisted away from a revenant as it stepped forward, but there was another beside it. They stood shoulder to shoulder, two deep in places, and behind them the water still rose.

"Let's go," Mangos said. "Even if we could kill them, we can't escape the flood."

It was like stepping inside a waterspout laid on its side. Water twisted around them, it sounded angry. Only an inch of sorcery held back death, and Mangos had little faith in it.

They went single file, for only a narrow strip of ground showed at the bottom, and nobody seemed inclined to step on the curved water walls that somehow circled the tunnel in spite of intersecting the ground. The revenants clustered behind them, expressionless, crowding them forward.

"Necromancers," Mangos muttered, aware of the stink, but not knowing if it came from the revenants or the river muck. "He's not making a good impression."

"They never do," Kat said. "They live on the borders, just close enough to grab people to use in their magic but far enough away to avoid important people's wrath."

Jalani and Celzez hesitated to climb out of the riverbed to the glowing door, but the revenants kept coming, dragging their feet through the mud and puddles. Even worse, the far end of the tunnel had collapsed and brown, frothing water followed the revenants toward them. "We can't stay here," Mangos said.

Celzez lifted Jalani up the riverbank. Kat followed. Mangos gave the revenants and the shortening tunnel one last look before climbing up and entering the necromancer's tower.

The door slammed shut, and water boomed against it as the tunnel completely collapsed. Water trickled around the frame, darkening the wood.

Silence, then the plink of water dripped from the rocks. The room was empty except for a set of stairs coiling up the far side of the tower to the next floor.

The revenants leaned against the outer wall and slumped, all semblance of life leaving them. Now they were just corpses piled against the walls, flaccid and motionless, all staring eyes, slack jaws, and rivulets of dried blood.

"We're underwater," Jalani said, looking very young and very scared.

We were before, Mangos thought, but didn't say it.

The water plinked again.

Black iron lanterns held globes of blue light. It gave the others a pale, sickly hue. *No different than the revenants. Is this what we'll become?* he wondered.

"I, ah, don't much like it here," Jalani said.

"We'll like it less when it floods," Celzez said. He stomped his foot and water splashed.

"We'd best be moving up," Kat said. She put action to her words, going over to the stairs.

Mangos gestured Jalani and Celzez forward. He followed them up, only stopping once to watch the water creeping over the corpses.

Kat was already prowling the second floor.

Shelves of bottles and boxes lined the tower. More bottles covered a table in the center of the room, and strings of dried...stuff—Mangos didn't know what it might be—hung from the ceiling. It still smelled of decay, but of spice and ash and something animal as well.

"Dragon's blood," Kat said as she studied the rows of bottles. "Tanis leaf. Heela spikes—that's impressive."

"You know these things?" Jalani asked.

Kat nodded. "Very rare, very dangerous, very expensive."

Jalani nodded, exhaustion etched on her face. She sank into a black chair half hidden by the table.

"Don't sit there!"

Jalani jumped up. Kat shook her head. "Arcane." She drew their attention to a large basin behind the chair with her sword point. "Quicksilver." She then pointed to a giant stone font. A wooden lid covered it. As she took the lid, she closed her eyes as if overcome with emotion. "Life," she said, "This is where the necromancer harvests his victims' lives to fuel his magic."

A warm yellow glow filled the room.

The lid slammed closed, seemingly by itself. Kat tried to open it again, but her hand slipped off.

"Do not touch what does not belong to you." A cloaked and hooded figure stood on the stairs to the third level.

"Then you shouldn't leave it out," Kat said. "It isn't really yours. It

belongs to those downstairs."

"You criticize me? Do you not know who I am?" He lifted both hands to lower his hood. It was the story-telling merchant from the inn.

Mangos felt his jaw drop open and he closed it with a snap. "Damn you! This was all to trap us?"

"Not just you," the necromancer said. "That story was aimed at every adventurer in the room. But," he shrugged, "you carried the trigger for the flood."

Mangos thought of the bronze *noblis* he carried. Then another thought crossed his mind. "You owe me five silver pieces!"

"Fool!" roared the necromancer. "I am the right hand of Death himself."

Jalani let out a soft whimper. Celzez stood in front of her. His hand shook as he lifted his sword.

"I am the devourer of souls!" roared the necromancer.

It seemed the darkness in the nooks of the tower grew deeper.

"I am the render of the creation." The man's words shook the very air.

"You own the tower where I'll be staying until the waters recede," Mangos said.

"I am ISAK YAN!" the necromancer shouted. "The waters recede when I say they'll recede, and you'll be staying much longer than that."

"Will you be serving dinner?"

"I don't think," said the necromancer, "you appreciate what is about to become of your life."

I think I do, thought Mangos, feeling the ice in his stomach and what felt like spiders walking on the back of his neck. *But if he can try to scare us, I can laugh at him.* Yet while Mangos felt scared, the necromancer wasn't laughing.

Isak Yan pointed to Jalani. "You are about to replenish my cauldron. Sit." When Jalani didn't move he said, "All I need do is call the revenants."

Keeping one eye on Isak Yan, Mangos went to the stairs. Something moved in the blue water, shadows that resolved into men and began to climb toward the surface.

The first revenant rose up, water dripping. Mangos slashed, opening a large gash that did nothing to slow it. He kicked it back into the water, but two more replaced it. He had to retreat.

The revenants were stiff and awkward but deceptively fast. While two attacked Mangos, others rushed past.

Celzez defended Jalani while Kat carved the hands from a revenant threatening her.

Isak Yan stood above them, watching. He lifted a hand.

Mangos's vision swirled, and the world tilted. The ground wasn't where his feet were, or so it seemed, and he fell. Across the room he saw Celzez fall before revenant feet, black and scabby, blocked his vision.

He rolled and rose, lurching and flailing as the room swam. "Beware sorcery!" he shouted as swung, somehow separating a revenant's head from its neck.

Kat dropped her sword and grabbed two large flasks from the table.

"No!" shouted Isak Yan. Mangos's balance returned as Isak Yan faced Kat and lifted his arms above his head. His hands sparkled as he thrust them toward Kat. Kat smashed one flask before the sparks enveloped her like a swarm of fireflies. The little, twinkling lights settled on her and she slowed and stopped moving, the second flask tilted and her free hand reaching for her dagger.

Isak Yan lifted his sleeve to mop his face.

A sharp scream pierced the air. Jalani struggled in the grip of a revenant while Celzez tried futilely to reach her.

"Give up," Isak Yan said.

"Not likely." Nearly surrounded, Mangos could only put the stairwell at his back and try to keep the revenants from grappling him.

Cold hands grabbed his wrists. A revenant climbing from below pulled his arms back. He felt cold, wet flesh pressing against his back, and the stench of rot filled his nostrils. He struggled, but the hands pinching his wrists, hard bone gripping through flaccid muscles, held him tight.

"You see how fruitless your struggle is?" Isak Yan said.

Mangos kicked backwards, hoping to catch the revenant holding him by surprise. He struck hard, but with no result.

"It doesn't seem you do. You'd better bring me his sword." Isak Yan gestured and a revenant tore the sword from Mangos's grip.

"Give it back!" Mangos shouted, renewing his struggle. The Marin blade was irreplaceable!

Isak Yan came down and took the blade. He turned it over and held it up to the light. "Very, very nice. You are, indeed, a man of taste and accomplishment," he mocked. He laid it on the table. "It shall go back in the ground for the next adventurer to find."

"Fool to bury it!" Mangos snarled. He needed a sword; he wanted that one.

Isak Yan shrugged. "Telling the truth helps lure otherwise suspicious folk."

Mangos lunged forward, but again could not break free. He could not expect help, either. Kat strained against the magic holding her, but couldn't do more than quiver. Four revenants hemmed in Celzez, and Jalani could not break free of the revenant holding her.

"Bring me the girl," Isak Yan commanded.

The revenant dragged Jalani over to the ebony chair.

Isak Yan came down the stairs, extended his hands over the bowl of quicksilver, and began to murmur arcane words.

Mist gathered over the bowl, silver and faintly luminous. It grew thick and began to swirl, spinning into threads and from threads into ropes.

Jalani moaned as the ropes drifted to her, wrapping around her arms and legs, binding her to the chair. She closed her eyes and seemed to grow smaller as she shrank back.

Isak Yan drew a long, black knife. He reached into a dark corner and seemed to cut the air. He pulled back a piece of darkness and pulled it over Jalani's head.

A hood of shadows, Mangos thought.

Celzez roared, bashing aside the revenants in front of him and rushing at Isak Yan. He raised his curved sword as he attacked.

Isak Yan lifted his other hand. "You…can't…win," he said, his teeth clenched and muscles tight.

Celzez slowed, as if he pushed against greater and greater resistance. He started to swing his sword, but it moved with glacial slowness and finally stopped altogether.

Isak Yan quivered with the effort of all his magic.

Kat's hand shook. The liquid in the flask she held crept over the lip. A thick, syrupy fluid, it caught the light as it stretched, slowly, to the floor. Smoke twisted up as it touched the spilled contents of the flask she dropped earlier.

The two liquids exploded, lifting Kat from her feet and throwing her across the room. The blast cleared everything from the table. Heat washed across Mangos.

With a cry of exertion, Mangos flexed to free himself. The revenant clung to his wrists; he was pulling it more tightly against his back. With an awful tearing sound, he pulled free.

He had torn off the revenant's arms; they still clung to his wrists.

He started to use them to club the revenants around him.

"Kill the necromancer," Kat said. She climbed to her feet, clothes singed and a dazed expression on her face.

With these weapons? Mangos wondered. *At least I'm armed.*

He knocked the revenants back, but couldn't stop them. The Marin sword had been lost in the explosions, blown somewhere out of sight. Kat had taken Celzez's sword and cut the head from a revenant, but she was barely holding back several others.

"I don't want them to kill you," Isak Yan said.

He just wants to kill us himself. Mangos needed to attack the necromancer directly, for the revenants would eventually win. He could not outlast the undead.

He avoided the blundering charge of an armless revenant. *Madness,* he thought. His eye settled on a sword hilt amongst the mess on the floor—his Marin blade.

Mangos dove forward and grabbed the sword; it settled into his hand, feeling like an extension of his arm. It was perfectly balanced, perfectly proportioned. *A man could do amazing things with this,* he thought.

Mangos uncoiled in a lunge, stretching as far as he could, and was rewarded by striking Isak Yan. Isak Yan parried too late, swiping after the sword had sunk deep into his chest.

The black knife cracked against the Marin blade. The knife dissolved into shadows that disappeared in the corners of the room. The Marin blade vibrated, letting off a low moan before it shattered.

Isak Yan gasped, and all motion stopped.

The revenants collapsed, the quicksilver ropes binding Jalani splashed to the floor, and the hood of shadows disappeared.

Isak Yan hunched over, clutching at his chest as if he could draw out the portion of blade still inside him. He dropped to his knees and collapsed completely.

"He broke my sword," Mangos said, staring at the hilt in disbelief.

Kat nodded. She went over to the window and opened the shutter a crack.

"He broke my sword," Mangos repeated.

"I heard you." Kat opened the shutter wide. "It stopped raining."

"That sword was worth a fortune."

THE SWORD OF THE MONGOOSE

Jalani blinked in the light. She seemed dazed. "You saved my life."

"But you cost her the wagon and all her trade goods," Celzez said.

"I lost my sword," Mangos said.

Kat stared at both of them and started to prowl the room. "Sell this," she told Jalani. "Instead of that junk you had, sell all of this." She stopped by the font. "Even the life essence."

Celzez protested, "We only want the value of what we lost. This is worth much, much more."

A small smile stole over Kat's lips, "Are you on her side or not? We're adventurers, not merchants; and you fought the battle too."

Their conversation barely registered with Mangos as he gathered the shards of his Marin blade. He cupped them carefully in his hands, thinking how few they seemed. He took them to the window and threw them into the receding flood.

THE SWORD OF THE MONGOOSE

The Valley of Terzol

Eight months after the fall of Alness.

"**D**o you think it's poisonous?" Mangos asked, prodding the snake with the tip of his sword.

"Almost everything else in this jungle is, why not that?" Kat answered.

Mangos laughed. The snake coiled and hissed, its white mouth contrasting sharply with its vivid green and yellow skin. It had inch-long fangs that folded up as it drew back and closed its mouth.

"It'd make a nice belt," Mangos said as he tapped the snake under the chin. The coil became a mass of frenzied movement, and there were three sharp "clacks" as it struck the sword. Mangos stepped back. The snake coiled and struck again, but Mangos twisted his sword, and the snake's head hit the ground and rolled away while the body thrashed on the jungle floor.

Kat cut away some branches at the far side of the clearing and glanced over her shoulder at him. "You may as well bring it now."

"Will you stop playing?" said a waspish voice. Andorholm Wallenoop stood up and wiped sweat from his face. "It's like I brought a child."

"If you're ready to go," said Mangos.

Andor snorted and jerked his head in a way that managed to say, 'It wasn't my idea to rest' when, in fact, it had been. Mangos and Kat had to slow considerably so they wouldn't outpace their employer.

Andor claimed to be an adventurer, but his skin was too pale, his hands too soft, and he cared about little inconveniences too much.

"I didn't bring you to play with snakes," said Andor peevishly. "I brought you to protect me." He looked at Kat. "I'm not even sure why I brought you. I don't even desire you."

Mangos sucked in his breath. In less than a year since he and Kat met, they had become known as a clever and dangerous team. He knew little of Kat's background, but he knew of her abilities. Andor was a fool to disparage her, but Kat merely looked at him, a slight flaring of her nostrils her only reaction.

"Had I known the Meerkat was a woman," Andor went on, "I would

63

have sought my bodyguards elsewhere."

"Have a care, little man," said Mangos. "Lest we return your money and leave you here."

"Oh, I'll keep you on," Andor retorted. "I've come this far."

"And how much further?" inquired Mangos, glad to change the subject. Kat still had not spoken.

Andor snorted. "You needn't know."

"We'll know when we get there," Mangos huffed.

Andor curled his lip. "I doubt you would recognize it even then."

"We're in the Terzol Valley," said Kat, her arm raised to cut another branch. Mangos blinked.

Andor swiveled his head and looked at her for a long moment before speaking. "We are."

"As Terzol is the heart of the world, so the Emperor's house is the heart of Terzol," she continued. It sounded like a quote. "He controlled religion, government, and commerce. We're going to the Imperial Palace."

Andor licked his lips. "That need not concern you," he said.

"Terzol is—" started Mangos.

"Not a myth," interjected Kat. She swung her machete and a branch fell to the ground. "Your people never had much commerce with them."

"I never said it was a myth," said Mangos, offended. He came from Arnelan, a narrow strip of land between the Western Sea and Callos Mountains. With fish, farm, and mines at hand, they needed little. Mangos only knew Terzol as an Empire months to the east that had fallen centuries before.

It wasn't that he had anything against learning. He even planned to get some sometime. And, if he was completely honest, he was a little jealous of Kat's knowledge. "I just wondered who said Terzol was the heart of the world."

Kat did not answer. Mangos looked at Andor, but he didn't answer either. He was used to Kat's mysterious background. When they first met she looked so haggard he thought her an escaped slave. Later when he discovered she could fight, he revised his opinion to escaped gladiatrix. Still later, as she haggled over supplies, he thought perhaps a merchant's guard. Now that he had seen her learning on several subjects, he admitted he didn't know what to think.

Kat beckoned with her machete, inviting Andor to precede her into the jungle.

"No," said Andor. "You go first." He glanced back the way they had come, a nervous habit that made Mangos wonder if he expected pursuit.

Kat stepped from the clearing back into the jungle.

Mangos watched her for a second before following. None could deny she was extremely beautiful. Yet he did not desire her, and it puzzled him. Since he didn't doubt his manhood, he suspected magic.

"What are you doing?" Mangos hissed. Kat was crouched over the sleeping Andor, both barely shadows under the protection of a leaning tree, several paces from the fire.

Kat didn't answer, and Mangos did not repeat his question. The long day's travel, a meal of roast snake, and a safe shelter had put Andor to sleep. His snores joined the symphony of insects to form the background noise of the jungle night. Mangos did not want to wake him.

Kat slipped back to the fire, not at all concerned.

Mangos frowned. She held a small brass scroll tube with shards of wax still clinging to grooves at one end. She worried out the wooden stopper to retrieve the scroll inside. Carefully unrolling the yellowed and flaked parchment, she turned it so it would better catch the light.

"You're reading his papers!" Mangos said.

"I got bored," said Kat with a little shrug. "Besides, he stole this from someone else."

"What if he wakes up?" But Mangos couldn't contain his curiosity. "What is it?"

"An old receipt and instructions for delivery. Very old, very fragile. My guess is the merchandise was never picked up, and Andor wants it."

"In Terzol?" Mangos flinched at the volume of his voice. He spoke more softly. "Is he mad?"

"A little, maybe," Kat replied. "But it was stored in the Palace-Temple, well protected, and could only be removed with a certain key. There is an impression on the paper where it wrapped around a seal. Again a guess, but the seal is probably the key needed to unlock a vault containing the merchandise. If the vault was hidden or strong enough, it might not have been looted."

"He has the seal?"

"I put it back around his neck this morning," Kat said; Mangos couldn't help looking at her in amazement. "What? I just wanted to look at it. It's very nice work; an antiques dealer would pay good silver for it."

Mangos thought a moment, glanced at Andor to ensure he still slept. "So what is this merchandise?"

"It doesn't say."

Mangos sat back, disappointed.

"But consider," Kat continued, "it was so valuable they would not name it in writing, and the Terzoli would not take responsibility to ship it. It is so valuable that somebody paid in full without delivery. No," she added before he could ask. "It doesn't say who paid, or how much." She rerolled the parchment and slid it back into its brass tube.

"Fools doing business," muttered Mangos.

"Fools because the Terzoli civil war made it too dangerous to fetch their merchandise." Kat smiled a smile that made her look a little feral. "Maybe somebody believed it was lost, maybe somebody died, but it was forgotten until our friend here found the receipt and key. And that," she said in a tone that suggested this was the important part, "answers why an accountant hired bodyguards to travel to Terzol."

"An accountant? How do you know he was an accountant?"

Kat laid a finger on her lips to indicate he should be quiet. She returned to Andor's side. Something in the night howled, and Andor stirred, his snoring interrupted. Kat froze. After a second, she slid the tube back into his pack and returned to the fire.

"He has ink stains on his fingers. He could be an archivist," she said as she sat down again, "but he doesn't seem the sort."

"If you would stop looking behind us and look ahead, you might see we have a problem," Mangos said to Andor.

A group of men, all carrying sticks, formed a half circle, blocking their way. They guarded a squalid village of branch and leaf huts, arranged around a muddy clearing. Only one building was of stone, a small structure against a hill with roots crawling over and in it. Grey stone people peered between the roots, part of elaborate carvings on the walls.

"We're going that way," said Andor, pointing through the village.

The center man, apparently the leader, spoke angrily and waved his stick. Mud-covered children watched the confrontation. The small children clung to their mother's legs while the older ones stared wide-eyed and open-mouthed at Mangos and Kat.

"Do you realize," said Andor, "I don't understand a word they're saying?"

"They're talking too fast," replied Kat. "You see the leader's helmet? That's old—imperial Terzol, I'd guess. The stone building too."

The center man, the largest of what Mangos now counted was a dozen men, wore a conical bronze helmet large enough to rest on his shoulders. He peered out the arched opening in front like a bird peering from a birdhouse. He had a spearhead tied to his club and wore strips of something cut to resemble greaves, pauldrons, and bracers.

He shouted angrily and gestured to the jungle behind them.

Mangos shook his head. "We're not going back."

Just then, a little boy, maybe six years old, ran out from behind his mother and kicked Mangos. Mangos caught the boy by the hair and lifted him off the ground. He started to scream and kick, but Mangos held him at arm's length. The villagers cried out.

"Yours?" Mangos asked, raised the boy a little.

The boy's mother wailed, raising her arms in supplication and falling to her knees. One of the men took a step forward and shook his club, shouting unknown threats. Mangos shook the boy a little and said, "Now we have something to talk about."

The boy started to cry and the man with the club waved it again.

"I think," said Kat, "you have his son."

"You'll get us all killed!" cried Andor.

Mangos drew his sword and bared his teeth. "If everybody on one side dies, it won't be us."

Andor spoke, haltingly, stumbling over unfamiliar words. The villagers clearly struggled to understand him.

"What are you saying?" Mangos demanded.

Andor didn't answer but kept talking to the villagers.

"He is begging them not to kill us," said Kat. "At least I think that's what he thinks he's saying. I wouldn't use the same phrasing, but I can only read Terzoli, I can't speak it."

"We don't need to speak Terzoli!" shouted Mangos. He dropped the boy, who scrambled into his mother's arms. "Is there a man here who dares face me?"

"Don't antagonize them!" squawked Andor.

"Careful," Kat said.

One of the men lifted a short, straight stick to his mouth and blew. There was a little buzz, a flash of steel, and a clank as Kat knocked a dart from the air with her sword. Two more men lifted their blowguns.

Mangos roared and charged. The villagers scattered. Kat and Andor followed, and the three dashed into the jungle.

"Bluff and misdirection and brute force," Mangos said as they pushed through the undergrowth. He glared at Andor, "works better than begging."

The village was long behind them with no sign of pursuit when dark clouds rolled across the sky. Kat and Mangos noticed and took out their cloaks. Andor didn't notice; instead he kept looking behind them.

The rain rolled after the clouds. One moment, it was overcast; the next, rain fell in sheets. Andor hastily pulled out his own cloak.

Mangos carefully turned so Andor couldn't see his smile.

"Cursed rain!" grumbled Andor. "Why does it happen now?" He sighed, the sigh of long suffering that made Mangos want to strangle him.

"Tell me of Terzol," Mangos said as they worked their way through the sodden jungle. Conversation would distract him from the fact the rain had found the seam between his cloak and hood and now trickled down his back.

"Why?" Andor snorted. "You don't need to know to do your job."

"Terzol controlled this whole valley," said Kat. "It was all cultivated, with a half-dozen cities and an extensive canal network."

Mangos wiped the sweat from his face. "You'd never know. Those trees look hundreds of years old."

"They probably are. The empire fell three hundred fifty years ago. Civil War."

"Let me guess," Mangos said. "Armies back and forth, crops don't get planted, trade disappears. Famine, fire, and a great stillness come over the land."

"And then the jungle covers it all," Kat said. "Although you told the tale without the high drama of treachery and tragedy." He heard her laughter over the dripping water from the jungle's canopy. "Ruins litter the Terzol valley," she continued. "Ruins of an empire that tore itself apart, fighting itself back into savagery, back to primitives huddling amongst the bones of their ancestors' greatness."

"You didn't make that up," said Andor. "That is from Teritum of Alomar's *History of Terzol*."

"Hmmm," Kat noted in agreement. "Maybe you're an archivist after all."

Mangos and Kat stepped out from under the canopy to the edge of the canal. They faced a hundred yards of rain-splashed water. On the far side, rising over the jungle, was the top of a great building, small in the distance, but visible by its height.

"We could swim," said Kat.

"Eh." Mangos didn't like the idea but didn't want to admit it.

"You can swim, can't you?"

"Of course," replied Mangos, but he wondered if he could swim that distance and how they would get their gear across.

The sound of Andor panting interrupted further conversation. They fell silent to watch him approach the canal. The sight seemed to strike him a physical blow. His mouth opened and closed, his eyes bulged in his pale and sweaty face. He struggled to speak. "I'm not swimming that."

"Do you have a better idea?" Kat sounded angry.

Mangos shaded his eyes and looked down the canal. "We could try the bridge."

It had been a grand bridge. It once spanned the canal in three arches, two short on each side with a long center span that barges could pass beneath. Much of the marble remained, though rust bled from the joints.

A long ramp rose out of the jungle to form the abutment and lessen the incline of the road as it rose toward the top of the bridge. The first arch still stood, crossing a quarter of the canal. The center arch had fallen; it was visible under the cloudy yellow-green water. The footings for another support poked out of the water, bits of the spandrels still clinging to it, but nothing more. The last arch had also fallen, and bits of it stuck above the water, forming stepping-stones to the far side.

Upon reaching the bridge, Mangos ran his hand over the stained marble. "The re-enforcing rods are likely rusted away," he said. "They sometimes used iron cages filled with crushed rock to fill the abutments and spandrels. It was cheaper and easier than moving larger stones from the quarry."

Kat looked at him incredulously; clearly amazed he would know that, perhaps even surprised he would know the terms. "I did not know that," she said.

"My father was a mason," he said, feeling his skin redden as he blushed. "He once worked on a bridge." He changed the subject: "I think if we get to the other support, we can jump from stone to stone to the far side."

"And just how are we supposed to get there?" demanded Andor. "I told you I'm not swimming."

"If we can wedge a branch with a rope tied to it on that support, someone can pull themselves across."

"That would be me," volunteered Kat. "I'm the lightest and not afraid of water." Her smirk told Mangos she suspected why he didn't want to swim.

It took Mangos a dozen tries before he lodged a stick on the broken support. He pulled the rope tight and tied it to the abutment.

Kat pulled on the rope. "This ought to work." She slid off the edge of the bridge and started to cross, moving first one hand than the other. Her weight caused the rope to stretch and sag.

"A little lower and I may as well be swimming," she said between breaths.

As her feet dipped near the water, dozens of fish rose to the surface, making ripples as they circled below her.

"I don't think you want to do that," Mangos called. "Swim, I mean."

Kat kept moving forward, dropping even lower as she neared the midpoint. A fish leapt from the water, missed her, and splashed back. More fish started to leap, and she swayed to avoid them.

"They're—oh!" she exclaimed as a fish narrowly missed her, but bit her cape and hung, thrashing but unable to extract its teeth from the cloth. "They have large teeth."

"Hold tight, I'll raise the rope!" Mangos called. He grabbed the rope and began to pull it. At the far end the stones shifted. Kat dropped, jerked to a stop.

"Don't!" she shouted.

He stopped, unable to pull or let go while the fish kept jumping. Kat gyrated wildly as she tried to pull herself across the canal.

A huge shape, perhaps twenty feet long, swam into view just beneath the surface. It had a blunt snout, four stubby legs, and a long tail. "Not good," Mangos said, "Not at all good." The crocodile rose, its broad back breaking the surface, and swam under Kat.

The fish ignored the crocodile and kept leaping at Kat. She hung no more than a foot above the water.

The stone shifted again and Kat dropped a few more inches.

The crocodile opened its mouth, four feet long and full of teeth. It closed it with a snap, and Kat let out a surprised cry. The crocodile turned

toward the far bank then circled back.

Kat stopped struggling, lifted her feet higher, and watched it pass directly beneath her.

The stone shifted.

Kat let go.

"No!" cried Mangos. His heart seemed to stop.

Kat dropped onto the crocodile's back, ran its length and sprang into a shallow dive. She knifed into the water; the fish darted away and immediately swarmed back. The crocodile twisted around, its great tail driving it in pursuit.

Mangos could only swear, over and over, as his heart hammered. He prepared to dive in, stopped, tried again—couldn't do it.

Kat broached the water at the ruined support, pulled herself up, clothes in tatters, blood trickling through the holes. She climbed as her life depended on it, ignoring the jumping fish.

The crocodile erupted after her, teeth flashing, tail thrashing, beating the water to foam as it tried to scale the support.

And then Kat was crouched on the top, dripping water and blood, watching the crocodile scrabble uselessly. A fish flopped at her side, still caught on her cape.

Mangos let out his breath, and it seemed his heart started to beat again. "That," he called, "is why I don't like swimming!"

Kat began to laugh. The crocodile stopped trying to climb the support and swam around it, opening and closing its mouth.

"At least it'll be easy to tie off the rope securely," she said, still grinning. "Then you can cross safely enough."

"Only after the crocodile leaves," said Andor. Mangos had forgotten all about him. "I'm not crossing until it leaves."

Nothing remained of the main gates of Terzol City but blackened rubble. They had been contested beyond their destruction; even the form of gates and towers had been destroyed. A partially cleared path allowed the victorious attackers, and centuries later them, to pass.

The wall slithered up to the ruined gates. It would be easy to think it useless, shaded as it was by the trees that rose high above it. Or maybe it was that much of the wall had been reduced to rubble, or that time and weather had failed to erase the mark of fire. Yet the wall still served as a boundary, and in places it still had grandeur; twelve yards high where it stood unbroken, banded in grey and purple stone. It must have been grand, Mangos thought as they passed into Terzol the city.

What war started in the city, the jungle finished. Trees grew around and through the structures. Their roots pushed apart walls and wrapped up buildings. Grasses sprouted in a thin layer of soil that partially covered the streets. All was peaceful in the shade of the tall trees.

"We have seen you safely to Terzol," Mangos said.

"There is no safety in Terzol," came a voice. They turned to see a man crouched on top of one of the pillars. "Even now."

Andor turned very pale. "Why are you here? I have done nothing."

"Nothing but steal from the Bursa," said the man.

"The Bursa?" Mangos demanded in shock. "You stole from the Bursa?" He had heard of him—merchant prince, king of thieves, the most powerful man in Alomar after the true Prince.

"No!" Andor exclaimed. "I didn't! Only a scroll. Worthless, not even in the records. It had fallen behind the paneling."

"Ah," the man mused. "The Bursa was right. He didn't know what you took, only that you must have taken something."

Andor closed his mouth, his eyes popping from his face as he realized he had just confessed.

"Nobody," said the man, now talking to Mangos and Kat, "quits the Bursa and hires bodyguards unless they have done something... wrong." He sprang off the pillar, landing lightly. With a sword in one hand and a long knife in the other, he advanced on Andor. "Now I will recover this scroll and set an example of you." Andor sank to his knees in fear.

Kat stepped forward. "We can't let you do that."

"We can't?" said Mangos. "He's a treacherous little bastard. We *should* have fed him to the crocodile."

Kat's eyes never left the assassin. "If we're that particular about clients, we'll have few."

"Admirable," said the man. "But do you know who I am?"

"I think so," replied Kat. "The Hand of Bursa, though I'd not thought to see you outside of Alomar."

"This took me further than I expected. Our little bird flew very far indeed. But the Bursa does not tolerate theft, no matter how small."

The Hand of Bursa moved, and Mangos blinked, for it seemed he had not moved so much as disappeared and reappeared next to Kat. Steel clashed. Mangos blinked again, for he had not seen Kat draw her blades,

73

but nonetheless she had two.

He drew his own sword but waited for an opening.

Kat and the Hand fought in style—fluid, graceful, their blades whispering when they met and slid. Neither seemed to have weight, and both used their feet as weapons. They locked blades; the Hand swept Kat's feet from under her, and they rolled together, long knives flashing.

Mangos stopped, unable to attack as they changed positions so quickly.

They both rose, each bleeding, Kat from a nick under her chin, the Hand from a cut on his arm.

"Almost had you there," the Hand said.

"Almost."

"My turn," said Mangos and jumped forward. The Hand met his attack with his sword, swung in with his knife. Mangos drew back and swung low, trying to use his sword's longer reach to his advantage. Again the Hand parried and drove in. Surprised, Mangos clubbed him with the hilt of his sword and kicked away. The Hand grunted and shook his head.

Kat moved in to engage the Hand, and the fight swirled away, past Andor who seemed rooted on his knees, staring at those who fought over his life.

"Faster," Mangos said aloud. He and Kat attacked, driving the Hand back. They could not hurt him, but they drove him away from Andor, back toward the jungle. He gave ground, further, further back. He seemed a touch slower, perhaps still feeling Mangos's blow. A couple more exchanges, Mangos thought, and we'll have him.

The Hand dove and rolled, and attacked Mangos. Mangos gave a step, and the Hand was past him.

"No!" shouted Kat, but she bumped into Mangos, and the Hand was between them and Andor.

Andor looked up, eyes wide, hands at his side as the Hand leapt over him. He lifted his head to watch, and the Hand slashed down, slicing his neck. Blood showered the paving stones. He fell backwards, landing on his pack with a heavy thud, and then rolled onto his side where he twitched as blood spurted from his neck.

Kat and Mangos stopped. There was nothing they could do now.

The Hand stood over Andor. "No need to fight now? Good." He cut the straps on Andor's pack and flipped open the flap with his knife. His eyes did not leave Kat and Mangos as he rummaged through the pack until he found what he wanted. He pulled out the brass tube, now crushed by

Andor falling on it.

"He *was* a bastard," Kat said.

Prying off the top, the Hand looked in. He started to laugh. "Ironic." He poured flakes and dust from the flattened tube – all that remained of the receipt. "Did he ever tell you what he sought?"

"No," Mangos answered. Kat shook her head.

"No, he probably didn't. He's not going to steal from Bursa and share with you." He dropped the tube. It bounced twice and came to rest in Andor's blood. "You can take your pay from his body." He bent to wipe his blade on Andor's shirt and slid it back into its sheath. "Terzol has been picked clean for centuries. He should have known it wasn't worth the risk."

"Not if the Bursa would send you halfway across the world to protect his reputation," Kat remarked, a hint of irony in her voice.

"Just so," said the Hand, inclining his head as he accepted the compliment. "Good day. And good day it is, for you live to see the end of it." He turned to leave but paused. "Andor chose well for bodyguards, but early, I think. Time. With time and experience, you will be formidable." He nodded before disappearing into the jungle.

Mangos let out his breath with a loud 'whoosh.' "That didn't go well."

"I don't like failing in a commission," said Kat.

"We can hardly be blamed, by the gods of Eastwarn! The Hand of Bursa!" He nudged Andor with his foot. "You made powerful enemies."

"Shall we see why?" Kat raised an eyebrow.

Andor never told them where they went, but that didn't mean they didn't know. Mangos started to chuckle. He pulled the chain from around Andor's dead neck and tossed it to Kat. "We shall."

The square could hold thousands, tens of thousands. Mangos couldn't even imagine how many people it would take to pack such a place. The jungle had taken the city and invaded the buildings to either side, but the palace remained untouched. A dozen leopard statues flanked the broad steps to the portico, steps that rose fifty feet to columns that rose fifty more.

Wide terraces surrounded each level so that each was smaller than the one below and the whole building formed a pyramid. At the top, seemingly brushing the clouds, was the broken and vacant home of the god-emperors.

THE VALLEY OF TERZOL

The emptiness made Terzol seem even larger, grander—too large for people.

Kat climbed the broad stone steps. The leopards looked down at her. Leopards, Mangos realized, who had looked down on the pageantry of emperors and treachery of generals. Leopards who had seen the wealth of an empire and the silence of centuries.

Kat wore that grandeur and sadness like a crown, as if she understood it and it was part of her. For a moment she was the Queen of a desolate country. Mangos shook his head to clear the image.

It took a day of searching through dark corridors that still stank of old fire and death, listening to their footsteps echo in empty halls, and picking through broken statues and the last rotting remains of furnishings. Finally, they stood outside a metal door leaning against its frame, one hinge broken and the other twisted by the door's weight. Kat ran her hand down the dented surface. "Here," she said, pausing to rub over a word barely discernable beneath a layer of red rust. "Mercantile vault."

She bent to pick up a battered lantern, lit it, and set it in an oddly-shaped mirrored box. Light bounced around the room, striking other mirrors and reflecting back and forth to illuminate a long chamber.

Broken pottery and chests littered the floor. Here and there a statue, masterfully carved, lay in pieces. Four heavy pillars obscured their view.

As they entered, their feet crushed shards of mirrors, broken glass from plates and vases, and shattered bones.

"It's been looted." Mangos stopped, looked and saw shadows on the far wall. "There."

They found six small vaults, each with a leopard's head snarling, black steel and cold, on the door. Four doors, a handspan thick and contoured to match the frame of the vault, were open. The vaults were empty.

Mangos squatted down to look at the lower of the two closed doors. "There is no keyhole." He reached inside the leopard's mouth. A faint noise, a creak of old metal, and he snatched his hand back just as the leopard bit down. The metal jaws clashed and relaxed, returning to their original position.

"That could—" He stopped as a thought crossed his mind. He peered under the metal fangs. Small holes in each. "Poison. Likely dried up, but you never know."

"Here," Kat said, handing him Andor's seal.

"Thanks," said Mangos. In the back of the leopard's mouth he could see an impression. It did not match the seal. "What if it belongs to a vault that's already open?"

Kat did not answer, and Mangos moved over to the other closed vault. The seal and impression matched. He grinned and then sobered as he lifted the seal near the leopard's mouth. "I really hope this works."

He pressed the seal into the back of the leopard's mouth. They could hear the sound of weights and counterweights tripping within the wall. Somewhere stone slid on stone.

The door swung open. The vault was a hollow in the wall four feet deep. Pushed to the back was a small leather bag, nicely filled.

All they need do was reach past a hole, as wide as the hollow and equally long, but of a depth Mangos could not tell. He wiggled his fingers and reached toward the hole.

"That would be foolish," Kat said.

There came a heavy rasping sound, as if called by Kat's words, and Mangos drew back is hand. The sound grew louder, and he could tell it came from the hole in the vault. A blunt nose appeared, poking up, and long tongue flicked out. A snake pushed up, out, and seemed to flow from the vault.

Mangos and Kat leapt back and drew their swords. The snake was pale green and yellow, and Mangos could not tell its length yet but he judged its width to be two feet. The snake lifted its head, fully as large as Mangos's. Its tongue flicked out as if tasting his smell on the air.

"I wouldn't count on its poison having dried up," said Kat.

It turned toward her voice and the light shone on its cloudy eyes. It flicked its tongue out. They could see more than twenty feet of snake and still it pulled itself out of the vault.

It struck.

Kat twisted as the snake shot by, curved, and she jumped to avoid its coils. She landed on its back, tumbled off and rolled, the snake striking just behind her.

"Why doesn't anything attack you first?" she complained. The snake struck again.

Mangos reversed his grip on his sword and plunged it into the snake. It thrashed, ripping the sword from his grip. Red blood welled around the sword and ran down its scales.

The snake raced away, taking Mangos's sword with it. He drew his long knife and drove it into the snake, edge toward its back. Bracing himself, he let the snake cut itself open as it rushed past. His teeth rattled as the knife bounced along the snake's ribs.

The tail whipped around, jarring him and knocking him back. It caught him again and knocked him over. Before he could rise a coil flopped on top of him. His breath left him but he struggled to free himself as the snake coursed over him.

It thrashed again; he didn't know what Kat did, but he rolled free. He knew he needed to get to the head. He couldn't kill the snake by beating its tail.

With a crash of broken glass, the room dimmed. The snake had knocked over several of the mirrors that lit the room. It reared its head and paused.

Silence. Mangos moved and it turned toward him.

"Make no noise," said Kat, hidden from view. "It's blind!"

The snake turned and struck at her voice. It vanished behind a pillar, and when it drew back, Kat was riding it, clinging just behind its head. She drew back her sword, thrust at its eye as it whipped back and forth. She missed, lost her grip and flew off, the snake after her before she struck the floor.

It scooped her in its coils, lifted her and opened its mouth to strike or eat.

Mangos grabbed its head. "If you let me attack first, this wouldn't happen," he grunted as he pulled back, his muscles straining. Kat couldn't answer, her face was red and arms were pinned to her body.

Mangos slipped down the snake, reached up, and grabbed a fang; it felt smooth and cool in his hand as he pulled himself up. He reached around with his knife and slid it into the snake's eye.

The snake went berserk and threw him off as it became a frenzied mass of coils. He pulled Kat free and they stumbled across the room to watch the snake convulse and die.

Kat lay against the wall and stretched her legs out in front of her, panting.

Her hair stuck to her sweaty face. She closed her eyes. "I'll be fine," she said. "Just need to get my breath back."

When the snake no more than twitched, Mangos returned to the vault, stretched his hand all the way to the back, and drew out the pouch. He carried it back to Kat, sat on the ground beside her and worried at the drawstrings. He tipped it over and shook eight large gems out onto the dirty floor.

Leopard eye emeralds—so pure it looked like the green elliptical inclusion floated. Legends said they were formed by moonbeams captured when the world was formed. Mangos felt himself smiling like a fool. Kat stared at the emeralds spread before her like a fortune-teller trying to read the future in the bones.

"I think," said Mangos, "I'll sell mine. I can live like a king, drinking Ambraisen wine in the most pleasurable company. And I'll have a sword made, a hand-and-a-half sword with one of the emeralds set in the hilt." He stretched, enjoying fantasizing. "And I'll buy a copy of Teritum's *History of Terzol.*"

Kat reached out to place a finger on a gem. She moved it aside and another that matched it exactly. "These two will be made into earrings. This one," she moved a larger stone next to the first two "will make a necklace."

"What of that one?" Mangos said, indicating the last emerald.
"This one," she rested her finger on her last stone and gently pushed it away from her, "will help buy an army."

MONGOOSE & MEERKAT

The Burning Fish

Ten months after the fall of Alness.

"This isn't the Burning Fish we need," Kat said.

"I know that!" Mangos retorted as he tried to push the fish off the hot stone. Smoke curled up, and the fish turned blacker and blacker. Finally, he drew his sword, slipped it under the fish, and flipped it onto a wooden plate.

Kat stood next to him, looking down at their burnt dinner. "I'd rather not be poisoned on this quest."

"If the worst thing that happens is our lunch, I'll be happy," Mangos said. But he laughed; there was nothing else he could do. "I turn my back for a minute…" He shook his head. Kat had been tending the mule that carried their gear and the special barrel that would let them transport a Burning Fish once they found one.

Baron Endelhorn wanted a Burning Fish because it was his family's crest, and he was willing to pay very generously for one. The true Burning Fish would burst into flames when it leapt from the water only to be extinguished when it fell back in. It was, Mangos had always thought, legendary, but after rummaging through old records in the ruins of Terzol, Kat said they might be able to find one.

"I thought I would save time," Mangos gestured to the well-stoked fire, prodding the plate with his foot. He would have to be starving before he tried to eat that fish.

"It was said the right sized fish would cook itself perfectly if it wasn't returned to the water," Kat said.

"Then the fish could cook itself better than I can cook it." He sighed. "How much further to the lake?"

Kat shot him a look that seemed to say, *if you learned to read, you would know this for yourself.*

Mangos threw dirt over the fire and took up the mule's halter. The journey was easy—plentiful fish and game, and pleasant shade under the forest canopy. It was almost like being paid for a pleasure trip.

Best to enjoy things while they were good.

Yellow flowers dotted the forest floor. They looked like little suns, globes of tightly bunched petals just starting to open. Their sweet smell tickled his nose and made the forest seem cheerful.

Presently he caught a glimpse of the lake far ahead, sunlight sparkling off its surface. They emerged from the trees on the east shore. The lake was half a mile across, and something more than that in length. They were closer to the south end of the lake than the north.

Grey stone buildings clustered at the north end, an enduring reminder of the former power and reach of Terzol. Vines crawled over half the buildings, and empty darkness gaped through their windows and doors. The rest had been cleared of growth and fitted with shutters and doors of rough-hewn wood to keep out the weather.

Made small by the distance, people moved around the buildings and on the beach. A few used large baskets to fish while others worked on the beach.

Mangos shaded his eyes, trying to see more clearly. "There are people here."

"People?" Kat came up behind him. "What kind of people? The only people in these mountains are hunters."

"Just people."

"They're not from the Terzol valley, and it looks like they're fishing for food, not trade."

"They must be crazy. This is nowhere. Go to Alomar, people," he growled. "You can *buy* fish in Alomar."

"Not Burning Fish," Kat remarked, her tone thoughtful.

An old man sat on the sandy beach, watching the fishers. Another man sat next to him, weaving a fishing basket. Several more people moved around, some carrying wood or fresh cut rushes. They all stopped working as Mangos and Kat approached.

"Are you pilgrims?" one of the fishing women asked. She was only a year or two older than Mangos, brown hair bleached by the sun, wearing a tunic that came to her knees, the bottom inch wet from the waves.

Pilgrims? Mangos wondered. "No," he said.

"Who are you?" Kat asked the group.

They turned to the old man to answer. He bowed his head in respectful greeting before saying, "We serve Tourlan, the goddess of the lake."

There was a stone table with a roughly carved wooden fish on it halfway up the beach. *That's a pretty poor altar*, Mangos thought. Did they expect pilgrims for that?

"Tourlan?" Kat raised an eyebrow. She appeared thoughtful. "You are far from civilization."

"We are. Yet the goddess is here, so here we serve."

"We won't bother you," assured Mangos. "We'll just get what we need and leave you to your goddess."

"What do you need?"

"A Burning Fish."

The crowd murmured and an angry, wordless grumble came from many throats. The old man's eyes widened a fraction, he glanced at his followers, and licked his lips. "The Burning Fish are sacred to Tourlan," he said. "You may not disturb them."

"The Terzoli served them for dinner," Kat remarked. She jerked her head around to encompass the village. Mangos wondered if these people even knew the origin of the buildings.

"And look what happened to Terzol," the old man retorted.

"You think there's a connection?" Kat asked.

The old man took his gaze from the buildings and turned it on her. "Yes."

"You eat fish," Mangos protested, pointing at the women fishing.

"Not the goddess's sacred fish," the old man replied.

"It's fortunate nobody wants to eat one," Kat said. "The earl wants one because it's the symbol of his family. It would be honored."

The woman who first spoke opened her mouth, her expression angry. The old man forestalled her by shaking his head and saying, "No."

The man weaving fish traps reached for a rusty sword lying beside him. "Darnow," the old man said. "That isn't necessary. They have traveled a long way. They may rest here before returning home."

Darnow glanced at the women in the water before drawing back his hand. He didn't say anything but still glared.

"Tourlan has given us more than we need." The old man gestured at the stone buildings. "You are welcome to use one." He looked coy as he said, "Maybe you'd like to learn more of our goddess."

Mangos ducked his head as he entered the small building. The thick slates forming the roof remained solid, successfully protecting the massive timbers that supported them. The heavy cut stones of the walls remained straight and true. Leaves gathered in the corners, but somebody had swept most of them out so it looked like autumn on the ground outside. An old blanket hung over the door.

"I don't think he's letting us stay from any feeling of charity," Mangos said. "He just wants to keep an eye on us."

"There are four people who matter," Kat said with a nod. "The High Priest, of course, and the old woman who sat next to him. She didn't talk, but she also didn't work, so she has some influence. The girl who was fishing in the water—she wants to be the new leader, you can tell by how she acts. The man weaving fish traps is the other. I don't know how smart he is, but he's clearly willing to fight. The rest are sheep."

Mangos scratched the back of his neck. "I'm willing to bet any of them could get a Burning Fish pretty easily. Maybe somebody will quietly sell us one."

"Can't hurt to try," Kat said. "Except the trap weaver is a fighter. A tough and dirty fighter, if I had to guess."

Mangos thought of the villagers. The High Priest was Barnor, and though he tried to hide it, his left leg was horribly scarred. The woman who stayed near him was Saralyn. The young woman was Danielse. As Kat said, Darnow was a scarred fighter, younger than Barnor, but still older and more experienced than Mangos. There were more who kept to the back. Barely individuals, together they gave strength to Barnor's refusal.

"There's a stream flowing from the east side of the lake," Kat noted. "It might be a good place to trap fish."

"I'll try to get a Burning Fish the easy way."

"Cooking it?"

Mangos laughed. "Getting one from those who know best."

I'll start with these two, Mangos thought.

Saralyn crouched at the water's edge, washing reeds.

Danielse carried a bundle of yellow flowers to the altar. Bowing her head, she arranged them around the fish carving. Dropping to her knees, she bowed her head again before brushing the sand smooth.

She rose and came to the edge of the water, humming a tune that wandered like a lost adventurer—going nowhere, but happy about it. She sat, putting her feet in the lake, and began to braid the flowers in her hair.

Saralyn frowned at her but didn't say anything. Danielse kept braiding while the older woman worked.

"Have you seen a Burning Fish?" Mangos asked.

"They're beautiful," Danielse said. "They leap high out of the water and burst into blue flame." She sighed, enraptured by her memory. "So lovely. The goddess favors me," she added.

Saralyn rolled her eyes. "So you keep reminding us."

"You saw one?" Mangos prompted.

"My first day," Danielse replied. Her smile was vacant, as if the past was still before her. "The spring rains had flooded my family's farm and drowned my parents. I tried to reach town, but I got turned around avoiding the floods and wandered until I ended up here. The goddess welcomed me with the sight of Burning Fish." She blinked herself back to the present and returned to braiding the flowers into her hair.

She's not going to give us one, Mangos thought. *The Fish are too holy*. He turned to Saralyn. "Have you seen one?"

Saralyn pursed her lips. "No."

"She cleaned the High Priest's house for years without the goddess revealing her sacred text," Danielse said.

"Don't sound so smug." Saralyn glared. "You can't read it. Nobody can."

"A text?" Mangos felt he was in the middle of an old argument and didn't know half the terms.

"A worthless old book," Saralyn spat.

"A sacred book," Danielse insisted. "It's written in the goddess's sacred script."

"So you claim!" Sarilyn retorted. "By the goddess, your foolishness makes me ill!"

"You," Mangos hesitated to suggest, "could leave?"

"Leave? Where would I go? Beyond fishing, I have no woodcraft. Besides, except for *her*, it's not so bad. Quiet. And I have a certain influence with Barnor." She smiled a prim smile at Danielse.

"What she means is she's a slave and can't leave," Danielse said.

Saralyn gasped. "It doesn't matter here," she snapped. "My life is no different from anybody else's."

Danielse smirked.

"*You* could leave," Saralyn said. Her tone betrayed her eagerness.

Danielse looked incredulous. "Go out in the world? Serve a baron or an earl? Why? Here I serve a *goddess!*"

This isn't helping, Mangos thought. *Danielse won't give a Fish, and it's clear Saralyn never leaves the village.*

At the edge of the trees, Darnow lurked. He caught Mangos's eye and motioned him over. Mangos gladly excused himself and trudged up the beach.

Darnow looked around. "How much will you pay for one?" he whispered.

Mangos looked up. Darnow could only be talking about a Burning Fish. *How much would we pay for one?* Mangos wondered. Better yet, *does he truly have one to sell?* It seemed too easy.

Darnow drew him closer, as a conspirator would. Mangos could smell smoke and sweat and rotting teeth. "How much?" Darnow repeated.

"You have one to sell?" Mangos asked.

Darnow scratched behind an ear, drew his hand down and pulled at his upper lip. "Course I have."

"And you're willing to sell the goddess's sacred fish?"

Darnow turned his head and spat in the sand. "If your gold is good."

He doesn't think much of the goddess, Mangos thought. *But he thinks a lot of that fish.* He wondered why Darnow needed gold. He couldn't spend it here. "You think a fish is worth gold?"

"You think a fish is worth coming all the way out here." Darnow smiled, showing not just his rotting teeth but several gaps. "Think about it." He stood, evidently having noticed Danielse fishing, and puffed out his chest before walking away.

"So," said Kat.

Mangos jumped, spun, and glared. He hadn't known she was sitting on the other side of the tree.

"Darnow is planning on leaving sometime," she continued. "And my guess is he wants to take Danielse with him." She snorted, a sound of skepticism. "He'll need luck and a new set of teeth for that."

"But he can get us a fish," Mangos mused.

"Can he? He might sell us a fish, or he might murder us in our sleep. I wouldn't bet either way."

They told each other what they had discovered. Kat went first, telling him there would be no fish in the outflow stream. The water level was too low.

Mangos told her of Saralyn and Danielse's argument, and she agreed there was little more to be gained there, though the book interested her.

"And," she said, "we need to talk to Barnor. Alone would be best."

They didn't get a chance until late afternoon when the beach was empty and Barnor was limping alone to the altar. He took out a rag and began to wipe the top.

"I'd like to talk to you about the goddess," Kat said quietly.

Barnor looked at her from the sides of his eyes then glanced over at Mangos. He repositioned his scarred leg to make it more comfortable. "Talk."

"Tourlan was a prostitute in Denoit, famous because she could—" Kat cleared her throat. "Never mind why she was famous. She might still be alive, but she'd be old, and certainly not a goddess. Also, the Terzoli harvested Burning Fish for generations and never mentioned deities. Strange that one should suddenly settle in now."

Ha, Mangos thought, *the whole thing is a sham.*

"I spent my whole life in these mountains," Barnor said. "When I was a lad, a few old men hunted here, but they died, and I was the only one. I got tired of it, lonely if you will. I was starting to look for something else when I ruined my leg." He slapped his scarred leg. "Hard to go anywhere then, worse now."

"Live somewhere else," Mangos said.

Barnor shook his head. "Maybe you would, maybe you bend to the world, but I bend the world to me. I knew about this village, of course, and of the Burning Fish."

Kat leaned back, smiling. She nodded. She must have guessed Barnor's story.

Barnor wadded up the rag and resumed wiping off the top of the altar. Mangos suddenly realized this was not really an altar, just a stone table once used for cleaning fish. It had a groove around the edge and a hole in one end to wash down the scales and offal. He couldn't suppress a snort of amusement, wondering how many of the goddess's sacred fish had been cleaned on her altar.

"So," Barnor said, continuing his story, "I made up the story of Tourlan, the goddess of the lake. I became High Priest and went out to recruit acolytes." He grinned, eyes twinkling. "The original Tourlan was something of a goddess, too, at least when I was a young man."

"And people fell for it," Mangos said, half a statement, half a question, for it seemed incredible, yet there they were.

Barnor snorted and smiled like a boy caught in a clever lie. "I had to buy my first follower because nobody would join. After that it was easier."

"Then it shouldn't be a problem for us to take a fish," Mangos said.

Barnor shook his head. "The High Priest loses face if he gives away the goddess's sacred fish."

"Nobody need know," said Kat.

"You still can't have one," Barnor shook his head again, "because there aren't any left."

The water lay flat, untroubled by wind or wave. A faint mist hovered over the surface. A large bird, a heron, glided down, wings not moving, coasting on the air until it nearly touched the water. It dropped its legs, flapped, and came to a stop standing in the center of concentric circles that rushed away from it. Further away, a fish jumped. A normal fish.

According to Barnor, it was four years since any there had seen a Burning Fish, and Mangos believed him. After confessing to making up the religion, Barnor had nothing to gain by lying about the fish.

How could Darnow sell us a Burning Fish if there aren't any? Mangos wondered as he leaned on the windowsill. Dusk was fast approaching. *What does he know?*

Kat came into the building, walked right to the lamp and sat beside it. She pulled a medium-sized book from under her cloak and opened it.

"You stole the goddess's book!" Mangos exclaimed.

"Quiet," Kat whispered forcefully. "I'm pretty sure the goddess can't hear you, but let's not take our chances with the others."

"Nobody can read the book," Mangos reminded her.

"That," Kat said, "is because they can't read Terzoli."

Mangos blinked, caught off guard. "Terzoli?"

"This is just a Terzoli log book. I told you they served Burning Fish at the Emperor's banquets and they built this village to supply the fish." She ran her finger down the first page.

"But—" Mangos started.

"It's the same thing we're doing," Kat explained. "They just had a system to do it regularly." She fell silent as she read. After a minute, she said, "And to ensure a predictable supply of fish."

"Well, it'd be embarrassing if the Emperor didn't have Burning Fish to eat."

"And therefore unacceptable." Kat turned the page, grimaced. "Some fool didn't mix the ink right. Look at this," she pointed half way down the page, where the words seemed to vanish. "It's so faded you can't read it." She flipped several more pages until coming to one with writing. "Ah, better. New ink, mixed properly this time."

"There is another lake," she said after studying the page for a moment. She looked over toward the window. "It must be on the west side because it flows into this one."

Mangos went to the window and looked west, where the mountains were further from the shore, looking for a break in the trees. He couldn't see anything in the dusk, so he turned his attention back to the book on the table.

Kat turned the page and groaned. "They let that idiot make ink again." She started to flip pages. Nothing.

"What can it tell us?" Mangos asked.

"Not enough. There was something important about the other lake. There were no Burning Fish in it, but the Terzoli did something, something they felt would allow them to control the harvest of Burning Fish."

"And?" Mangos prompted.

"And they ran out of ink. Finished the entry in a new batch, and it faded to nothing."

M angos found a break in the trees in a small cove. A shelf of rock sloped down to the lake. There was a hole in its flat surface about forty feet from shore. A pile of wilted flowers and a small cup of water sat next to the hole.

"Home of the goddess, I expect," Mangos murmured as he surveyed the offering.

He could see the upper lake while standing next to the hole. Its surface was three or four feet higher than the lower lake, the water held back by a natural dam of stone packed with branches and leaves, held in place by grass and small shrubs.

Mangos walked up the shelf of grey slate. Water trickled over the dam, making a river an inch deep and narrow enough to step over. The river vanished into the "goddess's home."

The Burning Fish never appeared in the upper lake, yet the Terzoli fish keepers felt the lake important, and required great care.

He climbed onto the dam.

The upper lake was deep. He didn't want to judge, knowing how water could distort distances, but it was at least ten feet deep near the sides, and in the center the bottom plunged out of sight.

Curious.

He just didn't know why it was curious.

He walked off the dam, brushed his feet through the leaves on the forest floor. He wasn't good at puzzles. Adventures were supposed to be about fighting and drinking and treasures and pleasant company.

He sighed. What was the connection between the upper and lower lakes? A pittance of a stream too small for fish.

But there were no Burning Fish.

Maybe, Mangos thought, there are no fish because there is no connection.

Walking back onto the dam, he realized he had only thought it natural. Under all the grass and dirt, the stones had been fitted together.

Curious.

He crouched down, pulled up some grass, and ran his hand over the mortared stones. There was no doubt. Should he get Kat?

He jumped off the dam and walked down to the goddess's home. Cool air and darkness rose from it. He could hear water dripping. Home of the goddess or work of the Terzoli? He crouched down to see better.

The wind stirred. Mangos felt it on his back. It blew through the forest and brought with it the smell of flowers.

Something very hard struck him on the back of his head, and he pitched into the hole.

Mangos opened his eyes. A dozen halos of light danced above him, slowly revolving down to one. The light felt painful. He shivered. He was cold. His muscles felt tight and his head pounded, but nothing worse. Lucky.

He sat up and felt water run from his hair, heard it drip. He was sitting in three inches of water on another slate shelf. Luckily, he had been lying face up, or he would have drowned.

He reached up and touched his head. His hand came away wet, but not bloody. Lucky again. A man had no right to expect such luck.

He was at the end of a cavern, the area around him lit by the hole above, the rest melding to darkness to his left. Water fell through the sunlight, like diamonds into darkness to splash beside him as mere water again.

A few feet away the rock shelf ended, the pool suddenly dark, and Mangos had no idea how deep it might be.

Branches and bones wedged in the rock wall showed the water had been higher in the past. Some sort of plant grew from cracks in the wall. It looked like kelp, with long vines and narrow leaves, and it trailed in the water.

As his eyes adjusted, he could see the further walls. Walls, he realized, that separated him from the two lakes on either side. He hoped they were thick.

A large fish swam up and nibbled a trailing plant. After a few bites, it swam away, but there were dozens more, appearing and disappearing in the dark water.

Mangos picked up a plant; it felt warm to his touch. He rolled it between his fingers, crushing the leaves. Heat flared on his fingertips.

There was a splash. Mangos saw a twinkle of light out of the corner of his eye. When he turned his head, all he saw were small waves rushing from where a fish had jumped.

Then another. The fish hung over the water, longer than he would have suspected, and he saw it clearly illuminated by blue flames. Then it splashed back into the pool, and the flames vanished.

Burning Fish! He scrambled to his feet.

The fish darted away, but he didn't care. He had found them!

His stomach growled. He didn't worry about starving, though. Not with all the fish around just waiting to cook themselves. He was more concerned with getting out. He had no idea how.

The hole was twenty-five feet up, high enough that he considered himself lucky not to have been injured when falling, but far too high to reach. The ceiling overhung the walls. He might climb the walls, but he couldn't stretch far enough to reach the hole.

He gave up trying and searched for some way to catch a fish. A shadow fell on the floor. Mangos looked up.

Kat leaned over the opening, her hair hanging down.

"Get me out!" Mangos called. "I found the Burning Fish." He told her of the fish, and the plants, and the inability to climb out.

A rope snaked down and splashed in the water. "Why did you climb down if you can't get back out?"

Mangos grabbed the rope and pulled himself up. "I didn't." He tilted his head as if she could see the bruise through his hair. "Somebody knocked me in."

That wiped the grin from her face. "Who?"

"I didn't see them."

Kat turned toward the village, as if she could tell Mangos's attacker just by looking. "Did they think the fall would kill you, or that I wouldn't be able to find you?"

"I don't know," Mangos replied. "They likely believed the fall would kill me."

"Then it's decision time," Kat said. Mangos looked at her in surprise. "We can grab a couple fish and take them to the Baron. Or we find who attacked you and sink them in the lake."

"That one." Mangos rubbed his head meaningfully. "We can get the fish afterwards."

Kat nodded.

Mangos felt, and heard, his stomach rumble again.

With a laugh, Kat dug into her pack and pulled out a small loaf of bread and some fish. "I got some dried fish from the village." She held up the food, but seemed distracted, perhaps her mind on the attack.

Mangos reached for the bread. Kat gave it to him and took the fish for herself.

"To the fish," Mangos toasted. They saluted each other with the food and took a bite.

Kat swallowed. She looked into the cavern. "Let's assume it's a combination of a particular type of fish eating the special plants that only grow in the cavern."

"If the cavern floods, some of the fish can escape," Mangos said. "Maybe without the dam it's always flooded."

Kat nodded. "That makes sense. And if the fish swim freely in the lake, they eat other things besides the right plant. By keeping the fish in the cavern, the Terzoi made it easy for themselves."

Mangos waved aside the conversation. "I only want two things," he said. "Find whoever pushed me and get a Burning Fish back to the Baron."

"If we can't figure who pushed you, I'm inclined to take the fish and leave." Kat grinned, her expression feral. "Or we can kill them all."

Suddenly she gagged, swallowed and gagged again. Her eyes went wide, and she stared in horror at the fish in her hand. She threw it out into the lake and immediately began to cough.

"What's wrong?" Mangos asked.

She could not answer, she was coughing too hard, looking to be on the verge of throwing up. She doubled over, clutching at her stomach.

Mangos didn't know what to do; something was very wrong. "Poison?" he asked, dropping his bread.

She nodded her head in jerky motions, slumped over, struggling to breathe.

"What can I do?"

Kat gagged and coughed. A trickle of blood leaked from the corner of her mouth.

Mangos scooped her up, lifted her over his shoulder. He started to walk, then jog, then run back to the village as Kat's coughing eased and she went limp.

"Don't die," he told her, "don't die."

Barnor was sitting next to the lake with the others gathered around him when Mangos reached the village.

"What happened?" Barnor asked.

Danielse and Darnow craned their heads, looking curious, then alarmed. "What bit her?" Darnow asked.

"Nothing bit her, she's been poisoned," Mangos said. "Help her!"

"Poisoned?" Saralyn leaned over to examine Kat. "She knows better than to eat unknown berries and roots."

"Somebody gave her poisoned fish. Somebody here."

Mangos slid Kat off his shoulder, set her down, and laid her back. Her skin felt cold. Her face was white, giving the streak of blood a ghastly appearance. Her eyes were closed, but her eyelids spasmed.

"Help her!" Mangos commanded. It felt like Kat was slipping away and nobody felt any urgency. "If she dies, I'll kill everybody here."

Darnow glared, clapped his hand to his sword and stepped forward, the stink of him filling the air. But Mangos eagerly reached for his own sword. It might not save Kat, but killing Darnow would be doing *something*.

"Draw that sword, and I'll turn the altar back to its original purpose," Mangos growled. "But it's you I'll fillet."

"Please," Saralyn interjected. "It's not that easy." She shook her head. "I don't know antidotes." She looked at the others.

"I do," Barnor said. "But I need to know what she ate."

Mangos glared at the small crowd. The poisoner knew what they used. Who was it?

Barnor? He was a liar and a fraud. If they took a Burning Fish after he denied them one, it would make him look weak. He could be pretending not to know.

What of Darnow? He could be angry they wouldn't pay him and afraid they would reveal his attempt to sell a fish.

Saralyn? Maybe she feared the group would disband if Barnor were to look weak. She could have done it without Barnor knowing about it.

Kat convulsed, then lay still. She would die soon.

Any of them could have poisoned her.

It would be the same person that knocked him into the cavern, he realized. They didn't expect Kat to find him because they thought she would be dead.

A breeze stirred the smell of fish and ash and fresh cut pine, and another smell he recognized...

"What did you use to poison Kat?" Mangos demanded.

Danielse shrank back. "Nothing! What makes you think I did anything?"

"Anybody could have poisoned Kat," he said, "but you're the one who knocked me into the pit." He curled his lip in contempt. "Barnor cannot walk that far. Saralyn doesn't leave the village—and Darnow? I'd have smelled Darnow. Instead, I smelled flowers."

Danielse clutched at her hair, let her hand drop, pulling one of the flowers with it. She lifted her chin. "You will not steal Tourlan's sacred fish."

"Damn the fish! What poison did you use? If she dies, you die."

"Then I will be a martyr for the goddess."

Mangos grabbed the flower from her and brandished it at Barnor. "She uses these for everything. Are they poisonous?"

"Yes."

Danielse glared, and Mangos knew it was true. "Can you cure Kat?" he asked.

Barnor nodded. "I think so. Aanerberry juice should do it."

"Let her die!" shrieked Danielse. "She would defame the goddess! Tell them," she implored Barnor. "Tell them it is true."

"I—I," Barnor faltered.

Mangos sheathed his sword. "Don't waste my time, and don't waste

Kat's."

"She's coming around." Mangos nodded to Saralyn, who came to sit next to Kat. The old woman readied a glass of water.

Kat opened her eyes. She seemed dazed as she looked around. She focused on Mangos and said, "There's something I need to do."

Saralyn gave her the water. "Drink. You need to drink."

"No," said Kat, "that's not it."

"You need to feel better. It will take some time," Saralyn said.

"What will make me feel better won't take long at all," Kat answered, pushing herself up. She wobbled a little and didn't look any steadier as she made her way to the door. She put her hand on the frame and paused, breathing heavily.

"You need to rest. The poison damaged your stomach."

Kat ignored her. "You'll want to come," she told Mangos. "She tried to kill you too."

Mangos nodded, he did want to come, but he opened his mouth to protest. He meant to say Kat should rest, but the look in her eyes and his own desire for revenge changed his mind. "I don't know where she is."

"What are you going to do?" Saralyn sounded both fearful and resigned.

Kat again ignored her. She walked to the beach, slowly, clearly concentrating on her movement. Barnor sat on the sand. He didn't say anything, nor did he try to stop her.

Danielse was not on the beach or in the water.

Kat brushed the wilted flowers off the altar as she walked toward the water's edge and around the west shore of the lake.

"Where's Darnow?" she asked.

"Gone," called Barnor from behind them.

"I wonder what he took," Kat said, but kept walking.

Realizing she headed toward the "goddess's home," Mangos moved ahead of her. His heart beat faster as he neared, expecting to see Danielse kneeling beside the hole in the rock.

It was empty except for a scattering of yellow flowers.

"She's not here," he said as Kat approached. He looked down. Something caught his eye.

He crouched at the hole and stuck his head down, waiting a second for his eyes to adjust. Danielse lay, face down, in the shallow water. Jumped, fell, or pushed; drowned or broken, Mangos couldn't tell, but she was clearly dead.

He straightened up and motioned to Kat. She came over to look.

"She found refuge in the arms of the goddess," Kat said. "One way or another."

The Golden Pearl

One year after the fall of Alness (and Mangos has forgotten all about it)

The muscles in Mangos's back creaked as he and Kat pulled the boat up the beach. The rollers under the boat crushed shells in concert with his efforts. He licked his lips, casting a covetous glance at the fruit hanging from the lush bushes above the high tide mark.

"Rare, eh?" he said.

"I'm sure," Kat answered. She sweated as she helped drag the boat.

"Valuable, too?" His foot slipped, and he had to grab the gunwale to keep from falling, sand spraying as he tried to get his feet back under him.

"Very."

"Better be."

They had just sailed for weeks in a small boat, and it better be for something more valuable than low hanging fruit, no matter how tasty.

The sun was hot, and he was hungry and thirsty, but it was golden pearls he really wanted. The pearls were a cure for any poison, and he and Kat figured that sooner or later they would need some. They had made many enemies during their time together, not the least of which was the notorious Bursa of Alomar. "Just making sure."

"As you have every day so far," Kat said.

"That should be far enough." He was thinking of how far he'd have to push it back out to go pearl diving.

Kat stopped pulling, looked at the tidemarks, and nodded. She was tanned by the sun, which also lightened the color of her hair. She brushed it from her face, and the sea breeze blew it right back.

Mangos climbed to the bushes, eyes fastened on the dark red fruit. He picked the largest, darkest fruit; it lay heavy in his palm, filled with juice. His mouth began to water. He lifted it and opened his mouth.

"That's poisonous."

Mangos blinked, looking around to see who spoke. Kat was looking past him, so he turned to see a young girl, about thirteen, holding a sheaf of dry palm fronds and a two-tined trident. "You can eat it if you want," she said, "but paligrates *are* poisonous."

Mangos regarded the paligrate, his mouth suddenly dry. It looked so good he didn't want to believe it was poisonous. *That's why we need Golden Pearls,* he thought as he threw the fruit into the ocean.

"Who are you?" Kat asked.

"Kimi."

"We're looking for Golden Pearls."

"Everybody's looking for Golden Pearls," Kimi replied with a shrug, as though the actions of the world didn't concern her.

"I'll bet they are," Mangos muttered. He glared at the rest of the red paligrates, offended that he couldn't eat them. "Then they could eat this fruit."

"No..." Kimi gave Mangos a puzzled look with her blue eyes, making him feel as though he didn't know the most basic thing about the island. "To give to the Killanei in hopes she will give them the Elibli fruit."

Nobody spoke, the wind, surf, and rustling leaves the only sound. Mangos tried to remember what Kat had told him about the island. A few miles across, one village, only place to find Golden Pearls: nothing about Killaneis or Elibli fruit.

"What are the Killanei and Elibli fruit?" he finally asked.

Kimi shifted her trident, keeping it between her and them. She frowned. "Why did you come if not for the Elibli fruit?"

"For Golden Pearls," Mangos said. "We said that." His stomach growled. "And something to eat."

"Why would you want the Pearls if not to give to the Killanei?"

"To cure poison. Just in case somebody feeds us bad fish." Mangos glanced at Kat, trying to see if she thought Kimi as innocent as she appeared. Kat smiled at his fish jest and shrugged to his unspoken question.

"If someone gave you bad fish, you would have been foolish to eat it, but they did it to make you eat your Golden Pearl," Kimi said.

"Kimi!" a deep voice called out. "Tell them no more. They are not your friends." An old man pushed his way through the bushes. He had white hair, his skin was dark and wrinkled. He had the same blue eyes as Kimi.

"I have no friends," Kimi retorted. "But they are strangers who do not know of the Killanei."

"They are liars," said the old man. He shook his fist at Mangos. "Leave her alone. She has nothing the Killanei wants."

"By the gods of Eastwarn!" Mangos swore. "What are you talking about?"

The old man curled his lip. He took Kimi by the shoulders and turned her away. "Go home," he commanded. When she hesitated, he pushed, making her stumble. She righted herself quickly and walked away, her back straight.

Once she was out of sight, the old man turned to Mangos. He pointed to the paligrates. "Have some. They're very good." Without another word, he vanished into the bushes.

Mangos raised his eyebrow at Kat. "Elibli fruit? Killanei?"

"I have no idea what they're talking about," Kat replied. She poked the fruit on the bush and looked after the old man. "Good for whom, I wonder?" She shrugged. "Let's find the village and see if we can buy some food."

"They'll probably try to sell us poison."

"And that's why we need the pearls," Kat replied.

Not knowing where the village might be, Mangos suggested the first thing that came to his mind—follow the path and the footprints into the jungle.

A bird landed in the bushes. It was blue—a blue the Alomari dye makers would have envied—with strips of yellow and orange on its wings. It screamed raucously, and another bird answered.

After two weeks, Mangos wanted something besides dried meat, something fresh. Counting a half dozen varieties of fruit he could easily pick didn't help. They all looked good, but he didn't know if any were edible.

People shouted in the distance, calling to each other in hard voices. The words were indistinct, but the tone was of dockworkers—men thrown together by the necessity of their jobs, not the desire for companionship.

Footsteps pounded on the trail behind them; Mangos turned. An islander pulled up to avoid running into them. He was flushed from exertion, his eyes dilated with pleasure. He scowled, but a smile kept tugging at his lips. "Who are you?" he demanded.

"The Mongoose and the Meerkat," said Mangos. "At your service."

"What do you want?" he was clearly trying to conceal his excitement, and failing.

"Golden Pearls," said Mangos.

"There are none," snapped the man. "They are a lie."

Kat raised an eyebrow, shook her head minutely.

Mangos let out a lungful of air. *Easier*, he thought, *to force the truth from the man*. But the man ran past them and disappeared down the trail. They followed after.

The voices grew louder, and with them came the smell of smoke. They rounded a bend in the trail and entered the village. Silence fell.

It was the silence of humans. The birds still sang, the leaves rustled, the surf still sounded in the distance, but the villagers remained silent, staring. Not motionless—they still moved about their business, but they were not paying it any mind. They stared at Mangos and Kat without a word.

They weren't afraid, Mangos decided. Not angry, either. Wary, like a mercenary might size up an opponent. He rested his hand on the hilt of his sword.

The jungle brush had been cleared, leaving the tall palms to shade bare dirt and dozens of huts. These were centered loosely on a communal fire but flung away from each other, as if the inhabitants wanted as much space as possible. The walls were made of woven branches, thicker than Mangos thought necessary, and most had a caged bird hanging before the door. The birds squawked like watchdogs when someone approached.

A large kettle hung on the fire, stirred by a stooped old woman who watched their every movement. A man sauntered toward them—a big man, taller, broader, and thicker than Mangos. He had dark, wild hair. He wore a cloth around his waist. Tattoo stripes covered his right arm from wrist to shoulder. They moved like snakes when he flexed his muscles.

"I am Marumbi," he said. It sounded like a threat.

"Mangos," Mangos answered, keeping his hand on his sword. "Kat." He jerked his head toward Kat.

"The Killanei doesn't give the Elibli fruit to strangers." Marumbi stopped just out of reach.

"We're not here to talk to the Killanei," said Mangos. "And if the Killanei doesn't favor strangers, you have nothing to worry about." *Especially since I don't know who the Killanei is*, he thought.

"I have nothing to worry about anyway." Marumbi slapped his waist, and Mangos noticed a long knife hanging from a leather belt. He grinned. "Strangers used to land here often." His grin made it clear unfortunate things happened to those strangers and that he enjoyed it. "They never found what they wanted. You won't either, but maybe you'll find what you *don't* want."

Marumbi turned and walked into the jungle.

Mangos watched him go. He didn't like being threatened. *I could take him*, he thought. He turned to Kat. "Leave now?" The idea amused him, and he had no intention of doing so. He smiled.

Kat shook her head. "If we leave without Golden Pearls, sooner or later, we'll die. Arrow, knife, or drink; somebody will poison us."

"But what about this Elibli fruit?"

"Let's ask her." Kat gestured. He followed her hand to see Kimi sitting across the clearing where the communal fire burned. There was no sign of the old man. Kat led the way to her.

"Thank you for warning us about the paligrates," Kat said.

Kimi nodded. "It's clear you don't know anything."

Mangos covered his annoyance with a cough.

"Will you get in trouble talking to us?" asked Kat.

"No. Grandpa only yells at me when we happen to meet. He spends all his time searching the island for a pearl somebody else hid." She paused, then explained. "He can't dive deep enough to get his own pearl oysters anymore. But when someone finds a pearl, they hide it so it won't get stolen. Grandpa tries to find those pearls."

"All this to give it to the Killanei?" Mangos asked.

"And we don't know what the Killanei is," Kat admitted.

"She is the spirit of the Elibli tree."

"People think a lot of the Killanei," Mangos said.

"It is all they think about," said Kimi. "Especially now, as the fruit grows ripe."

"What fruit is this?" Kat asked. "I haven't heard of it."

"The Elibli fruit? There is only one each year, and it must be eaten soon after being picked. It cannot survive a trip off the island. Everybody tries to convince the Killanei to give it to them."

"Why?"

"It can heal anything, but more, it gives health and vitality. It is like an extra year of life."

Mangos whistled. "An extra year of life?"

Kimi nodded, her blue eyes sad. "Marumbi is over eighty years old. The Killanei favors him often."

"Everybody would want that," Kat said. "Cure disease, heal injuries, live longer. The competition must be fierce."

Kimi looked down, made an arc in the dirt with her foot, and nodded. "Most people try to gain the Killanei's favor." She took a deep breath. "And they will try anything to get it. Marumbi has a stripe on his arm for each person he's killed."

Mangos's stomach rumbled. He blushed.

Kimi laughed. It reminded Mangos how young she was. "There is food." She pointed to the kettle on the fire. "Take some. It's for all."

"They'll let us?" Kat asked. "It is safe to eat?"

"Oh, yes," Kimi answered. "It is the one thing that is safe and free. You can't poison *everybody*."

Why not? Mangos wondered, but it sounded like poisoning the communal pot was taboo. Or maybe potential mass murderers just didn't want to cook for themselves. "And I thought it was because you like each other so much," he said.

Kimi looked puzzled, then smiled as she got his jest. "Of course not. But it's the only thing that brings people together. As much as we hate and fear each other, we desire company."

"The barest minimum to remain a community," Kat said. "You are a perceptive young lady."

A ll gathered to take their food, a type of stew made from wild pig and tropical fruit served in wooden bowls. Villagers made a large circle around the fire. Each spoke, a few with apparent warmth, to a particular person or other; one, Mangos assumed, whom they trusted. For the most part, though, they seemed wary, holding their food close and keeping an eye on their neighbors.

"You said the Killanei likes Golden Pearls," Kat addressed Kimi.

"Yes. Everybody dives for pearls. But nobody gives them to the Killanei."

Mangos paused from slurping his stew. "What? Why work so hard to get pearls for the Killanei and not give them to her?"

Kimi pointed to a man across the fire. "Karabi found a pearl," she whispered. Karabi, Mangos realized, was the man who had overtaken them as they walked in from the beach. "His wife was attacked by a shark and cannot walk. The Elibli fruit can heal her, so Karabi has hidden the pearl until he can give it to the Killanei."

"How can you tell?"

"He is too happy."

"That's bad?"

"Not that he wants to heal his wife," Kimi said. "Only that everybody knows he found a pearl."

Even as she spoke, Karabi slapped at his neck, plucked at the skin. His fingers came away red, and he stared in horror at the thorn he held.

"Poisoned," Kimi murmured.

"Damn you!" Karabi shouted at the jungle. "The fruit is not ripe, and she cannot walk to the Killanei—I must do it for her!" He rushed into his hut.

"He needs to speak with his wife," Kimi explained. "If he uses the pearl to save his own life, there is no hope the Killanei will give him the fruit." She shrugged then added, "He must hurry to decide."

Several minutes later, Karabi staggered out, doubled over and gasping. He pushed his way into the jungle.

Nobody said anything.

"Friendly," Mangos grunted.

"We have no friends." Kimi sounded bitter.

When Karabi returned, cured of the poison, he neither sat by the fire nor went into his hut. He sat just outside the door, legs curled to his chest and weeping.

"That is why people hunt pearls but do not give them to the Killanei," Kimi continued. "Perhaps he will have better luck next year."

Conversation began amongst the villagers as though nothing had happened. Marumbi swaggered into the village and went straight to the kettle to get food. He saw Karabi weeping and burst into laughter.

"Why talk to the Killanei?" Mangos asked. He spoke quietly so Kimi, who walked a few feet ahead of them, would not hear.

"She may know where people have been successful in pearl diving." Kat shrugged. "Or not. But it doesn't hurt to ask. Nobody else is going give away likely dive spots."

"There is her grotto." Kimi pointed. "People only speak to her once a year, to ask for the fruit." She stopped. "Otherwise, they do not bother her."

They didn't want to bother her, or just didn't want to bother? Mangos wondered.

Kat stepped around Kimi. "We'll claim ignorance." Mangos hurried to catch up. The silence behind him told him that Kimi did not follow.

"Let me talk," Kat said. "Killanei is a tree spirit. She will seem very young, but she is not."

Mangos agreed. Kat obviously knew more about this than he did.

The circle of large stones that formed the boundary of the grotto rose twelve feet. Vines of green leaves and orange flowers entwined them, binding them together. Water trickled over one of the stones, darkening it and sprinkling the leaves before pooling at the base and flowing into a crack in the earth.

Palms rose over the grotto, their fronds moving in the breeze, striping the ground with moving shadows. Inside a plant grew, maybe many but forming one growth, for it grew from many stalks. It had small leaves, no longer than Mangos's finger and wide as two. Yellow-orange blossoms alternated with leaf clusters.

Wind rustled the stalks, and a girl stood as if she had always been there. "Who are you?" She was slight, with large eyes and long hair. Her dress was leaf green with yellow-orange flowers.

"Are you the Killanei?" Kat asked.

The girl smiled a sad smile. "*The* Killanei? I am Killanei." Her expression hardened. "The Elibli is not ripe."

"I am not here for the Elibli," Kat said.

"Why then?"

Kat shrugged. "Courtesy."

Killanei cocked her head. "How very strange."

"Are your guests not courteous?"

"They come once a year, bearing gifts, professing their love of me, and telling me why I should hate the others." Killanei ran her hand down one of the stalks of her plant. "They lie, about both their love and their rivals, but they *are* courteous."

"And they bring you pearls."

Killanei snorted. "They make excuses for why they don't have pearls, and they promise me pearls if I will give them the fruit." Her expression became thoughtful. "Many years ago, there was a man who brought me pearls."

"Marumbi?"

Killanei's eyes grew dark. "No. Marumbi killed him."

Mangos and Kat exchanged looks. "I wonder where the man found all his pearls," Mangos said.

"I never found out," Killanei answered. "Only that he dove off the

northern point, outside the reef. It never mattered. I cannot leave my grotto." She sighed. "So few pearls now, and they are *so* pretty. I wonder what became of them."

"They are used by desperate people," Kat said.

"I have seen their desperation under Marumbi."

They were silent. Mangos shifted his weight. *The sooner we find our pearls, the better,* he thought. He had no wish to become involved in the competition for the Elibli fruit. Only the pearls would help them in the years to come.

Kat merely waited, a sympathetic expression on her face.

Killanei broke the silence. Her voice was hesitant, as if she wasn't sure she should confide in them. "Marumbi scares me."

"He should," Kat agreed.

"But he dares not push too hard, or I will not grow the Elibli fruit." She lifted her chin a little, a small gesture of defiance.

Clever, Mangos thought. Marumbi could influence but not control Killanei, the same as he could the villagers. So he created an atmosphere, a system almost, that favored him. He might not get the Elibli fruit every year, but he would get it most years.

Kat began telling Killanei the story of their journey to the island. It bored Mangos, but Killanei listened intently. She enjoyed their company, for she clearly got little, and Kat told the story in a way that made her laugh. One story followed another until hours had passed, and they made to leave.

"Must you go?" Killanei asked.

"Yes," Kat said. "But what do you like? What can we bring you?"

"We are not exchanging gifts." Killanei stretched her hand up, cupping it as if she could catch the sun's rays like she would the rain. "I eat of the sun's bounty and drink the water of the earth. I need nothing. But I thank you for your company."

"We can't dive here," Mangos complained. There was no bottom outside the reef, only the wall of coral falling away into the depths. For two days they had waited, unwilling to dive while the islanders watched from the shallows. But now the Elibli fruit was ripe, and everybody was begging Killanei, so Mangos and Kat were free to search untroubled.

"Wait." They drifted over an alcove in the coral, a sandy niche a few yards wide and a hundred yards long. "Here it is."

Mangos dipped his hand over the side. The water caressed him, surprisingly warm, like liquid air. He could see the bottom; it looked so close he thought he should be able to stand.

Throwing over the anchor, he watched it sink down, down. It struck bottom, and he pulled, dragging it along the bottom until it caught on the coral. "Fifty feet?" The depth surprised him.

Kat tied back her hair. "I'll dive."

Mangos nodded. He didn't like swimming. He could dive, but maybe not that deep.

Kat dove over the side, knifing into the water with barely a splash. Fish scattered from her. It looked like she swam without moving, but Mangos knew that was an illusion. She reached the bottom, moved about, fumbling along with her hands. She grabbed what looked like a rock, slid her knife under it, shook, and kicked up.

A moment later, she burst out of the water, grabbing the gunwale and gasping for air. She did not have an oyster. "That didn't work," she said. She held up a hand, and Mangos lifted her into the boat.

"It takes too long to dive." Without another word, she dove over the side again. This time she sank quicker, leaving behind a trail of bubbles. Almost immediately she returned, gasping harder than before.

"What did you do?" Mangos asked as he lifted her back into the boat.

"Let out my breath, it helped me sink faster."

Mangos laughed, "And left you without any air when you reached the bottom."

Kat gave him a sour look. "Yes."

"I'll just tie you to the anchor and let that take you down."

A smile spread on her face. "Do that," she said. "We have a spare anchor."

Mangos found the spare anchor, a small one, perfect for this task. Kat looped the rope about her wrist; Mangos thought that foolish in spite of his joke—he would want to be able to let go. He dropped the anchor overboard as she dove, and the two sank rapidly. She disengaged the rope once she reached the bottom.

This time when she surfaced, she dropped an oyster into the bottom of the boat. Mangos pulled up the anchor so they could do it again.

As she dove, he picked up the oyster. He took his knife and slit it into the shell and twisted. He moved the knife and twisted again.

"Open up, you stupid shell," he muttered.

Finally the shell opened enough for him to get his fingers inside. With a heave, he tore it the rest of the way open. No pearl.

Kat surfaced, panting, and dropped another oyster into the boat. This was the size of his head.

"Give me a rope," she said. "There's one the size of a bushel basket."

She dove and he opened the oysters, tossing them aside time after time without finding a pearl. He would finish opening an oyster and pull up the diving anchor just as she surfaced again.

Time and again; no pearl.

The day wore on, diving with periods of rest interspersed, but no pearl. The oysters began to pile in the bottom of the boat and Mangos started to feel frustrated.

During one of Kat's rests, he leaned on the gunwale, watching the fish. There was… he had to rub his eyes, surely the water and the waves were tricking him. No, it truly was—an oyster as large as his hand, but if it were fifty feet down, it must be as large as a man!

His excitement washed away his hesitation. This was a prize he wanted to claim. He grabbed the anchor and jumped over the side.

The saltwater stung his eyes, but he closed them. He knew where the oyster was, and he swam toward it, only opening his eyes for quick reassurances.

His eyes burned as he tried to find it, taking a second look because it was so large he thought the blurry shape had to be coral. The stinging look told him the oyster was open enough to reach inside. *Good,* he thought, *I could never haul it to the surface.* He reached in, groping, and felt a hard lump. He closed his hand on it just as the oyster closed on his arm.

He jerked back but was trapped. Bracing his feet, he pushed, but the oyster held him tightly. He was caught above the elbow and could not move in or out. His lungs started to labor; he needed to surface.

He tried to pry the oyster open with his free hand. It did not open. He felt his blood pounding in his head.

He looked up, the sun shone brightly, but the edges of his vision seemed dark. He kicked and pulled, pounded the oyster, but to no avail.

Kat was next to him, sliding her arm, smaller than his, into the oyster, cutting and twisting with her knife until the shell suddenly loosened. She pulled it open, and Mangos shot up, fighting to reach the surface before he passed out.

"You'll feel better if you look at what's in your hand."

Mangos blinked. He lay in the boat, looking up at the sun. He didn't remember climbing in, didn't even remember making it to the surface.

But he held a larger pearl than he ever imagined. His fingers stretched to hold it; it may have been five inches across, a perfect sphere. It wasn't really the color of gold; instead it was lighter, more lustrous. It had an iridescence; all the colors chased each other so quickly they were more a suggestion than a truth, leaving the pearl a shimmery gold.

"By the gods of Eastwarn," he said, awed. He had a hard time focusing his thoughts, so he just stared at the pearl. "With a pearl this large, we don't need any more. We can shave from this for years if needed!"

"I think," Kat said, "we should sail away sooner rather than later. A pearl like this is as good as a free year of life, maybe even the promise of next year's fruit too."

Mangos looked around, suddenly afraid they were being watched. He gave the pearl to Kat, who dropped it into a pouch and hung it on her belt. "Good thing everybody is talking with Killanei. Keep it hidden while we gather supplies for the voyage."

"I'll get provisions so we'll be ready to sail with the next tide," Mangos called over his shoulder. He raced up the beach, leaving Kat to anchor the boat in the shallows. He took great lungsful of air, still feeling giddy as he recovered from his dive.

The sound of the surf faded, and he thought of where to get food. It would be safest to trap a boar—no chance of poison, but that might not be easy and preserving the meat would take too long.

He dashed around a curve in the trail, saw somebody blocking his path, and skidded to a stop to avoid hitting them.

Marumbi held a spear with both hands; his long knife still hung from his waist.

"Why aren't you trying to get the Elibli fruit?" Mangos demanded.

Marumbi grinned evilly. "The Killanei will not give the fruit to any but me. She knows better."

"I'm not after the fruit." His head hadn't cleared, and he struggled to understand.

"I'm not a fool. I watched you. You knew where to dive; now you run to get the Elibli fruit. You must have a pearl."

"I am not running to get the Elibli fruit," Mangos said, reaching for his sword. It wasn't there. He had taken it off to dive.

"I will take the pearl from your body."

I can take him without a sword, Mangos thought. He kicked sand and lunged, but Marumbi closed his eyes and swung his spear. Mangos had to twist aside to keep from spitting himself.

Marumbi laughed. "I've been killing men for sixty years. I know all the tricks."

Like surprising them when they're unarmed, Mangos thought. He rolled away and threw himself back as Marumbi attacked. He came to his feet. He felt light, energized.

He laughed, and Marumbi laughed back.

They circled. Mangos heard a call behind him but didn't pay it any mind. He was in his own world, intent on the man before him: intent on the spear, which he intended to dodge, and the knife, which he intended to grab.

He feinted left, then right, danced back. Marumbi thrust low, and Mangos leapt high, over the spear, grabbing the knife. He tore it free and

swept it up and back across Marumbi's throat.

Marumbi wobbled. Blood spurted down his chest, but he held tight to his spear, and Mangos felt a tugging in his gut.

"There's a trick you don't know," Mangos said.

Mangos coughed a wet cough. He ignored it and drove the knife into Marumbi's chest. Marumbi let go of his spear. Mangos staggered. Marumbi's eyes rolled up, and he fell.

Mangos looked down. Marumbi's spear protruded from his stomach, angled up. He coughed again and wiped the spit from his face. It wasn't spit. It was blood.

"You fool!" Kat shouted. "Too long without air, you're still not thinking right. A minute more, and I would have been here."

"Didn't need you," Mangos said, finding it difficult to breathe. He took a deep breath. The pain surprised him. "Damn this thing." He grabbed the shaft of the spear and yanked it out. "That's better." He covered the hole with his hand to staunch the bleeding.

"Gods, you idiot!" Kat took the spear. "Lie down. I need to look at this."

Mangos shook his head. "Just help me get the food. We'll be on our way."

"Let me see the wound," Kat said, throwing the spear into the bushes.

Mangos did not sit down, but he let her peel back his fingers for a second to see the wound. He coughed again, his breath rasping in his lungs. "I'll be fine."

"No," Kat shook her head, "you will not be fine."

"If I eat a pearl, I won't need to worry about it festering. Somebody must be hiding a small one."

"A pearl won't heal this." Kat looked anxious, thoughtful. "There is a way. Stay here. Rest." She started down the path toward the village.

"Where are you going?" Mangos staggered after her. She did not answer; apparently she did not hear him. She ran lightly, with a haste Mangos didn't understand and could not match.

"A pearl will keep it from festering," he insisted. "It can heal on its own."

He reached the village, far behind Kat, and saw her on the path to Killanei's grotto.

"No!" he shouted. "Don't give her the pearl!" He could survive without the fruit, he knew he could, but a pearl that size could not be replaced.

He stumbled after her, coughing again and again, having trouble getting enough air in his lungs. "Don't give her the pearl!" His vision seemed cloudy, and he blinked to clear it.

Villagers clustered on the path to the grotto. Whether waiting to speak to Killanei or waiting for her decision, Mangos did not know. None tried to stop him; none offered to help him.

"Do any of you have a Golden Pearl?" he asked. He didn't want to use the large pearl if he could help it.

The villagers just looked at him.

Breathing didn't seem to satisfy him, and he couldn't fill his lungs. He needed to rest. A couple minutes and he'd be fine, but Kat would have given Killanei their pearl. He pushed on.

"Don't trade it," he gasped, but Kat was too far away to hear.

His legs failed him, and he pitched forward, darkness washing over him for the second time in an hour as he tried again to tell Kat not to give away their giant pearl.

He opened his eyes. Palm fronds waved overhead. He took a deep breath. "Damn. You gave me the fruit."

Kat, nearby as he knew she would be, said, "You would have died."

"I would have been fine."

"Not with a wound like that. It went through your stomach and up."

Mangos raised his head. He was in the grotto. Killanei watched from her plant, holding the giant pearl. Kimi stood next to her, smiling. The two had evidently been talking.

Sitting up, Mangos ran his hand over his stomach. The skin felt tight, but that was all. "You shouldn't have given up the pearl," he complained.

Kat didn't answer him directly. Instead, she looked at Killanei and raised an eyebrow. "Better than a pearl?"

Killanei laughed, the sound of running water. "Oh, yes. You were right." She handed the pearl to Kat.

"What?" Mangos asked, not understanding.

Kat looked toward the opening of the grotto, making sure nobody watched as she dropped the pearl into Mangos's hand.

He rolled it in his palm. "How?"

"She only gave me the pearl in case I didn't agree that her real offer was better," Killanei said.

"You needed the fruit immediately," Kat explained as she returned the

pearl to her pouch. "I hadn't time to fetch Kimi. Think of the pearl not as a trade, but a hostage."

Killanei laid a hand on Kimi's shoulder. "She offered a friend."

"On this island, friends are rarer than pearls," Kimi said.

"And more valuable," Killanei added. "But with Marumbi dead," she said thoughtfully, "maybe things will change."

hunt of the Mine Worm

Fourteen months after the fall of Alness.

"**B**ack!"

Mangos watched Stiefnu's mouth move, though he couldn't hear the word. The cascading chain and ore carts crashing down the shaft drowned the foreman's voice.

Mangos didn't need to be told. He might be willing to fight demons or jilted husbands, but being crushed by tons of mining equipment seemed a stupid way to die. He joined the others as they moved across the cavern.

Beside him, Kat had her cloak across her nose and mouth to form a mask as dust blown by the wind of the chain's impact enveloped them. In her other hand, she still gripped her spear, which was odd, Mangos thought, since she'd never used a spear before. Now, she refused to be separated from it.

Three other hunters, a man and two women—Mangos didn't know their names—moved further away to avoid the dust. They appeared calm, or as calm as one could expect while in the deepest level of a mine with the only way out collapsing before them.

It ended, the echoes of the fall bouncing back from the workings. Dust swirled through the wall lights, giving the lanterns halos.

"Doesn't usually work like that?" asked the man.

Stiefnu turned, glowering. "No, fool, and now we're trapped down here with the worm!"

The older of the two women snorted. "If we feared the worm, we wouldn't be here."

That, Mangos allowed, was true. The women stood next to each other, and judging from their features, they were sisters, the blonde a couple of years older than the brunette. The blonde had a rough beauty in her high cheekbones, curled lip, and strong chin. She wore a low-cut blouse, which seemed out of place hunting in the deep mines.

The brunette wasn't as rough. Her features were finer, more composed, her bodice not as revealing. She had a bow, a short re-curve with a wooden core and horn belly, and carried a short sword on her hip.

"It will take days, maybe weeks, to fix the lift," Stiefnu said.

The man shrugged. He had long black hair he tied in a ponytail. A scar twisted across his neck, as if Death had grabbed him but couldn't hold on. His left eye looked slightly askance, not quite the same direction as his right. He wore a great sword with scalloped edges strapped across his back. "Throw down rope. Tie to chain, lift back up. Easy."

"There isn't a rope strong enough to lift the weight of that chain up to the machinery in the upper levels," said Stiefnu. "We'll fix it, never you mind. That's our job. Yours is to kill the worm."

Stiefnu took a deep breath, but it didn't seem to calm him. The dust made him cough, and it took a minute before he could stop. "We're likely safe," he said. "The worm would have to cross the fissure to get here from the workings."

"So," said the older sister, "tell us of this worm."

Giving the pile of chain and ore carts one last look, Stiefnu nodded. He performed introductions by jabbing a thick finger at each and saying their name. "Mangos. Kat." The man was Corjon, the blonde sister, Daini, the brunette, Kairi.

"The worm," Stiefnu said and began to tick off characteristics on his fingers as he said them, "is eight feet in diameter. It has two sets of teeth, one to tear rock and another to grind it. It can breathe acid. While not fast, it can outrun a person for a short distance."

"It can out-crawl," murmured Daini, and Kairi smiled.

Stiefnu pretended not to hear. "It is immune to fire; no blade can penetrate its hide."

Corjon didn't seem interested. He wandered around the chamber. He looked into crates and tapped the sides of water barrels. He stopped at a stack of crates with words stenciled on the sides. Mangos had difficulty reading *NitroBarite*.

"Nothing we have tried has the slightest effect," Stiefnu was saying. "That's why we put out a contract."

"This makes the bangs?" burst out Corjon, thumping his hand on the crates.

Stiefnu pressed his lips together but gave no other sign of displeasure. "More or less, yes."

Corjon grinned, displaying a set of white but crooked teeth. "Worm go bang."

"We've tried—" Stiefnu cut himself off, shrugged. "Blow yourself up. It won't hurt the worm."

"Have you tried to asphyxiate it?" Kat asked.

Stiefnu nodded, as if reforming his opinion of her. "We have. But there's enough bad air down here that the worm can go without air for—well, we don't know how long."

"We'll find a way," said Daini. "Just fix that lift so we can get out when we're done and have our payment ready which," she added with a meaningful look at the others, "we're not sharing with anyone."

"Payment is made in silvecite. Twenty percent of all refined ore for the next two years will go to those who kill the worm. If you prefer cash," Stiefnu said, "we will arraign the sale of the silvecite and forward the proceeds to you."

Mangos wiped his sweaty, dusty face. It was hot this far down, and the air felt thick. He would face the discomfort and the worm for the silvecite, or rather the money from the sale. Silvecite was very rare, very difficult to mine, and made the best weapons, if you could find a smith competent enough to work it. The proceeds should be enough to buy friends and good times for a year.

"Have ye ever fought a worm like this before?" asked Kairi. All five adventurers headed toward what Stiefnu had called 'the workings,' the places where silvecite ore was actually mined and the worm lurked.

"Twice," said Corjon from in front of them.

"Somehow I doubt that," said Mangos, pitching his voice so only Kairi could hear.

"I heard that," Corjon snapped.

"Snake—yes," Mangos told Kairi as he ducked a lantern, "worm—no. You?"

Kairi shook her head.

"How much is silvecite worth?" Mangos asked, wondering how many drinks he could buy.

"Plenty," Daini said. "The Dukes of Endras mined it in the Karras Mountains until Balmis built a reservoir to help irrigate their northern farms."

"Why would that matter?"

"They accidentally flooded the mine."

Mangos glanced at Kat, who confirmed this with a nod.

This seemed to offend Daini, who apparently didn't like being doubted.

"So, no silvecite for almost fifty years until this seam was found," she said. "Small wonder Stiefnu doesn't want to give it up."

It also explained why most silvecite weapons and armor were old. Mangos knew his steel, and he knew most silvecite was really a steel alloy. Pure silvecite, while better, was too expensive and difficult to work.

"Twenty percent of the refined ore for two years," he mused.

"Look around," Daini said, a hint of a sneer on her face. "This whole level of the mine was opened to get to the silvecite. They built a new smelter for it, in case you didn't notice on the way down. They may be offering twenty percent because they're desperate, but they won't be losing money by doing it." She tossed her head. "Stiefnu's not offering so much because he wants you to be happy."

"Or," Kat said, "once the worm is dead, they shut down the workings for two years. Then you get twenty percent of nothing." She smiled sweetly.

"They wouldn't—" Kairi stammered.

"Stiefnu's not doing this because he wants you to be happy," Kat repeated mockingly.

"Do you really think they would do that?" Mangos asked.

"No," Kat said.

Kairi laughed, but Daini muttered, "Bitch. Thinks she's some kind of queen or something."

"Ah," said Corjon with a note of satisfaction in his voice. They had nearly reached their destination.

The miners had dropped the shaft down then tunneled horizontally to reach the seam of silvecite; because, according to Stiefnu, silvecite ore was so difficult to mine, they repeatedly opened new tunnels to approach the seam from different angles so they could mine multiple faces. Once they crossed the fissure, Mangos expected an extensive maze of tunnels to reach the workings.

Lanterns at each end, and one in the middle, illuminated a thin bridge while the fissure extended down into darkness. The bridge was a dozen yards of steel holding cart rails with a wooden walkway between them. There was no handrail. The workings, and the worm, were on the other side.

Corjon puffed out his chest and, with a grin on his face, stepped onto the bridge. The wooden slats creaked, and his grin vanished like he had dropped it. He faltered, just a little, and hesitated.

Kat stepped after him, one hand on the strap of her pack, the other holding her spear.

Corjon began to creep forward, flinching with every creak of the bridge. He shuffled his feet as if afraid to pick them up.

Excited voices came from the tunnels on the other side, and a pair of miners burst into view, running and shouting. Crazed, they dashed onto the bridge.

"No! No!" shouted Corjon, waving for them to stop and back up.

They didn't. The miners kept racing forward, screaming, eyes bulging in their grimy faces. One man clutched at his arm, which had no hand. Blackened bones protruded from the stump, itself blackened past the elbow and turning to angry red, mottled with huge white blisters. Too panicked to take care, he barreled into Corjon.

Corjon grabbed the miner, both shouting incoherently, swung him around, and thrust him behind him.

Right into Kat.

Kat gave a cry of surprise as the impact knocked the spear from her hand. It clattered on the cart rail, and the panicked miner kicked it into the abyss. In one fluid motion, Kat shrugged off her pack and dove after the spear.

"No!" shouted Mangos, jumping to catch her. Strong hands grabbed him.

"You'll fall too," said Daini.

Mangos pulled away from her, stepped onto the bridge and grabbed the thrashing miner. With a heave, Mangos threw him to safety, grabbed Corjon and steadied him, and held the last miner so he couldn't knock anyone else over.

"She," Kairi said, "just…dove."

"Didn't expect that," Daini agreed.

Mangos crawled to the edge and looked down. Kat hung to the underside of the bridge with one hand, feet dangling in the darkness.

"Was that necessary?" he asked.

Kat looked up at him, her brows knit and lips turned down. "I didn't catch it." She swung her free hand up as he reached down, and Mangos lifted her back onto the bridge. "That was our best chance to kill the worm."

"Will you at least tell me what it was?"

"A candeliere—a thrusting spear," said Kat as she retrieved her pack.

121

"It had a hollowed tip and shaft filled with poison. Nasty stuff, made from toad glands or some such thing. Kill you to even smell it." She looked outraged. "It cost a fortune."

"Can you get more?" Kairi asked.

"Can you climb that shaft without a lift?" Kat's voice was hard and mocking, and Mangos guessed she had placed more confidence in the spear than any other plan.

"Looks like you're not killing the worm, now," said Daini. She raised her eyebrows and shrugged.

Kat shrugged back. "We'll see how you fare." She finished crossing the bridge; Mangos followed a step behind. Daini and Kairi came last, Kairi cautiously peering over the side and shaking her head.

Corjon, now safely off the bridge, looked confident and eager again.

Mangos clapped him on the back and, feeling vicious, said, "Well, to make the worm go bang, you only need to cross that bridge at least two more times." Corjon blinked, and Mangos explained. "The nitrobarite is still on the other side. No handrails."

"I get later," Corjon muttered.

The tunnel divided shortly after they crossed the fissure. Down the right branch it divided again, giving them three choices.

Corjon did not hesitate. "I go this way, none of you follow. Worm be mine."

"Yes, Corjon," said Mangos, "the mine worm is mine."

"Not yours," said Corjon, glowering. "Mine."

Kairi stifled a giggle.

Corjon glared at her, bushy eyebrows drawing together, and rested a hand on his sword.

"Push off," said Daini, making a shooing motion. "Your worm is waiting for you."

Corjon stomped away, back straight, not looking back.

Daini ran her hand through her hair, sizing up Mangos and Kat. "Guess we're stuck with you for a bit, eh?"

"A little while," said Kat. "After that?"

The two women started down the tunnel, side by side, both clearly assuming their partners would follow, and Mangos and Kairi did just that.

"Daini and Kat seem a lot alike," Kairi remarked.

"And neither seems to like the other," Mangos replied.

"They both know where they're going."

"They're smart enough to follow the trail of blood from the wounded miners," Mangos said.

"Ah." Kairi touched a red drop with her boot. "That makes sense."

The blood spatters became more evident the further they went. They did not pass any other miners, and Mangos noticed the sounds of mining had stopped. No more steel on steel, no more distant shouts, only absolute silence filled the mine.

They came to a face wall where miners had been cutting away at the tunnel. Pickaxes, steel rods, a water barrel, and a giant bellows lay strewn about. A natural tunnel moved off to the right.

Daini sniffed. "No bad air. The bellows must be just a precaution."

"Here," said Kat, crouching down amongst large splashes of blood. A few feet away lay a pitted hammerhead, its handle eaten away by acid.

Kairi strung her bow and nocked an arrow.

"What are you going to use?" Mangos asked her. "Not the bow?" But he took a closer look and realized runes curled up and down the belly of the bow.

Daini heard his question and cut off Kairi's reply. "We're going to use our guts."

"Oh, you're going to overfeed it then," quipped Kat. She didn't even look at Daini but kept examining the tunnel wall.

"Kairi," Daini said, "If she's blocking your shot of the worm—take it anyway."

Mangos glanced at Kairi. Her eyes were wide. "I'm pretty sure she's joking," he whispered. Kairi nodded.

How, Mangos wondered, did they have a chance of killing the worm? He liked his odds in a fight with anything. *We'll see if its hide is proof against my sword*, he thought. But suppose it was... Corjon was going to use explosives; Daini and Kairi had a magic bow. Without Kat's poison spear, they had nothing.

Kat drew a heavy leather cloak and hood from her pack and put it on. It didn't make sense to Mangos until he recalled the acid eaten hammer on the ground. Kat started down the right-hand tunnel, Daini hurried to keep up, and again, Mangos found himself following.

They did not have far to go before they found the worm, or it found them. Another tunnel joined theirs, and just at the edge of the lantern light, the worm filled it. The worm was quiescent until they stepped into the junction—then it quivered, its tapered snout questing for a scent or taste. It started to move toward them.

Its back scrapped the ceiling, though Mangos wondered if it mattered which side was up. Its mouth, covered by thick, rubbery lips, closed down around the cone of its outer teeth. It drew back its lips, and its teeth opened and closed like stiff-jointed fingers. The smell of hot iron drifted toward them.

"Shoot it!" screamed Daini.

Kairi drew her bow, the runes flared orange, and the glow moved to the string and along the arrow. She released. The arrow shot true, sparkling across the mine to shatter on the worm's hide. Kairi drew another, released, and it too had no effect.

The worm rumbled forward, scraping lanterns from the wall, pushing darkness and small stones before it.

"What is it, really?" Mangos asked as he drew his sword.

"How should I know?" Kat said.

"You know everything!" Mangos stepped forward, putting himself between the worm and Kat. "I thought you might know because the fourth king of Terzol kept one of these as a pet or something."

Kat laughed. "The fourth king of Terzol was Alhemtzol, and he kept miniature lemurs. That's why he was overthrown."

"You actually know who the fourth king was? You really do know everything!" Mangos stopped bantering as they backed down the tunnel, further into the mine.

Kairi still drew and shot arrows while Daini stood beside her, sword ready. Finally, Kairi lowered the bow and said, "It needs to cool down."

Daini grabbed her and dove aside, back the way they had come. The worm reached the junction and turned toward Mangos and Kat, grinding its way around the corner and blocking them from the others.

The worm probed toward them. It retracted its foreteeth, exposing a second set of wedge-shaped teeth, tightly closed to form a disc. These teeth opened, and a stream of liquid shot out.

Mangos spun aside while Kat dove forward to attack with her sword. The liquid hissed as it splashed against the tunnel wall. Kat's attack skittered along the worm's side to no greater effect than Kairi's arrows.

Mangos lunged, sword extended, and stabbed the worm in the mouth. His sword passed in and stuck, jarring his arm. The worm closed its inner teeth and broke his blade. It closed its outer teeth on the remaining end and flicked up, tearing the hilt from Mangos's hand. The worm opened its mouth, dropping the useless sword, and breathed out a spray of acid.

Mangos threw himself back, and the acid settled over Kat.

"Kat!" he shouted.

The worm moved forward again, and Kat scrambled to escape. Smoke swirled off her cloak as she tugged at the clasp and let it fall. Angry red spots covered her hands.

The worm worked its mouth back and forth, moving lips and teeth. Finally, it opened both sets of teeth and twitched, sending the tip of Mangos's sword shooting past them.

"Seen enough?" Mangos asked.

"For now," Kat said. She began to back slowly away.

"Faster than a man can run over short distances, remember?" Mangos said.

"You suggest we run?"

"Yes." Mangos spun, and the two raced away. The walls shook, and Mangos hazarded a glance behind him. The worm filled the tunnel, growing larger in his vision as it drew nearer. He wondered how long "short distances" actually were.

The tunnel curved, and they came up against a dead end. The worm slowed down as it approached. It flexed its rubbery lips and opened and closed both sets of teeth. A long round tongue, as big around as Mangos's arm, cloven-ended and rough-textured, snaked out.

Mangos grabbed the last lantern off the wall and swung it, but the worm didn't flinch.

"Time to go 'Bang,' Mister Worm!" Corjon shouted nearby before lobbing the explosive.

The worm didn't react, but the tunnel rocked, and small stones fell from the ceiling. Mangos staggered, the light dancing as he swung his arms to regain his balance.

"This way!" Kat cried, grabbing him and pushing him toward a tight crack in the wall. Mangos didn't question if it was opened by the explosion or just overlooked. He held out his hand and followed the lantern through.

"Keep going," said Kat, "so Corjon doesn't catch us in his next 'bang.'"

Down, far below, something glowed deep orange, almost red. Heat rose up, more intense than the already hot mine, along with the smell of sulphur.

Mangos moved carefully, feeling his way downward. The tunnel fell away steeply, and only his care and strength saved him when he stepped on a loose stone. If he hadn't been steadying himself with his free hand, he would have followed the stone down.

At the bottom, they stepped onto a small ledge overlooking a half-cooled lava field. Cracks ran like veins through the darker cauliflower-like surface. Small pools dotted the chamber. The light of lava crept through the cracks and pools, giving the chamber a hellish atmosphere.

An explosion rumbled above them. Mangos could feel it through his boots, and a few stones clattered down the tunnel. "The first bang must not have killed it," he said.

Kat stepped forward, turning her head back and forth, testing the air. "This air is too cool, and it moves. There's another opening somewhere."

"Are those diamonds?" Mangos pointed to the lava pools and the crystals encrusted around the edges.

"Noooooo," Kat said thoughtfully. "But they may be..." She lowered herself onto the crust of the lava field and moved over to the nearest pool. The glow illuminated her face from below, and rising heat lifted her hair. She pulled on a glove and reached down to break off a crystal.

Pulling back from the updraft, she studied it. Mangos approached and looked over her shoulder.

"What is it?" he asked.

"Nushadir Salt," she said. "Alchemists use it, but never as pure as this." Up close it didn't look like a diamond, rather a mess of interlocking icicles. "Now, we have something to try. We need as much as we can carry."

"Is it poisonous?" Mangos asked.

"No." She did not wait for his next question but began to gather more crystals, working quickly.

Another explosion made the chamber tremble, and stones rained down. The largest drove into the crust and stuck.

"Hurry," Kat said, "before Corjon brings down the roof."

Mangos set down the lantern so he could help. The heat seared his throat, and just touching the crystals made his fingers burn. The bottom of his feet prickled on the hot crusted lava.

He glanced up. "I wonder if the worm can come down here."

"Hopefully, it's enjoying playing with Corjon."

Mangos wiped sweat from his face. "And it doesn't like its food well done." He kept picking crystals.

"That's enough," Kat finally said. "Gather them up, and let's go."

Mangos juggled the last crystals to make them balance in a one-armed load so he could pick up the lantern. Kat prowled about, trying to follow the cooler air.

"This way," she said.

Another explosion staggered both of them. Kat went down to a knee and rose up with an exclamation. Stones, detached from the roof, showered down. Mangos looked up to see a large shadow resolve into a stone and plunge through the crust, splashing molten lava a dozen feet in the air.

The crust rippled like jelly, and a wave of intense heat slapped them. They hurried, Mangos first, to discover another ledge and a steep tunnel up. Warm air rose with them as they climbed, but mixed with cooler and more tolerable air. When Mangos squeezed through a crack and fell into another mine tunnel, the air was no worse than a hot day.

Kat leaned against the wall, hair hanging in sweaty lengths, breathing heavily.

"Now what?" Mangos asked.

"We need to get some nitrobarite if Corjon hasn't used it all going 'bang.' You get that. I'll get a fire, a barrel of water, and two of those big bellows."

"They overthrew him because he kept lemurs?" Mangos asked as he ground the nushadir salt into powder.

They worked in a dead end, perhaps the start of another approach to the silvecite. Kat had chosen it because she found two bellows, massive things that could push air great distances, which the miners left there.

"Who? Oh, Alhemtzol of Terzol," said Kat. She had heated the nitrobarite before dumping it in the water barrel. Now, she fished white crystals from the water and laid them out to dry. "Well, lemurs were sacred to the moon goddess. Keeping them as pets was an insult. The priestesses led a revolt, and while Alhemtzol tried to put it down, his cousin overthrew him to become Albalada the Second."

After testing to see if they were dry, Kat began to grind up the white crystals, being careful to keep her powder separate from Mangos's growing pile.

"Then," she continued, "Albalada had the priestesses killed and the moon temples closed," she said.

Mangos laughed, appreciating the irony of Terzoli politics. His laugh echoed back to him. A thought wiped the smile from his face. "I haven't heard an explosion for a while. I wonder if Corjon killed the worm."

"It's possible," Kat allowed. "Not likely."

"It would save your life if he had." Daini approached, limping, sweaty, and grimy. Blood trickled from several small wounds, streaking her face. Kairi appeared behind her, one arm hanging limply at her side, barely holding her bow in loose fingers. Her other hand clutched her shoulder, but it didn't begin to cover the blood that soaked her tunic.

"Looks like you've been badly used," Kairi remarked.

"Us?" said Mangos. He glanced at Kat and realized how tattered she looked. With her singed hair, drawn and sweaty face, and charred clothes she did indeed look badly used.

"Giving up?" Kat asked, ignoring Kairi's comment.

"Regrouping," Daini replied.

Kat paused from grinding her powder and studied each of them. A slow smile crept over her face. Rather than speak, she merely shrugged and resumed grinding.

Daini curled her lip. "Go crawl back into whatever hole you hid in."

"What are—" Kairi stopped as a faint scraping sound came from the down the tunnel. "The worm!"

With a quick look around the dead end, Daini said, "To the bridge before we're trapped." She reached out to help steady her sister, and the two hurried away.

Mangos started to rise and follow them.

"Fill up your bellows," ordered Kat. She started to shovel powder into the back of her bellows. "We can't risk the worm destroying this. We'll do it now."

"Do we have enough?" Mangos asked. Almost a third of both the nushadir salt and the heated, soaked nitrobarite remained unground.

"Pray we do and that this works."

The worm came around the corner. It made straight for them, slowly, as if it knew they couldn't escape.

"Wait behind me," said Kat, turning the bellows and lifting the handle. The worm bore down, making her look small. She began to frantically pump the bellows.

The powder billowed through the air, enveloping the worm and clinging to its rough skin. It took a ghostly appearance from the grey coating.

"Now!" shouted Kat, abandoning her bellows and diving away.

Mangos had a clear path to the worm.

He began pumping his bellows. The worm came closer, acid drool dripping from its mouth. Fear shot through him; he wanted his sword. As it was, he felt like a baker having a flour fight.

Mangos's powder covered the worm, overlaying Kat's coating. When the last of the powder puffed up, Kat yelled, "RUN" and he didn't need to be told twice. Acid sprayed over the bellows as he turned to flee.

"Run where?" he shouted as he realized the worm blocked their way to safety. Kat already stood with her back against the tunnel wall.

"Now what?" he asked as he grabbed an iron rod and turned to face the worm. Panting and sweating they pressed back as the worm came toward them.

Kat didn't answer, but she watched the worm with an intensity that told him she expected something.

The worm ground forward, pushing cool air before it.

Cool air? Mangos couldn't believe it, but he shivered. A pungent smell filled the tunnel.

"Die, you bastard," Kat breathed.

The worm shuddered, making small stones jump. It crept closer, more slowly, its tongue probing sluggishly. Mangos ducked and parried. Suddenly it slapped its tongue at him, and the blow tore the rod from his hand.

Water beaded on the worm's hide. The pungent smell clung in Mangos's nose, clawed at his throat. The air was *cold,* and it looked like ice was forming on the worm.

Slowly, ponderously, the worm rolled. Its tongue lolled out of its mouth, slapping the ground with a wet smack. A shiver ran its length, and it lay still.

Mangos couldn't believe his eyes. "How did you do that?"

"Magic?" Kat suggested with a raised eyebrow.

Mangos snorted. "You may know magic, but you can't cast it."

Kat laughed. She rubbed her arms against the cold coming from the frozen worm. "Alchemy, then. This thing is used to the heat. Not surprising that it can't stand the cold."

"So we…"

"Froze it."

Mangos toed the worm's tongue. Seeing no reaction, he ground it under his boot. "I would never have believed it."

"Some things you mix together and get heat," Kat said. "Some things you mix and get cold."

"Mr. Worm," said a voice, "you are about to go bang."

"A little late for that, Corjon," Mangos called.

"What you mean?"

Mangos stuck his head around the worm. "We just killed it."

Corjon slumped a little at the news. He held up a sack, "Biggest bang yet. You sure worm is dead?"

"Very sure, and very dead," said Kat.

"Maybe Stiefnu will let you keep the bang," Mangos said.

"Not as good as money," Corjon muttered.

Mangos smiled, for he agreed completely.

The Grain Merchant of Alomar

Sixteen months after the fall of Alness.

The rope tore Mangos's hands. His arms and legs protested, so he stopped to rest and look up. Only ten feet to go. Forty feet down. He took a deep breath and lifted one hand, felt the rope's coarse fiber prick him, and pulled himself up. He pinched the rope with his legs and reached with his other hand.

Only a few more feet, and if the rooftop watchmen remained oblivious, he would be safely inside. Other mansions rose to near his height; other watchmen scanned the night. They, unlike the men above him, would not raise the alarm. Henrik did not pay them, and they did not care to protect his property.

Two more heaves and Mangos grabbed the window ledge. He pulled himself up and over, pulled the rope into the room, and collapsed against the wall, breathing heavily. He sank down to rest.

The marble floor was cool on his outstretched legs. The furniture in the room was bloodwood and mahogany, the coverings on the bed were silk. The ewer and basin on the nightstand were of delicate glass with gold filigree. Woolen tapestries, royally dyed, decorated the wall, either chosen to match the ceiling or the ceiling was painted to match them. Mangos neither knew nor cared.

The door opened enough for Kat to stick her head in. "You could use the slaves' entrance."

"Why are you using a door?" he demanded. "You could be caught sneaking in that way. Do you know what Henrik would do if he caught us living in his house?" Mangos didn't know exactly, but rumors said Henrik enjoyed others' pain.

"Henrik would never go into the slaves' quarters," Kat said. "It's beneath him. And the slaves don't care. If we don't make work for them, they won't make trouble for us."

Mangos rolled his eyes. Then he smelled food. "Did you get something from the market?"

Kat opened the door further to show the bowl she held. "No, the cook gave it to me. I've been bringing her fresh vegetables and some spices she can't afford with the budget Henrik provides."

"If Henrik won't pay for his cook's spices, how can you afford them?" Then he realized she didn't pay for them. "Never mind."

Kat smiled, green eyes dancing. "Henrik is happy for the better food, Cook is happy she can pocket some of the grocery money." She lifted the bowl and inhaled deeply. "And I get really good food."

Mangos struggled to his feet. He stretched. "Better not let Henrik or his *Fedai* catch you." Henrik owned ten *Fedai*, warrior/guards who had their tongues, and other parts, removed to assure their discretion. He didn't know Mangos and Kat had taken residence in his guest suites. The house was so large they never saw him or his wife, Polonia.

Mangos's stomach growled. "Is there more food?"

"I think so, if you ask nicely." Kat started to withdraw but paused to ask, "Did you get a contract?"

"No. Nobody here has even heard our names." The whole reason they came to Alomar was for prestigious, high paying jobs. The fact they hadn't found any would have to change, Mangos thought.

Kat laughed, no doubt thinking she had told him that very thing. "If you want fame, we need work to prove ourselves. You," she said in a jesting tone, "just need work. You can barely climb a wall."

"Something will come up."

"No doubt," said Kat. "Hopefully before you get too fat to fight." She left, and Mangos heard her enter the next guest suite—the rooms she had taken as her own.

Three weeks hadn't dampened Mangos's fascination with the main market of Alomar. Everything from in the world and out of it, people said, and every day he found it to be true.

"Goods from the deep places," murmured a wizened old man standing on a box and still no taller than Mangos's shoulder. A half-dozen open trunks held merchandise of hammered brass and copper.

"Water!" called another seller. "Water infused with moonlight! Makes your soups taste better—water!"

Mangos took a cautious breath. He could smell spices and sweat, fresh fruits and flowers as well as the gutter filled with waste, both human and animal. The smell of rot, rubbish piled on rubbish until the lower layers began to dissolve, wafted from the alleys.

Shops lined the open market. Tailors, cobblers, scriveners; these he expected. The alchemists surprised him, for he always thought them emaciated men in towers chanting by moonlight. He puzzled at the shop dealing in "domestic tranquility" until discovering they sold devices to punish one's slaves, but as a discrete sign pointed out, they worked equally well on spouses.

He could not resist a shop labeled "Bizarre." Inside, junk piled the shelves and counters and mounded on the floor. He walked carefully to avoid sending mounds of old jugs or tangled piles of lamp holders across the narrow shop. Stuffed heads of exotic animals (and one gladiator) filled a shelf. Another was nothing but battered iron pots, some with gilded runes around their rims, others decorated only by rust.

The door opened to allow a man entrance. Neither large nor small, he seemed perfectly ordinary, and only when he walked up and asked, "Are you the Mongoose?" did Mangos more than glance at him.

"Yes," replied Mangos. He wondered who could know him and why they might want him.

"Good," said the man. "I've been trying to find you. My employer, a very rich man, has need of you and your partner."

"Really?" Mangos couldn't repress a smile. So he was known in Alomar! Kat was wrong after all. "What does he want?"

"He'll tell you. You just need to come and listen." The man held up a small gold coin. "For your trouble."

Mangos reached out, stopped. "I may not agree."

The man leaned forward and pressed the coin into Mangos's palm. "That is understood." He smiled, a smile both condescending and satisfied. "It is the way business is done in Alomar."

Mangos turned the coin over in his fingers. It felt warm and slick. Truly, he thought, a strange but welcome practice.

"At this time of day, he will be home," the man said. "He lives up the hill."

Mangos wanted to say, "So do I," but held his tongue. If the gold coin had not told him his prospective employer's wealth, the reference to his home's location would have.

The man led him through the market and up the hill to the mansions.

Mangos tensed when he realized they not only headed toward the mansion district, they headed toward Henrik's mansion. Was this a way of luring him into a trap? Some revenge for living in the guest wing?

Mango had never entered the front door before, and as they passed through the main entrance, two *Fedai* fell in behind and followed them through the house.

The man led him to the library where Henrik sat at the large table in the center, ledgers piled about him. He was short, thick, and broad. He had a flat face and short black hair that didn't hide the blocky nature of his head. He initially frowned at the interruption, but when he saw Mangos's escort, he broke into a smile.

"Ah, this must be the Mongoose," said Henrik, rising. "How do you like Alomar? No more than the usual trouble?"

"A marvelous city," said Mangos.

Henrik nodded acceptance. "Be careful. It would be a shame for you to die before anybody even knew you were here, before you could make a name for yourself." He looked about. "No Meerkat?"

"She's elsewhere," said Mangos. Maybe upstairs, but he didn't know.

"No matter. Your word will be sufficient for me. I have a job for you."

Mangos relaxed just a bit. This didn't have to do with their living in his house, after all.

Two *Fedai* quietly closed the door. Mangos noticed two more, stoic and deadly, flanking the door to the garden. While Henrik seemed friendly, Mangos nonetheless felt a threat. "What job?" he asked.

"First, I must ask that you keep what I am about to say in strictest confidence," Henrik said. "I have worked with several other merchants to help keep the price of grain stable." He made a throwing away gesture. "It is a little thing, but everybody benefits when the price doesn't go up and down."

Especially you—when it doesn't go down, thought Mangos. He waited silently.

"I believe," Henrik went on, "Laromar, one of the other merchants, has betrayed us. He is selling his early harvest in my market, and buying contracts we agreed would go to others." He paused, waiting for Mangos to say something.

Mangos did not.

"I want you to find proof," said Henrik.

"What would be proof?"

"Contracts for winter white wheat, agreements with my suppliers, anything." He placed his hands on the table, leaned forward, scowling, "I want this done." A threat was evident in his stance.

Mangos glanced at the *Fedai*. "We can do that."

Henrik nodded as if he expected nothing less. "Tomorrow, Laromar will meet with the other members of our group. While he is out, you and the Meerkat will find the evidence that proves his guilt."

Mangos stroked his chin. "Let us set our own time. We need to prepare, to view his house."

"No," said Henrik. "It must be tomorrow. Not only is it safer for you, knowing Laromar will be gone, but he will not suspect me, for I shall be at the meeting too. His study is atop the west tower. The evidence will be there. If you can't do it, then I'll find others who can."

Mangos nodded, not seeing much choice.

"These things need be done quictly," Henrik added. "Much can be done in shadows if one can pretend it never happened. Otherwise, the Prince must hang you."

The Prince of Alomar did little unless he had to. "And what must he do to you?" asked Mangos.

"To me?" Henrik shrugged. "I would not be invited to next season's balls." He walked to the bookshelves and paused to ponder an empty spot. He shook his head and continued to a curio shelf where he picked up a small pendant. "I trust you will be able to get in, but to get out, rub this and say, 'Come, release me from this place.' My mage shall do the rest."

Mangos took the pendant by the leather thong. I was a bit of stone cut to resemble a fang in a circle. "Come rel—"

"NO!" shouted Henrik. "It only works once. Do not waste it."

Mangos nodded and tucked it into his belt. "And payment?"

"I am a rich man," said Henrik. "Do this for me, and I'll make sure you never need look for work again." He beckoned to the man who brought Mangos. "See the Mongoose to the door. No doubt, he has plans to make." To Mangos, he said, "Tomorrow. The meeting is scheduled for the ninth bell in the morning."

"He insisted?" Kat said. "He insisted we do this now?" She leaned against the doorframe of his suite as he, once again, panted on the floor, having climbed in through the window.

"He said the grain merchants were meeting at the guildhall, that

Laromar would not be home, and it would be safer than any other time. It makes sense if he wants to eliminate a rival before he loses too many contracts."

"And he told you where to look."

It wasn't a question, but Mangos responded anyway. "In the west tower." He stood up, flexing his fingers to work out some stiffness.

Kat shrugged, making light of her questions. "We've a job. We do it well, and more will follow." She straightened up. "According to the slaves, Henrik is a cruel master."

Mangos raised an eyebrow. Henrik's reputation was well known—why did she mention it now?

"They've learned his rewards usually benefit himself more than others." She shrugged before leaving him to his thoughts.

Mangos moved over to the window. He never tired of the view. Finally they were in Alomar, living in luxury. Somebody else's luxury, but luxury nonetheless.

Alomar. One scribe described Alomar as the "Rot that Endures." Mangos tried to think of the writer, but couldn't bring him to mind.

Power and mercy have no connection in Alomar, Kat had said.

In Alomar nothing matters but Alomar, he had read.

From his own brief observations, he already knew that in Alomar the laws were for the benefit of a few and were applied according to their humor.

Alomar, uncaring to the point of cruelty, gathered wealth and its trappings, and Mangos could see it. Not just in the room around him, but the city. The mansions of the wealthy rose fifty, sixty feet in the air. Built of colored stone, they competed with each other in their extravagance.

Further away, he could pick out the domes and spires of temples. Alomar kept a lively pantheon of deities, both false and true. The citizens treated them as pets; gods to be stroked and fed and humored with largesse, a comfortable accouterment of time and wealth.

Far away, down by the quayside, visible between the towers of the mansions and the temples, lay the true power of Alomar—the flat-roofed warehouses. Everything in this world or out of it came to Alomar. The raw materials for Alomar's craftsmen, the grains and other foodstuffs to feed the citizens, the wines they consumed in vast quantities, the slaves that did the work, all these and more passed through the warehouses.

And amongst them all, hidden by the skyline, were the craftsmen and the markets and the taverns and the slums.

This, he told himself, *is the pond we're in, a pond where even the minnows are sharks*. He snorted, deciding he needed to distract himself.

Mangos turned from the window and picked up the copy of Teritum lying open on his bed. He closed it, smelling the vellum and ink as he did, and ran his hand across the soft leather cover. Another benefit of living with a wealthy man. Henrik had a full library of fantastically hand-illustrated books which, as far as Mangos could tell, he never read.

It was time to get another book. He slipped from the room and made his way toward the library.

The house had the quiet of fear in it. The slaves might have been mice; they scurried about never making noise and never seen but from the corner of the eye. The *Fedai* were absolutely loyal because of training, the slaves provisionally loyal because of the *Fedai*. Fortunately, the *Fedai* usually guarded the entrances to the mansion, and if he was careful, Mangos could easily move about inside.

The library was empty when Mangos entered. He slid the book into the empty slot on the shelf and began to browse for something else to read. He smiled when he heard the singing, forgetting for a moment the risk of being caught.

"*...and green shall the valleys grow, when spring sun melts the winter snow...*"

He recognized an Alnessi children's song. The singing was beautiful, pure, and somewhat familiar. He cursed. How could they remain undetected if Kat started singing?

He followed her voice to the garden, a sanctuary of sorts used by Polonia, Henrik's wife. It was a rooftop garden, on the western end of the house. Mangos entered through the library, but the family's private suites also opened on it.

As he opened the glass door, Mangos felt the warmth of the late afternoon sun and smelled roses. Roses of every color filled the garden, their odor covering the stench of Alomar.

Kat sat next to the fountain, singing to two children, a boy and a girl, both older than six and younger than ten. They stared as if never having seen anything so beautiful. Polonia stood in another doorway, drawn by the song.

Mangos froze, afraid Polonia would call the *Fedai*.

The children smiled and laughed as Kat finished her song. "Another!"

they cried, "Sing another!"

Polonia stepped closer. She had straight black hair tied back with strands of pearls. Contrary to Alomari fashion, she wore long sleeves and a high-buttoned collar. Her face was too long, her nose too hawkish, her eyes too close together for beauty, but her gaze was unsettlingly sharp. She seemed caught between boldness and hesitance.

"Who are you?" she asked Kat. "Are you another of his purchases?" Without waiting for an answer, she began to think out loud. "No, all they care for is his money and later their skin." She came out of her reverie. "Who are you?"

"I am the Meerkat," said Kat.

"I have not heard of you."

The girl dashed over and threw her arms around Polonia, who winced at the contact. "She sings!" the girl said, "She sings real songs, like you told us about. Like Father never lets us hear."

Polonia demanded an explanation with a raised eyebrow.

"Songs of home," said Kat. "A few simple tunes only."

Polonia nodded, her mind clearly wandering. "Those damned goats." Mangos noticed two white goats eating rose bushes. "I'd have them for dinner, but he won't allow it. His prized white Ilyrian goats; he loves them more than his children."

Mangos thought she might be jesting, but she appeared completely serious.

"This is *my* garden, my only place, and I can't do anything about the goats," Polonia said. "I can see my children like you, Meerkat, but that won't help you with him." She lifted her chin. "I was a princess once." She held out her arms and the boy reluctantly went to her. "Enjoy what time you can with him." She led her children into the house, leaving Kat, Mangos, and the goats amongst the roses.

"I can't believe you were singing to them," Mangos complained as they approached Laromar's mansion the next morning.

"They surprised me," Kat said, not at all perturbed. "I needed to make them like me, otherwise, they would run screaming to Polonia who would call the *Fedai*."

"Instead, Polonia thinks Henrik bought you for his pleasure."

"But she didn't call the *Fedai*, or tell Henrik," Kat said. "Which is curious." After a pause she added, "And I'm not sure she thinks I'm a slave."

"She seems daft to me," Mangos said. "And I'm not sure why she didn't call the *Fedai*."

"Maybe she's daft," Kat said, "or maybe a wily woman in a hostile home. She could have any number of reasons for not wanting to disturb the routine of the house." Kat shrugged and smiled. "Maybe she even liked my singing."

"That's it, the west tower," Mangos changed the topic by pointing to a mansion not much smaller than Henrik's, a fortress of grey and pink stone surrounded by an iron fence.

"Window, then, I think," said Kat.

Mangos nodded. They wouldn't need a rope, for vines grew over the rough stone of the tower. Both would help make the climb easy.

"Why," mused Kat, a few minutes later as they rummaged through Laromar's study, "would Henrik seek us out? There's a whole guild of thieves he could hire."

"Maybe he doesn't want it known he hired a thief," said Mangos. He opened a book and rifled through, looking for papers stuck between the pages.

"They'll know he got the evidence somehow," said Kat. "And how did he know of us?"

"We have—"

Kat waved her hand to silence him. "Alomar doesn't care what happens elsewhere. Any reputation we have is from you bragging in the taverns. Why us?"

Mangos kept looking through the books while Kat coaxed open a locked chest with a piece of twisted wire. "At least Henrik could tell us when Laromar would be away."

Kat rubbed behind her ear, a sure sign she was thinking. But her questions started Mangos thinking. He could not answer them, so he took comfort in the gold coin and promises Henrik gave them. The offer must be genuine because nobody would throw away gold.

"Have you found anything?"

"No," said Kat. "He might have something in his bedchamber, but I don't think he's cheating Henrik." She stopped, cocked her head, listening.

The door burst open, and a dozen men swarmed through. A small, bald man standing in the hall shouted, "There! Just like we were warned!

Arrest them!"

"Time to leave," said Mangos. He pulled Henrik's pendant from his belt and rubbed it.

Kat's eyes grew large as he said, "Come..." She opened her mouth in a 'O.'

"Release me..." he continued as she dove for the pendant.

"...from this place," he finished as she knocked the pendant from his hand.

"Oh, gods," she said, grabbing his tunic and dragging him toward the window. The guardsmen crowded the room after them.

A pinprick of light appeared above the dropped pendant, growing larger and brighter. Two clawed hands emerged in the center, grasped the light like the inside of a hoop, and forced it open.

"Let's go! Let's go!" Kat shouted as she climbed out the window. Everybody else stared at the massive arms, horned head, and winged torso that followed the hands from the light.

Mangos threw his leg over the sill, then hesitated. It was a long way down, and he had his sword. "I can fight this," he muttered.

The demon stepped completely through the gate. Seeing the guards, it roared, and Mangos felt the sound vibrate through him.

"It will kill you!" Kat called. Mangos looked down to see her a few feet below the window, climbing down. "It *will* kill you!"

Mangos looked back in time to see the demon punch its fist through a guard's boiled leather breastplate and draw out coils of intestine.

Men started to scream, those nearest the door turning to run. The demon grabbed another man and flung him back, knocking Mangos away from the window.

Mangos scrambled to get to his feet, watched as men hacked futilely at the demon, as one after another fell torn and dying at its feet. The demon, momentarily ignoring the commotion by the door, started to turn to the window.

Mangos rolled over the windowsill, grabbing for any unevenness in the wall to help climb down. Screams came from the room. He slid and grabbed, his feet hit a ledge, and he bounced out. He flailed wildly as he fell and just managed to catch the ledge.

"Maybe not that fast," said Kat as she climbed past him. "But don't just hang there. That thing is on a twenty-minute killing spree, and there's nothing to be done about it."

A body sailed out the window above them. It crashed into the next building and rebounded down to the street.

"When it's done there, it'll look for more," Kat said. The demon roared again, and they felt it through the marble wall. "Maybe faster is better." She let go, dropped the rest of the way, landed lightly, and rolled.

Mangos dropped after her, and together they raced away, screams and roars drifting after them.

"That double-crosser," Kat said.

They stopped, panting, looking back at the top of Laromar's house. Although it hadn't changed, the windows seemed darker, the ivy more like strangler vines. "What was that?" Mangos asked.

"Killgate demon," Kat replied. "Henrik must have figured we wouldn't know what it was."

"We didn't," said Mangos. "Well, I didn't." He caressed the handle of his sword. "We were supposed to take it with us, then when we found the evidence, the demon would kill us? That doesn't make sense."

"I think," Kat said, "the plan was we take the Killgate demon into the house while Henrik tells Laromar somebody is robbing him. Laromar rushes home to catch us. Trying to escape, you summon the demon, and it kills Laromar *and* us. Henrik eliminates a rival and all witnesses without risking being near the demon when it's unleashed."

Mangos thought about it. "I've never yet killed an employer, but we should pay Henrik a visit."

Kat nodded. "Not through the front door, of course, and not now. Henrik will hear of the massacre, but nobody can identify our bodies, so he won't know we escaped."

Mangos took a deep breath. Henrik must have wanted unknown adventurers so nobody would note their absence when they died. Anger boiled inside him, but he merely nodded. *Wait until evening,* he told himself, *when Henrik is sure to be home.* He grinned. Henrik didn't know how easy it was to get near him.

That night they climbed into Mangos's room, a room he knew so well he didn't even bother to light the lantern.

"We'll do this with style," he said as he poured water into the basin. "No sense looking disreputable when we're trying to build a reputation."

Kat shrugged, clearly not willing to argue, and slipped to her own rooms to clean and change.

Mangos stretched, took his time, enjoying the cool water on his face before stripping off his clothes and donning clean ones. As he reached for his bracers, he heard a scrape at the window. He froze.

A man pulled himself up, dropped over the sill. Mangos could see him clearly against the window. A black hood covered his face, and he wore black clothes to blend into the night.

An assassin! Mangos thought. Henrik must have learned they survived after all. Mangos lifted his sword from the bed, waited.

The assassin stepped away from the window, but Mangos could still see his outline. He could sense the man waiting, listening. Did he know where Mangos stood or was the room too dark?

One shout would bring the *Fedai*—perhaps more difficult for Henrik to explain, but Mangos couldn't give the assassin the opportunity.

The assassin stepped closer, silent. He drew his knife, paused, and stared at where Mangos stood. Mangos yanked his sword from its sheath and swung in one motion, swung with all his strength. The assassin crumpled, his head striking the floor and rolling away.

Mangos stepped over the head as it came to rest and stormed into Kat's room. "Henrik sent an assassin to kill us."

Kat, in the action of cinching her belt, saw blood drip from Mangos's sword. She buckled the belt, nodded, and took up her own swords. "Let's go talk to him about it."

The house was quiet. The slaves, like mice, were out of sight. A lone *Fedai* walked the corridors; he was easily avoided.

"It is too early for Henrik to be taking his pleasures," Kat whispered. "Let's check the library."

They crept to the library door, Mangos reaching it first. He peered in.

Both Henrik and Polonia were in the library. Henrik smiled as he walked about, talking, sometimes waving his hands. He paused by an open ledger and let his finger follow a line of numbers. He seemed delighted by what he read, for he began to laugh.

Polonia sat stiffly, primly, watching the wall as if it would fall if she didn't.

Mangos strode in, holding his sword loosely, so the last of the assassin's blood dripped onto the expensive carpet.

Henrik yelped; his face went pale then red. He stammered something unintelligible, swallowed, and tried again. "Have you proof of Laromar's betrayal?" he asked, his voice slightly squeaky.

THE GRAIN MERCHANT OF ALOMAR

"Not his," said Mangos, "but yours."

"Mine?" said Henrik, his face contorted by a smile so unnatural it made him look bestial. "I do no treachery."

"The demon? You wished to kill a rival and all witnesses. And when that failed, you set an assassin at us."

Polonia blinked slowly and turned her head to look at Mangos. She licked her lips, her brows pinched. "What of this assassin?"

"Quiet, woman," Henrik barked. He laughed, high pitched like his voice had become, not at all confident. "You're daft, man." He drew a deep breath, but Mangos prodded him with his sword.

"If you shout, you will die," said Mangos, turning his sword so it caught the light.

Henrik let out his breath but seemed to take courage from the fact he lived. "So. Tell me of this demon." He sounded more confident, his voice deeper. "Tell me of this assassin."

Polonia furrowed her brow, as if trying to determine the meanings behind the words.

"You know of the demon," said Mangos. He was aware Kat had come from behind him and now stood next to him. "The assassin lies dead upstairs, surprised even as he sought to surprise me."

"Dead?" Polonia asked.

"In this house?" said Henrik. With a smile and elaborate shrug, he said, "I know of none of this. What will you do? Will you kill me before my wife?" He stepped back, away from Mangos and behind Polonia, standing close to her for protection.

Mangos opened his mouth to answer, but Kat forestalled him by placing a hand on his elbow.

"Why would we kill you?" Kat said. "You've taught us a valuable lesson in Alomari business. Did you not say if we did this for you, we'd never have to worry about working again? I think that's what Mangos told me. Very clever."

Henrik frowned, looked from Kat to Mangos, studying both.

"We've done what you asked," Kat said.

"You will let him buy his way free," Polonia said, her voice flat.

"Shut up," Henrik said. He sounded very confident now. He clearly knew this game. "How much do you want?"

Mangos opened his mouth to speak but Kat nudged him with her foot. "We don't know Alomar well. I'm sure you have a better sense. Give us a dozen gold coins, and you can go back to all your pleasures."

"A dozen gold?" Henrik said. Mangos couldn't tell if he was relieved or surprised.

"Is that too much?" Kat asked. "Maybe ten? Surely ten gold to put this behind us, let you get back to your slave girls... and of course, we interrupted an evening with your wife. I'm sure you were looking forward to spending time with her."

Polonia shuddered.

"Ten gold," said Henrik. "As you say—"

"NO!" screamed Polonia. She twisted and thrust, a short knife somehow appearing in her hand even as she pushed it up under Henrik's chin. "You will NOT!" she shrieked. "Not one more night!"

Henrik's eyes bulged; he flailed with his hands. Bright blood gushed around the hilt and flowed down his neck. He knocked her hands away and pulled the knife free.

Blood showered them both before he sank to his knees.

"You will not live to do those things to me again," whispered Polonia.

Henrik fell back, tipping over a marble stand and sending the vase on top to shattering doom. Mangos and Kat moved forward to watch him die.

"How did you know to bait her?" Mangos whispered.

"It was clear he didn't send the assassin," Kat said, "she did. Once I recognized that, it wasn't hard to guess why." She turned to Polonia and said, "I'm sorry we killed your assassin. Bad fortune he chose to enter the same way we did."

"I'd just—had—enough. I've seen him kill rivals before. It would be natural for a rival to kill him. Nobody would have suspected me." Polonia held up her blood-splattered hands. "I don't care what happens now. You have no idea what he liked to do."

"No, I probably don't," said Kat.

"What will happen to her?" Mangos asked.

"She could return to her family, if they will have her," Kat said.

Polonia drew herself up, gathered her dignity, and Mangos saw, for the first time, a woman who was a princess once. "They will take my children, but they will not take me. A husband slayer has no place." She smiled, a bitter smile. "Like a mercenary who kills his employer, I will be outcast."

"All this," Mangos said, meaning the house, the slaves, the guards, the grain business, "what will happen to it?"

"It will be taken by the Prince of Alomar," said Polonia.

"Not at all," said Kat. Mangos and Polonia looked at her in astonishment. She sheathed her sword.

"Claim that Henrik sent the assassin after us and we killed him for the double betrayal. It's understood that mercenaries can kill those who betrayed them."

"But that's—" started Mangos.

"An excellent solution," Kat interrupted, a hint of a growl in her voice. "We are justified, and Polonia can inherit everything."

Polonia looked suspicious. "You—you would let me—?"

"I think you can manage the business well enough," said Kat. "After all, you were a princess."

"Well enough," Polonia said. "But why would you do this?"

"Word will spread. It will be known we escaped a Killgate demon, slew an assassin, and avenged a betrayal." Kat shrugged. "A small step toward fame. And, I think, it will be useful to have a well-positioned friend."

Polonia smiled. "Yes, you will have a friend."

"Then," Kat said, "I think it best we moved out. It would be awkward to be living in the home of a man we supposedly killed."

"I know a very nice place," Mangos said, "that recently became vacant."

MONGOOSE & MEERKAT

The King's Game

"Nice," Mangos said, drawing out the word as he looked around, and everything he saw confirmed it. From the marbled floors to the frescoed ceilings, everything was impressively ornamented. Gilding covered the finials on the tapestry rods, the capitals of the reeded columns, and the high relief carving that circled the rotunda. Everything spoke of wealth and influence, and he finally understood why, if you wanted to make a name for yourself in Alomar, you came here.

"The last of the great Regum arenas," Kat said.

Regum was the sport of power, and those who played well were powerful, in part because their wealth allowed them time and access to learn, but they were also powerful because they played well. The skills of Regum were skills that made one successful: boldness, subtlety, and resolution; and Alomar respected that. Here, then, were the people to impress.

Mangos shifted his sword to ensure it would be seen. Nobody would fear it; that wasn't his purpose. It was a Marin sword: very old, beautifully crafted, and extremely valuable. It said more about the man who carried it than he could say himself.

"Names and information," Kat said, and Mangos nodded.

Not only did they want to impress people, they needed to be knowledgeable about Alomar's elite. What better place to meet the powerful than the Regum Arena? And the gossip they could overhear would be of a very different nature than that of the taverns.

He wandered out to the arcade. The haze in the lower city blurred the slums, but up here on the headlands, the blue sky was dazzling and view breathtaking.

He could smell spiced lamb and mint eel, but vendors did not entreat customers. The Gilt Arena was too civilized for that. Wealthy sportsmen strolled along the arcade, enjoying the sun, the food, and the drink. Mangos drifted closer, trying to hear their conversation.

MONGOOSE & MEERKAT

A small band of musicians played—something elegant and boring, and too loud because it drowned out the sportsmen's conversation. Mangos moved off, seeking quieter places.

People might eat and drink here, they might pause to watch one of the sideshows, but they came for Regum—the King's Game.

There had been six great Regum Arenas. Here, in the interior arches of the arcade, were painted each of the other five arenas as they had been at their greatest glory. The Leopard Arena in Terzol, now overgrown by jungle. The Coral Arena, built of rose coral in Barliol, now called the Arena of the Fishes by those who cared to dive down to see it. The Queen's Arena, which had been sacked and burned at the fall of Kalidome. The Arena in the Clouds still existed and functioned, but the games had moved on since the diamond mines played out. And the oldest and greatest of them all, the Arena of Onyx and Alabaster, which had vanished when the gods made the desert swallow Anhunkten.

The King's Game. Mangos knew how to play; anybody who pretended to culture did. The allure of Regum came from the complexity of the pieces and their powers. Each player had seven pieces: Knight, Archer, Priest, Mage, Assassin, Dragon, and Monarch. In this respect, all players were equal, but in the Great Arenas, as one advanced in Regum, they unlocked new powers, one-time skills that could change the course of the game. These skills were so old, so bound into the magic of the Arena, that nobody knew them all, but many a younger player used to playing on un-enchanted tavern boards had fallen to these unexpected powers.

The allure of today's games was the Grande, the monthly game featuring the best players. It drew the wealthiest spectators, and a man with open ears could learn much that was useful.

For a moment, Mangos entertained the fantasy of playing—that would be the way to impress people—but he quickly dismissed it. Bookmakers thrived among the spectators, but the real gamblers were the players. Each must stake a bet to play. Even the Petite Games would flatten his wallet.

Across the rotunda, people were gathering for the next game, the Grande—the game that required the highest stakes.

There were several men, each carrying a small pouch or box, and one woman. She, as far as was apparent, did not carry anything to bet, and her tight clothes left few places of concealment. She led a small dog on a leash. Maybe she would wager that.

Kat pushed past him, headed toward the group. Surprised, Mangos followed.

"What are you doing?" he asked.

"Playing."

"What? Here?"

"Here. Now."

"But," Mangos trailed off as they approached the office. "Now? You brought a wager? Why didn't you tell me?"

"You didn't ask. Besides, you spent all your money on wine, pleasurable company, and antique swords," she said.

She was right, but it still stung that she hadn't told him. "I know how to play," he said. "Well enough to impress potential clients." Actually, he doubted that, and Kat knew him well enough to know whether it was true or not, but his pride made him say it.

As they joined the four people by the Croupier's door, Kat said, "You have nothing you're willing to lose, and you can't hear gossip in the arena."

Mangos shrugged, still not willing to let go of his pride.

The Croupier surveyed the small group. "Good, we have six." He clearly knew the other players, for he greeted them by name. "Talex," he greeted a small, bald man who wore a red silk shirt with a yellow vest, "Always a pleasure to have one of our stronger players." Talex smiled without showing his teeth and nodded. "Hartwick, of course, you have no need to fear strong competition." Hartwick was a burly man with dark, curly hair and a slight sneer.

"Ninix San" wore long robes and smelled of the perfumed oil he used on his hair. Mangos recognized Ninix San as the Alchemists Guild archivist. A thousand secrets lived in his head, and a million more in his care.

"Valdora," the woman, was the most remarkable of the other players. She wore little, and she wore it well. Her dress would grab a man's attention and, with the ties patterned like a spider's web, ensnare it. She reminded Mangos of a spider in her web, but one so alluring that men would go rejoicing to their doom. She wore a small circlet of gems and platinum in her raven black hair.

"And you are?" the Croupier looked at Kat.

"Kat."

"And?" he prompted.

"Sometimes called the Meerkat."

"Charming. And you?" Now the Croupier stared at Mangos.

"Mangos, better known as the Mongoose," Mangos said.

"If you're known at all," said Valdora. The others laughed.

Kat may have wanted to say something—she looked like she did—but Mangos turned his head. He didn't want people to think he couldn't act on his own.

"Make sure their bets are worthy," Hartwick said.

Ninix San snorted. "You're one to talk, Hartwick. Did you really think your unsold slaves and mangy arena animals would be deemed worthy?"

Hartwick shrugged. "It was worth trying."

Ninix San rolled his eyes. "I hope you have something better this time."

"You know, of course," the Croupier said, his gaze lingering on Mango's clothes, "a wager is expected."

"Of course." He had, in fact, forgotten. He reached for his pouch to count his coins.

"Not money." The Croupier sniffed. "Money is gauche. Bets should be interesting for their value and uniqueness."

"Ah, of course," he said, but what could he offer?

"Not sure this is a good idea," Kat said quietly. "The only thing you have is your sword. And only one of us needs play."

Could the stakes be that high? This was his second Marin sword, and it had taken almost all his money to buy it. Could he possibly pull out? Could he let Kat face this game alone?

Why not? It's her wager. But, he reminded himself, if she embarrassed herself, it hurt both their chances of employment.

"Of course he's not playing," Valdora said. "He's not bold enough." Her gaze lingered on his sword. "Likely, it's not even his sword—or even real."

I'll be damned if I let this woman think me a coward or a fool, Mangos thought. With that, he realized the truth—backing out would be just as bad as losing. "Of course I'm playing." He tried to match Valdora's tone as he spoke.

Kat rolled her eyes.

The Croupier ushered them into his office, and Mangos found himself moving along. When the door closed, it was too late to quit.

It wasn't an office at all, but a waiting room. They entered opposite a closed door and curtained enclosure; otherwise the small room was empty.

"Step up to the table and place your wagers," the Croupier said. He pulled back the curtain to reveal a velvet-covered table against the wall, under a window that opened to the crowd.

"Your wager?" the Croupier prompted Mangos.

I do keep it if I win, Mangos reminded himself. He laid his sword on the table. "A Marin sword." There was a rumble of appreciation, and he realized the crowd could see and hear through the window.

The Croupier took the sword and examined it closely. He raised an eyebrow. "Indeed. A worthy wager." He turned to Kat.

She brought out a round flask of cut crystal. A silver stopper held in the thick red liquid. "A quart of Royal Dye," she said.

"An entire quart?" He took the flask and held it up, rotating it to make the dye move. "And undiluted. We've never had this before. Worthy."

"You can have it back after I win," Mangos told her. He'd be damned if he thought of failing, or at least showing his thoughts of failing.

"Don't count on him for that," said Talex as he readied his stake. He dropped an exquisitely crafted, gem-studded statue on the table. "A stupid gold statue of no particular use except it was made by that goat-chaser Gildi."

The Croupier pursed his lips and drew his brow together at Talex's comment. "Worthy." The word barely made it past his disapproval.

Hartwick placed his bet on the velvet table. "A sardonyx hardstone carved libation plate from sunken Barliol." Again the crowd murmured their appreciation.

"Worthy," said the Croupier.

Ninix San dropped a pouch onto the table and said, "Six white river rocks, six black casting stones, six red child's blocks, and six small painted bones."

"Ninix," growled the Croupier.

"Oh, very well. The black and white stones are bound Dalizi prophecy stones, the child's blocks are rubies, and the painted bones are illustrated dragon's teeth."

"Worthy," the Croupier said with a touch of exasperation. "You could have just said so. Valdora?"

Valdora took the coronet from her head. "Jewels from the jewel of the north. The Crown of Alness."

"Again?" Talex shook his head. "Doesn't Bardor give you anything else valuable?"

Valdora curled her lip. "No one has won it yet." Her gaze flicked around the group. "It's not likely to happen today either." She lifted her nose and turned to the croupier. "Declare it worthy."

Strange world, Mangos thought. The banker Bardor underwrites Ryghir's conquest of Alness and is given the royal crown in appreciation. He gives it to his mistress, who then bets it in the Regum Arena.

"King's crown for the King's game," said the Croupier. "It is worthy." He then announced to the crowd, "The bets have been placed," and drew the curtain around the table. Those in the arena would be able to see the bets, but not the rest of the waiting room.

Mangos expected either some last instructions or for the game to begin. Instead, everybody stood quietly. "Why are we waiting?" he whispered.

"For the bookmakers," Kat said.

Mangos nodded. He wished they could get started. He had a feeling he really shouldn't have joined the game, and waiting made it worse. Winning might impress people, but he didn't want to think about losing.

"Adventurer. New to Alomar. Trying to make a name. Bold." Ninix San looked at Mangos as though he were reading a book. "But foolish."

"Ha!" Hartwick let out a quick laugh. "True enough. We'll send you back to the gutter, boy. You too, girl," he said to Kat.

"Or whatever corner of the world you crawled from," Talex added.

"If they win, they will have contracts aplenty and can set their price," Ninix San said.

"They're not going to win," Hartwick said. He turned to Mangos. "Somebody's walking out with a Marin sword, and it won't be you." He glowered at Kat. "Waste of winning, if you're just going to bet some dye. Can't believe that's worthy."

"You can always sell it," Talex said. "Well, *you* can't, Hartwick, because you won't win."

Valdora took a deep breath and ran her hands up her sides, accentuating her figure. "I think I look good in red."

"It hides the blood." Talex didn't look like he was joking, merely making a statement he had no strong opinion about.

"Carefully, little man," Valdora purred. She leaned over, pretending to pull her hem a little lower.

Is she trying to distract us? Mangos wondered, *Because it's working.*

THE KING'S GAME

Valdora wiggled as she straightened, raised an eyebrow at Hartwick and ran her tongue over her lips. He swallowed and nodded minutely. Valdora shot a smug smile at Kat.

That's my sword on the table, Mangos reminded himself. *Don't allow distractions.*

The times he had played, he had played aggressively. Those had been on miniature boards in taverns where you could see over the obstacles, and the pieces had no higher powers for advanced players. While his very nature told him to be aggressive, Mangos knew doing that would be the same as stretching his neck out on a headsman's block.

The door to the Arena swung open, and crowd noise flooded in. The Croupier stepped out. In a deep, booming voice he announced the players.

"Talex!" The crowd cheered as Talex stepped out.

"Hartwick!" Boos mixed with the cheers.

"Ninix San!" Feeble cheering but mostly apathy from the crowd.

He was next. He stepped into the bright lights and got his first sight of the fabled Regum board of Alomar.

Many different stones made the board, beautifully laid in patterns meant to confuse the unwitting eye. Pieces could be overlooked amidst the geometry. The obstacles, the mountain and the lake, were breathtaking. The rose quartz mountain almost touched the ceiling, and pearly white fog rose from the azure lake.

"The Mongoose and the Meerkat!"

Mangos stepped out, amused they didn't even warrant separate introductions. Nor did the crowd seem impressed. There was a slight, speculative buzz, but clearly they needed to be shown why they should care about new players.

"And the reigning Regum champion—Valdora!" There was wild cheering, but an undercurrent of hisses ran through the noise.

Reigning champion? Mangos thought. *By the gods of Eastwarn, we've wagered for trouble, haven't we?* He looked at Kat, but she had already started out into the arena.

A raised walkway with six evenly spaced rostrums ran around the arena. Each rostrum had a lectern from which the player controlled their pieces. Above them, rising into darkness, were row upon row of spectators.

Mangos took his position, Kat to his left, Ninix San to his right. He could see Valdora directly across the arena, but the fog blocked his view of Talex and the mountain his view of Hartwick.

MONGOOSE & MEERKAT

A schematic of the arena covered the lectern. He could control his pieces by moving their symbols across it. He also had an optic window allowing him to see what was visible from the position of the Monarch. If he wanted to risk his Monarch to see what lay behind the obstacles, it would show on the lectern. This was a far cry from tavern boards where you could see the whole board and moved your pieces by hand.

"Please state your preferred Monarch," the Croupier called. Players could choose to defend either a king or queen.

"King," Hartwick called.

"King, please," said Ninix San.

"King," said Valdora, with a smirk. "I'll show you what I can do with a *man*."

"Bardor has his hands full with that one," a man in the crowd behind Mangos said. The others around him chuckled.

"King," came Talex's voice.

"Queen," said Kat.

"King," said Mangos.

"You have three minutes to position your pieces." The arena went dark, and a small light illuminated each Rostrum as a magic shield rose and blocked out the noise from the crowd and prevented them from watching the players move. The players could still hear each other, but nothing outside the arena.

Mangos had drawn black pieces. He started with the basic positions. He placed his King near him with his Priest nearby. The Priest could detect invisible pieces—vital protection to keep close to his King, for if he lost his King, he lost the game.

The Mage could turn one piece invisible. Mangos used the power on his Assassin before placing the Mage forward. The Mage and Priest could not be placed together. He put his Knight midway between the two. The Knight protected either from the Archer, but since the two couldn't be together, it couldn't protect both.

He placed his Archer as far forward as he could, shading right toward the mountain. The Archer was a support piece; it could attack Mages, Priests, Assassins, or other Archers, but not Knights, Dragons, or Monarchs.

That left his Dragon and Assassin. He was not good at using the Dragon. It could fly and carry one other piece but could not attack Monarchs and was vulnerable to Mages. He placed it next to his Knight.

His Assassin, now invisible, he put center forward. Kat wasn't his partner in this, but he trusted her more than Valdora, and placing an invisible Assassin in her path made him feel better. The Assassin could also be made to look like any other piece, a useless skill Mangos believed, for who wouldn't be suspicious of two Dragons, or two Archers? One of the strengths of the Assassin was that it could counterstrike. It killed any piece attacking it except Archers or Mages. Its weakness was that once it was identified, either in disguise or invisible, it could not attack.

The lights came on, and Mangos started moving his pieces. Archer, as fast as possible to the mountain. Assassin, to the center of the board, placed near the lake. Knight, shading closer to the right. A Knight-Archer combination could be deadly, but he didn't want to let his Knight go too far from his Priest.

He glanced left. Kat played gold, her Queen held back. She had a Knight-Mage-Archer combination forward and left, not threatening him.

A quick glance to the right told him Ninix San played indigo. He, too, kept his King back with a Priest nearby.

An azure Dragon burst over the mountain, dropping an Archer on the peak. Somebody wanted the longer range the mountaintop afforded.

Mangos grinned. His Archer was already in position.

His Archer drew his black bow and shot the azure Archer. The azure Archer toppled off the mountain and vanished as it plummeted. He never dreamed the set could be so expressive, that so much magic could be bound into a game.

Talex swore, loudly.

A pair of Ninix San's indigo pieces advanced. Mangos attacked with his Archer. The black arrow broke uselessly on the Knight's shield, and Mangos realized it was a Knight-Archer combination he could not beat. He tried to withdraw his Archer, but an indigo shaft ended that, and his piece vanished.

"Damn!" He thought himself clever, and he had been, but he also left himself vulnerable.

An emerald party edged around the lake, just visible as it emerged from behind the fog. That had to be Hartwick. A Knight-Archer—and, yes, damn, a Priest! His Assassin would be detected. He slid it over, under the shelter of the mountain, and pushed his Knight closer to his Mage.

A flurry of movement told of another person trying to take the mountaintop. Mangos only caught the color, emerald—likely the Mage, though Mangos couldn't be sure. A weak piece, but it would make it hard on the Dragons and thus protect the group by the lake. Hartwick had a strong position in the center of the board.

Directly across from him, Valdora flashed her teeth. "Don't worry, puppy, I'm not coming for you yet."

Mangos frowned. Valdora wasn't emerald; she was crimson. He could see her King and Priest before her.

I can't just react, he thought. He brought his Knight closer to his Mage and slid both left, closer to the fog but, hopefully, out of Hartwick's sight.

Lose quickly and nobody will respect our ability. Lose quickly and never get high paying contracts. Do anything but win and lose the sword.

Kat brought her gold Knight-Archer-Mage group closer.

She wouldn't attack me, would she? The answer was, of course she would; that was the point of the game. But not yet. They wanted to impress people with their skill. Knocking each other out early would defeat that.

So she was going after Hartwick's Knight-Archer-Priest, which was vulnerable to a Dragon, but not really, for the Mage on the mountain protected it. Somebody needed to pluck down that Mage with an Archer.

Ninix San's indigo Archer did just that. It moved forward, brought down Hartwick's Mage, and retreated as the indigo Dragon raced toward the lake, only to veer away at the closeness of Kat's Mage.

Kat's gold Dragon flew to the top of the mountain, circled, and retreated.

By the gods of Eastwarn, Mangos thought, *she dropped an invisible piece on the mountain. That's clever!*

"Think it's clever?" called Valdora. "A way to get attention, little girl? Something to make up for the way men don't look at you? Somebody clear that mountain!"

"Do it yourself," shouted Talex.

"If you tell me what's up there, I might do it," Ninix San said.

Hartwick's emerald battle group retreated since they no longer had protection from the Mage, and Kat's gold group followed them, bringing them close to Mangos's Knight-Mage group. Suddenly they turned and raced away. Trouble coming from the other side of the fog, no doubt.

Mangos brought his Assassin back away from the mountain.

"Damn you, Valdora!" shouted Talex.

"I don't like it when men don't pay attention to me."

Valdora's crimson Knight appeared across from him. Talex's azure

Dragon swooped down, a sure kill. But the Knight flared brightly. It bulged as if it were too large for its armor, reached up, and plucked the Dragon from the air. It slammed it against the floor twice, and the beast vanished.

"That's your problem, Talex," Valdora said. "You get angry. You knew I could do that."

I didn't know anybody could do that, Mangos thought. He took comfort that once used, a power couldn't be used again.

"The azure Monarch has been killed," announced the Croupier. Somebody, Kat or Valdora, had gotten to Talex's King.

Mangos didn't have time to think about it because Ninix San's indigo Priest strayed too far from its King. Not by much, but enough so Mangos could sneak his Assassin past. He slid his Assassin over. This would be an easy kill.

As he readied a strike, the Assassin symbol on his lectern glowed and froze. He had been detected, but how?

He tried to pull his Assassin back, but of course it couldn't move, and the indigo King reached out and killed it.

Mangos blinked. The indigo Priest *was* too far away. How had that happened?

Damn! He realized the Priest he could see was really the Assassin in disguise, and the real Priest was standing near the King—invisible. He shuddered. He had never thought about what traps an invisible Priest might lay.

How did you kill an invisible Priest? With another Priest and anything else. Was he willing to—no, not with that Archer still there. He'd lose the Priest and leave his King vulnerable.

Hartwick swore. Something was happening behind the mountain. Mangos could send his Dragon over—but he didn't know what Kat had on the mountain.

Valdora's crimson pieces came toward him across the center of the board. Hartwick's emerald pieces circled from the right side of the mountain. Mangos pulled back, worried, but Valdora slid her group past him, threatening Ninix San.

Ninix San pulled his pieces back as crimson and emerald pieces flanked him. His indigo Knight and Mage attacked Hartwick's emerald Knight-Archer-Priest while the indigo Dragon picked up the King and flew away from the attacking groups.

Light flickered, and Ninix San's indigo Archer and Assassin came back, slightly luminous and insubstantial. They joined the attack on Hartwick but didn't seem to do much.

Mangos rushed his Knight and Mage over to help. It was clear Ninix San was on the run, but if they could take out the emerald Priest, it would help.

Mangos swarmed the emerald Priest, taking satisfaction in seeing it vanish. He turned his Knight on Hartwick's emerald Archer and drew back his Mage. *Kill them when you can!*

Ninix San's reborn Archer and Assassin flickered out. They had done nothing; were merely ghosts or illusions, another one-time power, and a weak one at that.

The indigo Dragon emerged from behind the mountain, still carrying the King. It flew across the board and vanished into the fog. Valdora's crimson group moved closer to the lake, waiting for the Dragon to fly out of the fog. It didn't.

"Damn you, Ninix," shouted Valdora. "I'll make sure Bardor never does business with your guild again!"

Easy enough kill, Mangos thought. Even as his Knight chased Hartwick's Archer, he brought his Dragon up to pick up his Mage and sent them both into the fog. His target could be anywhere in the fog, but he doubted Ninix had changed height. Mangos matched altitude and began to scour the fog with Mage attacks.

There was a splash, and a second later the Croupier said, "The indigo Monarch has been killed."

A few seconds later, he said, "The emerald Monarch has been killed."

Ha! Hartwick is done, Mangos thought, *Kat has been busy.* He wished he could have seen the kill, but the mountain blocked his view.

"You said you'd cover my Monarch if I pushed my Priest forward!" Hartwick shouted.

"Oh, calm down. It's not like you were going to *win*." Valdora called back. Her pieces turned to attack Kat. "Now to slaughter the peasantry."

Kat needs my help! Mangos thought.

Crimson and gold Archers traded shots, each blocked by protecting Knights. Kat's gold Knight stumbled into smoke, and Mangos cursed. Valdora's Assassin had struck! Mangos rushed his Priest forward, but, without the gold Knight to protect the group, Valdora killed Kat's Archer. Mangos's Priest couldn't help.

Mangos drew his Dragon from the fog, dropped his Mage, and attacked the crimson Archer. His Dragon tore the Archer to wisps of smoke, but as his Priest arrived, he realized the crimson Assassin had moved. Where was it?

He hesitated. Valdora's crimson Knight cut down Kat's gold Mage. Valdora laughed, and magefire lanced through Mangos's Dragon. He hadn't even noticed her Mage against the pattern of the floor.

Valdora was carving up them both. Only his Monarch, Mage, and Priest remained. Kat had lost her entire Archer-Mage-Knight team. He had managed to kill Valdora's Archer; that was all.

Mangos started to slide his pieces left, trying to join them with Kat, but Valdora pushed her Knight and Mage in the gap. Her Assassin was somewhere, too. Where was it?

"The black King has been killed," the Croupier said.

Mangos rocked back. There it was. His Priest was too far away. Valdora had used her invisible assassin to knock him from the game. The magic shield around him dropped, and he could hear the crowd.

He had lost. Lost his sword, lost his chance.

"Bastard!" somebody shouted. "I had you to be the first one out!"

"Not bad," said a man in the first row behind him. "Tentative to begin. You *would* have been meat if they went after you first."

"Valdora will destroy that other woman," said another man, and the spectators nearby agreed.

The crimson pieces began to circle Kat's Queen, which was protected by her Priest.

Valdora's crimson Knight stood apart from the others, maybe too far from the Mage. Vulnerable to a Dragon.

"Don't do it," shouted the man behind Mangos. "Don't do it!" Of course Kat couldn't hear; her screen was still up.

Why shouldn't she do it? Mangos wondered.

Kat's gold Dragon raced across before the crimson Knight could move, grabbed it, and rended it to nothing.

Valdora crowed and clenched her fist. She worked her lectern. The patterned floor where the Knight had stood began to glow, and he rose out of it, now a dark, almost black shade of red. He was gaunt, almost skeletal.

"Revenant!" said the man behind Mangos. "Now she's in trouble."

The Revenant rotated twice. It faced Kat when it stopped and began

162

to shuffle forward.

"What does it do?" Mangos said over his shoulder. He had never heard of this power.

"Kills. When a player's Knight is killed, they can convert it to the Revenant. They aim it and set it loose. Once moving, it can't be controlled, and it will kill everything it nears."

"What kills it?"

"The only way is for somebody to sacrifice their Priest. The regular players know she has this power. That's why they leave her Knight alone."

A nasty piece indeed, for a player without a Priest couldn't reveal the invisible. Valdora's Assassin would rule the board.

Kat clearly knew the piece and didn't hesitate. Her Priest moved forward and grabbed the Revenant. Smoke swirled and they both vanished.

Move your Queen! Mangos leaned forward. He *knew* that an invisible Assassin stalked Kat's Monarch. *Why don't you move your Queen?*

Valdora laughed, a low, cruel laugh, filled with condescension and false pity that drew Mangos's attention across the board. "Were you just hoping to distract me?" She brought her Priest out from behind her King, flaunting her trap. "You didn't really think an invisible Assassin could save you? I know all about them."

Mangos groaned. Kat had been focused on the wrong side of the arena and, as his had been, her Assassin was frozen.

Valdora chuckled, a low, throaty chuckle and moved her hand across her lectern.

Kat's Queen sprang into action, striking the air next to it. An invisible piece swirled into smoke. Valdora's crimson Assassin was gone.

"What?" screamed Valdora.

Only one piece could counterstrike. The Assassin. Kat had disguised her Assassin as her Queen.

"You can't do that!" Valdora protested. "If that's not your Queen, where is she?"

"The Queen is out killing people," Kat said. Her invisible Assassin, which wasn't her Assassin at all and had only feigned immobility, struck Valdora's King.

"The crimson Monarch has been killed," said the Croupier.

The crowd rumbled, a mixture of appreciation and anger. Most of them

163

must have lost money on Kat's victory.

It felt like a weight had been removed from Mangos's chest, and he laughed.

The players filed out of the Arena. Hartwick glared at Valdora but didn't say anything. Ninix San appeared amused. Talex seemed to be appraising Kat as if she just now was worthy of consideration. Valdora shook with anger.

"A nice ploy," said Ninix San to Kat. "Pretending to place an invisible piece on the mountain. I'll have to remember that."

Hartwick blinked and Talex laughed. "You never did figure it out, did you?" Talex said. Hartwick growled at him.

Mangos didn't admit he hadn't either.

The Croupier stepped forward. "These, surprisingly, are yours," he told Kat as he drew back the curtain from the wager table. "And well-earned."

Mangos eyed the table and all the wagers. "So, ah, what are you going to do with your winnings?"

Kat's face was bland as she picked up the Crown of Alness.

"I hope you don't plan on wearing that." Valdora curled her lip. "It really doesn't suit you."

"I would have given you back the dye if I had won," Mangos said, hoping Kat would get the implication. It was a Marin sword, after all, and he didn't know if he *could* replace it.

Kat looked up from the crown and smiled. "Take your sword. We'll need it now that people know what we can do."

Valdora snarled like a dog that won't admit when it was beaten. "Bardor will make sure you never work in Alomar."

Ninix San stroked his chin. "Alomar is like Regum. Everybody is in it for themselves."

Talex nodded. "Bardor is a banker. He measures his actions against his profit, and petty spite makes no money. If your goal is fame and fortune, you've made a good start."

Mangos buckled on his sword and picked up the sardonyx libation plate. "I'll wager this would make a passable drinking cup," he said hopefully.

MONGOOSE & MEERKAT

Too Many Mangos

Twenty Months after the fall of Alness.

The wind howled, biting Mangos's face and stinging his eyes. It tore his breath from his mouth and pushed his fur-lined hood back from his head.

He grabbed his hood and pulled it forward, shuddering as snow slipped off and down to his neck. "Snakes, worms, and sorcerers are fun toys," he said, raising his voice so Kat would hear him, "and any small risk adds to the excitement. But cold is a miserable foe."

Kat turned, her eyes looking overlarge in the opening of her hood. "Easier beaten."

Mangos laughed. "Yes. Go south."

"Pytheas is not to the south."

And that, Mangos thought, *was it*. They wouldn't head south until they fetched the *wilinear* from the Pythean smiths.

"Strange. You normally like adventure," Kat said.

"It's not normally so cold."

Kat laughed. "You don't normally complain like a child. At least now I know the cold makes you act strangely."

The great shaggy dog Kat bought in Alness bounded out of the swirling snow. The beast actually enjoyed the cold. Mangos didn't like the dog, which seemed fair, as the dog didn't like him.

"You're getting rid of it in Pytheas, right?" he asked.

Kat scratched the dog's ears. It was a massive thing, an Alnessi mastiff that weighed as much as Mangos did.

"Yes," said Kat. "Pytheas uses them as guard dogs, but they can't have bought any for two years now."

"At least it won't be growling at me for the trip south," Mangos said. He didn't like this job; it was courier duty, nothing more. With nothing but snowy mountains to the east and a precipitous fall to crashing surf to the west, the trail threaded its way north. *North*, Mangos thought to himself, *ever north*. So he amused himself remembering taking the job.

The breeze had felt cool to him at the time, wafting through the wizard's chamber, smelling of the last roses of autumn and picking up the musk and unidentifiable odors of sorcery. Mangos savored the memory.

"It is an expensive and delicate work," Snader had said as the memory rolled forward. "Long in the making, and only done in Pytheas."

"Pytheas?" Mangos had asked the sorcerer. "Why there?"

"They know more about smithing than any others, and the earth fires they use allow them to do marvelous things. They sent word my *wilinear* is ready, and I want you to fetch it for me."

"What is a *wilinear*?"

"You don't need to know, you just need to fetch it," had been Snader's answer.

Kat had smiled, and said, "Why us?" with a feral grin Mangos recognized as meaning the situation had more possibilities than it appeared. He wondered about it then, and he wondered about it now.

Snader had looked at her, long and steady, a look that made Mangos wonder if wizards saw more than normal men. "Unlike others, I know of the world beyond Alomar, so I know something of you. My job is easier done by somebody who is familiar with the north."

Mangos remembered leaning over, trying to look dangerous because he didn't want to leave Alomar. "You don't need us. Any good teamster would do. They'd be cheaper, too."

Snader had chuckled, completely unconcerned with Mangos's bluster. He sobered. "They might be cheaper. But there are other wizards, particularly Youlia, who don't want me to have a *wilinear*." He had risen and placed his fingertips on his desk, which glowed where each one rested. "Youlia will want the *wilinear* for himself, or at the very least try to destroy it."

The breeze had come again, smelling of roses, and Mangos inhaled deeply to enjoy. The icy air knifing through his lungs brought him out of his reverie.

"I should have walked out when I heard that," he said, plodding through the snow. "Wizards and cold make a bad combination."

He hurried to catch up with Kat, but the mastiff growled at him. "I can take you, dog," he said.

Kat laughed, stroked the dog, and murmured to it in Alnessi. It wagged its tail and lowered its ears—a little—but watched every move Mangos made.

"The reason the dog is so healthy," Kat said, in a tone that implied what she said meant more than her words, "is it has been eating

Rhygirians."

Rhygirians: the mercenary soldiers who had overthrown and occupied Alness almost two years before. And Alness, once the jewel of the north, still smelled of smoke and death. The people—those who had not been killed or sold or fled—lived in frozen squalor. Dirty, starving, and abused, the people were mere shadows compared to the dog.

"I would have bought two," Kat said, "but the dogs are doing good work."

"Perhaps the people should be eating the Rhygirians, too," said Mangos.

Kat shot him a frown. "It is likely some of them are." She started down the trail again, leaving Mangos to follow a safe distance from the dog.

The trail curved, following the shore around a spur of rock. The spur stuck far out into the ocean, ending in a point that the trail hooked around.

The dog growled.

Kat stopped, hand resting on its back. "There must be people ahead of us," she said as he approached.

"Good," said Mangos, drawing his sword. "A little exercise will warm me."

"Maybe they're friendly."

"I'm not friendly, I'm cold. That's all that matters."

"I'll go with the dog," Kat said. "They're probably just around the bend. If you can't stay close, don't get too far behind."

Just where the trail turned around a spur of rock, men leapt down, landing between them and driving them down opposite sides of the spur.

Half a dozen men faced Mangos, blocking the trail and pushing him back. He gave ground as he gathered himself, glancing behind to make sure there were no other attackers.

He retreated to the narrowest point in the trail to stand his ground. Kat could take care of herself for the moment.

The men advanced, interfering with each other's swings and jostling to get into position to attack. Mangos easily parried them.

Another man dropped onto the trail behind the attackers. "Quiet!" he said, his voice pitched low. The attackers drew back a little.

It took Mangos a moment to realize the man dressed as he did, same style of cloak and trousers and boots, same pack. He was much the same size and build as Mangos. He had the same color hair, the same unshaven chin. He, and Mangos stared hard to be sure, looked *just like Mangos*!

"What sorcery is this?" Mangos demanded. The resemblance was exact, down to his windblown hair and the stains on his tunic.

"Sorcery indeed," said the imposter. "I'll be taking your place. At least until the *wilinear* is in my hands and we're away from Pytheas."

The imposter spoke to the bandits. "I'll join the woman. No loud noises until we're gone. He must not attract her attention; he must not escape."

"He's already dead. It'll just take a few minutes before he stops twitching," said one of the men.

"Be sure you're right." The imposter spun away.

"Kat!" Mangos shouted. "KAT!"

"Yell as you wish," said a bandit. "You're too far away, and the rock is in the way." He was less concerned than the imposter about noise; given the distance, rock, and howling wind, he was probably right.

Kat would never fall for an imposter, Mangos thought. Would she? What could he do about it?

First, escape. Second, rejoin Kat. Third, kill the imposter.

Now that he had a plan, it was time to act. He turned and ran down the trail, feet slipping in the snow, but he did not fall. He could hear the pursuit and the shouts to climb the ridge and cut him off so he could not go north.

A quick glance back told him he was stretching his lead, but he knew each step took him further from Kat. His pursuers were clustered together; he could not turn and kill them one at a time.

He turned uphill, scrambling into a ravine that opened on the trail. The snow was deeper and slowed him down, but he pushed through it.

Reaching the top, he shivered as he left the protection of the ravine and the wind hit him full force. The pursuit had fallen back a little, so he took the time to shade his eyes and look north.

The snow let up, allowing him to see the trail below, and how it followed a bay until disappearing around another ridge further north. He could see two figures on the far side of the bay.

It can't be her, he thought. *She would never fall for an imposter*. But then he saw the mastiff beside the front figure and remembered Kat would pass off any strange behavior as his dislike of the cold. *She doesn't suspect*, he thought, *and the dog won't help because he doesn't like me anyway*.

I need to reach Pytheas before they do.

A shout came from below. Men climbed the ridge in front of him, men who must have been climbing parallel and were now between him and the trail. A glance back confirmed men were still making their way up the ravine. He had no choice except to go east, higher along the ridge, and try to get around them.

But that was not the way to Pytheas.

Mangos looked over his shoulder. He was safe for the moment. His pursuers were out of sight, and if the wind didn't scour the ridgeline down to bare rock, it quickly filled his footsteps with fresh blown snow.

He shivered.

He tried remembering the jungles of Terzol. He told himself about the heat in the deep mines where silvecite was mined. His mind balked, and his body didn't believe.

Because he could not remember what it felt like to be warm, he took to saying, "the wind is my friend," over and over through gritted teeth. The tree branches grew on one side of the trees, only where the trunk protected them from the wind. He did not expect it to let up now.

"I need to get out of the wind so I don't freeze to death," he said aloud.

"You wouldn't be the first," said a voice, and Mangos spun around in surprise.

At first he thought it was a talking bear, but then he realized it was a man, so bundled in furs as to appear a beast. "Who are you?" Mangos asked.

"Don't look so surprised," said the man. "People on the ridges as night approaches usually need help. I'm Dahmeade," he said. "And who are you?"

"Mangos."

"Need help?"

The sun touched the western horizon; it would be getting *really* cold soon. Reluctant, but seeing no other choice, Mangos nodded.

"There's a cave nearby," Dahmeade said. "We can shelter there while you tell me what brings you north."

Mangos followed him off the ridge and through boulders strewn about until he ducked behind a large rock that protected an opening in the hillside.

Mangos stepped inside, glad for the protection of the cave. "Better," he said. "One could die out there."

Dahmeade pushed back his fur hood, revealing his face for the first time. He had an enormous salt and pepper beard, a nose red from the cold, and lively eyes. "One could die in here, as well," he said.

Mangos tensed. Had he been lured here to be killed? He rested his hand on his sword.

Dahmeade didn't seem to notice. He jerked his head toward the back of the cave.

Warily, Mangos took a step, glanced at Dahmeade, and took another step to the rear of the cave.

A woman and her child huddled, frozen, in the corner. The mother wrapped around her daughter as if to be the blanket they both lacked. The daughter's face rested above her mother's arm. Blue-white skin showed through tattered clothes. The daughter may have died while sleeping, but the mother's frozen eyes were still open, watching over her child.

"And what brings you north, Mangos?" Dahmeade asked. "Is it the hunt for gold or furs?"

"No," said Mangos, still looking at two bodies.

Dahmeade sighed, a melancholy sound at odds with his bearlike appearance. "Alnessi. They're everywhere. I find them; frozen solid for two years, but I still find them. Alnessi fleeing the Rhygirians. Damn fools to run north, but when you're being chased by fire and sword, you're not likely to know or care."

He gave a great sigh. "Mostly women and children. The men stayed to fight, to buy their families time. There are so many the wolves can't eat them all."

"You know a lot about this," Mangos said.

"I used to sell my furs in Alness. They were fair in their trading and generous to strangers." He shrugged. "I've heard some say that's what made them weak." His face turned hard, angry, "But they were not weak. They fought long after the walls were breached, long after the King and his family were slain, long after it was hopeless.

"So," said Dahmeade. It sounded like a challenge. "Why are you in the north?" The Alnessi obviously meant a great deal to him, and he clearly didn't want to talk about them, yet almost seemed compelled to.

"Travelling to Pytheas to fetch something back for a wizard," Mangos said.

Dahmeade seemed happy with the new subject. "You *are* turned around. Pytheas is on the coast to the northwest. You're a good bit east.

Quicker to make for the coast and take the trail than to cut across country."

Mangos swore. He would never catch Kat now. "Can you show me? I need to get there quickly—before my partner does."

"In the morning," Dahmeade agreed.

"Why not now?"

"You aren't that far from Death," Dahmeade said, "You want to go back out and greet him? Travelling through the valleys at night is foolish."

Mangos didn't like it, but Kat wouldn't be travelling at night either. He watched Dahmeade pull a pack from beneath his furs and rummage through it until he pulled out a tin canister and two pouches of powder. He mixed some of the powders in the canister and set it on the ground. Mangos could feel heat coming from it.

"Magic!"

"Alchemy," Dahmeade said.

Mangos didn't argue; he was glad to be out of the wind, and the canister warmed all but the very front and very back of the cave. "We passed through Alness on our way north," he said carefully.

Dahmeade grunted.

"Kat bought a dog, a mastiff she intends to give to Pytheas. The city is in ruins, frozen mud and desperation in equal portions. The people—"

"Stop!" barked Dahmeade. "I've seen too many dead. I have no wish to hear the plight of the living."

Darkness gathered in the cave, for Dahmeade's tin gave only heat, not light.

"I do not wish to offend," said Mangos. "All I know of Alness is what I saw. Why..."

"In time," Dahmeade cut him off, "people may talk of the tragedy of Alness." The shadow that was him in the dim light moved as if he shrugged. "But we live with ghosts here, and the jewel is too recently shattered to put it back together in memory."

Ghosts indeed, thought Mangos with a glance toward the back of the cave, now completely enshrouded in darkness. "What can—"

"Nothing can be done," said Dahmeade. His voice dropped. "Not even bury the dead. The Rhygirians have already left us nothing to do but mourn." Mangos could hear him shift. "You need not mourn; you are not Alnessi. But tell me why you must reach Pytheas before your partner."

172

Mangos told Dahmeade about the *wilinear* and the imposter, and the fur trapper again agreed to help him. But, he confirmed what Mangos already knew, Kat's headstart would be difficult to overcome.

"We must," said Mangos. "We *must*. Good as she is, Kat can't fight if she's not prepared."

"Hmmmmm," agreed Dahmeade. "Good thing she has that dog. It'll watch while she sleeps."

The cold down Mangos's back had nothing to do with the weather. He knew Kat planned to give the mastiff to the smiths at Pytheas. Once she did that, she would be entirely at the imposter's mercy.

Mangos woke early, stiff and cold. No heat came from the tin. He rose, rubbing his hands and arms, and stepped to the cave entrance. Approaching dawn made the sky grey, but it was the grey before sunrise, and it was already shading toward blue.

"Anxious?" asked Dahmeade. Mangos turned to see him tapping the now-dead powder out of his tin. "Then let's get started." Mangos glanced toward the back of the cave. Dahmeade shrugged. "Can't bury them, and it would take forever to find enough rocks under the snow to make a cairn."

Mangos understood. For now, it was more important to reach Pytheas before Kat.

Hours later, as they trudged through the snow, Dahmeade said, "Now, look." He pointed ahead of them. It was clear and cold, the sky pale blue and the sun bright on the snow. They could easily see the coast curving away from them. "The coast road follows that curve west because hidden by the ridge is a whomping big lake. Even if you could haul a cart up the ridge, you can't cross the lake."

"Ah," Mangos thought he understood. "Is there a boat? We could use it to save time."

Dahmeade shook his head and muttered incoherently.

"Well, it's too cold to swim," Mangos said.

"Are you sure?" Dahmeade said, knocking ice off a nearby rock. He smiled slyly, "I've been told city folks need special clothes just for swimming, but around here we strip down and jump in."

"I don't like swimming."

"Fortunately, you won't have to," said Dahmeade. "Come along, I'll show you."

TOO MANY MANGOS

When he first saw the lake, Mangos felt stupid. "The lake is frozen."

"'Course it is," said Dahmeade. His beard didn't hide the smirk on his face. "But you can't cross it in a cart—in summer."

The lake stretched across like a great frozen field. Miles of snow, edged to the east by snow-covered evergreens marching up the slope of the mountains. He could not see the sea to the west, just more evergreens and blue sky.

Mangos followed Dahmeade along the shore until they came to a small hummock. Dahmeade rolled several stones toward the lake, stooped down, grabbed something below the snow, and stood. He had the edge of a canvas tarp, and as he lifted, Mangos could see that what he had taken as a large rock was really a snow-covered tarp stretched over something he didn't recognize. It reminded Mangos of the crossed sticks of a kite.

"This," Dahmeade said as he grinned a grin that split his huge beard, "is going to be fun."

Mangos helped him drag the object to the edge of the lake. It had a small center platform, not much more than two planks nailed together. A wide crosspiece held heavy blades on each end, and two blades supported the back end of the platform. Dahmeade dropped a mast in a hole where the crosspiece intersected the platform. It had a boom with a sail tied to it. "Ice yacht," he said.

Dahmeade untied the sail and pulled it up. The wind caught it, making the boom swing, and the small craft chattered forward across the uneven ice. "Hold it!" Dahmeade called as he pulled back and began to tie off the sail.

Mangos ducked under the swinging boom and grabbed the platform to keep the craft from scooting away.

"Get on," Dahmeade said, "and hold on!"

Mangos did, Dahmeade likewise, and the ice craft began to move across the lake. It picked up speed as Dahmeade drew the sail in.

"Hope you got your warm small clothes," Dahmeade called. "It's going to be a chilly crossing!"

"By the gods of Eastwarn!" Mangos swore as the ice yacht tore across the lake. He almost slipped off as the constant vibration bounced him on the narrow platform.

His eyes watered from the cold wind and his face felt numb. The ice yacht lurched, tipping up on two blades, and banged back down. His feet slipped sideways and off the platform. He dragged them back on, clinging to the mast as hard as he could.

Dahmeade pulled the sail in tighter, and this time when the yacht tipped up it did not drop back. "Wondering how fast we're moving? Look up!" he shouted, "Look UP!"

Mangos looked up, not sure what he was supposed to see. A white speck, a snow kestrel, seemed to drift just ahead of them. As he watched, they caught up and passed the bird.

Dahmeade leaned back, balancing the yacht and laughing like a maniac. "Faster than your Kat can travel!" he shouted.

If this is what I must do, Mangos thought, *then I'll do it*. He just prayed he could reach Kat before the imposter killed her.

"How much further?" Mangos asked as he struggled to make his stiff limbs obey him and help stow the ice yacht. It felt like forcing the words out, his jaw stiff and flesh too cold to help form the sounds.

"Over the ridge," Dahmeade said. They both staggered with their first steps, their muscles too cold to function properly. "Not far, but it's a difficult climb."

The ridge looked imposing, steep, and forested.

"I'll get the yacht tomorrow," Dahmeade said as he led the way up the ridge. "Over this ridge, across a valley, and over the next ridge; Pytheas is in the second valley. On the second ridge is a small trail we can follow down to where the coast trail turns east to Pytheas."

Mangos nodded. He rubbed his arms as he climbed.

Dahmeade sniffed the air, testing for something Mangos couldn't smell. "It's going to warm up."

"Great!" said Mangos. He blew on his hands. It would be good to have a break from the cold. Perhaps it would make the climb easier. "Weather changes quickly around here."

"Aye," said Dahmeade. "Best we get as far up the ridge as we can." He did not seem heartened by his own forecast, but Mangos climbed with new energy.

"Rain?" Mangos exclaimed. "It's raining?"

A steady drizzle fell, already leaking through the seam where his hood met his cloak.

"Still think the warm is good?" Dahmeade asked.

"I wouldn't call this warm." His breath puffed through the rain. He shivered. "Let's go. Maybe this will slow Kat down."

A thin layer of ice began to form over the exposed rock, making footing treacherous. It grew thicker and spread over the bushes, then formed a crust over the snow so their steps crunched as they broke through. Ice even began to form on them, thickening until their movement broke it free.

As it darkened, they slipped more often. Mangos cut staves and sharpened the points so they had something to hold when they slipped. It would be wiser to stop, Dahmeade said, a broken leg would come easily with the ice, but Mangos wanted to push on as long as they could see the ground.

Eventually, they had to stop. They sheltered under a tree, serenaded by the icebound branches clacking together.

The next morning the rain had stopped, the temperature dropped, and the sun came out. It looked like the world was covered in diamonds, so bright it hurt Mangos to look at it. He took a tentative step; his feet shot out from under him, and he landed painfully on his backside.

Dahmeade snorted. "I usually prefer the cold; that rain's a bitch."

After guiding Mangos down the ridge, Dahmeade left, shaking his head and offering luck. Luck wouldn't help against the bandits camped beyond the gates of Pytheas. Their presence gave away their plan. Kat and the imposter were inside. Once they left with the *wilinear*, the bandits would spring their trap.

Eight, Mangos counted. *I wonder how smart they are.*

He circled around the camp, making sure the gates of Pytheas stayed closed. If Kat and the imposter appeared now, it would ruin his plan, and thinking about it, to best eight men he would need as much luck as skill.

"Get up!" he called as he walked into the mercenaries' camp. "I've the *wilinear*! We go south, and not soon enough for my taste. Let's go where it's warm!"

The men reached for their weapons but then relaxed. "Doncar," said one, "thought you were the idiot. I'll be glad when you get your own face back."

"So will I," Mangos said. *I'm an idiot, eh? Who's fooling whom?*

The mercenaries gathered around him, murmuring questions, wondering where the woman was and how he got the *wilinear*.

176

Mangos laughed. "An accident, if you believe it." He gave them a wink. "She stumbled into an acid vat."

The men laughed. "Dangerous," muttered one. "What if they caught you?"

"I told you," Mangos said, pushing the man. "It was an accident. Now break camp! Hurry, so the fools in Pytheas don't see us here." *And I don't have to call any of you by name.*

"Let's go, boys," exclaimed one. "We don't even need to kill the woman."

The men scrambled to gather up their belongings and shove them into their packs. By the tone of their banter, Mangos could tell the only thing they liked better than easy money was easier money.

He could see the ocean far down the trail. A quick glance confirmed that Pytheas remained closed. *Hurry,* he urged the men. He needed to get them away in case Kat and the imposter left those gates.

"Doncar!"

Mangos blinked. *That's me!* "What?"

"What's wrong with you? I want to see the *wilinear.*"

"Just thinking what to do when we get paid. And no, not this close to Pytheas. Later."

The man grumbled, but Mangos kicked him. "Come on. I'll leave you behind."

The bandits followed, the slowest still stuffing clothes into their packs.

"Love working for wizards!" one of the men said. The others looked at Mangos expectantly.

His stomach suddenly cold, Mangos searched for words. *Was it a comment about easy money?* "He didn't take your face!" he said, trying to sound aggrieved. The men laughed, and Mangos relaxed.

They turned south, following the trail closer to the ocean. Winter gulls rode the deep water. Waves crashed against the cliff below the trail.

Mangos picked up the pace. He needed to get them further away. He needed to get back to help Kat. The men must suspect him; it seemed inconceivable they wouldn't.

Once they reached the ocean, Mangos sighed and began to walk more slowly, drifting to the back of the group. The sun had melted much of the ice, but patches still remained. Perfect.

Nudge. A scream. *Seven.*

"What happened?"

"Talmar fell!"

Push. *Six.* Drag and thrust. *Five.*

Mangos drew his sword, slashed another, who went down in a fountain of blood. *Four.*

He lunged, stabbing another. He yanked his sword free and twisted in time to parry an attack. *Three and a half.*

"Traitor!" screamed the bandit.

"No," Mangos said, breathing heavily. "I'm not Doncar. Trick cuts both ways, doesn't it?" He moved further away from the cliff's edge, backing up so the remaining mercenaries couldn't encircle him.

The man cursed as he attacked. Mangos beat his sword down and thrust into his throat. *Two and a half.*

Two men faced him; the third stumbled away, clutching his side. Mangos leapt forward, cloak swirling, parrying the landward man while crashing into the seaward one. The man fell, causing Mangos to stagger.

Mangos tore off his cloak, letting it settle over the fallen man as he attacked the other. He paused long enough to run this sword into his moving cloak. *One and a half.*

"It's just you left fighting," Mangos said.

The man made the mistake of running. Mangos caught him quickly. *One half.* Even as he thought it, the wounded man stumbled, one foot landed on the edge of the cliff, and he pitched over the side.

Done.

"That worked," he said aloud. Now he needed to return to Pytheas.

He retraced his way northward, hurrying and wondering how to save Kat. He was steps away from turning east again when he ran into somebody coming the other way.

Mangos stared at his own face, startled as Doncar drew his sword and charged Mangos shouting, "Sorcery! The black arts won't help you now, mage's pet!"

Mangos drew his own sword, only to have it torn from his grasp by Doncar's heavy swing. "I don't talk like that!" Mangos said, grabbing Doncar's sword arm, wrapping a leg around him, and driving him to the ground. Doncar caught his shirt, and they both fell.

Mangos pounded Doncar's hand on a rock, making him let go of his sword, then they were both rolling, grappling, flailing at each other with their fists.

"I'll kill you both."

Both men stopped fighting. Kat stood over them holding her sword. They let each other go and stood up. Seeing Kat reminded Mangos of all that was at stake.

"I see," Kat said. "One of you is false. The attack was stupid if Mangos initiated it, brilliant if it was the imposter."

"How can you have doubts?" said Doncar. "It's a good ruse, I admit, but I'm surprised he fooled you for a second!"

"Don't fall for it!" Mangos burst out.

"Fine spell casting," Kat said. "And divination too."

The imposter must have been primed with magically gleaned information about their past, Mangos realized. He could not prove himself with information only he and Kat would know.

Kat moved between them, examining each closely, pushing each a little further from the other. "Very nice spell casting," she said.

She took a small box from her pack. "The *wilinear*." She set it on the trail and stepped to the ledge, an equal distance from the two Mangoses. "Now," she said, "I shall know you by your actions." She stretched out her arms and almost nonchalantly lay backwards, over the edge to the sea.

Doncar leapt, grabbing, a cry of surprise on his lips, and caught Kat's hand just as she fell toward the rocky sea below.

Mangos, a half-second slow, stopped to watch, not wanting to ruin the rescue and have Kat fall.

"What are you doing?" said Doncar, pulling Kat back onto the ledge.

Kat smiled. "A test, to see who would save me, and who would take the *wilinear*."

Doncar chuckled, a sound that made Mangos want even more to kill him. "Brilliant. That imposter would have let you die. Well done. And even better that he didn't even think fast enough to grab the *wilinear* and run."

Mangos opened his mouth to speak but closed it. He didn't know what he could say that would affect anything. If he tried attacking Doncar, Kat would fight against him.

"I've wanted to kill him since we were separated," Doncar said.

"I'm sure you have," Kat said, and it sounded like purring. "Go ahead."

Doncar smiled, picked up one of the swords. Mangos looked around, but his sword lay too far away. He tensed, ready for one last desperate

TOO MANY MANGOS

leap.

Kat followed behind Doncar, hooked her foot around his leg, and drove her dagger into his back. He arched even as he tripped, and Kat twisted her dagger free, kicking him so he landed on his side.

Mangos flinched as she slid her dagger up and under Doncar's chin then yanked it across his neck in one motion. "It's a little disturbing to see you kill me so easily," he said.

Doncar's features rippled, his eyebrows grew shaggy, his nose larger. Pocks marked his cheeks, and his teeth, visible in his open mouth, turned and darkened. "Death sheds enchantments," Kat said.

Mangos scratched his chin. "I'm not sure why you thought he would save you."

"His only chance was to fool me into letting him kill you," said Kat. "Had he taken the *wilinear* and ran, we would have hunted him and killed him."

"What if he wasn't smart enough to try and fool you?"

"Then *you* would have caught me while he took the *wilinear* and ran." She shrugged.

"If he's smart, he saves you. If he's dumb, I save you," Mangos said as he worked it out aloud. "But you can't tell which way it is."

"But if he catches me, you stay here. If you catch me, he takes the *wilinear* and runs," Kat said. She stuffed the *wilinear* into her pack. "It had more to do with the person who didn't catch me than the person who did. You stayed, so I knew the man who caught me was the imposter."

"Let's go to Alomar," Mangos said. They started south, and he shook his head and laughed as he thought of her audacity. "What if neither of us managed to save you?"

"I," Kat said, "can swim."

TOO MANY MANGOS

The Wreck of the Cassada

Twenty-two months after the fall of Alness.

The heat brought out the smell of everything: the fruit in the market stands, the offal in the gutters, the vomit and stale ale about the tavern entrance. Mangos covered his eyes and winced, his head pounding. He didn't mind missing the best produce by sleeping through the morning, but he wished he could miss the worst by sleeping through the afternoon, too.

The enormous lady who sold vegetables sat against the wall of the building behind her, as far under her canvas tarp as she could get, and still the sun roasted her protruding belly. Sweat beaded on her face, and instead of greeting Mangos with a cheery voice, she watched him as she did the flies buzzing about her stall.

Mangos walked past, trying to marshal his hung-over brain into telling him why he came down to the Alomar market. He hoped it wasn't for the overripe fruit, spotted and oozing in the sun, or the meats, three shades too brown and covered in flies.

He gagged in front of the fish stall, his stomach protesting the stench. Worse, he remembered he had come to get fish. A fellow drinker had told him a cure for hangovers that required raw fish.

The fish hung heads down, eyes glassy, mouths open. Try as he might, Mangos couldn't step closer. Instead of curing his misery, the mere thought of eating one of these things compounded it.

"Fish?" said the seller, a man almost as glassy-eyed as the goods he sold.

Mangos looked them over—none appeared better than any other. Even the small shark hung limply, looking like something found on the shore instead of freshly caught.

"I think I prefer my fish fresher," Mangos said.

"Grab your weapons," said a voice. "You'll need them."

Mangos spun around, drawing his sword as he turned, searching for the threat. A man, older, dark hair with grey at his temples, obviously fit, armed with a sword on his hip, stood regarding him with an amused expression.

"He didn't mean now," Kat said as she walked up behind the man. She carried a pack over each shoulder, pulled one off and tossed it to Mangos. It landed at his feet.

"What?" he said.

"Job," said Kat. "The *Cassada* went up on the rocks last night, and we're to help." She nodded at the pack. "Just in case you get wet."

Mangos didn't put his sword away. Something about this man seemed familiar, a little threatening. "Have I tried to kill you before?"

The man laughed, low, companionable. "Is that what you call it? I wasn't sure."

Kat snorted. "Don't bait him," she told the man. "He's not at his best."

"He'll need to be," the man said.

Mangos lowered his sword but kept it extended, a low guard. "What job? Who are you?"

"I'll tell you as we walk." The man turned toward the docks, clearly expecting them to follow.

"What job?" Mangos mouthed to Kat. She just smiled and started after the man, leaving Mangos to curse and catch up.

"How much do you know of ship's salvage?" the man asked over his shoulder.

"Some," said Kat.

"Nothing," said Mangos. Each step jarred his head, making it pound worse. Buildings crowded the streets, holding in the heat, making Mangos feel there was too little air to breathe. The taverns, normally raucous even in the afternoon, exuded quiet. Nowhere, it seemed, was immune. "Why hire us if we know nothing?" he asked.

"I've seen you work," the man said. "I think you can do this. You're better than most of the local talent."

"Fair enough," said Mangos, perfectly happy to believe the exalted status assigned him. "But you say you've seen us..." He trailed off, trying to remember where he might have met this man of good manners and unconscious menace.

"Terzol," the man supplied.

"The Hand of Bursa!" The memory burst through Mangos's headache, and he could almost smell the jungle from his first meeting with the Hand. "So the Bursa wants something off the ship?"

"The Bursa wants *everything* off the ship," the Hand said. "The *Cassada* carried bales of silk, fine tableware, raw silver, even a consignment of silvecite. Wreckers might take off small articles, but to salvage it properly you need to use cranes and barges to lift the bulk goods. The wreck is too close to the harbor to do that illegally."

"Who owns an abandoned ship?" Kat asked.

"Alomar naval law says the original owner does unless the Naval Court assigns it to someone else."

Mangos shook his head, trying to sort this out. Either you could take it legally or take it illegally. Clearly, he didn't know enough about maritime law. "Why does the Bursa care if it's legal or not?"

"There is a delicate separation that must be maintained," the Hand replied. "Certain types of activities should not be publicly acknowledged. It's bad manners."

Mangos snorted.

"Appearances matter in Alomar," the Hand said. "It is not what you do, but how it appears."

"So it needs to be legal," Kat said. "But the Bursa wouldn't hire us if it were as simple as going to the court and bribing a judge."

The Hand let out a sharp bark of laughter. "No, he wouldn't. To be granted ownership you need the keel plate."

"Keel plate?" Mangos asked.

"A metal disc attached to the keel when it's first laid in the shipyard," the Hand said. "You show it to the judge to prove possession of the wreck."

"We're not sailors," Mangos said. "Why us?"

"Fighting. There are plenty of scum from the wharfs who will take anything they can carry, but the real danger is the crews working for a banker or merchant prince. Especially Bardor," he added. "If anybody tries anything clever, it's likely to be Bardor."

Kat turned her head slowly, her face unreadable. "The banker?"

"Yes, he's a nasty bastard, but clever," the Hand said. "Always finds a way to do something you don't expect."

Kat nodded, her green eyes veiled, expression thoughtful. "So we go get the keel plate and bring it back?"

"Why not wait for somebody else to get the keel plate and take it from them when they bring it back?" Mangos asked.

"Two reasons," said the Hand. "The plate is much harder to catch in someone's hand than it is on the keel. Secondly, prior to the Naval Court bestowing ownership you must swear before a Priest of Gelean that you checked to ensure the wreck was abandoned."

"Ah," Mangos said. The Priests of Gelean could always tell when a person lied. "What if the ship isn't abandoned?"

"Then you make it abandoned," the Hand said.

They approached the port, long stone quays jutting out, ships tied along them. Heat shimmered on the dark stones paving the quays. The water rose and fell lazily, as if doing so only because it must. A few sailors moved about, but mostly it was quiet; it was too hot in the inner harbor for strenuous work.

"Can you swim?" the Hand asked Mangos.

"Not out to where the wreck is," Mangos said, shading his eyes and searching the port. "I don't see it."

"It's beyond the lighthouse. We'll be rowed out. Can you swim?"

"I don't like to," Mangos admitted.

The Hand turned his gaze to Kat. "Yes," she said.

"Good. You'll be the one to get the keel plate." He led them out one of the long piers to a skiff tied amongst the merchant ships. Two men waited, a bulky pack next to them. When they saw the Hand, one climbed down into the skiff and the other handed him the pack.

"Climb in," the Hand instructed.

"What of the pay?" Mangos asked. Once aboard the skiff, they wouldn't be in a strong bargaining position.

"When dealing with the Bursa," the Hand said, "you take anything he will pay."

"No," said Kat, "that, we won't do." She jumped off the quay, landing lightly in the skiff. "But it might be useful to have him indebted to us."

Mangos frowned, "Your word it will be fair?"

The Hand seemed amused. "My word."

Mangos looked to Kat. "Can we trust him?"

"One of the few in Alomar. He's a professional. We should be more concerned with the wreckers."

The sun was already halfway down the sky as the rowers pulled away from the quay. Ahead of them, the Outer Point lighthouse stood at the end of a spit of land that formed the north end of the harbor. The spit had fallen, Mangos knew, so that in times of high tide and storms the sea broke over it. But the builders of the lighthouse had left nothing to chance. Massive blocks of granite formed the base of the lighthouse. More blocks formed the house, a square building, tall and strong, with a round lantern room at the top.

Mangos turned back to look on Alomar, sweltering in the heat. Haze filled the streets, smoke and fumes of everyday living, turned golden by the lowering sun. On High Hill, the Prince's palace rose above the haze, but the rest of the city seemed ghostly, half-obscured, as though it would vanish if the wind dispersed the sunlit fumes.

"You don't see that when you're in the city," Kat remarked.

"Competition," said the Hand, ignoring Kat's comment. He pointed ahead of them, and Mangos turned to look. Another skiff cruised from behind the lighthouse. It carried six men, and the man in the bow spotted them. The oarsmen pulled faster. "They're a lot closer than we are."

Kat sat in the stern, the weak breeze lifting her hair. She pushed it back. "Only part of this job is a race. You have to survive the rest."

"I'd rather fight on something more solid than this skiff," said the Hand. "The tide is high and ebbing. We can take a shortcut."

The oarsmen steered them to starboard, and they rode the tide over the old lighthouse road, saving the trip around the lighthouse itself. The waves were higher outside the harbor and a stiffer breeze cooled them.

The Hand stood up to get a clear view of their destination. Dozens of rocks stuck from the sea, some small islands, some no larger than the boat in which they rode. All rose from the ocean as vertical fingers of stone. One could step off them into thirty fathoms of water.

The Hand balanced in the bow, tense, watching the other boat like a hawk. The oarsmen grunted, driving them forward so the waves slapped the hull with each stroke. Kat sat, hands on the gunwale, watching the sea that ignored them all.

The sea, Mangos thought, following her gaze. *What about it holds her fascination?*

A crate rose and fell with the waves, a gull riding on top. Some distance away floated a barrel, half-submerged. There were smaller things: boxes, clothing, and bits of wood that bobbed in and out of sight amongst the crests and troughs of the waves.

"Shark," Kat said.

THE WRECK OF THE CASSADA

It took Mangos a second to spot the giant fish. It cruised below the surface, a vague threat. "That's why I don't like to swim," he said.

The Hand said something to the oarsmen. They turned toward the bow to look and, when they turned back, adjusted their strokes to move more toward starboard.

The other boat turned sharply and quickly closed the distance between them. Mangos drew his sword and rose. He swayed a bit.

The man standing in the bow of the other boat brandished a harpoon. "Don't think to steal our spoils!" He drew back his arm and threw. The harpoon flew true, passing between Mangos's legs and thudding into the side of the skiff.

The prow of the other skiff struck their own, throwing Mangos and the Hand down. Two men leapt into their boat; two more clambered past their oarsmen to follow.

Kat appeared over Mangos, blocking the swing from a man with a double-edged billhook. As Mangos climbed to his feet, another man leapt into the boat, heeling it over and throwing him back down. The others fell, leaving only the man who leapt and Kat standing.

Again, Mangos gathered his feet beneath him and rose. One of the attackers grabbed Mangos's ankle and pulled. It wasn't enough to pull him down, but he shifted his weight, causing the boat to rock enough to topple him once more.

"These men are used to this kind of fighting," said Kat. She somehow managed to avoid the billhook, but she was too close to use her sword.

The man fell on Mangos, and he could not tell what else happened. The man's sweaty, unshaven face filled his vision. A flash of sun on steel and Mangos barely caught the hand driving a knife toward his head.

The boat rocked, and water sloshed over the gunwale.

Mangos flexed his muscles, forcing the knife away. The man grabbed his throat—not a good grip, but enough to make breathing difficult.

The boat rocked again, and more water rushed over the side, filling the bottom before the boat settled upright. The water soaked Mangos as he struggled to free himself.

Mangos pushed, forcing the man away. He tore the man's hand from his neck and rolled. Water splashed, and the boat pitched as they struggled. Now, Mangos was on top, twisting his attacker's arm behind his back and forcing his face into the water filling the bottom of the boat.

"You're going to drown him in ten inches of water," said the Hand.

Mangos didn't look up. He pushed the man's face down harder. "Is that a problem?"

"Not for me." There was the sound of water splashing, and the Hand said, "Don't bail until Mangos is done with the water." The splashing stopped.

After the man stopped struggling, Mangos looked around. The two oarsmen leaned on their oars. The Hand stood in the prow over two more bodies.

A couple dozen feet away, Kat stood in the center of the other boat twirling a sounding line. Two dead men floated in the water that half-filled the boat. A third man leaned against the stern, eyes wide, clutching his side. The dark stubble of his beard stood out on his pale face.

Kat let go of the line, and the lead weight dropped neatly into their boat. The weight caught on the gunwale, and Kat drew the two boats together.

"Dump the bodies into the other boat," the Hand said.

"We can dump them overboard," Mangos said.

"That'll excite the sharks," the Hand replied. "Kat doesn't want that when she dives for the keel plate."

"Makes sense."

After putting all the bodies in the other boat, Mangos pushed it away. It rode low with five dead men and one dying.

"That was just one group," said the Hand. "There are others."

The wreck lay on the seaward side of a rock island. Only the masts angling toward them and the starboard rail were visible above the salt-encrusted stone.

As they came around the island, Mangos could see the *Cassada* was caught near the bow, thrown up by high seas or caught when the tide was higher, and the stern sloped down until the decks disappeared underwater. It was a large ship, easily over one hundred fifty feet, but Mangos couldn't tell how much more.

They could see much of the hull, even some of the keel near the bow, and Mangos thought this might be very easy. Then he noticed the skiffs pulled up on the rock. "More competition."

The Hand laughed. "There is half a million worth of goods here. You still think we'll be the only ones after it? The first thing is to make sure nobody is on deck to interfere with diving for the keel plate."

"I have a feeling," Mangos said, "a few people are about to abandon it."

Mangos, Kat, and the Hand climbed onto the island in the shadow of the bow. One of the oarsmen tied the skiff while the other tossed the Hand's pack out on the rock. Then they both settled down, apparently to wait.

"Aren't they going to join us?" Mangos asked.

"They've been paid to row, not to fight," said the Hand. "The three of us will look over the ship, then Kat will get the keel plate while you and I go through the lower decks to make sure she's deserted."

The ship canted toward the island. Bales, crates, and other goods lay jumbled against the port rail. They climbed up the slope of the deck until they could hold on to the starboard rail and look down the length of the ship. Men shouted below decks, the continuing struggle to ensure the ship was abandoned.

A voice called, drawing Mangos's attention before he could truly survey the ship, "This be your only warning. The *Cassada* be ours. Leave whilst you can."

Mangos noticed a man standing with one foot on the bulkhead of the deckhouse and the other on the deck. "The men below decks disagree."

"Fools they be. Whether you be a fool, I'll be able to say in a minute," the man answered. He held a large three-hooked gaff in one hand and an oversized scimitar in the other.

"Not fools—," the Hand said.

"Beware in the rigging," Kat said, quietly so only Mangos and the Hand could hear. A man lay on the sloping mast, out beyond the deck of the ship but close enough that he could join any fight.

"—but here to claim the ship nonetheless," the Hand finished, giving a small nod to show he had heard Kat.

"Fools you be, and death to follow," said the man. He seemed to recognize the Hand. "Didn't expect you to come in person, Hand."

"Do I know you?"

"Reckon not. I took over from Lannel."

"Bardor's men," the Hand murmured so Mangos could hear. He lifted his voice to the man on the deckhouse, "Too hot in the city."

"You'll be cold soon," the man said.

"You've given us a warning," said the Hand. "It would be a discourtesy if we didn't give you the same—an opportunity to leave alive."

The man on the deckhouse laughed. "There be five of us here, and another half-dozen below. Another be coming for the keel plate." As he spoke, the man on the mast gave them a jaunty wave.

Five? Mangos only counted four. Kat gave a cry of surprise. Mangos looked behind to see a fifth man slide off Kat's blade and tumble down the sloped deck, leaving a trail of blood until he came to rest against the rail with the other debris. Blood ran down Kat's leg.

"I deserved that," she said through gritted teeth. "Should have checked the bow."

"You're lucky you're dead," Mangos growled at the man who had wounded her. "You okay?"

Kat nodded.

The Hand reached behind his head, casually, as though to scratch an itch. And everybody exploded into motion. The Hand whipped a flat knife at the men below him. Kat leapt up on the starboard rail and ran along it. Mangos let gravity help him run toward the men at the port rail, one of whom clutched the Hand's knife in his shoulder.

Mangos barreled into the wounded man, knocking him over. The second man swung a belaying pin. Mangos instinctively dodged, but when the man swung again he caught the pin in one hand. He jerked the man closer, then drove him back with a blow to his head. The man let go of the pin as he collapsed.

A shadow made Mangos look up, and he saw Kat dueling, driving her opponent up the sloped mast toward the crosstrees. He did not watch long: instead he reached down to pick up a crate. He strained to lift it above his head.

"No, mate, you don't be wanting—" The scavenger raised his arm as he spoke. Mangos half-flung, half-dropped the crate, ending the man's sentence.

Mangos went over to the man the Hand had wounded. It seemed a little cold-hearted to kill him, helpless as he was.

Before either could act, a man landed on the wounded scavenger with a chorus of broken bones. Kat smiled down from the mast. "He didn't have good balance."

"Is scavenging always this deadly?" Mangos asked.

"The *Cassada* has a very valuable cargo," said the Hand from where he crouched on the deckhouse. "The fighting didn't start when we arrived, and we're not the first to kill. Let's go after the keel plate before Bardor's other man arrives."

A drop of blood sparkled as it fell from Kat's leg. Its movement caught Mangos's attention as it fell past him to splash at his feet.

It was a shallow cut, but it bled copiously. Kat quickly bound it, tying it tightly and testing it. It didn't seem to bother her.

"You're going to have to get the keel plate."

Mangos looked around. The Hand was looking at him. "Me? Kat's going to get it."

"I can get it," said Kat. "This wound is—oh." She cut herself off.

The Hand nodded. "Sharks."

Mangos frowned. Kat couldn't go into the water while bleeding. He would have to do it. "My price for this job just went up," he muttered.

"If the Bursa gets ownership of the *Cassada*, he'll be *more* than fair," the Hand said. "But we need that keel plate." He looked around, scanning the waves. "Before Bardor does something clever."

They gathered below the bow. Mangos pulled off his boots while the Hand opened the pack that still lay on the rocks. He pulled out a flaccid bladder with a long tube coming out of one end. Next, he took out a small bellows. He inserted the bellows into the tube and inflated the bladder. It was larger than Mangos expected. Then the Hand put a small clip on the tube and detached the bellows.

"The bladder floats; you put the tube in your mouth and use it to breathe," the Hand said as he pulled the last thing from his bag. "It won't last long before the air becomes stale, but it'll give you several minutes. Work quickly, and it should be more than enough."

The Hand gave Mangos a small object. "What is this?" Mangos asked.

They were two small pieces of glass, each set in a tiny cup of greasy leather. A small strap held them together, while a long string connected the opposite edges. Mangos turned them over in his hands, noting a small cylinder inside the leather, giving it rigidity, but cushioned by the leather on the open end.

"Underwater glasses," said the Hand. "Put them on, and you can see underwater."

"Clever," said Mangos. The water looked dark. He would be working in the shadow of the wreck. "I hope they help."

"Just grab the keel and work your way down until you find the keel plate," Kat said. She stood on the side of the hull, looking down along the ship toward the underwater stern. "You should have enough breathing tube to get down that far." She paused, clearly thinking. "Unless it's all the way down near the rudder."

"I—," Mangos didn't continue. He didn't like it, but he could do it. Just swim down, find the plate, and use his knife to pry it from the hull. What could go wrong?

A couple minutes later, Mangos lowered himself into the water. He shivered and could feel goosebumps rise all over his body. A wave broke on the rock, splashing his face, and he tasted salt. He pulled down the glasses, wiggling them so the supple leather formed a seal around his eyes. He took a deep breath and put the tube in his mouth, took off the clip, and ducked underwater.

The world changed, turning black and grey. Sounds seemed deeper, fuzzy, and muted. *Better hurry*, he thought, *before I run out of air and it's too dark to see.*

As he started to swim, something caught his eye. Two glowing dots approached, evenly spaced, moving as one, as eyes would move. *What is that?* he wondered. They were large, as big as his head, and headed toward the ship. As they neared, he saw small glowing bubbles rising up behind them. He felt a momentary panic, not knowing what kind of creature this could be.

As it drew nearer, he saw a face inside one of the eyes, a man, peering out, illuminated by the light. Now, he could make out two long, skeletal-looking arms ending in claws sprouting from a dark outline that grew clearer as it approached. Runes pulsed, barely visible, around the portals, near where the arms attached, and along the top edge, revealing a ship much the size and shape of a coffin.

The ship coasted to a stop, and the small bubbles ceased. The man piloting it moved from portal to portal, obviously getting his bearings.

An undersea magic boat! Mangos thought. *It's after the keel plate.*

Mangos kicked toward the hull. His movement must have drawn the pilot's attention, for he looked surprised. The bubbles started again, and the boat started forward.

Mangos tried to outswim it, but a claw closed on his ankle. He kicked hard, making the undersea boat rock, but he couldn't break free. The pilot grinned as he worked controls.

The second claw extended, reached for Mangos's head, and snapped

closed as Mangos jerked back. The claw reached again, missed high, and closed.

Mangos's lungs hitched, trying to draw air that wouldn't come through the tube. He reached up and grabbed the claw, felt it clamped on his air tube.

The claw was too blunt to cut, but it pinched the tube closed so he could not breathe.

He started to thrash, instinctively trying to break free. He felt the claw on his foot, chafing, tearing at him, and the sharp sting of salt in an open wound, but he could not escape. His lungs started to burn.

The pilot drew in the claws, bringing Mangos closer. He smiled, clearly enjoying Mangos's struggles and wanting to see them better.

Mangos struck, smashing his fist against one of the portals. The water slowed him, dampened his blow, but he struck again and again. He gave up trying to free himself but began pounding on the glass with both fists. Water began to trickle down the inside of the glass.

A look of horror crossed the pilot's face. He moved frantically, and the claws both released and pushed, but just then, Mangos broke the seal of the portal completely. The runes flared and vanished as the glass blew inward on a rush of water. Great bubbles of air forced their way out, and the undersea boat began to sink. A burst of glowing bubbles rose from the back. Still it sank. The bubbles stopped, the inside light vanished, and the undersea boat disappeared into the depths.

Mangos floated, drawing huge breaths. In spite of the numbing cold and the burning sting in his ankle, he felt happy, almost light-headed.

A shadow passed over him. He looked up.

Shark! A big one, drawn by the blood from his ankle. Mangos needed to find the keel plate quickly.

He kicked and reached to grab the hull as the shark circled at the edge of his vision, drifting downward until it was at his same level. He grabbed the keel with both hands and ran them along it, pulling himself along as he searched for the keel plate. Barnacles flayed his skin, but he didn't stop.

Deeper he edged, and it grew darker. He hoped the plate wasn't completely covered in barnacles, or he might not feel it. The shark passed, languidly, and Mangos felt the water stir from its passage.

There! The smooth edges of a circle, the ridges of a design, and a rough-edged barnacle slid under his touch. He ran his fingers around it once then pushed his knife under it. He twisted the knife.

The keel plate *may* have moved, he couldn't tell. He twisted harder.

A quick glance told him the shark was moving faster, more aggressively. He knew it smelled his blood. He twisted again and felt the edge of the keel plate rise. The shark swam away, dropping slightly, and he hoped it might leave, but it turned back and rushed toward him, rolling over as it approached.

Mangos drew up his legs just in time, but the shark brushed against him, jarring him. The knife handle slipped from his hand. *Gods of Eastwarn!* he thought as he grabbed for, and missed, the sinking knife.

He could not see the shark, but he knew it must be near. He stuck his fingers under the keel plate, placed his feet against the hull, strained. The shark tore out of the darkness toward him along the hull, rolling to bring its open mouth to him.

The keel plate came away, and he pushed away from the hull. The shark rushed past, barely missing his feet. He kicked, stroked, and thrashed his way to the surface. He spat out the breathing tube and sucked in fresh air as he tried to climb the curve of the *Cassada's* hull.

He slipped off, thrashed his way toward the bow where he could climb onto the island. "Shark!" he called. "Shark!"

"Hurry, then, lad," shouted one of the rowers, climbing into one of the skiffs and reaching toward him.

Somebody appeared over the curve of the hull: Kat, staring down. He ignored her, swimming as best he could, so slowly, toward safety.

"HURRY, LAD!" the rower shouted. Mangos's heart pounded. "HERE IT COMES AGAIN!"

Kat ran down the hull, a harpoon in one hand. He lost sight of her in his own splashes, but then he saw her foreshortened feet, and she struck the water beside him. Miraculously she stood, half out of the water, now moving forward, and she plunged the harpoon down. She then, somehow, leapt and grabbed the gunwale of the skiff and pulled herself in.

Mangos swam the last few strokes to the skiff. The rowers each grabbed a wrist and pulled him aboard. He set the keel plate on one of the seats and shook his head as he tried to catch his breath. "I hate swimming," he said.

"It's not so bad," Kat said.

"You *like* this?" he asked her.

"As long as it's the shark swimming away with a harpoon in its back and not me." She laughed, wiping her wet hair from her face. "You may want to choose your playmates more carefully."

Mangos laughed, which turned into a cough. "Where's the Hand?"

"Finishing abandoning the ship. I thought I'd check on you. The men below decks had mostly killed each other already."

Mangos nodded his gratitude. "Good thing. What if others come?"

Kat shrugged. "We don't care, as long as we can swear it was abandoned when we last saw it."

Mangos picked up the keel plate and ran his fingers over the inscription: *Cassada eijn Dex lentern.* He translated it, "The Gods give *Cassada* safe journeys." That hadn't happened.

He set it back down, looked out over the sea, and realized his hangover was gone completely. Maybe there was something to that fish cure after all.

The Flying Mongoose

Two years after the fall of Alness (but Mangos doesn't indulge in history).

Death, blood, and ash: all signs of a dragon. Mangos looked up, half expecting to see the beast swooping from the clear northern sky. Beasts, he reminded himself; there were two of them, and no sane man would confront even one.

But if the reward were great enough, one could excuse oneself from sanity. The Pythean smiths, Mangos knew, could offer rewards to make his heart flutter. They only needed to kill the dragons that kept the smiths trapped in their mountain.

"You do have a plan that will work against dragons, right?" he asked Kat.

"I have one I'd like to try," she said.

"You make it sound—uncertain."

Kat shrugged. "Adventure or death, adventure and death. What's the difference?"

"Death."

She laughed. "And the ability to enjoy your rewards." She lifted her face to the sky. "But dragons… you're right. Legends are made of dragon slayers."

The great iron doors of Pytheas, sheltered between two arms of the mountain, were open, welcoming all who might offer assistance. That nobody stood watch told of the Pytheans' expectations. Instead, a secondary gate had been drawn across, and a large dog lay inside.

"The doors are open, yet nobody guards?" Mangos raised an eyebrow.

"There's the dog," Kat pointed out. "And the dragons."

"And the dragons," Mangos echoed. "They must indeed be large if they can't fit through these doors." He tried to shake the memory of burnt caravans and instinctive fear that kept all but the bravest or most foolish from travelling this road.

The dog climbed to its feet as Mangos and Kat approached. It was a massive thing that made Mangos glad for the gate between them. It barked once, a deep rumbling bark that Mangos could feel as well as hear.

"Hush," said Kat. She spoke to it in Alnessi, and it took a step back,

198

its ears up and attentive.

A man emerged from the tunnel inside and peered through the railings. "What have you done to Judge?" he asked. He gave the dog a disapproving frown. He was a big man, broad-chested and thick. He was bald, and the top of his head was pale, as you might expect from one who lived inside a mountain. His bushy beard covered his neck.

"Let us in," said Mangos. "We're here to kill your dragons."

The man snorted. "And I wish you the best of luck. Best you carry a cask of dipping sauce. You'll taste better that way."

A voice drifted out of the mountain, "Turn them away, Naan, or feed them to the dog. Save us the food."

Naan grimaced. "You'll have to excuse Thorgul. Short rations make him irritable."

"We'd heard Pytheas didn't want the dragons, but you've an odd way of welcoming help," Mangos said. He did not even try to keep the sarcasm from his voice. "Shall we leave them with you?"

Another man appeared from the dimmer light of the tunnel. Thorgul looked similar to Naan, stocky and bearded, but that was all, and if they were related it was likely as cousins or more distant kin. He glanced at the sky as he neared the gate. "Everybody else has. They come and announce they will kill the dragons. Instead, they eat our food and are then eaten themselves."

"Surely," Kat said, "you don't regret the last meal to dying men?"

"I do," said Thorgul, "since we've little enough now."

"We've a plan." Mangos spread his hands and smiled.

Naan sighed. "Come in and tell us." He unlocked the inner gate and opened it. "Before the dragons come," he prompted.

Thorgul grumbled, but he, too, looked up with a fearful expression. He led them into the mountain, leaving Naan to close the gates. "At least your story will be entertaining. They always are. We had the fellow who killed the mine worm in Kalahar give it a try. Thought he could blow a dragon up."

"What happened to him?" Mangos asked.

"Same as the rest. You can find him if you want to sift through the dragon droppings. Tell me, why will you be the ones to kill the dragons?"

"Because," Kat said, "we're smarter than they are."

Thorgul snorted. "If you were really smart, you wouldn't be here." He looked over his shoulder and called to Naan. "Light the lanterns in the first chamber, then tell Friedal we've guests."

Naan nodded and hurried ahead.

Unlike other underground places, lanterns lit Pytheas and warm air brushed past Mangos as it circulated through the corridors. His nostrils tickled with the smell of sulfur and hot bronze.

After several sharp turns, the main corridor shot straight through the mountain, level and true. The ceiling arched up to twice his height. Occasionally, massive supports and crossbeams reminded him he was underground, but it seemed more like a castle corridor than a mine.

Smaller corridors branched off the main one, and it was into one of these Thorgul led them. It led to a chamber with a table and some chairs. A pair of tapestries hung on the walls, and a thick carpet covered the floor.

Thorgul gestured toward the chairs, and they sat. "Let's talk dragons."

"Remind me, exactly, what you are offering to those who kill them," Mangos said.

"We'll make anything you want," Thorgul said. "Anything we can make, we'll make for you."

"A Marin sword?" Mangos raised an eyebrow, for nobody could make an antique sword.

Thorgul snorted. "Marin was a Pythean smith. You want one of his swords?" He leaned forward. "Kill the dragons. I'll give you four. But," he leaned back again, "we've learned a lot since Marin. We can make better now."

Kat laughed. "A choice between vanity and utility. Poor Mangos."

"The reward has gone unclaimed for a reason," Thorgul said. "Tell me how you plan to get killed by our dragons."

"I want you to build us a polybolos," Kat said.

Thorgul snorted. "For free, no doubt."

"Do you want the dragons killed or not?" Mangos demanded.

Kat reached out to calm him. "We will contract for one," she said. "But you do have something else we would like for our hunt."

"I knew it!" Thorgul slapped his palms against the table. "Every time an adventurer says, 'please make us a silvecite spear.' Or, 'four dozen triple forged arrowheads should see us off;' they're the ones who *don't* get killed by the dragons. They just disappear, taking our weapons and not fighting the dragons!" He looked like he would tear his beard out. "We promised rewards *after* the dragons were killed, not before!"

Thorgul's attitude bothered Mangos. "Look," he said. "You're done here. I counted all the burned wagons between here and Alness. You can stay until you die. Eat the dog first, but in the end you'll still starve. You can lock the doors and try to slip away one or two at a time like we did getting here. Might work, but all this precious crap you have in the mountain? It's worthless as long as the dragons are out there."

Thorgul growled. He rested his hands on the table, big smith's hands. Standing, he leaned over and opened his mouth.

"What Mangos means," Kat said in a quiet, straightforward tone, "is don't be an idiot."

Thorgul's eyes bulged and his face turned red. "Four generations of smiths have carved out this mountain," he said, his eyes smoldering with anger. "You have *no* idea the loss this would be to us."

Kat's expression hardened, her voice turned cold. "You dare say that to an Alnessi?"

Thorgul blinked. Mangos had the impression the smith's anger was his hammer, and he had just struck a diamond.

Pytheas was threatened, but Alness had fallen. Pytheas could close their gates, but the enemy lived inside Alness. Pytheas looked toward a bleak future, Alness already endured Hell.

Kat continued in a milder tone, "We will pay for the polybolos, and if we need to *buy* anything else, we will." She looked calm, but Mangos saw a slight curling of her lip and a faint crease on her brow. She was angry. "Then we'll discuss your lives as a separate business venture."

She snapped her fingers and was suddenly holding a silver coin. With a contemptuous flick she tossed it onto the table where it spun, flashing in the lantern light. "Is that how you value your lives?"

Thorgul stared at the spinning coin. "It is not so simple. But you, as an Alnessi, know this."

"Forgive my old ears, but what is it you want made?" said a voice from the door.

Mangos turned to look. An old man came in, shoulders curved by long hours over an anvil. He squinted as a smith would after a lifetime of grinding and polishing small objects. His arms were bare, his skin loose as though he had lost weight.

Kat didn't even turn. "A polybolos."

"A repeating crossbow." The old man nodded. "A clever idea, but still dangerous to use. Look at me, child, that I may gauge your temper."

Kat turned and met the old man's gaze. After a minute he nodded and turned his scrutiny on Mangos. Mangos smiled confidently.

The old man turned to Thorgul. "See to it." Thorgul opened his mouth to protest, but the old man cut him off. "We will make her anything she wants."

Thorgul frowned and shook his head. "Naan can do it."

"Naan can," the old man said, "and you can help." He turned to leave but paused to say, "Alness has been good to Pythias in the past. May it be so again."

"That's why we're here," Kat said.

Naan came in, settled into a chair and said, "Father said you wanted something built."

"I want a polybolos," Kat said. "I saw the remains of some in Endgras that looked large enough to kill a dragon."

Naan scratched his beard. "Endgras, eh? Chances are we made those. Long time ago. Not me, of course, it would have been my great uncles." He closed his eyes and thought. "Those were likely cavalry polybolii—sized to take down a horse. That might kill a young dragon, but it isn't even enough to annoy the two troubling us."

"Make it larger," Mangos said.

Thorgul curled his lip. "Don't teach us our trade. Larger and it's too large to aim. If you can get the dragon to lay down in front of the polybolos and sit quietly until you shoot it, well, then you'd have something."

"Then we'll try something else," Mangos said.

"We'll need to improve the design," Kat stated.

Thorgul sneered.

"Not just the design," Naan said ignoring Thorgul's expression. "We'll likely need different materials. But we've done some things with alloys that might help. Have to work on some gears, though…" He trailed off, his expression thoughtful.

"And how would you hunt these dragons?" Thorgul demanded. "You can't move a polybolos fast enough."

Kat nodded. "They fly."

"Everywhere. Only in their lair don't they fly. Will you chase them there so they can have breakfast in bed?"

Kat cleared her throat. "That's the other thing: I know you've been working on an airship. A basket and balloon thing. Do you still have it?"

Naan focused on her. "Well, yes, but…you're mad!" His mouth dropped open, his eyes grew wide. "Surely you can't be serious! To fly against these dragons is folly!"

Mangos laughed. *That* was her plan! An airship. "Flying! Sorcery!"

"It is risky," Kat admitted.

"No!" Thorgul exclaimed. "You will take our polybolos, and then you will take our airship!"

"Not sorcery," Naan said to Mangos, ignoring the other two's comments. "A semi-rigid balloon that floats, carrying a gondola—a basket that carries people."

"But it could carry the polybolos?" Kat pressed her question.

"It could," Naan said. "It hasn't been flown in years—even before the dragons came. There was some trouble with the steering wires."

"When you said you were smarter than the other adventurers, I believed you," Thorgul said. "But now I see you're just crazy."

"Resourceful," Mangos countered. "Our plans work." He didn't mention the plan was Kat's. "And when they don't, well, there's a first time for dying, but we haven't found it yet."

"Dragons," Thorgul said menacingly. "Dragons are a fine way for dying."

Naan led them through the mountain, past forges and workshops. Pytheas was vast, but except for the clash of unseen hammers or the roar of the furnaces, Mangos might have thought it deserted. "The airship," Naan said, his voice cracking. "I—I would hate to see it destroyed."

"I'm sorry," Kat said.

"No, no, it's all right. It's just—it's all right. Better a fiery death than sitting inside this mountain, trapped." He stopped at a closed door. "It's in here, where we can inflate it and tow it out of the mountain. This was a natural cave before we joined it to the rest of the complex. It's a little bright after being underground." He opened the door.

The sunlight was painfully bright. All Mangos could see was a dark shadow outlined by an aureole of bright light. The light dimmed as his eyes adjusted and he could make out a huge, baggy curtain of silver-grey silk suspended from the cavern ceiling. Thick straps wrapped the silk and attached to a long board—which on a ship would be called a keel. Under the keel was the gondola.

"It looks like a giant bathtub," Mangos said. A closer look told him the gondola shared the shape of a tub, but little else. Teak and brass glinted in the light. Mangos could smell the oil used to polish it. He walked through a jumble of trunks and worktables to see it more closely.

He paused to run his hand over the side, as smooth as the silk that made the balloon. The joints were perfect, the grains of the boards flowing together. The brass work was bright, ornately cast with, ironically, dragons on the fittings. The brass, too, was smooth; no bubbles or roughness from the molds remained.

"This is a work of art," Kat said, echoing his thoughts.

The basket had large windows, two on each side, one on each end. Mangos pressed his face against the glass to look inside. He did not know why brass tubes ran across the top, or what the box against the ceiling held, but he recognized a small brazier situated in the center.

"We'll need to take out the windows and mount the polybolos," Kat said.

"There are other things it needs," Naan said. "You can help while I make the polybolos."

"Can you make it swivel-mounted?" Kat asked.

"Gods, yes." Naan pulled his hand over his face. "You'll have enough trouble without having to wait for the dragons to fly in front of you. This thing doesn't steer well."

The brass dragons felt cool under Mangos's fingers. "This really flies?"

"After the envelope is filled," Naan said. He looked at them, his expression thoughtful. "You'll need to learn to fly it," he said, nodding toward Kat. "The polybolos will need Mangos's strength."

"You won't be coming?" Mangos asked, a little sharply.

"The airship won't carry that much weight. And," Naan rubbed the back of his neck, "I'm a smith, not a warrior."

He coughed and went on briskly. "I'll have you re-string the control wires for the rudder." He pointed to the wires crisscrossing from the steering lever to the flat rudder. He opened a nearby chest and rummaged through, pulling out coils of wire and setting them on the table. "Use this."

Mangos picked up the thin wire. "This? I can pull this apart." He wrapped it around his hand and began to pull, testing it.

"No, you can't pull it apart," Naan said. "You'll only cut yourself. I'll show you how to attach it." He quickly demonstrated how to feed the wires through the pulleys and clamp them in place. "Make sure the set screws are tight," he said. "If the wire slips, you have no steering." He paused and added, "Not that you have much anyway."

Mangos fumbled with the tool Naan gave him. "My hands were made for swords," he complained.

66 I can't believe it's taken so long," Mangos said as he tightened the last screws.

"Third time lucky." Kat loaded metal polybolos bolts into the storage locker.

It was, indeed, the third time Mangos had strung the steering wires, interspersed with helping take out the gondola's windows, working bellows as Naan forged parts, and other tasks to prepare for hunting the dragons.

He clipped the extra wire and coiled it. There wasn't any place to put it, so he slipped it into his tunic until he could return it later.

Naan pushed a two-wheeled cart into the room. "Here's your polybolos. I made it as small as possible." He positioned the cart so the polybolos pointed at the stack of crates against the far wall.

It was still a big weapon. The limbs of the bow, horizontal like a crossbow, were no longer than a horseman's bow, but made of metal Mangos did not recognize. A rack on the top held metal bolts, each as long as his forearm.

Mangos reached out to turn the crank on the side. It took more effort than he thought, but turned smoothly. A catch drew back the bow, just as it reached the end of its draw, a bolt dropped into a groove, the catch released the string, and the bow fired with a loud "thwang!" The bolt slammed into a crate, punching through the side and disappearing inside.

"I'll just pretend that wasn't reckless," Naan said. He opened the polybolos's side, exposing gears and a chain. Turning the crank set it all in motion. "It has extra gears to multiply the force to draw the stiffer bow. The slide is internal so you can stand behind it to try and aim."

Mangos nodded his understanding and appreciation. They were not aiming at ranks of soldiers, but a single agile target. He rotated it on its stand, swung it down, then up.

"Better block the upward swing," Kat said. "We don't want him shooting the airbag."

"I'm not going to shoot our own airship!" Mangos exclaimed. "Will it kill a dragon?"

"Test it a bit," Naan said. "Then let's mount it in the airship. Tomorrow will be a fine day to fly."

For a second Mangos thought he had said, "a fine day to die." Only when he sorted out the correct words did he realize Naan hadn't answered his question.

The airbag almost shimmered as the men pulled it into the sun. Ropes creaked as they winched the airship down and tied it securely to iron rings set in the stone.

Kat stepped lightly into the gondola. Mangos felt a chill as he entered the shade of the airship. He looked up, but the sky was clear of clouds and dragons.

"Might get a few clouds as the sun gets higher," Thorgul said as he finished tying off the last line. "Not much. Should stay calm. That's the main thing. Only time we had this up in any sort of wind, it didn't go well."

Mangos wished the smith would shut up.

Naan approached. "One last thing," he said. "Should the dragons destroy the airship, which is likely, and you survive, which is unlikely, these gliders are your only hope of reaching earth alive."

He had what looked like two closed parasols, but he opened one to reveal a very large, triangular kite. A folding brace snapped in place to lock the arms apart. He folded down a pair of handles. "You won't need to be reminded to hang on when it's five hundred feet or more to a messy death."

"Can you steer it?" Mangos asked.

"If you twist the handles, you can make it bank one way or the other. It's not much."

"And you've tried this?" Mangos tried hard to keep the skepticism he felt out of his voice.

"No, of course not. But if you're down to using these, your chances aren't worth much anyway." Naan closed the glider and passed both into the gondola. "Are you ready?"

"Luck." Thorgul didn't specify which kind, and Mangos suspected he would just as soon see them have the bad variety.

"We're ready," he said with more conviction than he felt.

His pulse quickened in the crisp air. They climbed above the mountains. The peaks were so close it seemed they could touch the snow. The valleys fell thousands of feet into green forests. Clouds, thin wisps like raw cotton pulled apart, glowed gold in the morning sun.

A marvelous feeling: the world at his feet. He never dreamed of looking down on the mountains.

Kat laughed, a carefree sound. "Ready?"

Mangos grinned. "Yes."

"Good. Because here they come."

They looked like crows at first, but they were too large to be crows. The dragons were iridescent black, a black that had trapped all other colors. Large hind legs, muscular and clawed. Front legs as long, but not as muscular.

The nearest one's tail stretched twenty feet behind it, about as long as its body. Mangos estimated its neck to be eight-to-ten feet long and very thick, as it needed to be to support the large head.

Its eyes sat deep in their sockets, protected by bony ridges and thick, scaled lids. It had a mouth like a crocodile with teeth that looked longer than his fingers. From nose to tail, it had to be fifty-five or sixty feet long.

The wings were hard to judge, for they were always moving, but he knew what looked like slender bones from a distance would be as large as his leg. The wingspan was probably the same as the dragon's length.

The second one looked just as large.

The dragons closed on the airship. Mangos cranked the polybolos as fast as he could. The limbs drew back, the bolt rotated into place, and the whole polybolos shuddered as it released, immediately starting to draw back again.

The bolt whirred away, carving a path behind the dragon.

"Ahead of it!" Kat said. "Aim ahead of it!"

Mangos swung the polybolos just as it fired again. Closer, but still behind it. The polybolos, which fired so rapidly before, now seemed to draw and reload with agonizing slowness.

He jerked back just as the third shot launched, sending it wild. He cursed, steadied the polybolos, and kept cranking.

The dragon swept close.

The next bolt slammed home in the dragon's flank with a sharp *crack!* The dragon flinched, rolled away, and they could see the steel bolt embedded in its leg. The next hit at the base of its neck, and the next soared over it.

"Over there!" Kat exclaimed, and Mangos swung, marveling that he knew which "there" she meant. Miss.

"Faster," he muttered, trying to crank faster as he turned the polybolos to follow the dragon. He could see individual scales. Hit, just behind the head. Hit on the neck. Hit on the neck. Hit on the shoulder.

"Yes!" he bellowed triumphantly as the dragon banked away.

"The first one's coming back!" Kat shouted.

No longer curious, the first dragon circled toward them. Mangos felt his arm beginning to tire but kept cranking. "What if he runs into us?"

"He won't! Worry about his flame!"

The bolt flashed across the sky. Miss. It fell in a graceful arc. Hit, near the dragon's mouth. Hit, punching a hole in a wing before tumbling down. Miss—how had he missed with the dragon so close?

The dragon roared and snapped.

The airship rocked. Mangos stumbled, kept cranking, shot the dragon's belly as it passed. It flicked its tail, sending the airship skittering across the sky. The ship rolled; Mangos gripped the polybolos as the deck turned. Kat gripped a support, her legs dangling until gravity brought the basket vertical again.

"Fun, eh?" Mangos said. No longer cranking, he scanned the sky for the dragons, craning his head to look above and below.

Kat scrambled to the locker, took out more bolts, and dropped them into the hopper.

The basket rocked gently, the only sound the wind. Where were the dragons?

Mangos cranked, drawing the limbs back and letting a bolt rotate into position, stopped just before it fired, holding ready.

An ear-splitting screech pierced the air, and the airship jumped, then dropped, stopping suddenly but immediately starting to settle again. One of the dragons soared out from overhead. Mangos turned the crank, but the ship started to plummet. Rapidly.

The airbag sagged and wrinkled as the ship fell.

"That's not a steering problem," Mangos shouted. "Can we fix it?"

Kat shook her head. "No!"

Mangos grabbed one of the little gliders and passed it to her. "Looks like we're going to test these!"

Kat took the glider. She checked her knives.

Mangos grabbed the other glider. He leapt away from the basket as he would dive into a lake. He snapped open the glider, praying it would work, that it would hold his weight, that he wouldn't plummet to his death in one of those far-below valleys.

The triangle opened, grabbed the air, *lifted* him. His shoulders screamed at the sudden change of direction. His feet flopped down, swinging wildly below the glider. The handles twisted and the glider heeled left, cutting through the air and arrowing down.

He twisted the other handle, and the glider jerked right. For a second, its nose rose then dropped, and the glider spiraled down.

He twisted again, fighting the urge to panic, trying to keep the twist small. The glider's nose lifted, and by making more small adjustments, Mangos was able to stop its rapid descent. The noise of rushing air lessened, then he heard the cries of the dragons.

They're smarter than we think, Mangos thought, for it seemed the dragons talked to each other. One circled him while the other banked toward Kat, who had set her glider into a slow, sweeping spiral.

His dragon passed in front of him, giving him a glimpse of scales before the draft from its wings sent him bouncing across the sky.

The dragon turned and came right at him, mouth open wide. Mangos twisted the left handle to send his glider down, but the dragon was too close to escape.

It snapped, crushing the glider in its jaws. The glider didn't break apart; it folded under the dragon's jaw, slapping Mangos against the beast's belly. For a second, he hung there, then he reached up and grabbed one of the embedded polybolos bolts. He pulled himself up until he could reach the next and grabbed that one, too. The dragon gnashed its teeth, and the glider fell away in bits, leaving Mangos clinging to the bolts.

The dragon rolled so Mangos lay partially across it. He grabbed the next bolt before the dragon rolled back, sending him dangling once again.

He could see the clouds beyond the arch of the dragon's neck, and knew they were closer than the earth. He could almost touch them if he tried. He stretched out his hand, grabbed the next bolt, pulled up, and could finally reach the first bolt with his foot.

A second later, he was astride the dragon, legs clamped around its neck, leaning over so he could still hold a bolt.

"By the gods of Eastwarn!" he swore. Now what did he do?

The dragon turned and rolled. Mangos clutched the bolts tightly and

THE FLYING MONGOOSE

pressed himself against its neck. Its claws flashed before his face, and he shied away, only to grab the bolt in terror as he slipped. A second harrowing pass of claws told him the dragon could not quite reach him. Were they on the ground where it could use its back claws, however...

He couldn't leap off, that was obvious.

He tried to wiggle the bolt, but it was deep in the dragon's muscles. He didn't really want to pull it out, for he couldn't puncture the dragon's scales by himself anyway. And he needed it as a handhold.

Where was it vulnerable? Eyes, ears; both places he couldn't reach. He couldn't think of anywhere else.

He had no sword, no dagger. He had nothing. He tentatively took his hand from a bolt and patted his tunic, hoping to find anything that might help. Nothing except the bit of steering wire he had tucked in the inside pocket.

Using one hand, Mangos pulled out the wire. He wrapped and tied the wire around the bolt in the dragon's neck. He flipped it around the neck, caught it, and drew it tight. He had to stop to ride out another twisting effort of the dragon to dislodge him. Then, inching the wire up, he slipped it under the long scales protecting the front of the neck.

He pulled tighter, forcing the wire further under the scale. He strained, and the wire bit in. "Now we're for it."

Mangos wrapped his cloak around his hand, three, four, five times, and wrapped the wire around twice. He took the wire in his free hand so he could pull with both. Drawing his feet up, he levered himself into a crouching position.

He pushed with his legs and pulled with his arms. The wire tightened on his hand.

The dragon twisted its head, rolling as it did, but Mangos, every muscle tight, stayed planted. The dragon snapped at him, Mangos flinched, but it couldn't twist far enough to reach him.

He could feel the wire cutting into the dragon's neck, but it stopped, caught on the edge of a scale or a bone. Mangos jerked harder, something snapped, and the dragon screamed. Blood sprayed into the air.

The dragon stopped screaming; instead it made a whistling, gurgling sound. It convulsed, throwing Mangos off.

The wire jerked him back, slamming him against the dragon as it tumbled in a welter of wings, claws, and blood. He fell free again. The world became a spinning mélange of sky, dragon, and fast approaching mountain. Then he swung back against the dragon and everything went black.

It was quiet; not an absolute quiet, more a restful quiet as if the world was muffled or far away. Mangos felt neither hot nor cold. He felt no pain, and, for the moment, he thought no thoughts.

Presently he remembered the feel of the wind, the splash of blood, and the onrushing ground. He forced his eyes open, and his body exploded with pain. The blue sky was darker, the lower half of the mountain in his view was shadowed. *The sun is going down, and I'm still alive!* He tried to turn his head. *But, oh gods, I hurt.*

Maybe I should have waited until it flew lower before killing it.

He tried to separate the pain but couldn't. He felt like he had been pounded all over. He rolled over, a new, sharp pain flaring through his right shoulder, and raised himself to his knees. Mangos forced himself to stand up, wobbling on legs that didn't want to support him.

The dragon lay broken at the foot of the cliff, body twisted and folded, neck stretched out, and the mess of its head lay amongst the rubble of its impact.

"By the gods of Eastwarn, what a ride!" Mangos laughed as he staggered over to the dragon.

Something thick, clear, and oily leaked from the dragon's mouth. Blue smoke curled from it, and Mangos felt heat on his raw flesh.

"I have no idea where I am," he said to the dead dragon.

Night would fall in a couple hours. Summer nights could still be freezing.

What of Kat?

He suddenly had a cold feeling. There had been a dozen ways to die, and he couldn't even be sure how he found one to live.

"Is it alive?" Somebody was shouting to him.

He turned, wincing as the movement drew his skin and muscles tight. "Me or the dragon?" he called up.

"We'll start with you," another voice, Kat's voice, shouted.

Mangos felt a rush of relief. "You're alive!"

She leapt off a rock and landed in front of him. She looked fine, her green eyes dancing. "You have a big decision to make."

"I do?"

"Naan says they have the first silvecite blade Marin forged. That's an amazing collector's item. On the other hand, they can make you something new—a better weapon."

"You killed the other dragon?"

"Better," Kat said, and the fire in her eyes burned like dragon flame. "I *caught* it. Bone, blood, and fire; you can do amazing things with dragons."

"How did you catch it?"

Kat laughed. "I lured it into the airship, and the airbag entangled its wings. It fell like a rock, but survived. I just rode down on my glider. But if I hadn't seen your ride, I wouldn't have believed it. So, dragonslayer," she said, "Which is it going to be? The original Marin blade, or something equally amazing?"

Mangos groaned, holding his hand to his head. "Don't ask me to think right now. I'll decide in the morning."

THE FLYING MONGOOSE

Death and Renewal

Twenty-seven months after the fall of Alness.

The sun shone overhead.

Not the real sun, that had long set, but a crystal enchantment suspended on a golden chain slowly moving its way down the grand cathedral hall in imitation of the seasons. The sun was still in the first quarter of the hall, shining brightly to signify spring.

Mangos pushed through the room, lost amongst thousands of Alomar's citizens gathered in the vast indoor garden to celebrate the Renewal Festival. He ignored the women in their colorful dresses and the men in their finest tunics as he searched for Kat.

Instead he saw the Bursa, the man who hired him, seated in a high-backed chair near one of the great columns that marched down the nave. The Hand, his administrative assassin, stood behind him, half in the shadows.

The Bursa lifted a hand, beckoned him with his fingertips.

"Damn," muttered Mangos, wondering what could be said that would help. He pushed his way forward, shoving harder than he needed, but angry that he didn't know the answers to the questions the Bursa would surely ask.

"Mangos, my friend," said the Bursa.

"Bursa, you have news?" Mangos asked to forestall any of the Bursa's questions.

The Bursa chuckled, but without humor; worry lurked in his eyes. "I hoped you had news for me. You haven't much time." He pointed to the crystal sun. "At the end of winter, when the sun reaches the end of the gallery, the mute spell on Manchil breaks, and he can talk again."

Mangos nodded. He knew this. He knew somehow the gladiator/slave Manchil had passed from the Bursa's ownership to the Prince of Alomar. The Bursa had already made it clear Manchil could not be allowed to give information to the Prince—something that would be possible at the end of the celebration. Mangos didn't want to hear it again.

"I have no doubt Kat is doing her part as we speak," Mangos said. *I just don't know what it is. So don't ask.*

"No doubt, no doubt," said the Bursa, obviously not convinced. "A bright girl, Kat, and I'm already in her debt. But it's worth remembering, yes, it is; it's worth remembering if the Prince can move against me, I won't be able to pay my debts. That is certain. But," he hunched in the chair, leaning forward, "I can make sure those who failed me share my downfall."

Mangos ground his teeth as he forced a smile on his face. *Don't threaten me, old man*, he thought, *I'm not in the mood for it.* "I can make sure Manchil never talks again."

Shaking his head, the Bursa replied, "No, no, no. My Hand should have made that very clear." He twisted to look up at the Hand, who nodded. "Yes, very clear," the Bursa continued. "The Prince said if Manchil dies— no matter how he dies—I will be held responsible. And again I will—"

Make sure those who failed me will share my downfall, Mangos thought, not even listening as the Bursa spoke the words. He knew this! Hearing his problem didn't help him find a solution. *We've been hired to kill a man we're not allowed to kill.*

The Bursa smiled. "I hope you succeed. I really do. So does my Hand."

Mangos didn't trust himself to speak. He lowered his head, just a bit, to give the impression of respect, then spun to go.

He climbed the stairs to the first balcony and looked down the length of the cathedral's five hundred foot long nave. He could not see into the transepts, each large enough for its own permanent festival functions. The northern one held a gladiatorial arena with seating for hundreds; the southern currently held a runway stage used for theater and the fashion show.

With a sigh, he glanced up. He imagined the stained glass windows would be beautiful during the day, but at night they were flat and dark. The crystal sun illuminated frescos painted between the ribs of the vaulted ceiling, scenes of the gods and the seasons.

"Go, look around," Kat had said. "Enjoy the festival. I have an idea I want to work on. Be ready, I'll get word to you."

By the Gods of Eastwarn, she can be frustrating! he thought.

"I've a note for you."

Mangos turned. The Hand stood next to him, a folded piece of parchment in his hand, which he held out. Mangos took it.

He unfolded the paper.

MONGOOSE & MEERKAT

It has been arranged for you to fight Manchil during the gladiatorial contests in late summer. You are NOT to kill him. He must be embarrassed.

—Kat

Spring fashion, summer games, autumn feast, winter dance; that was the order of the Renewal Festival.

He crumpled the message. They had not been hired to embarrass Manchil. How would this solve their problem?

If they could make Manchil disappear... Without a body, maybe the Prince wouldn't punish the Bursa. Then everybody (except Manchil) could enjoy the festival. He sighed. Things didn't work that way in Alomar.

Where was Kat? He had been around the hall twice without finding her.

"Everything in order?" the Hand asked. He leaned on the balcony rail, smiling slightly and looking the length of the hall.

"Why aren't you the one taking care of this?" Mangos demanded.

"I presented three plans to the Bursa concerning Manchil. He chose the third."

A smile curled the edges of Mangos's mouth. At last he would find something out. "What is the plan?"

"To hire the Mongoose and Meerkat."

"What?" Mangos's good humor vanished. "That was your plan?"

With a shrug, the Hand said, "I came up with nothing. It is a cunning trap. In truth, the Prince thinks he has won and is enjoying the Bursa's discomfort. By showing Manchil in public, he mocks the Bursa."

"How did the Prince get Manchil in the first place?" Mangos asked. "And how did the Bursa cast a spell that would keep him silent, and why is the spell only good until the New Year?"

"I'm not the one telling you, but it involved too much brandy, what the Bursa thought was a winning hand of cards, and a hurried spell by a less than competent mage."

Drinking while gambling. Mangos could understand that.

He let out an angry breath. It didn't matter, anyway. They had taken the job. "Where's Kat?"

"She went to see Snader," the Hand said, referring to one of Alomar's more powerful wizards. "I think she wants to know if the mute spell on Manchil can be made permanent, or another laid on top of it." He shook his head. "She'll be disappointed. I already checked.

"Come," the Hand clapped Mangos on the back. "She said she'd be at the fashion show."

Mangos twisted away from the Hand's grip, glaring, but followed down the steps, returning to the main floor.

"The Prince will be at the show also," the Hand added. "Have you ever seen Manchil?"

Mangos shook his head, realized the Hand wasn't looking at him, and said, "No."

"Now's your chance."

They made their way into the south transept, working through the crowd to emerge just behind the reserved seating.

A temporary runway jutted from a doorway on the south wall, extending into the transept so the models could be seen from three sides. Extra lights, bright burning "sunflower" lamps, shone onto the runway, making everything else dim by comparison.

The show set the tone for Alomar's fashions for the next year, Mangos knew. A well-received design meant sales, and sales to Alomar's elite meant wealth. The worlds of high fashion, treachery, and murder intertwined in Alomar. Two designers had been killed in the last month, and another's studio burned.

"Do you see Kat?" Mangos asked the Hand.

Instead of answering, the Hand said, "The Prince has taken his seat. The show will begin soon." He nodded, drawing Mangos's attention to the Prince and the favored slave beside him.

Mangos could only see the top of the Prince's head over the back of the throne facing the runway. He had a better view of Manchil, whose chair lacked the high back of the Prince's throne.

Manchil hulked in his chair, neck as thick as his head. The edge of a tattoo showed above his silk shirt—an incongruously light yellow shirt. He was bald and missing half an ear. Even from the back, he looked like what he was—a gladiator. Unfortunately for Mangos and Kat, he was also a slave who knew too much information about a former owner.

Embarrass Manchil? Manchil was the most dangerous gladiator in Alomar. Embarrass him? Seeing Manchil, Mangos couldn't help but think, *I'll be lucky to survive, and Kat's instructions be damned.*

"The show is going to start," the Hand said.

I need to learn that trick, Mangos thought, *how to be so unconcerned.* It was clear that if the Bursa fell, he would take not just Mangos and Kat, but the Hand, too. Yet the Hand seemed only interested in the show.

The tip of a sword parted the curtains. The rest of the curved sword followed, then a slender, white-gloved hand. It rotated, making the sword spin and twirl, sparkling in the light. Another sword-wielding hand joined it, and the two weapons performed together for a few moments before parting the curtains to allow the model to walk out, still twirling the swords.

"Can't I just make it an accident?" Mangos asked. "Do it, some way the Prince can't possibly blame on the Bursa?"

The Hand snorted. "The Prince made it clear if *anything* happened to Manchil he would hold the Bursa responsible. I think that's why Kat wanted you to fight Manchil—to make sure somebody else doesn't kill him." The gladiatorial games were timed so they didn't overrun their season, but there was a death bonus if one gladiator killed the other before time expired.

Mangos blew out his breath, frustrated. He seemed to be doing that a lot lately.

The model performed an empty routine designed, not to show her prowess with the swords, but her beauty and that of her dress. She was beautiful, and so was her dress, though Mangos no more than noticed. The crowd applauded politely when she finished.

"Maybe I should make a renewal offering," Mangos said. "For luck." He didn't have anything else on his side; he may as well have luck. The Temple gathered small gifts early; would luck begin when he gave the gift or when it was presented to the gods at midnight?

The Hand glanced at him. "Did you bring anything?"

"No, but I can give something and buy it back when they sell the gifts." Many temples sold donated items so they could pay expenses.

"Don't give anything you want," the Hand said. "You'll never get it back. *This* Temple doesn't sell anything for revenue and, once given, gifts are beyond anybody's influence."

"I can't even buy luck for this job," Mangos muttered.

The next model walked out, a man dressed in tight-fitting trousers that flared out at the cuffs. A circle of wire held each cuff in shape and made it look like he wore two cones. He had to bow his legs to keep the cuffs from rubbing together. The sleeves of his shirt flared in a similar fashion. Swirling shades of orange and green covered both trousers and shirt.

A man behind Mangos murmured, "I'd never wear that."

Mangos endured a steady procession of men and women in clothes he could not comprehend. A few he thought were dressed to appeal, but others, like the woman with stuffed, purple-dyed lemurs on each shoulder, mystified him.

Where's Kat? He could not find her in the crowd and started to move to see the other spectators better. Everybody gasped, and he looked back to the runway.

A woman had come out and seized the attention of every person watching. She wore a cape of snow lion fur, luxurious white and three-quarter length that caressed her as she walked. All else that she wore was swim clothes, two small pieces made of snow snakeskin, mottled white and cream, and a mask over her eyes.

Her hips swayed as she walked, and walking was too pedestrian a word. She had a feline grace, an elegance that held the crowd spellbound. She stopped to twirl, causing the cape to lift and the audience to draw in its breath. She flashed a smile and a wink at the Prince.

Mangos had never seen a woman so captivating—or had he? Could that be—Kat? He cursed under his breath. It could be, because it was, but it was also true that he had never seen a woman like this.

Kat had always felt like a sister, had always been ignored by men. This—this was *so* different. Every *person*, but especially the men, stared. The air practically dripped desire.

Kat ran her hands down her sides, over her hips, pushed them out, and rotated them. The rotation traveled up her arms, through her chest, and down. Mangos swallowed, conscious that he suddenly felt warm. He had a hard time believing those limbs were the same that fought and killed so effectively.

Kat raised her arms, inhaled. The man next Mangos whimpered softly.

That's my partner? Mangos thought. When Kat wrapped the cape around herself, it was almost as if she were giving the audience permission to breathe.

She sashayed up the runway, looking coy above the thick fur. She reached the curtains, drew one across her as she let the cape fall back, so only her head and bare shoulders showed. With a smile, a wink, and a wave, she slipped out of sight.

Applause thundered through the transept like a spring tempest.

Mangos closed his mouth. He hadn't been aware it was open.

From the whistles and calls, it was clear everybody wanted to see Kat again, and Mangos knew he had an excuse.

What had changed, and why? He didn't know if it was because of their job or an instinctual reaction, but Mangos needed to see Kat, and quickly.

He finally found her seated next to the Prince outside the transept. The Prince was a lean man, about fifty years old, with a long face and high forehead. Manchil stood behind them while four palace guards kept people away.

Kat and the Prince burst out laughing. Manchil shuffled his feet and looked down, the top of his head red.

Kat still wore her modeling clothes, little though they covered her, and the guards couldn't keep the stares from her. The Prince did not seem to mind that her garb drew attention from his flamboyantly colored tunic. He was clearly more interested in flattering her with his undivided attention. She, in return, appeared to be entertaining him at Manchil's expense.

Mangos started toward them only to have a guard drop a spear in his path. "No one approaches the Prince," the guard said.

"I could care less about the Prince, I want to talk to the woman."

A sly smile crept across the guard's face. "You and me both. But you can't compete with the Prince."

"You miss my intention," Mangos said while trying to catch Kat's attention. She finally looked up and saw him. She laid a hand on the Prince's arm. With obvious reluctance, the Prince called for the guard to let Mangos approach.

"What are you doing?" Mangos demanded. Beside Kat, the Prince stirred, frowning at Mangos, but Mangos didn't care.

Kat cut him off, presenting him to the Prince as etiquette demanded. "This is Mangos of Arnelon, a formidable adventurer and sometime gladiator." She laid her hand on the Prince's arm again. Mangos ground his teeth. "And this," Kat said with a flick of her hand, "is Manchil, the greatest gladiator in Alomar, which is good because he isn't the smartest man I've met."

Manchil flushed bright red, and Kat laughed. "Isn't that cute? It just goes to show wits aren't everything."

She did not introduce the Prince, which reminded Mangos of the expected manners. "An honor, Your Grace," he said. The Prince merely inclined his head.

Mangos glared at Kat. "A word?"

"You just took two, and you want another?"

The prince laughed as Mangos blushed. Kat smiled, "Just one."

Kat stood, turning as she did to face the Prince. His eyes seemed glued to her chest as she rose. "I'll be right back," she said.

Mangos stalked away, sure she would follow. Once far enough away he turned, "What are you doing?" He felt anger, and if he were honest, jealousy boiling inside him.

"Why aren't you getting ready?" she demanded, not answering his question.

"That's not the question! What do you think you're doing dressed like this, playing up to the Prince? Do you think he will give you Manchil as a gift?"

"No," Kat said. "Manchil's too valuable both as a gladiator and informant against the Bursa."

"Then what?"

"I've been baiting Manchil, making him look foolish."

Manchil glowered in his seat while the Prince looked from him to Kat, an unhappy expression on his face. Mangos frowned, not sure how this would help kill Manchil. The prince wouldn't forgo retribution just because Kat made Manchil look stupid. Even if Kat convinced him Manchil *was* stupid, it wouldn't help.

Kat struck a pose and took a deep breath. "Do you like the latest fashion?"

His eyes snapped back to her. "Yes! NO!" he said, he didn't know what to think, how to react. It made no sense that Kat should suddenly become so appealing.

Kat laughed softly, enjoying his discomfort. She looked up at the sun. "It's almost mid-summer. Prepare."

"Manchil hasn't prepared, and I'm a better warrior than he is."

"This isn't knives in the dark or hunting worms. Nobody knows the arena like he does," Kat said. "This is the most dangerous gladiator in Alomar, and he is very angry right now."

"I'm not happy myself."

"You must not kill him," Kat said. "You must *humiliate* him."

"The Bursa wants him—"

Kat interrupted him. "You must not kill him."

"Just tell me your plan!"

She glanced over her shoulder at the Prince. "No time. The Prince *mustn't* get anxious." She returned to her seat, brushing against the Prince as she sat down. She spoke in quiet tones, laughing and ignoring Mangos until the Prince relaxed.

"But I want to kill him," Mangos muttered, and he would have been perfectly happy if the Prince were in the arena too.

Humiliate without killing? Did she even know what she asked? He sighed. She usually did. Well, he thought, he wouldn't beat Manchil; he would mock him. He might get killed doing it, but it would be funny.

The sun was yellower now, losing some of the warmth of high summer. The crowds had moved to the arena—Mangos looked up from the sands, understanding finally that this was different from his normal fighting. Seeing the crowd told him how alone he was in the arena. Nobody could help him; the hourglass timing the fight would not stop to rescue him. His only friends were those he brought with him: his sword and the whip fastened to his belt.

Kat sat in the Prince's box; he had no idea how she had arranged this fight. The Prince pointed toward him. Kat began to clap, and those near her took it up. The applause barely overcame the buzz from hundreds of people talking. He had hoped for more, from her and the crowd.

Manchil stepped out onto the sands, lifted his arms to the crowd who stopped talking to cheer their approval. He no longer wore the light yellow shirt; instead, he wore a full brassard on his right arm. A tattooed dragon coiled from under his left arm to climb over his shoulder and out of sight. He wore a short loincloth fastened with a golden clasp and carried a wide sword in his left hand, a short-handled scythe in his right.

Well, Mangos thought, *time to begin*. He pointed at Manchil, lifted his own arms in the air, and began to wiggle his butt like a cheap tavern whore. The crowd roared.

Manchil clashed his sword and scythe together. He looked like he would like nothing better than to measure the length of Mangos's intestines.

Mangos blew him a kiss.

The bell sounded. Manchil charged forward, intent on killing.

Mangos caught the sword with his own and let the force of the blow push him back as he dropped and rolled out of reach of the scythe. He sprang up, Manchil already on him, swinging again—appallingly close.

Mangos parried the sword, parried the scythe, and danced away from the kick Manchil aimed at his knee. The crowd roared, but he didn't know for whom. Again, Mangos had to parry, once, twice. Pain shot through his arm, and the crowd roared louder.

Blood flowed down his arm. The point of the scythe had curved around his sword guard and, though he parried, cut into his forearm.

He parried the sword, parried the scythe. Manchil kicked, lifting sand into his face, into his eyes, blinding him. Mangos leapt back, blinking, wiping his face, backpedalling, moving to avoid the blur that was Manchil until he could see again. He parried and knew he was lucky.

Who's getting embarrassed now?

His eyes stung, but he could see well enough to parry again. He was starting to get the rhythm of Manchil's attacks. Sword, scythe, other. Unbelievably fast, fueled by Kat's poor treatment of him before the Prince. Sword, scythe, other.

Mangos readied a parry, disengaged, which fooled Manchil into over swinging. Mangos put his free hand on Manchil's shoulder and pushed, turning him further and exposing his back. *I could kill him now.*

Mangos took two steps and leapt, one foot on Manchil's back and a quick step up to stand on his shoulders. Mangos threw up his arms in triumph and jumped away as Manchil ducked and flailed his sword. Waves of laughter rolled down from the crowd.

Manchil spun, attacked, nearly purple with rage. Sword, scythe, scythe. Sword, scythe, kick. Even knowing the pattern Mangos could barely parry.

Be patient, Mangos told himself. Sword, scythe, sword. He knew the pattern and couldn't believe Manchil didn't realize it. Surely everybody realized it. Manchil was well trained for sure, but stupid. *Wait for the right moment.*

Sword, scythe, and the kick for his knee. *There.* Mangos rolled away, planted his hands and one foot, kicked the leg Manchil stood on. Manchil collapsed.

Mangos rose, stepped away, and took his whip from his belt.

Manchil stood, favoring his leg, moving slowly.

With a quick flick of his whip, Mangos snapped the clasp at Manchil's waist. Manchil's loincloth fell to the sand, leaving him naked and vulnerable to the crowd's laughter. Mangos straightened to attention and

gave his foe a mocking salute.

The hourglass ran out, and the bell sounded, ending the match. Mangos had done what Kat wanted, but he still didn't know how it would solve their problem.

Mangos feasted well. While he hadn't killed his opponent, the crowd feted him like a king, moving him to the second table where he could be lauded by all and served immediately after the first table.

Two priests, a man in black representing the old year, and a woman in white representing the new, sat in the center of the first table, presiding but not eating. The Prince and his guests filed to the chairs on either side. The Prince was still dressed in his flamboyant tunic. Kat still wore her snow lion cape, but she had changed into loose cream-colored trousers and a light green blouse; a blouse, Mangos knew, that would bring out the color of her eyes.

Manchil sat with them, looking both angry and despondent. He wore a restrained maroon shirt, open at the neck, with leather bracers, and charcoal grey trousers held up by a broad leather belt. Mangos couldn't help smirking as Manchil stared down at the table.

Kat would not meet his eyes. She spent her time flirting with the Prince, laughing, laying her hand on his arm, batting her eyes. When she wasn't doting on the Prince, she consoled Manchil. She leaned against him to whisper in his ear. This seemed to cheer him some but appeared to frustrate the Prince, and it infuriated Mangos.

A poison, he told himself, *she's going to poison him*, but he didn't believe it, for there would be no point in embarrassing Manchil if she just meant to poison him.

Mangos wondered if it was too late to donate his sword. He wouldn't need it anymore tonight, and could use all the luck he could get.

The sun passed beyond autumn as the revelers rose from the table. Some headed toward the southern transept where the runway had been cleared away to make room for dancing. Others wandered up and down the nave where entertainers performed.

Mangos found himself with the dancers, not that he felt like dancing. Kat would be there. They could run away. They'd never walked away from a job before, but they'd never had a job like this. And he'd never felt such attraction to Kat, either. It was affecting his thinking.

It must be the festival. Once they got away from Alomar, they could return to just being partners. Right now, he wasn't sure if that was what he wanted—he wasn't sure of anything.

The dance floor was awash in colors from the expensive gowns and jewels as couples spun to the music. The press of dancers parted, and he could see Kat walking toward him.

She was stunning. She wore a long, cream-colored gown that hugged her tightly. It had one shoulder strap and no belt, though it fit her waist perfectly. Jewels sparkled as she walked, priceless leopard-eye emeralds at her throat and on her ears.

Mangos smiled as he saw her, his heart beating faster. "By the gods of Eastwarn," he murmured. "By the gods of Eastwarn." He moved across the floor in a daze, noticing others just enough to avoid them as he held out his hand to take her in his arms and dance.

While he was still ten feet away she turned her head, lifted her hand, and swirled away in the arms of Manchil.

It felt like being struck in the gut. He dropped his hand. The dancers closed in around him, Kat and Manchil vanished in the crowd, and he shuffled off the dance floor.

Anger built as he stepped off the floor and turned to look over the dancers. The Hand came to stand next to him.

"Peace," the Hand said. "Find another woman for dancing. She is not the only one here."

Mangos shook his head. "I have saved her life countless times. We've traveled far lands together. Yet *she will not dance with me!*"

The Hand smiled, a tolerant smile. "If it makes you feel better, she would not dance with me, either."

"You asked her?"

"I, and every man here," the Hand said.

"But she dances with that fool, whose intelligence she mocked and whom I exposed as fraud in the arena!" By chance, he caught sight of Kat through the press of dancers. She was pressed against Manchil with every appearance of intimacy. "I'll kill him."

The Hand grabbed his shoulder before he could move. "And the Prince will visit retribution on the Bursa," the Hand said. "Here comes the Prince now."

The Prince cut in, taking Kat from Manchil's arms. He tried to draw her close, which she allowed, though not as close as she allowed Manchil.

A popping sound surprised Mangos, and he realized it was his knuckles as he clenched and unclenched his fists.

"You will not kill *him,* either," the Hand said, nodding toward the Prince.

"No," sighed Mangos, feeling hollow. "Gods, how can she do this? What happened?"

"The Bursa hired you," the Hand replied.

"And damn him for putting us where she would meet them."

The Hand nodded toward some chairs where the Bursa sat with a frustrated and angry expression. "Carefully," the Hand said.

Mangos curled his lip, sneering at the entire situation. The Bursa would fall; he saw no way around it. But Kat was safe; the Prince would protect her. She was making sure of that.

If he was honest, he really didn't care. The image of Kat dancing close to Manchil burned into his mind. He wanted to get very, very drunk.

The Hand stood next to Mangos, watching as the priest started the offering ceremony. "When the offering is completed, the new year begins," he said.

"I know," Mangos said.

The priests approached the altar. Behind them, a pair of slaves drew carts of offerings—small coins, pottery, a cage of chickens, Mangos's sword—the gifts of people not important enough to present them individually.

"When the new year begins, the spell is lifted from Manchil," the Hand said. "He will be able to speak."

"I know," Mangos said. Why not just say they would have failed?

"If Manchil can speak, the Bursa will make sure you feel his pain."

Mangos snorted. There was a time this would have intimidated him. It might be true, but he'd be damned if he suffered alone. "It's your plan," he said. "You hired the Mongoose and Meerkat."

"The Bursa reminded me of that, too," the Hand said.

Neither spoke as devotees approached the low altar wall separating the nave from the chancel. The black-robed Old Year took their offerings and bore them to where the white-robed New Year sat enthroned at the altar.

These were costly gifts; given by prominent citizens, but except for a few given by the truly devoted, Mangos didn't see anything that would be missed. Alomar didn't take the gods *that* seriously.

The Prince stood next to the altar wall; it was customary that he be last. Manchil waited next to him, holding an iron-bound chest that contained the Prince's offering. Kat stood too close to Manchil for Mangos'scomfort. He was not the only one, either. The Prince glanced from her to Manchil, frowning slightly, before looking back to the ceremony.

Maybe, Mangos thought, she's going to kill Manchil and trust the attraction the Prince feels for her to protect them. But the Prince would cheerfully ignore Kat's role (if it pleased him) and cast the blame on the Bursa as he promised.

The sun, now dim, approached the back of the chancel. The last citizens brought their gifts, and all eyes turned to the Prince. He stepped forward, Manchil trailing after him holding the coffer.

"This plan didn't work," murmured the Hand.

The Prince lifted the coffer from Manchil, tucked it under his arm—and pushed Manchil past the altar wall.

Manchil looked back in confusion. Murmurs ran through the crowd. The priest of the old year took Manchil's arm and guided him to the altar; he followed like a bewildered child.

Mangos blinked. "What happened?"

The Hand laughed quietly. "The Prince just donated Manchil to the gods. He's a temple slave now!"

"But he's not dead..." Mangos trailed off.

"He may as well be. As temple property, he is immune to the laws of the city. He is beyond the Prince's reach. That will satisfy the Bursa."

The light in the crystal sun went out, and fireworks lifted off, filling the vaults with explosions of color and light, signaling the successful renewal and anticipation of the real sun rising again in the morning.

Not knowing whether to be happy they fulfilled their contract or despondent that Kat had barely talked to him, Mangos drank. He was trying to convince himself it was all a bad dream, but three ales in he wasn't making much progress.

The true sun would rise in a couple of hours, bringing a new day and a new year. He couldn't care less. The bar was empty except for him. Even the barkeep had gone to bed.

The door opened, and Kat came in. Sat down across from him. The old Kat, hair drawn back, dressed as she used to dress. As beautiful as any work of art, and one that he could view without a trace of desire.

Mangos looked at his mug, wondering if he were drunk now, how to interpret earlier. He looked at her, trying to conjure up the desire and jealousy he had felt. He couldn't do it.

"You did perfectly," Kat said.

"I don't understand." *About a lot of things, which is,* he thought, *an understatement.* But it was safest to ask, "Why did the Prince donate Manchil to the Temple?"

"What good is a weak, stupid slave?" Kat asked. "You might keep him because he's expensive, but when he's also a competitor for the attractions of a woman..." She shrugged. "It's better to just to get rid of him."

"So you made the Prince—"

"It's easy to make powerful men jealous," Kat said.

Pushing the mug away, Mangos sorted his thoughts. "Making Manchil look stupid made the Prince doubt his ability to give evidence against the Bursa."

Kat nodded. "And in the arena, you made the Prince doubt Manchil's value as a gladiator.

"And he wanted Manchil out of the way," she continued.

"*I* wanted Manchil out of the way too," Mangos admitted.

"For the same reason, maybe," Kat said. Mangos couldn't read the expression in her eyes. It seemed less important now.

"He couldn't kill Manchil himself," Kat continued after a moment, "because he would still have to punish the Bursa for Manchil's death— which would be too much even for Alomar."

Mangos laughed. He couldn't help it. "I bet he thought he was clever when he decided to donate Manchil."

"I'm sure."

Mangos toyed with the mug, spinning it idly on the table but not drinking. The world was a more familiar place now. "You had Snader place a glamor on you to become more desirable?"

"No, quite the opposite," Kat said. "But the job is done, and all is returned to normal—no matter anybody's desire otherwise; mine, yours, or the Prince's."

Fight of the Sandfishers

Twenty-nine months after the fall of Alness.

I'm bored.

I wouldn't be writing this if I weren't. It's the first story I've ever written, and I don't even know how it's going to end.

Kat and I are riding in a merchant's wagon travelling to Hafiz. The merchant is Jalani, a young woman orphaned in the fall of Alness. The man who guards the wagon is Celzez, who also worked for her father. Celzez is from Hafiz.

The wind is hot and dry, the desert stretching out ahead of us. Tall obelisks mark the highway, red sandstone taken from the quarries of Hafiz so travelers know the way even when sand covers the roads.

It's not the quarries that give the people of Hafiz their name, though. It's the lake. They catch *fallo* fish in the shallow, warm water lake that somehow exists in the desert. They dry the guts, grind them to powder, and sell them as a spice. So the people of Hafiz are called Sandfishers.

Celzez is a Sandfisher returning home to denounce another man. To denounce is to accuse somebody of being dishonorable. This will lead to a fight because honor is *very* important to the Sandfishers.

Jalani does not want him to do this. Although she's a prosperous merchant with many teamsters working for her, she's accompanying Celzez to try and change his mind. And sell some goods.

I've agreed to help her. Not that I really care—I try to avoid other people's fights—but Jalani is pleasant to look at, and I'm bored.

Hafiz crowds around the end of Xelin Lake. The red sandstone buildings form a crescent, the largest along the shore, then they get smaller and smaller as they get farther from the lake. By the edge of the city, they are nothing but shacks of salvaged stone with canvas stretched across to keep out the sun. It's not a large city, as cities go.

I rode up front with Celzez when the city first came into sight. Looking down from the dunes west of the city, our shadows lay in front of us.

Celzez held the horses tightly reined in, for the covered wagon slid in the sand on the steep dune face. While Hafiz lay close below, it would take

232

until mid-afternoon to reach it.

"How long has it been since you've been here?" I asked him.

He held the horse's reins, staring down over the city, as if sorting my words and placing each one in his mind before answering.

"Seven years," he said.

Well, I thought, *it had been years since I left Arnelon, and I didn't have any plans to go back*. "Why now?"

He snapped the reins, telling the horses to go faster. They swished their tails together, almost as if they had practiced. The wagon wheels squeaked in the sand as they had the entire journey.

"The time is right," Celzez answered.

Obviously nobody felt the need to hurry.

Except me. "Why is the time right?"

Celzez glanced at me, not moving his head, just a quick darting of his eyes, and I sensed his disapproval. "There is a thing that must be done."

"So Jalani said. She doesn't agree. You want to challenge a man, but if the grievance is seven years old, why bother?"

"You are not a Sandfisher."

Just like that—I wouldn't understand.

I tried to think of what to say, but the silence drew out, leaving only the squeak of the wheels.

"It hasn't been seven years; two years, five months," Celzez said, surprising me with this gift of information.

I glanced over, expecting him to elaborate, but he did not, just kept guiding the wagon down the face of the dune toward Hafiz.

About two and a half years ago. What happened two and a half years ago? I had just left Arnelon, hadn't even met Kat—it seemed like an eternity ago. Stupid, I told myself. It wasn't what *I* was doing two and a half years ago, it was what Celzez was doing.

Two years and five months... it struck me, of course, Alness fell. Jalani and Celzez had been there when Rhygir's mercenary army took the city.

It shouldn't surprise me that something might happen in the plundering of a city that would make one mad. But over two years? And Celzez is just a hired guard. If anybody should want revenge, it should be Jalani.

I twisted around to look at her.

She rode in the wagon amongst the crates of goods, sheltering from the sun. Kat sat at the far back, her feet hanging over the edge, her hood up as protection against blowing sand.

I crawled into the wagon. "Did this offense happen in Alness?" I asked Jalani.

"Yes."

Kat turned her head, just slightly, but enough that I knew she listened. "So why are you coming here?"

"This is where Sandfishers make denouncements," she said. "Once it is made, he wants to return to Alness to make his kill."

I shook my head. Celzez was coming here to *say* he intended to kill another man—a man not even in Hafiz. *Perhaps I can convince him this is a waste of time,* I thought. It certainly seemed so.

Jalani took a deep breath. "It is not just another Sandfisher." She looked down and brushed her leggings, hard, as though forcing the sand away from her. "It's a Kingsfisher."

The name sounded familiar, but I couldn't place it.

"The Kings Guard of Alness were called Kingsfishers," Jalani explained. "It was the honor of Hafiz that the King would draw a dozen men for his personal guard from the city. They were considered," her voice practically dripped irony, *"absolutely* reliable."

Obviously, they had not proven to be. I glanced at Kat. She still listened. "You know of the Kingsfishers?" I asked her.

"Every Alnessi knows the Kingsfishers," she said. "They were the King's best fighters, his most loyal servants."

I opened my mouth to ask another question but shut it. *Think,* I told myself. *You can figure some of this out yourself.*

I remembered Alness, the grey streets, the rubble, the smell of fire and death. I recalled the tales of fighting so savage it took weeks to secure the city. The King and his entire family had been killed, it was said, and if they died, their guards should have died as well.

Clearly that had not happened.

"A Kingsfisher survived," I said, "and Celzez wants to denounce him. Because he survived, or something else?"

"Something else," Celzez said. His voice was strong and angry, louder than I had ever heard. "Teriz, son of Razen, betrayed his King and his honor. He aided the invaders and even killed a Prince of the House."

I scratched my collar where sand stuck and rubbed with every move. I was still missing something. Celzez served a merchant. "Why do you care?"

Celzez did not answer. Clearly, if I had to ask, I wouldn't understand.

I looked at Jalani, but she just sniffed and brushed nonexistent sand from her leggings.

"Maybe he'll win," I said.

She shook her head.

Well, it will take a while to get to Hafiz and prepare to denounce. I have time, and I will need it, for Celzez clearly doesn't want to talk.

Hafiz looks deserted as the full heat of the day begins to simmer in the early afternoon. Occasionally somebody will venture out on some errand, but the streets are mostly empty. The sun reflecting off the lake will drive right through your eyes and make your head pound if you are unwise enough to look.

Celzez stopped the wagon in front of a small house with large windows, now shuttered against the heat. He led us to the door, which was open a crack.

Celzez pushed the door open and called out.

Inside, a woman carrying a deep bowl stopped in surprise. She asked a question I did not catch.

"Sharin," Celzez said, his tone chiding.

"Celzez!" The woman dropped the bowl, and fruit rolled across the floor. She hugged Celzez, talking excitedly in Hafizi, laughing at the same time, even as tears ran down her cheeks.

A boy appeared in the other doorway, a lad about ten, with wild, dark hair and dark eyes. He frowned until the woman called to him, beckoned with her hands and spoke rapidly. A huge smile lit up his face, and he came forward, a little hesitantly, but Celzez swept him into the hug, and the three laughed together.

"My brother's wife, Sharin," Celzez introduced the woman. "And my nephew, Johin." Johin batted at his hand as he ruffled the boy's hair.

"Welcome," said Sharin. I could barely understand her because her accent was so thick.

Celzez spoke to Johin, a quick exchange in Hafizi, then said, "Johin only speaks Hafizi." He smiled at Sharin. "Sharin, too, mostly."

Sharin flushed but did not argue. She spoke to Celzez, and they launched into a prolonged conversation. It grew more and more animated until Sharin burst into an angry tirade. *Good,* I thought, *the more who oppose his foolishness, the easier it is to change his mind.*

It didn't take a genius to figure out she didn't like the idea of Celzez denouncing anybody.

Celzez cut her off with a sharp question, to which she responded indigently.

"You can stay here," Celzez told us. "It will be more comfortable. I will stay with the wagon."

It seemed strange that he still felt the need to guard in a city where, by all accounts, no one stole. But, I reflected, that was his job.

Celzez stroked his chin, spoke softly to Sharin, and nodded at her answer. A couple words sent Johin dashing from the house.

"He has gone to get a translator," Celzez said.

Johin returned with a slightly built man named Halmas. Halmas would stay with us until nightfall, then return in the morning. He would translate Hafizi for us, mostly for me, since Kat didn't seem interested.

Unlike me, Kat had made no promises. She did not argue with Celzez. Instead she seemed distracted, enmeshed in her own thoughts. If I was struggling to understand what would sway Celzez, she was struggling with something else entirely.

When Sharin took Johin to the market to buy extra food, Celzez drove the wagon to the caravan grounds, and I was alone with Jalani and Kat. I asked, "If this is about Alness, why now?"

"The north stirs," Jalani said. "There are rumors that one of the Princes survived. There is a feeling that something can be done."

Kat sat, leaned back in one of the corners. Sunlight slanted through cracks in the shutter to lie across her legs, but left her face in shadows. "Perhaps *that's* why Celzez chooses now to make his denouncement."

"I thought all the royalty died when Rhygir took the palace," I said.

"It was a large family," Kat said, "and there was much confusion that day."

Jalani nodded, her brows drawn together, uncertainty in her eyes. "Rhygir wants people to believe all the royals died."

"Do you believe it?" I asked. They were *her* monarchs, after all. I had no interest in whether they survived.

Jalani shuddered. "I have tried to block memories of that day. There was so much blood. For months, I believed everybody left in the city must have been killed." Her bottom lip started to quiver. "I *want* to believe one of the Princes escaped. But gods," her eyes misted over, and a tear stole down her cheek, "oh gods, I *watched* them kill the children."

I knew Celzez had saved her, taken her from the burning city, but I never knew she had still been there after the King had fallen and Rhygir was butchering the royals in the streets.

I glanced at Kat, unsure what to say, but she gave me no guidance. I cleared my throat. "Then the rumor is false. The royals are dead."

"There was so much confusion," Jalani whispered. "And there were twelve of them. Who can say they were all the right ones?"

"So," I said slowly, still piecing the thought together as I spoke. "Celzez could be doing this to help a surviving prince. If one survived," I added.

"He could." Jalani sniffed and wiped her cheek with the back of her hand.

"And Teriz was responsible?" I asked, remembering the name of the offending Kingsfisher.

"We saw him kill one of the Princes," Jalani said. She lifted her chin. "There was no mistaking it."

I nodded, starting to feel like I would soon have enough understanding to argue Celzez out of his denouncement.

"Which one?" Kat asked, her voice flat.

"Kalin."

"Kalin was thirteen," Kat said.

It suddenly occurred to me there was another Alnessi in the room. "Were you in the city when it fell?" I asked Kat. I couldn't see her face, for the shadows hid her expression.

"Yes," Kat sounded reluctant, whether to remember or answer I could not tell.

"You've never told me."

Kat stood up, prowled through the shadows around the edges of the room. "To what end?"

"To help me understand," I said. It struck me I did not understand. I did not yet understand Celzez, I did not understand Alness's dogged refusal to accept Rhygir's rule; and in spite of years of adventuring together, I feared I did not understand Kat. "To understand Celzez and all this anger simmering in the north." *To understand you,* I thought.

"Do you care?"

"Ye—" I bit the word back. It was easy to say, but did I care? Not just about Kat, who is like a sister to me, but about the Alnessi? Did I care like Celzez cared? Right is what you're strong enough to enforce, good is what benefits you; that is the way of the world. I know the fall of Alness troubles many, but I don't really understand why. Nations fall, people move on.

"Perhaps," Kat said in this silence, "that is why I never told you."

I said nothing then, and I can think of nothing now. What might I learn if I were to ask, and why do I not? Why should I fear to be drawn and bound to the turmoil in Alness as Celzez inexplicably was?

In the morning, when the desert air is still cool and the air over the lake is warm, the *fallo* fish are close to shore. The men wade in the water, casting their nets and calling to each other. This is when the fish are caught, before the heat drives them to deeper water. This is the good time of day, when food is gotten and the work is light. The stench of processing the spice, or the sweat of mining red sandstone, comes later. The Hafizi savor early morning.

Celzez stood with one hand resting on a stone wall, looking over the water. He did not face me, but spoke as I approached. "Do you hear them, the fishers calling each other? When I am too old to fight, I shall return to wade in the shallows as I did as a boy. Time will stop, and all that moves will be the water and the wind and the fishers. The heat of the desert shall steal over me, and I shall go nap in the shade." He smiled at the thought. "I shall bake the mountain's cold from my bones."

He fell silent and after a minute slapped the wall with his open palm. "But there is much to do before then." He turned to look at me. "There is a man here you should meet. A man I admire greatly."

"Who?"

"An old man with enough honor for any three men."

He clapped me on the shoulder and went inside, once again leaving me with questions instead of answers. Only after we broke our fast and Halmas appeared did Celzez announce his intention to visit Inark.

"Inark?" Kat said. "He's alive?"

"You know him?" Celzez looked interested.

Kat shook her head. "No more than I know other Kingsfishers." She chuckled. "I do remember when he retired and a new Kingsfisher was selected to replace him. Though," she added, "I was very young. I'm just surprised to hear he is still alive. I assumed he was old then and would have died by now."

A Kingsfisher. A former Kingsfisher, really, but I couldn't help feeling a sense of anticipation, having heard so much about them recently. This would be his fight, not Celzez's. I added it to my list of arguments to use.

"Inark lost a leg serving Alness," Halmas explained, trailing a step behind as we crossed the wide street and approached a small house near the lake. "Like all the Kingsfishers, he is very well respected."

The door was open, and Celzez knocked on the doorframe. A voice called out. Halmas didn't translate the word or the words Celzez used to greet the old man sitting in the cool dimness inside.

The old man answered—Halmas began to translate, but the old man stopped him. "We need not use Hafizi," he said, "if there are others here."

He must be blind, I thought. We filed inside, blocking the light from the door and making the house even darker. The only light threaded through us to fall on the old man.

Inark turned his head so that it caught the light a bit, and I could see white clouds of age in his eyes.

Celzez bowed respectfully. "There are, Kingsfisher. Jalani, a merchant."

Why does he bow if the man is blind? I wondered.

Inark nodded greeting.

"Mangos, an adventurer." Inark nodded again.

"And Kat, an adventuress."

Inark started to nod, but paused. "Where are you from, Kat?"

She stirred, dropped her hood. It seemed her answer came from deep within her, and it took a long time for it to come out. "Alness. It is a common enough name, as I'm sure you know."

"Among the children, I've been told," Inark said.

"Even so," said Kat.

Inark bowed deeply to her. "And Halmas, who I heard at my door translating."

"Honor to you, Kingsfisher," said Halmas.

Inark snorted. "Are the rumors true, Celzez? Are you here to denounce?"

"I've only spoken of it to family and friends."

Inark chuckled, a dry and angry sound. "There have been stories about Teriz—but nobody knew for certain. Nobody *saw*, nobody could denounce. You were in Alness then, and you return here now. Of course rumors start."

"Tell him," I said. "Tell him it is foolishness." Inark turned his head toward me but did not answer. The silence drew on, grew long. *This place is filled with silences,* I thought.

"I reached the fifth marking stone," Inark said finally.

"What?"

"The day we heard Alness fell I reached the fifth marking stone before they found me and brought me back."

"You did not try again?" Kat seemed to already know the answer, and I felt she asked for my benefit.

She had spoken mildly, but Inark recoiled as though slapped. He dropped his head. "The second day, I became confused by the heat and lost my feel for the sun. They found me in the desert."

Again silence surrounded us.

"You do Alness great honor," Kat said.

"I failed them. I failed them by getting old." The bitterness in Inark's voice filled the room, enduring beyond his words and mixing with the next silence.

I tried to clear my thoughts. "What? Why?" This man did not owe Alness anything.

"Because I am a Sandfisher, and because I was a Kingsfisher. Age has robbed me of my honor, leaving me waiting to die."

He held up a fist, wrinkled skin covered with brown blotches, tendons standing out from his withered muscles. "Were I able, I would find out the truth..." He dropped his hand. "It would do me no good."

"I know the truth," said Celzez.

"Then you must act," said Inark. "You must act before you no longer can."

I expected Celzez would rush off and make his denouncement, but when we left Inark, he merely turned toward his sister's house.

"Why *does* he wait?" I asked Halmas as we followed Celzez toward the main square. Not that I minded, I needed the time.

"Denouncements occur at sundown," he replied, "for that is a time of endings."

"Huh," I said. "Why should that matter?"

Halmas gave me a frown at odds with his usual stoic helpfulness. "It is a matter of honor. To kill a man without warning of your intention is murder. You must allow a man to defend himself. Or," he added, "another to defend him. There is a ritual."

It shouldn't have surprised me there would be a ritual, but why make it difficult? If you're going to kill somebody, just have at it.

"What is this ritual?"

"You must stand on the denouncement stone at sundown and wait ten minutes."

"Ten minutes?" I exclaimed. "Why?"

"To prevent people from jumping on the stone and muttering their charge before anybody knows of it. And the charge must be spoken clearly in a loud voice."

"You may as well announce it to the world."

"How can honor be a private thing?" Halmas said.

I wasn't sure if he expected an answer, but I didn't have one in any case.

After a short silence he continued. "Somebody may challenge the denouncement. It needs be one with knowledge of the person's honor." He shrugged. "Then there is a fight."

"What if no one challenges the denouncement?"

"The man who made it will hunt and kill the man he denounced."

"If he can," I said, thinking at that point all the rules would be over.

"If he can," Halmas agreed.

So, I thought, *since Teriz was not here, he could not challenge Celzez.* "What happens if the first man doesn't hunt down the man he accused?"

"There is much shame and loss of honor in that."

The Sandfishers seemed to have covered everything. Still, Celzez would be free to hunt Teriz down without rules. That wasn't so bad.

Sundown. I glanced up. Almost half a day remained to fulfill my promise to Jalani. I felt a prickling down my spine as I realized I might not be able to change Celzez's mind.

Kat went I knew not where. Jalani returned to the wagon to sell her wares, urging me to keep trying. I had until evening when Celzez would utter words that could not be taken back.

Sharin and Johin went with Celzez to a small cemetery on the edge of the desert. Halmas and I followed along but stood back when we approached a lone grave in the shade of the red sandstone wall.

"My brother," Celzez said as he crouched next to it. Without apparently thinking, he tugged on a string about his neck, drawing something from under his shirt.

It looked like a shield, twice the size of his thumbnail, light-colored with an iridescence that I wasn't the only one to notice.

"Are you still wearing that?" Sharin asked. Halmas murmured a translation only I could hear.

Celzez nodded. Sharin snorted, curling her lip.

"What is it?" I asked.

"Nothing," Celzez said. He turned toward the grave in the shade of the wall. "Something my brother gave me. When we were boys." Halmas quietly translated into Hafizi, speaking to Johin, who watched with wide eyes.

"What is it?" I asked again.

"A *fallo* scale." Celzez rubbed it—a gesture so practiced and smooth I knew it must be a habit. He held it out to me, and I saw it bore the head of a kingfisher, nearly worn away. "He told me it was a shield. That it should remind me of my goal and someday I would trade it for a real one."

"There are no Kingsfishers anymore," Sharin snapped.

Celzez shrugged. "It reminds me of the type of man I want to be."

"A man who would leave his sister-in-law and nephew alone in the world," she said.

"I shall leave you money."

"Damn your money! For years you have sent us money."

Celzez hung his head, staring at the grave. "You do not know," he said quietly. "You have not seen Alness. You have not seen the people suffer. They leave bloody marks when they walk. You have not heard Jalani cry in the night."

"Must I cry too?"

Celzez lifted his head and looked her in the eye. "No. Pray I do not fail."

We left the cemetery, Sharin and Johin returning home while the rest of us headed down to the caravan grounds adjacent to the main square and the lake.

Celzez stopped by the wagon and watched Jalani dicker with a customer. She pointedly ignored him and only glared at me. There was no reason to be there, so Celzez wandered over to the lake and kicked off his boots.

I took a deep breath. Now. Now was my best chance to try and change his plans. "There is no proof a prince survived," I said. "And if one did, you need not serve him." I licked my lips. "This will not make you a Kingsfisher."

Celzez smiled over his shoulder as he took a step into the lake. "I know."

"I promised Jalani I would talk you out of this. Think of her."

Celzez moved his feet, watching the waves he made disappear amongst the larger waves of the lake. "In Alness they call it Trust. It is the obligations the people have to each other, and some have special Trusts. Duties: the soldier's Trust to defend the country, the judge's Trust to be fair. The King's Trust to rule well."

A strange place of honorable fools, I thought. "You are not from Alness," I pointed out.

"No. I am a Sandfisher."

"Another Trust." I sneered.

"If you wish. A Trust to all those who take pride in what it is to be a Sandfisher. And for those who were Kingsfishers whose honor was betrayed. There is a reason the Kings of Alness drew the Kingsfishers from Hafiz, and a reason we were willing to serve."

"You want to do this," I accused him.

He sighed and closed his eyes for a moment. "No. I *need* to do this." After a long silence, he opened his eyes and asked, "Whom do you stand with?"

His question caught me by surprise, and I had no answer. Celzez continued to wade in the lake, wandering away from me as I groped for words.

This story isn't turning out as I expected.

The Denouncement Stone sits in the square at the heart of Hafiz, next to the lake. It's about eighteen inches tall, just enough for a man to be seen by a crowd. Like the rest of the city, it is red sandstone. There are no carvings on it. Like honor itself, it is an unassuming part of Sandfisher life.

I had expected more.

Men already gathered in the square. Some browsed the wares of the shops and merchant wagons. Others talked in small clusters, but all knew Celzez planned a denouncement.

Celzez walked to the Stone, looking neither right nor left. He paused next to it, looked out over the lake, took a deep breath, and stepped up.

A few men dashed off. Their shouts drifted back, summoning friends to the spectacle. The others came forward, forming a circle around the stone. And they waited.

Celzez looked like a statue on a plinth, standing quietly, hands loosely at his side. More people gathered in the square. I looked for Jalani, but having failed to change Celzez's mind, she didn't want to watch the denouncement.

Inark came. He used a crutch, and the men made way for him so he could stand near the stone. He did not look at Celzez—it wouldn't have mattered—but he kept his head tilted as if listening to every sound.

Finally Celzez spoke. "I denounce Teriz, son of Razen, as an oath breaker. He—"

"No!" exclaimed a deep voice. A huge man stepped forward.

"That's Ranas, Teriz's brother," Halmas murmured.

Ranas stood nearly as tall as Celzez, but Celzez stood on the Denouncement Stone. Ranas shrugged off his robe, stood in billowing pants and a sleeveless vest. He wore metal bracers on his arms. "I will not hear of dishonor. Not in the same sentence as Teriz's name." He moved to the center of the square.

I moved so I could see both Ranas and Celzez's faces. Neither seemed surprised.

"I will not retract," Celzez said. It sounded like he read from a script.

"Then we shall test your words." Ranas stretched his arms and drew a scimitar of enormous size.

Celzez stepped off the stone, suddenly looking very small.

"Is Teriz as big as Ranas?" I asked Halmas.

"They are twins," Halmas said. "But Teriz is far more dangerous."

I didn't know if that was good or not. Better chances now, worse later. Ranas clearly knew his work. He had the strength to use his gigantic scimitar, and he moved it quickly as he loosened his muscles.

Celzez drew his own sword. The two saluted each other, and the fight began.

Celzez moved well, like a veteran fighter. He kept his feet under him, his weight balanced. He moved away when Ranas tried to close. He engaged Ranas's scimitar, tapping it without attacking.

Ranas swiped at Celzez's sword, but Celzez disengaged and lunged. Ranas stepped back and delivered a great, sweeping backhand, but Celzez recovered from his lunge and moved aside.

All very formal, I thought.

Celzez leapt forward, his sword twisting and cutting, again and again; but each time Ranas tapped it aside. Celzez came close, too close to cut. Ranas punched, sending him reeling back as the crowd murmured.

Blood ran from a cut on Celzez's face, staining his shirt. He parried the next blow, and the next, but the third tore his sword from his hands.

With his free hand, Ranas grabbed him by the throat. He lifted Celzez until only his toes touched the ground. He drew back his scimitar. Celzez's face was turning red.

Celzez kicked right for Ranas's groin. Surprised, the larger man dropped him and twisted to protect himself. Celzez stumbled toward his sword.

Ranas swung, catching Celzez behind the knee. As Celzez sprawled on the ground, Ranas thrust down with enough force to part his ribs and plunge the heavy scimitar into his heart.

Ranas jerked his scimitar free and used his foot to turn Celzez over. "The fight is over." He turned around, looking at each of the watchers. "My brother's honor has been defended."

Johin pushed through the crowd and raced across the sand to crouch by his uncle. *Don't do anything,* I urged him in my mind. He brushed the sand from Celzez's face. Slowly he reached down, pulled on the string about Celzez's neck, and drew out the *fallo* scale shield. He wiped it clean of blood.

No, no, no. I feared what he might do.

He snapped the cord and held the scale in his fist. Lifting his head, he stared at Ranas and reached for Celzez's sword.

"The fight is *not* over."

The crowd murmured. I blinked, for Halmas spoke, translating words Kat had spoken. *She speaks Hafizi!* I realized.

Kat glided into the square and positioned herself between Ranas and Johin. She looked tiny.

Ranas started to laugh, but he saw something in her that made him stop. He hefted his scimitar and cut the air.

The men around me murmured. Halmas didn't translate, but I could tell they thought this an unfortunate waste of life.

"You cannot help," Halmas murmured, and I realized I had not just taken a step forward, but half-drawn my sword as well. "This is within the process. Should she die, you may act."

I knew Kat, had seen her fight a hundred times; but she looked so small, and Ranas had killed Celzez so easily.

Kat circled, Ranas turning with her, letting her do the work. She feinted, but he did not respond. She crept closer. He watched.

Suddenly, he swept his arm up, and Kat darted closer, raising her sword as if she would protect herself. Ranas swung down, but Kat was too close, he brought his arm down onto her sword, cutting deeply. Kat's left hand twitched, and a dagger appeared from some hidden sheath. She drove it into Ranas's side.

Ranas twisted away, the dagger caught in his ribs, swinging to keep Kat away.

She began circling the opposite direction. She flowed, she glided, she moved like a force of nature. Ranas followed her, blood dripping.

"Kill him," I growled.

She dove in, twisting and feinting. Ranas tried to follow her, but bad footwork put him off balance, and Kat grabbed her dagger and yanked it free. She swept past him, driving the dagger into his back. He arched up, and she dropped her sword to take the back of his collar. She yanked, over-tipping him. He tried to turn, but as he fell, Kat used her dagger to cut his throat.

Silence, another type of silence, the silence of surprise, filled the square.

"Do you accuse Teriz?" called a voice from the crowd, and the men murmured, agreeing on their right to know.

Can she do that? I wondered. I never asked if she witnessed Teriz's treachery.

Kat prowled over the paving stones like a cat looking over a gallery of songbirds, selecting its next meal. "I assert that Celzez is not a liar."

Another man stepped forward. Though not as tall as Ranas, there was a resemblance, a brother perhaps, or cousin. The man behind him grabbed his arm. "There's a difference. In what she said, there's a difference."

There was, I realized. Kat did not accuse Teriz, but left the accusation open. Celzez could not pursue it, so nothing would come of it. But would anybody push the question of Celzez's honor?

The first man paused as he looked at Kat, who grinned. Her grin sent a shiver down my spine, and from the crowd's reaction, I was not the only one.

By the gods of Eastwarn, I thought, *is he fool enough to take up this fight?* He was not. He left, half-turned to show he was not afraid. I snorted at that lie.

I could not shake the feeling something had happened here. Something about honor and deciding whom you will stand with. Something that *mattered* to me. Given time, I might figure out what.

MONGOOSE & MEERKAT

FIGHT OF THE SANDFISHERS

The crowd began to break up, and the men drifted away. The men furthest away leaving first, then more and more until only a few people remained: Halmas, who stood quietly next to me; Inark, who faced Kat with a question on his face but not his lips;

Kat, her eyes hooded, thinking I knew not what; Sharin, who stood crying beside the Denouncement Stone.

And Johin, holding a *fallo* scale shield tightly in one fist, who slowly took his uncle's sword as his own.

Thunder in the North

Thirty-one months after the fall of Alness.

"Are you with Karn?" The man shot the question at Mangos like an arrow, and he didn't know the right answer. Karn lurked somewhere outside of the city of Alness, looking for his opportunity to re-take the city from Rhygir's mercenary army. Mangos didn't know who these men were—Karn's loyalists, or the mercenaries hunting them.

The parchment tucked into his tunic seemed to burn him. That message to Karn, which Mangos hadn't even read, would be enough to kill him should the mercenaries discover it.

But were these men mercenaries or loyalists?

Two men faced him. *There could be more in the trees,* he thought. Scouts. Lightly armed, with only leather jerkins as protection. Mangos was sure he could kill them. But for these two to accost him so boldly, they must have comrades around.

"If he's alone, he's not one of ours," said a new voice—a woman's. Something about the voice tickled a memory, and Mangos turned to face the newcomer.

There were two more, both women, and they *looked* familiar. Unlike the men, they wore Rhygir's emblem on their jerkins. Where had he seen them before?

"But this is simple," said the woman who had spoken. "We take him in and torture all sorts of interesting things from him."

"I'm not partial to torture," Mangos said. "At least not when it's done to me."

The woman tensed, Mangos could see her regarding him. She glided toward him, her hand on her sword. "I know you," she said.

Mangos nodded; he recognized her, but still couldn't recall from where. "And I you."

The second woman came forward, carrying a bow with an arrow nocked and half drawn. "Mangos," she said.

"Mangos," repeated the first. She drew his name out as if savoring a memory along with the word. "Last I saw you was in Kalahar, gloating

249

over a dead worm. Missing something, are you?"

Suddenly Mangos remembered their names. Daini and Kairi—sisters. Time had changed them. A new hardness showed in the crease between Daini's eyebrows, the slight downturn to her lips, and the chill in her eyes. Kairi had lost her left eye and now wore a black patch to cover it. She still carried her rune-covered bow, and Mangos knew she could kill anybody in the clearing before they could take two steps.

Daini's question caught Mangos off guard. "Missing something?"

"Little girl, green eyes, second class fighter, first-class bitch," said Daini, the elder, blonde sister. "Kat?"

"She's not here," Mangos said.

"Why are you?" Daini demanded.

"Here?" Mangos asked. "I'm, ah," he thought furiously, "here to buy a dog."

"A dog." Daini looked at him, her eyes flat and hard.

"An Alnessi mastiff," Mangos said. "There's a breeder in Alomar who is afraid the unrest will hurt the stock. He wants another stud to protect his bloodlines."

"A dog." Daini shook her head slowly, her eyes still hard. She half-turned to face Kairi. "He's here for a dog."

Kairi shrugged.

Daini chuckled, looked around the clearing at the men still holding their swords. "There's rebellion brewing, and he wants to buy a dog." The smile fell from her face as though dropped. "I have a dog to show you."

"You—," Mangos floundered, unsure what she had in mind. "You do?"

"Yes," she smiled again. "Follow me. It's inside the city."

Mangos didn't want to go inside the city. Karn was supposed to be somewhere in the forests east of Alness. While he had passed through Alness several times in the past, the city had become a very dangerous place since rumors of Prince Karn had surfaced. It was said to be a place of quiet knifings and open retribution, where both sides considered everyone the enemy.

Mangos hesitated. The message to Karn felt stiff under his tunic, and he hoped it didn't show.

"What's the problem?" Daini asked. "You do want a dog, don't you?" She jerked her head to Kairi, who lifted her bow a little. It still didn't point at Mangos, but it nearly did.

"Of course," Mangos pretended to be offended. "That's why I'm here."

He wanted to go anywhere but the City of Alness, but it looked like he didn't have a choice.

"Where is Kat?" Daini asked as she led them through the forest. She looked ahead but watched him from the corners of her eyes. "Strange she's not here and you are, she being Alnessi after all."

"She's in Alomar," Mangos said. That, at least was the truth, though he didn't know why she stayed there or why it was so important that he deliver her message to Karn. "She hates dogs."

"That's too bad. She'd love the dog I'm going to show you."

Mangos grunted. Kat had been unusually forceful in what she wanted. Whether Karn was a true prince of Alness or a pretender, Mangos should deliver the message. Though she had not said it, Kat made it clear, this was very important.

"And tell me if he is a true prince," she had added.

"How will I know?" Mangos had asked.

In typical Kat style, she had smiled and said, "You'll know." And with that he had to trust she would be right, as she usually was.

Daini sidled up to him, drawing him out of his memory. "So you're still with her then?"

"I'm not real happy about her not coming north with me," Mangos said, "but we're still partners."

"Mmmmmm," Daini smirked. "Maybe you should follow me." She walked ahead, swinging her hips, and cast a glance back over her shoulder. "Not that you have a choice."

Mangos fell into step with Kairi. He thought she wouldn't notice, for he approached from her blind side, but she surprised him by turning to nod and give him a small smile. Her bow was the reason he wouldn't risk running, and her perception meant he wouldn't test her.

"When did you join Rhygir?" he asked.

"Last year," she said. "When we returned from the southwestern desert."

Perhaps it was his association with Kat, perhaps it was his previous trips through Alness, but Mangos didn't like what Rhygir did to his conquest. "Why?" he asked. "I mean, why did you join?"

Daini overheard his question. "You have no idea," she said, "what this place was. The pile of treasure Rhygir has is *enormous*." She grinned a grin of pure avarice. "He pays bonuses from it every year. We're always finding caches of gold hidden during the overthrow. We knock down the mansions and sell the marble in Alomar. We sell the statues, the tapestries, and the furnishings. Even the craftsmen had wealth, even the workers. It will take years to pick the city clean."

Mangos grimaced. *Why should this bother me?* he wondered. *I have sought treasure in the ruins of Terzol.* But the blood of Terzol was old and long dried.

"We had hoped to find Anhunkten," Kairi said, her voice quiet as she took her turn answering his question. She shook her head. "That didn't work, and we barely made it out of the desert alive." She touched the patch over her eye. "The Alnessi had hurt Rhygir badly, and he was offering bounties to any who would sign up with him." She shrugged, maybe ashamed of the job, maybe indifferent.

They came to the top of a hill, and there was a break in the trees. To the north, he could see the city of Alness, but smoke rising to the east drew his attention. He took a couple steps in that direction.

"Hey!" Daini barked. "You're not going there! You're headed to Alness to the dog you want."

The two men, whom Mangos had almost forgotten about, flanked him, one stepping in front of him to cut off his view and herd him north.

Mangos's palm itched, and he longed to draw his sword. *I can kill you all*, he thought, even Kairi, if he was willing to take an arrow in the process. When did he start to think like that? With a rueful smile and a shake of his head, he started toward the city. He always thought like that; the real question was when did he start to question it?

He didn't really want to kill Kairi, or even Daini. He would find another way to escape and deliver the message to Karn.

He had been in Alness before, always passing through, and he was always glad not to stay long. It had been called the jewel of the north once, a prosperous capital to a prosperous country.

That was until Rhygir overthrew the king. Now the smell of smoke and feces and rotting flesh hung heavy in the air. Large sections of the city were empty, the inhabitants fled or dead.

But murdered mercenaries, abandoned children, and discarded women still lay where they crawled or were dragged to die.

A scream made Mangos wince: a woman's scream from somewhere out of sight.

"A daughter," said Daini. "The women don't scream for themselves anymore. But they still do when the men take their daughters."

"And you?" Mangos asked. "You are not bothered?"

"The tunic gives some protection," Daini tapped Rhygir's symbol on her tunic. "My sword provides the rest."

Mangos had thought Alness destitute before; it was worse now. Every shop had been looted, few re-opened. Broken glass still sparkled in the cracks between the cobblestones where boots and hooves could not grind it into powder.

They stood at the crest of a hill, looking down at the lower city.

The canals, the pride of Alness, radiated from the Grand Plaza. They twined through the lower city and connected it with the harbor. The canal gates were closed, which meant the Grand Plaza was dry. The water behind the gates was dark and stagnant. Garbage clung to the sides while a dark, gritty substance coated everything. Hazy outlines of other things lurked under the water: rubble, statuary—the debris of war. At least Mangos hoped the bodies were statues, there were an awful lot of them.

The palace rose above the other buildings in the inner city. It had once been cream-colored and shone in the sun like a jewel. Now, it was greyed by smoke from when the city burned. Darker streaks ran up its sides from its own fires, but the stonework remained intact. It only looked like it wept.

There was also a tension in the air, an expectation.

"That's the dog you came to see, isn't it?" Daini demanded, pointing to the Grand Plaza.

"By the Gods of Eastwarn," Mangos whispered.

Bodies carpeted the plaza, mounded four or five feet high in places. A broad lane ran from the opposite side to the steps of the palace. There, at the foot of the steps, a man had been crucified, bound and nailed to a large timber "X," facing the charnel house that the plaza had become.

Mangos licked his lips. "Karn?"

"We caught him yesterday," Kairi said quietly. "Rhygir nailed him up last night."

"Is he dead?"

Nobody answered. Mangos felt his stomach sink and grow cold. The letter in his tunic rubbed against him, mocking his failure to deliver it.

Daini stared at him, an expectant expression on her face.

What do I do now? The message meant little, or so he supposed. But the memory of Kat's green eyes and the promise he made to deliver it made him reluctant to give up.

If he confessed to seeking Karn, he would be killed as a spy. If he denied it, he would have no choice but to move away.

So he laughed, making light of the city, and the bodies, and the man dying in the plaza below. "Was he so fearful you named him the Mastiff of Alness?"

Daini looked puzzled. "What do you mean?"

"I said I needed to buy a dog, a mastiff, and you show me Karn. From here, I see a boy who's too young to endanger a tavern wench's virtue. Nothing as dangerous as a mastiff."

"Danger?" Daini's face turned red. "Do you have any idea the danger of just being in this place? Every Alnessi is a murderer, just waiting to slit our throats. And when Karn appeared it got ten times worse."

Mangos nodded toward the plaza and Karn. "Maybe Rhygir will sell him to me. He's sold enough Alnessi as slaves already."

"You're a fool," Daini said. "This is Rhygir's city, and if you cross him you'll end up like that."

Come on, Daini, it has to be your idea! Mangos snorted and rolled his eyes. "And what will he do to me?" He jerked his head toward the plaza. "From here that doesn't look so bad."

"Not so bad?" Daini opened her mouth to say more, but no words came out. She sputtered for a moment before turning to stomp toward the plaza. "Follow me," she said. "You'll see bad!"

After an appropriate show of hesitation, and being sure to keep his face impassive, Mangos followed her.

Kairi walked beside him. "You have good eyes if you can see Karn's youth from this distance."

She didn't seem angry, and if she suspected he had ulterior motives, she didn't show it. Mangos cleared his throat. "She seems..." *crueler, less balanced,* "changed from Kalahar."

Kairi nodded once, acknowledging a truth. "I think the desert affected her." She paused. "And Alness is... *different*... from what you would expect. The people kill our men in the most hideous fashions if they can catch them. If you ask them why, they say, 'We stand with the King.'"

"But the king is dead," Mangos said. *Or soon to be, if that's a true prince crucified in front of the palace.*

255

"We all choose who to stand with," Kairi replied.

Mangos followed her gaze to Daini's back, and he knew what she meant. He opened his mouth to speak, but the sharp sound of stone striking stone stopped him. It came again, from somewhere out of sight. Not loud, it nonetheless carried through the air.

Another tapping joined it, from a different location. Further away, a third tapping started.

"What's that?" Mangos asked as the noise multiplied, coming from dozens, hundreds of spots.

"Death," said one of the men. He looked scared, his eyes darting from building to building.

Mangos ran to keep up. "What is it?"

"The Alnessi. They start doing this when they're going to kill."

The noise crashed through the empty streets. It grew *thicker*, deeper, more penetrating as it spread throughout the city. Mangos could picture people sheltering in the rubble, listening to the noise, picking up stones, and joining in. It felt like a physical thing thundering over them, the anger of a people in hiding.

"Who are they going to kill?" Mangos asked.

"All of us!" Daini snarled. "They do this to confuse us."

Kairi had an arrow nocked and half-drawn as she scanned the buildings around them.

"But never the whole city," said one of the men. "They're going to do something *big*."

"They're going to kill us all," said the other.

They turned a corner, and the buildings seemed to close around them. Somebody had scrawled "KARN IS COMING" on a wall; which, though ironic, struck Mangos as ominous.

"We have to find safety," the first man shouted.

Mangos could feel the pounding in his bones. *The Alnessi will kill me too. I'm a fool for trying to get the message to Karn now.* A corner of the parchment dug into him as he moved as if chastising him for the thought.

A scream rose above the thunderous pounding. It sounded like it started in the person's toes and was dragged slowly through their entire body before coming out their mouth.

This is for Karn, Mangos thought. *They stand with the King.*

"I'm not staying here," said one of the men. With an oath, he ducked into an alley and started to run.

256

"Fool!" Daini shouted, but the second man followed the first. Now they were three, and that much more vulnerable. She looked angry and confused, not sure which way to turn. Kairi was spinning slowly, bow raised, jumping at any movement.

Don't stop here, Mangos thought; *we were going where I wanted to go!* "I'll fight them if they wish," he shouted to Daini, "but not in the streets. I'm going to the plaza where there's space to fight!"

Daini nodded. "Yes!" she shouted back, and the three began to run.

They quickly reached the inner city and raced over canals and through the twists and turns until they came to the terrace surrounding the sunken plaza.

"Stop!" Daini cried, grabbing Kairi and pulling her to a halt. Mangos skidded to a stop just as a group of mercenary guards turned on them, swords out and spears leveled. "We don't want to get killed by our friends."

Close, he thought. He just needed to get past some scared and confused guards.

"What's that?" Kairi asked.

Mangos looked around, unsure what she meant. Finally, he heard it, a deeper pounding almost hidden by the clashing stones, but getting louder. "What *is* that?"

Daini started to laugh. "Oh, that will teach them a lesson. Give Rhygir credit, I'll bet he planned this."

The pounding grew louder, more distinct. It was the tramp of thousands of feet, all in unison, like hammer blows on the cobbles.

"Gods," muttered Mangos as rows and rows of men appeared on the High Street, marching toward the plaza. These were not Rhygirian mercenaries. These were *Fedai*, the eunuch warriors he had seen as guards in Alomar. They were trained to do nothing but kill, and they were absolutely loyal to their masters.

The thunder of the *Fedai's* boots clashed with the striking stones, throwing it back. The clashing stones faltered, and as they did, the sound of the boots grew to fill the space. As the *Fedai* flanked the plaza, only a few sounds of clashing stones from the further areas of the city remained and the tramp of the boots overwhelmed them.

The *Fedai* ringed the terrace, three men deep, facing the city, cutting Mangos off from the plaza. They were impassive, a wall, almost daring the people of Alness to break themselves in an effort to rescue Karn. With a

257

last, ringing, stomp, they halted. Silence fell over the city.

Karn lifted his head and looked about. From his vantage he must only be able to see the piles of bodies and bloody cobbles, the steps up to the terrace, and the backs of the *Fedai* ringing him in. His head fell.

Daini laughed. "He knows there's no rescue. And there won't even be the mercy of a knife."

She was right, Mangos realized. Should he even still try to deliver Kat's message? Whatever it said, it meant nothing now.

As he looked over the cordon of *Fedai,* a towering figure came out of the palace. He wore mail of enameled white chain with pauldrons, couters, and cuisses of plate. He still wore the kingfisher on his tunic. Teriz, the betrayer of Alness.

Rhygir followed Teriz. Rhygir wore silver plate armor, but not just silver, and not just mirror bright. The surface looked liquid, like quicksilver.

It was, Mangos realized, an entire suit of unalloyed silvecite. The value boggled his mind. It wasn't just the scarcity of silvecite, it was the difficultly of working it in its pure form. Light and strong, the silvecite armor made Rhygir nearly invulnerable.

Rhygir dragged a young girl to Teriz. The child, maybe five or six years old—it was hard to tell from across the plaza—struggled in his grip.

"Who's the girl?" Mangos asked.

"Just a lesson," Daini said.

"In case all the others didn't make an impact," Kairi added, with just the faintest hint of bitterness in her voice.

Rhygir and Teriz strode down the steps, pulling the girl, who lost her balance. They did not wait, merely dragged her along, her feet smacking each step as she tried to pull them under her. At the bottom, the small group circled Karn and stood in front of him.

Rhygir grabbed the girl's hair and pulled her up until her toes barely touched the ground. He drew his knife and held it to her throat. Karn turned his head away, but Teriz grabbed it and jerked it up.

Rhygir said something, but the plaza swallowed his words. With a final laugh, the mercenary leader sliced the girl's throat and held her while she struggled and bled.

Karn was being forced to view the price of his failure.

Rhygir held the girl until she was dead. He shook her body, as if making sure all her blood was drained, and tossed her onto the nearest pile of corpses.

Rage flared in Mangos. He couldn't rescue Karn, and he wasn't suicidal, but he had to do something to support Alness, and the only thing at hand was the message. It might be symbolic, and worthlessly symbolic, but he would find a way to deliver the message before Karn died.

He knew of two people who could grant him access to Karn. "I have a message to deliver," he growled.

"What are you talking about?" Daini demanded.

"I have a message to deliver," Mangos said over his shoulder as he approached the line of *Fedai*.

"Fool!" Daini hissed. He could hear her footsteps. "They'll kill you."

The *Fedai* in the front row drew their swords, those behind them lowered long spears, making Mangos draw up with a steel spear tip inches from his chest.

He gently took hold of the tip and tried to push it aside, but the *Fedai* held it firmly in place. *Impressive strength* and *discipline*, Mangos thought, knowing they didn't need an excuse to kill him.

"Teriz!" he shouted.

Daini hissed. "What are you doing?"

"Teriz!" Mangos shouted again. "I have a message!"

Teriz and Rhygir turned, and Mangos waved. "I have a message," he shouted again.

"I thought you were here to buy a dog," Daini said, her voice angry.

"No, you didn't," Mangos replied.

"I should kill you now."

Recalling her over-the-shoulder gaze and swinging hips, Mangos smiled. "But you won't." At least he hoped she wouldn't.

"Damn you."

Rhygir called out an order, and the *Fedai* parted enough that he could squeeze through.

A pair of mercenary guards moved to intercept him.

"Get out of my way," he growled. "I have an important message."

The mercenaries sneered, and both drew their swords. The nearest slapped the flat of the blade against Mangos's chest, making him stop.

"Teriz!" Mangos shouted. "Teriz!" He pushed aside the sword but both men blocked his path.

Teriz and Rhygir spoke, and Rhygir called, "Let him approach." The guards stepped aside, but Mangos felt their presence as he walked down the path between the mounds of bodies.

Mangos felt his heart pound as he approached Teriz. He stopped a couple steps away and nodded politely to Rhygir before looking up at Teriz. A mercenary's sword slapped up against the back of his neck.

"I have news for Teriz," he said.

Teriz's eyes narrowed, and he glanced at Rhygir. "Who are you?"

"Mangos of Arnelon," Mangos said. "I've recently been to Hafiz."

"And you have news, you say? Of what?"

"Of your brother."

Teriz stiffened, and Mangos wondered if he had made a mistake. "What of my brother?"

"He's dead."

Teriz nodded, almost to himself, and then to the mercenaries. They moved back a couple paces. Teriz said, "I knew this."

Mangos relaxed a tiny bit. "I saw it. A man named Celzez denounced you. Your brother defended your honor."

Teriz waved his hand. "I know all this. Ranas killed Celzez only to have a woman renew the claim. Few know who the woman is. Celzez's sister, a merchant, and old Inark; but none will say her name. I will see that she is killed. Do you know her?"

Mangos hesitated. It was curious nobody would tell Kat's name, almost as if they were protecting her. "No." He needed something to offer, some information Teriz might not have. "But she did not renew the denouncement. She only asserted Celzez did not lie."

"Did not lie?" Teriz scoffed. "What do I care if he lied or not?"

Mangos shrugged. "It just means she has not bound herself to come after you."

"Why do you bring me this news?" Teriz asked abruptly. "Who pays you? Or do you hope I will give you gold?"

Mangos shook his head. *Now for it.* "I wanted to be able to fulfill my other task. The other reason I came north was see if Karn is a true prince of Alness."

"You know him?" Rhygir said, the first words the mercenary leader had spoken to Mangos.

"No, I was given a description."

"Who wants to know?" Rhygir came closer. Wind stirred in the plaza, lifting his long hair, but also bringing the smell of the dead. Rhygir scowled, his hand resting on his sword while his other hand smoothed his magnificent moustache. His eyes were dark, so dark Mangos couldn't tell his pupil from his iris.

Mangos's mouth went dry, but he forced himself to use an easy tone. "A jade merchant in Alomar," he lied. "His mother was a distant cousin of the royal house. He didn't want to become involved in the fighting, but if Karn were a true Prince, he might be obligated."

Rhygir looked at Teriz, who shrugged. "Possible," Teriz allowed.

"Who is this merchant?" Rhygir demanded.

"He'd rather I not say," Mangos said. "If Karn is false, he can go back to making money without having made any enemies."

Rhygir snorted. "Typical merchant." He looked at Karn, whose head hung limply against his chest. "He's not truly Karn. He's a pretender."

"He is?"

"He is," Rhygir's voice held a hint of steel. Evidently he didn't like being questioned. "Isn't he, Teriz?"

Teriz looked surprised by the question. "Yes," he said. "Yes, he is, and I should know."

Since he was entrusted to your protection and you killed at least one of his brothers, Mangos thought. "I believe you," he said, but something about Teriz's hesitation told him otherwise. "And the merchant *wants* to believe it too. In fact, he strongly suggested that I would discover Karn was a pretender. But I need to swear I examined him closely, or I won't get paid."

Rhygir closed his hand on the hilt of his sword.

Mangos held up his hands, palms out. "I'm not interested in rescuing him, or in a mercy killing. You'd only kill me after it."

"You're right about that," Rhygir said. He glared at Mangos. "I don't trust you."

"If he carries word back of the pretender's fate, fewer will claim legitimacy in the future," Teriz said. "And his news from Hafiz is true."

Rhygir turned his glare on Teriz, then back to Mangos. He drew his sword a couple inches and let it fall back into its sheath with a *snick*. He drew it again and let it fall back. *Snick.* "If he dies here, we don't worry about a thing." *Snick.* Suddenly he laughed. "This is *my* city. Take *that* message back." He waved his arm, encompassing Karn, the *Fedai*, and the plaza full of bodies. "Tell everybody what happens to those who oppose me."

Mangos nodded. It sounded like he had just been given permission to speak with Karn. He took a step, hesitated, and when Rhygir didn't protest, walked over to the crucified man.

Dried blood made webs on Karn's arms, cutting through dirt and soot, crossing the deep bruises that covered him. Fresh blood glistened on the spikes in his hands and feet.

He hung loosely, held by the ropes and nails. His head lolled on his chest, and if it weren't for the rasping sound of his breathing, Mangos would have thought him dead.

Karn lifted his head, though his eyes were closed. His lips were cracked and swollen. His right cheek was cut and bloody, his left eye blackened. His hair was plastered to his head; the impression of his helmet was still evident.

How should I know if this boy is a true prince of Alness? Mangos wondered. Yet there was something about the cast of his bones, the structure of his face, that Mangos found familiar.

Knowing he could not give it to Karn, he took out the message and opened it up. He read it, glancing from the parchment to Karn and back as if he were comparing the two.

"I was told to give you a message," he said softly. "I don't expect it matters anymore. Not here. Not now. But I promised I'd do my best to deliver it."

Karn stirred. He licked his lips and his eyelashes fluttered. He moaned.

Mangos tried to picture Karn without the wounds or swelling. *What is it about you that raised an army?* "The message is from a woman named Kat. I don't suppose you know her. She says, 'The time is not right.'"

Karn opened his eyes. They were bloodshot, and blood pooled in his left one, but they were emerald green, and for a second Mangos saw Kat's face overlaying Karn's.

"The time wasn't right," Mangos repeated. "I'm sorry." He swallowed, the world shifting beneath his feet; nothing would ever be the same. He felt like a child who looks up from his games to find he is grown and the games he played were not games at all.

Karn was trying to speak. There was only a whisper of air in his lungs as he said, "It ends here."

"No," Mangos said. "It only starts. It is your sister's turn." Kat, Princess of Alness. Mangos understood, not everything, but enough. "Her footsteps shall thunder in the north when she reclaims her own."

The Feast of the Fedai

Mangos had been moving toward home since leaving Alness a month ago. The familiar stench of Alomar filled his nostrils, wafting up from the docks, the gutters, and the alleys. Alomar—home—the decadent, the corrupt, where every virtue and vice from this world or, it was bragged, any other could be had for a price.

He shouldered his way through Alomar's crowded market, where the smell of sweat and spoiled food mixed with the other odors of the city. He nodded greetings to the vendors, not sure if they recognized him but sure they didn't care. It was just good to be home.

He let his gaze stray on the fruits in one stall and, in consequence, slammed into a man who came the other way.

"Sorry," Mangos muttered.

"You ought to be," the man said, pushing Mangos.

Mangos bristled; he didn't like people pushing him. "I've apologized," he said. "Keep your hands to yourself."

"I'll do what I please with my hands." The man was solid, a bald man without much neck and a thick chest. He looked made for fighting, but he dressed like a dandy—clothes of velvet, and lace, and linen.

Two men trailed behind him, thugs by their look, and not as well dressed. "Hey, it's the Mongoose!" one of them said.

The bald man, without taking his eyes off Mangos, turned his head slightly to ask over his shoulder, "What?"

"It's the Mongoose, you know, the one Bardor told—"

"Shut up!" said the bald man.

Mangos let his hand stray to his sword as the bald man glowered at him.

"Well, Mr. Mongoose," said the man, "it was by good fortune that we met."

"Was it?" Mangos asked. "Whose?" The two thugs started to flank him to either side. The crowd, sensing trouble, ebbed away.

"Mine," said the dandy.

Mangos backed away, keeping all three in view.

"Hey! Stay away from here," said the woman inside the fruit stall. "I don't want you ruining my fruit with your fight."

"Not my fight," Mangos said, but it was, whether he wanted it or not. He thought to put a building to his back, but without looking, he backed right into an alley.

"That's right," said the dandy, following in after him, "let's take this someplace more private."

Mangos drew his sword and hazarded a look behind him. Apart from a rain barrel and a layer of garbage, the alley was empty. An iron gate blocked the far end. "Damn."

The two thugs attacked; Mangos gave ground, parrying. He could beat either of them, but both together... and he needed to keep an eye on the dandy.

He put a wall to his back and held off the thugs. A crowd of people gathered at the opening of the alley, but nobody called the constable; they just watched.

"Gods, two of you, and you can't kill him," said the dandy, drawing a small tube from his pocket. "Step aside. I'll finish him."

The thugs scrambled back. Mangos's heart pounded.

The dandy smiled and sauntered forward. He pointed the tube at Mangos. "It's almost too easy."

A fine mist shot out of the back of the tube. As it spread and enveloped the dandy, it burst into flame. He threw the tube away from him with a shriek and danced back, slapping at his face and shoulders, then his hands, as the fire stuck to him and spread.

Screaming, he turned to his men. With one hand clutching at his chest, he reached out and staggered toward them. The words "help me" emerged from the flaming ruin of his face.

The men shrank back. "Gods, no," said one. "Stay away from me."

As if the words were a trigger, they broke and ran. The slower stopped at the corner and looked back. He doubled over to vomit, started to run again, slipped, and tumbled out of sight.

The dandy fell and dragged himself to the rain barrel. He grasped the rim and, with hideous effort, threw himself head-first into the barrel.

Water overflowed onto the street. Steam rose, but the fire didn't go out. Flames danced within the barrel and the water began to bubble. The dandy stopped struggling and settled in deeper until only his feet stuck out.

"Didn't expect that," Mangos said. He gingerly picked up the fallen tube. "I'm going home now," he announced. Seeing no objections, he strode out of the alley, carefully avoiding the pool of vomit, and turned toward home.

M angos paused on the portico. He drew in a deep breath, now savoring the clearer air. The mansions of the wealthy looked down on the rest of Alomar, perched on any one of the many hills where the breeze cleared the heat and stench of the city.

Some things are natural transition points, he thought, his hand resting on the door lever; *things you pass through and nothing is the same again. Doors can be one. Questions can be another.*

He snorted. *The world is the same. Only the people have changed.*

He hesitated, stalling, by looking over the city. He would find his answers soon enough and know if the people had indeed changed.

Down in the harbor, almost lost amongst the carracks, galleys, cogs, and caravels, a small fleet of dromonds was tied to the northern quay. *Fedai* warriors crossed the extended gangplanks and formed ranks on the stone quay. Bardor's private slave army; they, too, were returning from Alness, though their journey would have been quicker and, presumably, less eventful.

Enough. Go in. Mangos opened the door and passed into the house.

The sound of voices drew him to the parlor. Kat's, and a man he didn't recognize. The door was open, but again he paused, staying out of sight of those inside as he listened to their conversation.

"You know nothing of war," said the man. "That was a task for others."

"Those so trained can no longer fight," Kat said, an edge in her voice.

"Do not join them in their graves. You have done well in Alomar."

Mangos looked proudly around the entry of the grand home. Alabaster columns, marble floor: yes, they had done well.

"If they even have graves," Kat muttered.

Mangos squared his shoulders and entered the room.

Kat looked up from the table where she sat and smiled, a broad grin of pleasure that he couldn't help but return.

"Who is this?" demanded the man with her, and Mangos turned his attention to him. The man was a bit shorter than Mangos, broad of shoulders but thin. He had dark hair salted with grey, and a narrow face with a worn expression.

"Mangos," Kat said, "This is Grel. At one time he served as assistant quartermaster of the Alnessi army."

"And now a slave," Grel muttered.

"I keep no slaves," Kat said evenly. "Even though I paid for you." Grel lifted his hand to his neck and rubbed a ring of raw flesh where a slave's collar had recently been. He looked down.

His eyes still on Grel, unsure of what to make of the man, Mangos said to Kat, "I delivered your message."

Kat drew in her breath sharply. "I assumed you didn't reach Karn in time."

"The time wasn't right, just as you told him."

"Yet Karn proceeded," Grel said, his voice had a nasal quality that reminded Mangos of a wasp buzzing.

"Karn was already crucified when I gave him the message," Mangos said. "But he was a true prince of Alness; bound and nailed to a timber 'X' in the Grand Plaza of his own city." He looked Kat in the eye. "He was your brother."

"Younger," she admitted.

"He's dead."

"I know. Word reached us nineteen days ago."

"You knew," Mangos accused her, suddenly angry. "You knew he was your brother!"

"I wasn't sure, but I suspected."

Mangos glared at her, and she stared back. "You don't care about your brother's death?"

Now Kat flashed anger. "Of course I care! But I've known for almost three weeks, and I already mourned him when Alness fell." She looked away. "I find it hard to grieve anymore."

Mangos weighed this. "You never told me you were a princess," he said.

A small smile played on her lips. "You never asked."

"By the gods of Eastwarn," Mangos couldn't help himself; he chuckled softly. "I wouldn't have thought I'd need to." He raised an eyebrow. "What happens now?"

"Now, I take back my country."

"Perhaps you can talk her from this reckless course," Grel said. "She is not prepared for this."

Kat ignored him. "Once the *Fedai* return from Alness, we can begin."

"They arrived today," Mangos said. He rubbed his hand on the back of his neck, his mind racing. "Do you have an army hiding somewhere?"

"Not yet."

"Anybody else know you're a princess?"

"Bardor."

"Bardor?" Mangos shook his head; that was bad. Bardor bankrolled Rhygir's conquest of Alness and sent five thousand *Fedai* to bolster the mercenary leader against Karn's army. They had returned, but he would send them north again to fight any army Kat might raise. "How did he find out?"

"One of his Alnessi slaves saw me and told him. She used to be married to one of the junior officers. The officer was killed, and she was passed amongst the mercenaries before being brought to Alomar and sold."

"You've no hope if he knows your intentions." Mangos said. He thought of the assassination attempt. "I met some people on the way here." He dug the dandy's fire tube from his pouch. "They offered me a warm reception."

"Yes, those were Bardor's boys. They like those because of the horror they create—a bad way to die," Kat said. "Careful which way you point it. They're tricky and expensive toys."

With a snort, Mangos slid it back into his pouch. "Bardor should hire better people to use it then. Now, about that army..."

"You'll start it for me," Kat said. "If you're willing."

Mangos was stunned she needed to ask, and he realized sometime in the last three years he had made his choice without ever knowing it. "I will stand with you."

A slow smile crept over Kat's face. "Good. Let's get started. Talgon is having a 'Toast the Host' banquet in a week."

Mangos didn't know Talgon, and it must have showed, for she said, "Talgon trains and sells *Fedai*. He is returning to Alomar in a week, and the banquet is his way of announcing he has more *Fedai* to sell."

"You'll buy *Fedai*?" The idea surprised Mangos, and Grel too, by his intake of breath.

"Not a whole army," Kat said, "that would cost too much, and Talgon doesn't have that many ready. But all the easy recruits in Alness are already dead. We need a core of fighters to give ourselves credibility—something to convince prospective recruits we have a chance.

"And no," she added. "I'll not buy the *Fedai*—you will. I have other things to do at the banquet."

"Toast the Host" banquets, Mangos knew, started centuries before when Alomar still engaged in empire building. A particular Prince of Alomar, Mangos couldn't remember which one, celebrated a victory by passing out free wine to the masses and hosting a great feast for the wealthy. The masses, in a gesture of spontaneous glorification, broke into the feast and toasted the Prince with their flagons of free wine.

So began the custom of the wealthy and powerful hosting a meal where the guests were expected to bring their own chalices for toasting the host. Like much else in Alomar, they were an opportunity for both the host and guests to impress each other. The feast was expected to be worthy of acclamation, and guests vied for the most impressive goblets. It explained the unusual number of goldsmiths specializing in drinking vessels.

"We need glassware," Mangos said. They had inherited the house, fully furnished, from the previous owner, and apart from the silver tankards, he didn't know what kind of drinking vessels they owned.

"I had some made," Kat said. She drew a leather box from under the table. It was tightly made, with a leather handle and bright brass clasps. She set it on the table and opened it.

Two goblets rested in red silk. Kat handed him one.

The goblets' bowls were a light and lustrous shade of gold where innumerable colors chased each other too quickly for the eye to register. Carved crystal vines, rooted at the foot, formed the stem and entwined the bowl. Lapis lazuli fruit hung from the vines and, presumably, hid the fasteners that held the bowl to the stem.

"Is this made from the Golden Pearl?" Mangos asked. Awe thrilled through his body. A person drinking from this couldn't be poisoned.

"Honor to our host," Kat lifted the other goblet in a mock toast.

"Indeed." Mangos examined the exquisite craftsmanship. "These are beyond price." He glanced up. "These could buy many soldiers."

"They've saved my life twice in the last month," Kat said.

"Not for sale, then." Mangos put his goblet back into the box.

That evening in the mansion's tower study, Mangos pored over the ledger Kat had given him. He needed to examine the long columns of numbers and know the categories, for the *Fedai* would be expensive.

The numbers represented Kat's share of their treasure—a fortune, and he felt guilty he had so little. Drink, wagers, and pleasurable company had claimed the larger amount of his share. Kat appeared to have kept every copper coin. "This is unbelievable," he murmured. She must have been planning this for years.

"A moment of your time?"

Mangos looked up. Grel stood in the doorway. Although he asked, it hadn't sounded like a question, more like a demand. Mangos remembered Kat's description of the quartermaster: *a petty mind, filled with nothing but numbers and charts. But he's good at that. He could tell how many daggers should be in the armory and number their nicks.*

"Yes?" he said, beckoning Grel into the room. He closed the ledger he had been examining. If Kat's accounts were Grel's business, she could show them herself; Mangos would be damned if he did.

"Do you even know what it takes to field an army?" Grel asked.

"It takes men," Mangos said. "And nothing else matters if you don't have them."

"And if you have the men, you need to feed them, to arm them, to move them about. It is no small task, and no task for a woman, especially one untrained."

Mangos resisted the urge to strangle him. "Do you even know who you speak of?"

"Better than you, evidently."

"I wonder."

"I'll tell you one thing I do know," Grel said in his rasping, buzzing voice. "Armies need to be fed. Contracts are settled seasons in advance. You cannot buy enough food for an army on short notice."

"The grain merchants—"

"Already have the harvest under contract," Grel said. "If anybody has any grain to sell, you'll only get it at famine prices."

Mangos leaned back. He couldn't argue with Grel's logic.

"Convince her to give this up," Grel pressed. "You don't want her killed."

"No," Mangos agreed. "But she's not easy to kill." Suddenly he thought of a solution. "Fortune has it that I know a grain merchant, and she is in our debt. Contact Polonia."

Grel frowned. "*She* suggested Polonia also. But we shouldn't waste money on a venture so clearly doomed."

Mangos felt his fingers twitch. He really did want to strangle the man. "Doomed?"

Grel snorted. "Even if you can feed the men, without weapons and armor, they're doomed. She doesn't have the knowledge or training for this."

"You don't seem properly grateful to the woman who freed you."

"Free?" Grel blinked, as if the word surprised him. "I carry three years of nightmares, three years of beatings, three years of hunger and loss since Alness fell. I am not free. But please excuse me if I don't care to add to that burden."

Mangos sighed and relaxed his hands. He could not argue with that, but neither would he hold up Kat's plans. He said, "Another thing an army needs is everybody working together. Contact Polonia."

Grel opened his mouth, perhaps to protest, but closed it without saying anything. He nodded once and turned to leave.

"And, Grel?" Mangos said as the quartermaster reached the door. "*She* has a name."

Grel hesitated, but didn't turn and didn't speak.

Mangos glared at the empty doorway; then, opening the ledger, he scanned the columns. There, buried amongst "non-currency assets," were the neatly written words, "125 tonnes silvecite ore—located in Pytheas."

So Kat never sold the silvecite they earned by killing the mine worm; instead she shipped it to Pytheas, where the smiths owed them for defeating the dragons.

Shaking his head, Mangos began to chuckle. Clever, clever Kat. The army would be very well-armed indeed.

If he could get it started with the purchase of the *Fedai*.

Talgon's walled mansion was well-situated, high enough on one of Alomar's hills to lift it above the haze that hung over the slums and workshops. There was very little space between the perimeter wall and the building, just enough for some ornamental trees and a few patches of well-trimmed grass. The house looked like a fortress, as suited a man whose influence came from brokering warrior-slaves.

Instead of gargoyles, a half-dozen *Fedai* perched atop the outer wall: three on each side of the gate.

A doorwarder, dressed in festive red and gold, stepped forward and held up his hand to stop them. "It is the tradition of this home that you surrender your swords," he said.

Mangos looked at him in surprise.

"Your safety is guaranteed while you're a guest," the doorwarder assured him.

Mangos closed his hand on the hilt of his sword as if he would shield it from the man. "This is a unique weapon," he said. "It's Marin's first silvercite sword."

The doorwarder bowed slightly. "I would direct your gaze to the words above the gate." Mangos read the words above the wrought iron gate as the doorwarder quoted them, "This is a house of honor."

Mangos eyed the scrawny man and wondered if he *could* keep the sword safe. It didn't matter, he decided. This was Talgon's house and Talgon's honor, and Talgon's *Fedai* would see to the keeping of both.

Kat unbuckled her sword. With a sardonic smile, she offered it for keeping. Much more reluctantly, Mangos followed suit.

"The words on the gate are true," Kat said, "but misleading. In Hafiz, honor is a way of life; for Talgon it is a front for business."

Two more *Fedai* guarded the house's main entrance, where an old butler directed guests further into the house. He bowed as they approached. "The Mongoose and the Meerkat?"

"Yes," Kat said.

The man smiled and beckoned them forward, then pointed. "Through the hall, dinner will be served in the courtyard." He lowered his voice, now sounding like a kindly grandfather. "You have your toasting goblets?"

Kat patted the box at her side.

"Good, good," the old butler said. "Sorry for asking, but adventurers have a certain reputation." He chuckled, almost to himself. "And it isn't for their manners."

"Thank you," Kat said. She led the way through guests who loitered in the hall, and they emerged under a portico that surrounded the courtyard.

In the center of the courtyard was a green bronze fountain of a dragon, wings unfurled, breathing a jet of what looked like red wine into the pool below.

Mosaics covered the rest of the courtyard, dragons and unicorns and lions, all entwined with geometric patterns. A large urn filled with flowers sat in each corner.

Couches ringed the mosaics, pulled to the edge of the portico where they sat, two between each column, each with its own slave. Another row of couches ran along the walls of the house. These were for less-favored guests, Mangos supposed, because of the obstructed view and only one slave served the many couches.

Though it wouldn't be dark for some time, lanterns hung from the

271

columns, sending light and sweet perfumes into the dark corners under the portico. Musicians on the roof began to play.

Mangos had never met Talgon, but he had a description and didn't doubt he would recognize his host. He saw Hartwick, who sold gladiators and animals to the arenas. Ninix San, the archivist of the alchemist guild, he knew, but others he didn't recognize. He didn't recognize the thick-necked man wearing emerald-studded bracers, or the bald man with a tattoo on his head. While he didn't know the young woman in red, he wouldn't mind meeting her. Her dark hair hung over one eye and cascaded around her shoulders. She adjusted her wrap as she moved, which only seemed to enhance the movement of her hips.

Mangos let his gaze linger on her before resuming his search for Talgon.

Another butler drew his attention by gesturing to one of the couches. "This couch is for the Mongoose," he bobbed his head at Mangos. "And that for the Meerkat."

Each couch sat at an angle, head toward the fountain. They were frames of burnished bronze covered by a thick mattress with pillows to prop up the guests. Each had a small table next to it and a slave behind it.

"Talia will serve you," the butler told Mangos with an elegant flourish of his hand to indicate the tall woman behind his couch, a woman made strong and fit by her labor in Talgon's house.

"Evard will do your bidding," the butler said to Kat, indicating the stocky slave waiting beside her couch.

Mangos tested the couch, appreciating the view of the courtyard and the clear view of the more honored guests. A quick twist and glance confirmed less fortunate guests had a superb view of his feet.

"Mangos!"

The Hand of Bursa, the Bursa's administrative assassin, lifted a hand, and Mangos walked over to him. "There are rumors," the Hand said. "Bardor is taking an unusual interest in you and Kat."

Mangos looked around. "Is that right?"

"Bardor only cares for money, and he makes it in two ways—predatory banking and fencing Rhygir's loot from Alness. Which one do you threaten?"

"Who wants to know?"

The Hand looked over his shoulder. The Bursa reclined on a couch in the corner deepest in shadows. It was impossible to tell if he watched them or not.

"This business with Bardor doesn't involve the Bursa," Mangos said.

"Yes, it does," Kat said, breezing past them.

The Hand turned to watch. "Only she can walk past me like that without my killing her."

Mangos laughed and clapped the Hand on the shoulder. "And I have my own business."

There, the man by the door, the one talking with the short fellow, must be Talgon. He stood almost a head taller than Mangos. He showed his prosperity in his enormous girth that almost hid his broad shoulders and deep chest and his toughness in the strong bands of muscle that even the thick slab of fat couldn't conceal. When Talgon started moving, it would be wise to stay out of his way.

"Time to buy an army," Mangos muttered and started through the crowd.

His movement drew the attention of the woman in red. She moved out of the shadows, and the torchlight danced over her, making her chiffon wrap seem aflame and her wreathed in fire.

He thought their paths would diverge, for he had business with Talgon, and she couldn't possibly have business with him, but she surprised him by approaching and resting a hand on his arm. Her touch was dry and warm.

"I've been told the Mongoose is one of the most dangerous men in Alomar." Her voice was low, slightly breathy, yet rich in tone.

"I can't imagine who would be telling you that, or why," Mangos said. A quick glance showed Talgon still deep in conversation with the short man.

"Tell me," the woman drew close enough that Mangos could feel her heat and ran her hand over his upper arm, "what makes you so dangerous?"

Mangos glanced at Talgon's back. The woman's caress distracted him. He opened his mouth to ask what she wanted but realized that was a very stupid question.

Her hand closed on his elbow. "Show me the fountain." She steered Mangos into the courtyard, pausing by one of the flower-filled urns. "So beautiful," she purred. "I love these flowers."

They were bright yellow flowers, globes, like suns. Mangos recognized them as the same flowers that grew in the mountains west of the Terzol

Valley. Beautiful, yes, and very poisonous; did the fact she loved them mean anything?

"Very nice." Even he wasn't sure what, exactly, he was complimenting, but he did know he needed to get away from this woman. Somewhere amongst his swirling thoughts was the belief that nothing in Alomar was innocent. "Very nice," he repeated, pulling his elbow free. "But I'd like to talk to somebody before dinner."

The woman hooked her arm through his and reached up to pat his cheek. "Of course. Business." She took a deep breath, half-turning to make sure he noticed, "My loss. But surely it can wait?"

By the gods of Eastwarn, Mangos thought. "No. I'm afraid it can't." He pulled his arm away and headed toward Talgon.

"Wait," she said, but her footsteps stopped, and he didn't look back.

"Talgon, I'd like a word," he said just as Talgon nodded and shook hands with the small man.

"I don't believe I know you," Talgon said.

"Mangos of Arnelon."

"Ah, yes, the Mongoose." Talgon looked around, surveying the crowd, apparently looking for 'the Meerkat.' "Glad to have you here tonight." He smiled broadly. "Having thieves and adventurers here reminds people why they need to buy *Fedai.*"

"Actually, I'd like to buy *Fedai* myself."

"Really?" Talgon tugged at his lip. "Huh. I didn't expect that." He looked down at the man next to him and back at Mangos. "When do you want them?"

"Now."

"That, Mangos of Arnelon, is unfortunate, for I've none to sell."

Mangos felt his stomach go cold. "None to sell?"

"None. Bardor here just purchased all I had."

"Bardor?" Now it felt like Mangos had been punched in the stomach. That shrimp of a man was Bardor? He had pictured a grossly overweight octopus, a man fat on the flesh of others with his hands in a dozen different pies. Bardor looked like an evil child next to Talgon, if the child was bald, wrinkled, and had a chin so sharp it made his face look like a hatchet. "He has five thousand already."

The banker lifted his goblet in a mock toast. "I like to be prepared. If I can't remove the trouble before it starts, at least I'll be prepared to deal with it."

"What of them?" Mangos said, pointing to the *Fedai* stationed about the courtyard.

Bardor laughed, a shrill, 'hicking' sound and waved his hand in front of his face as if Mangos's question had left a funny, but noxious, cloud in the air.

"My house guard are not for sale," Talgon said.

"When will you have more?"

"I have already spoken for those." Bardor stepped very close, though he only came midway up Mangos's chest. He lifted his chin to glare upwards. "There will never be *Fedai* available for you, or that orphan princess either. Your days, and the days of your rebellion, are numbered."

Mangos sat on his couch, glaring at the mosaic floor, trying to puzzle out the situation. He needed to buy those slaves. Kat couldn't build her army without the credibility they brought.

Talia, the slave by his assigned couch, intercepted him. "My Lord," she said, holding up a broad, shallow brass bowl, "I have sea lemons in light syrup."

Mangos shrugged.

"The sea lemons cleanse your palette and prepare you for the next course," she explained. Fishing out a slice of lemon, she held it up for him.

Mangos regarded the dripping fruit, not sure he wanted the syrup on his hands.

Talia smiled, clearly experienced in the protocol of the feast and how to handle guests. She lifted the fruit to Mangos's mouth and fed him. Then, glancing down, she sucked her fingers clean. "Now, My Lord, you are ready for pre-dinner delicacies."

"Thank you." Mangos pushed himself up. He needed to talk to Kat.

He approached the Bursa's couch, where Kat still talked to the Bursa, oblivious to all else. The Hand stepped in front of him and stopped him with a hand to his chest and a gentle push.

"They are busy," the Hand said.

Mangos's irritation flared. "I know that," he snapped. "It's important."

"They," the Hand repeated with emphasis, "are busy."

Mangos slapped the Hand's hand from him and made to push his way past. The Hand snapped his fingers in Mango's face, and a dagger appeared as if by magic. The Hand snapped again, and the dagger vanished.

Spring-loaded forearm sheath hidden by his sleeves, Mangos thought. There was a time he would have feared the Hand, but that time was past. Still, the fact the Hand would warn him like that made him pause.

The Hand nodded. "Now that I have your attention, listen. Kat's calling in everything the Bursa owes her, and the Bursa doesn't like it— he's resisting." The Hand looked over his shoulder at the two in conversation. "If you interrupt now, there's a good chance she won't get what she wants."

Mangos nodded his reluctant understanding.

"Good," the Hand said. "Whatever you needed, you'll have to do it yourself."

Mangos munched spiced fowl, acutely aware of the empty couch next to him. The courses came and went, each dish chased by a slice of sea lemon, finger-fed by Talia, but he had no ideas about buying *Fedai*. The largest band of *Fedai*, after Bardor's army, was Talgon's house guard, and none of them were for sale.

Bardor sauntered past, paused. "The Mongoose and the Meerkat," he sneered. "So little you know, so little you understand."

Mangos climbed to his feet.

Bardor didn't flinch. "Haven't you learned? My information is always good." He snorted. "Crawl back to your couch and finish this farce."

Mangos clenched his fists and jaw.

Bardor laughed. "I am the one who is honored to toast our host. I hope you have a worthy goblet. But I doubt it." He walked away, smiling warmly at the woman in red as he passed. With every familiarity, he plucked one of the yellow flowers and tucked it into her hair.

The poisonous little bitch! She delayed me on purpose! Yes, the flower suited her.

Suddenly, he had an idea. *This is a house of honor, is it?* He pulled the Golden Pearl chalice from his pouch, and while Talia fetched the toasting wine, plucked one of the poisonous yellow flowers. He needed to finish a farce.

He shredded the flower over the sea lemon, taking care to let the pollen cover the floating fruit. Next, he pulled the flame tube from his tunic and dropped it on the ground. He brushed off his hands just as Talia returned and filled his goblet.

"One last entremet, so you can appreciate the wine," Talia said. The pollen blended into the yellow of the lemon, unnoticed except by Mangos. Death. Talia watched him expectantly. He rubbed his thumb over the cool side of the goblet. Life.

He ate the lemon from Talia's fingers.

Bardor raised his hand, turning so everybody could see him, no matter where they sat. "Friends," he said. "Now is the best time of the dinner. This is when we get to toast our host." He made a great show of lifting his goblet from the pouch at his side and holding it up. The gold cup gleamed in the torchlight. Rubies flashed like blood between his fingers.

"Friends," Bardor said, "a toast. To Talgon, may his *Fedai* grow ever more dangerous."

Mangos snorted. *That's a self-serving toast. I drink instead to life.* He started to take a sip.

"And now you pass your goblets to the left," Bardor called.

Mangos froze, the goblet halfway to his lips. Nobody around him drank, instead they did, indeed, pass their goblets to the left. The fat old man to his left held out his ring-encrusted hand impatiently.

Mangos's breath caught in his throat, his chest spasmed as he drew in air that would not come. His throat throbbed. He needed that drink, must have it! *Damn manners!* He started to drink again.

But the old man snatched the Golden Pearl chalice from his hand, and Mangos raised only air. He couldn't even squawk his protest. The edges of his vision already darkened.

Kat lifted the goblet out of the old man's hand, deftly replacing it with a silver chalice. "Did you just poison your own food?" she whispered angrily as she held the Golden Pearl chalice to his lips and helped him drink.

Mangos took in wine, feeling it soothe his throat, opening it again. He gasped, letting wine spatter in his rush to breathe.

Heads turned their way. He didn't care.

"What do you hope to accomplish with this?" Kat demanded.

Mangos coughed, but before he could answer, there was a crash of falling trays. Talia clutched her hands, trying to stop them from shaking, then she started to tear at her throat, her face turning red and her eyes bulging. Her fingernails dug furrows in her neck and blood trickled down her body.

Evard, Kat's servant, stared in horror.

"Give her a drink," Mangos wheezed, holding out the goblet.

"She can't swallow!" Evard protested.

"Give it to her anyway!" Talia was turning purple, and her neck was bloody. Mangos grabbed her and forced her head back. He poured wine into her mouth.

She paused, frozen in her panic. With a gag and gasp she spat out the wine, but then took several labored breaths. Mangos gave her the goblet and she swallowed all that it held.

"What is this?" Talgon stood in the center of a cluster of guests at the edge of the portico.

"Somebody has poisoned your slave," Mangos said. Kat stood next to him, her eyes darting from him to Talgon.

"There is no point in poisoning a slave," Talgon said, his eyes were narrow, and he looked around the courtyard as he spoke.

"I think she was just in the wrong place at the wrong time," Mangos said.

"Who would do this?" Talgon demanded. He stepped closer, his gaze going to the lemons, then to the crowd around him.

Mangos raised his eyebrows. "Somebody who cares little for your guests or your honor."

Talgon nodded, still looking around. He stooped down to pick up something. He held up an assassin's fire gun. "Yours?" he asked.

Mangos shook his head and waited for Talgon to reach the desired conclusion.

Talgon's knuckles turned white. He jerked his jaw toward Talia. "You saved her. What saved you?"

Mangos held up his goblet. Talgon took it, turning it over in his hand. "What is this?"

"Half a golden pearl," Mangos answered. "Hollowed out and made into a goblet."

"Incredible!" Talgon examined the goblet, wonder on his face. "You could never be poisoned while you have this. I've never heard of such a thing!"

"What chalice is more unique or valuable?" Mangos said. "I do you great *honor*." He loaded the last word with irony, and Talgon flinched. "Let's talk honor and guarantees of safety."

Talgon drew a deep breath and let it out in a gust. "There is nothing more to see," he told the clustered guests, and when they moved away,

turned to Mangos. "I know what you want. The only *Fedai* I have are my house guards. There are fifty. How many would you like?"

"All of them," Mangos said.

"You shall have them." Talgon waved Talia toward the kitchens, then shot a swift, malevolent glare at Bardor. "But," and he turned back to Mangos, "With them I buy my honor and your silence. Bardor may hold me in contempt, but I can't afford to cross him. Damn his blood."

Mangos nodded.

"We'll make arrangements when I hire new guards." He thrust the goblet back in Mangos's hand and spun to leave, as if not wanting to draw more attention to their conversation or just wanting to put the episode behind him.

Kat laughed and leaned in so others couldn't hear. "And did you plan to poison his daughter, or did you just get lucky?"

"His daughter?" Mangos glanced at the kitchen door, but of course Talia wasn't to be seen.

"She didn't get that nose from her mother," Kat said. "Talgon wouldn't be the first man to have children in the slave's quarters. He loves her, though he hid it well."

Mangos leaned forward and lowered his voice. "You think it lucky I poisoned his daughter?"

"You didn't," Kat said. "Bardor did—and it was careless of him to drop his fire gun like that. That might have been too clever, by the way. If Talgon wasn't so angry about his daughter, he might have suspected a frame-up."

"It showed Bardor was near the lemons," Mangos said. He changed the subject. "The goblet switch nearly killed me."

"I thought you knew about the chance. The crowd at the first banquet was quite rowdy and free-spirited with their drinking. It's up to the toaster if they call for the switch or not. Sometimes they switch, sometimes they don't."

"Did you get what you wanted from the Bursa?" he asked.

"Yes." Her expression didn't change but her eyes exulted, and Mangos knew she had accomplished something important. "We must be ready to move quickly now."

Several days later, they were ready to move north. They would march, but equipment and supplies would follow on wagons. Jalani, the

Alnessi merchant, was only too willing to aid their cause.

Mangos waited in the study to do one last task.

Kat stuck her head in, Grel behind her. "We're ready to march," she said.

"I'm not ready quite yet," Mangos said. "Grel," he called. "I'd like a word."

Grel came in. "What?"

"You won't be going north with us," Mangos said.

Mangos drew his dagger and, with a quick step, drove it into Grel's stomach and up. "Somehow Bardor knew Kat wanted *Fedai*. He even knew to delay me, not Kat, so he could buy them. Somebody told him."

Grel doubled over and looked up, his eyes wide. He looked toward Kat, but she didn't move to help him.

"I talked to the slave who told Bardor about Kat," Mangos said. "She confirmed my suspicions.

"The slave girl gave away Kat's identity because she had no hope," he went on. "But you betrayed the hope that stands before you. This is your *Queen*."

Grel fell to his knees, still clutching his wounded stomach.

"By the gods of Eastwarn, you're Alnessi. You're supposed to be faithful. Three years of burdens don't change that." Mangos snorted his contempt. "Kat deserves better than you. *Alness* deserves better than you."

Grel's eyes held his answer, an expression of sadness, remorse, and helplessness, but also defiance. He opened his mouth, moved it as if unsure what to say, or just struggling to speak. Finally, he gave up with a slight shrug and jiggle of his head. He collapsed completely, reaching out with one bloody hand while he kept the other pressed to his stomach.

Mangos wiped his dagger and re-sheathed it. "Now, I'm ready to march."

Kat nodded, her expression thoughtful. "You are indeed ready."

Trapped in the Loop

In the Current Time

Mangos stood on the small rise of grey schist at the neck of the Loop. The river All ran deep and swift around him. The field formed by the Loop was coarse sand and gravel, sometimes interrupted by sawgrass, sometimes by the underlying schist pushing upward. Makeshift scaffolds stood in the center of the field. A dozen bodies, or parts of bodies, hung from the scaffolds.

"Kill the birds if they won't give up their meal," Siln ordered from behind him. "Nasty things," he added, stopping beside Mangos and pointing to the carrion hawks perched on the bodies. "We never had them in Alness until Rhygir came. They're drawn by death and will fight to defend the food they claim." As the first soldiers of Kat's army approached the scaffolds, the hawks flapped their wings and squawked their indignation.

Mangos nodded his understanding as he and Siln surveyed the Loop. It was nice to have one of the few experienced Alnessi commanders so close. He was sure to be able to answer Mangos's questions.

The men fanned out across the field, pausing to look down. Now Mangos noticed the bones strewn about, as well as pieces of faded cloth and rusted iron: the bodies of Karn's Alnessi army and whatever wasn't worth looting.

Trees hedged the far banks, making a double barrier with the river. The only way in or out of the Loop was over the neck of land where Mangos stood.

It seemed crazy they wanted to fight a battle here when every fiber of his body screamed: "Trap!"

"The river cannot be crossed?" he asked, though he knew the answer. He could *see* the answer. Near the shore, the water foamed around rocks or fallen trees, but further out it ran dark and smooth. He could *feel* the answer, too; the wind that stirred across the field carried the tale of its coldness.

"There is a ford several miles east," Siln said.

The carpet of bones showed how helpful that was.

"How many of Karn's army survived going into the river?" Mangos asked.

"Damned few."

"Let's form up ranks," Mangos said. "When the men are in position, I want markers laid for each squad. Each man must be able to find his place quickly. After that, form a detail and start to gather the dead."

The mounds of bones doubly disturbed Mangos. First, that they should be so large; they reached his waist, and when new bones were added, they clattered as they rolled down the sides. But secondly, thousands of men had followed Karn into this loop, and all that remained were these piles of bones that only came up to his waist.

A few hours' work, he thought, *will finish this task.*

He put his shoulder against one of the scaffolds and pushed. The post tipped, the end spraying sand as he ripped it loose. The whole scaffold twisted, the lashings broke, and it collapsed in a clatter of wood and bones.

"How do you deal with bodies in Alness?" he asked.

"Bury them, mostly," said Siln.

Mangos grunted. The land was too low here. If they dug graves, they'd hit water or schist, which they couldn't dig through anyway. "The Norfins consign them to the sacred river."

Siln grunted in turn. "That'd be easier, but it's never been the tradition. Nobody wants bodies fetching up on shore or cluttering up the bay."

The breeze picked up, turning the leaves on the trees. Mangos froze, straining to hear. For just a moment, he thought he heard a doleful moan, a mourning whistle as the wind whipped through the piles of bones.

What words would these dead wish to speak? Would they offer encouragement? Would they call for vengeance? Or would they shout warnings?

"The dead will favor us, buried or not," Siln murmured. "But this is a bad way to prepare for battle. It reminds the men how they died."

A soldier came forward with another armload of bones. He cradled them as a mother does her child. Arm and leg bones jutted out of the rib cage like bread loaves in a basket, and the skull balanced precariously on top. He lifted the skull with one hand as he gently lowered the rest of his burden onto the pile.

He stood looking at the skull, his face as expressionless as the one he held, but Mangos could almost read his mind. *Will this soon be me?*

The soldier set the skull atop the other bones. It wobbled and started to roll down the side. He steadied it, making sure it was stable before taking away his hand.

Satisfied, he turned and saw Mangos watching him. "When will the Rhygirians attack?" he asked.

"Soon," Mangos said. "They have scouts. They know we're here, and they think they know why. But not tonight."

The night air held just a hint of chill and carried enough moisture to tell Mangos there would be dew in the morning. The sky seemed abnormally black and the stars preternaturally bright. The sound of running water enveloped him, coming, as it did, from three sides.

He flipped a stone into the black water. The water claimed the stone, and the current erased both splash and waves. How many of Karn's men had thrown themselves into the river here, furthest from the neck of the loop?

"What are you doing?" Kat asked as she came up behind him.

"Making peace with how we came here in the noose of the river," he mused. "In case we should die."

"Is that what they're calling it?" Kat asked. "The noose of the river? It has a name, Cannai, but the noose is apt enough. Are you at peace with how you came here?"

"There are a few questions that trouble me," he said. "I agreed, but you chose the path."

Kat laughed. "Not such a bad analogy. If I were to say yes, I've been working toward this since the fall of Alness, would that answer your questions?"

Though he knew, Mangos was still amazed. He hadn't even suspected until recently, and there would be plans within plans that he didn't suspect even now.

"You might have told me," he said, though he wasn't really angry.

"Would you have helped? If I said every step I took was preparation to fight Rhygir?"

Mangos remembered first meeting Kat and how worn and dirty she looked. "I would have thought you mad."

"I had the resources I took away from Alness," Kat said. Her tone was mild, but held a hint of steel.

She had escaped Alness with her dagger, her clothes, and her life. She didn't mean any of those things. "You had more skill than the average refugee," Mangos observed. "Yet no more fame."

"I'm a princess," Kat said as if that explained her skill. "But I would not be Queen; my older brother Kel was to inherit the throne. I was tutored and trained to represent Alness, not to rule it. But I have an aptitude even my teachers did not suspect."

"Why hide it?"

"It is important that the heir to the throne be the most suited to sitting on it," Kat said. She smiled, "Or at least thought to be. It didn't bother me, for Kel would have been a fine king. Only Father knew the truth."

The smile fell from her face as she continued. "That is why, when only we remained, he threw me into the canal and turned to face Rhygir so I might escape. I'd have taken Rhygir in with me and gladly drowned us both, but there would have been none to redeem Alness."

She moved, drawing his attention. "Let's see to the men."

"One last question," Mangos said, thinking of something that occasionally puzzled him. Something he never dared ask. "Why don't men desire you?"

"Spells were cast on me to protect my virtue, magic that turns aside men's lust. Before the fall, it was mostly a formality, but since then, it has helped avoid… distractions." She looked him in the eye. "Perhaps when this is over, we'll have the spell removed."

Mangos smiled, not sure why, only that he felt he should. He knew he should want the spell removed, but he didn't *feel* it. He let out a short, ironic laugh. Yes, the spell was working.

Gravel crunched as Kat shifted her weight. "I'd like to check the mood of the men."

Mangos nodded.

The encampment was quiet—quieter than one would expect of so many soldiers. The men were uneasy; Mangos could feel it. Too many mutterings; too much staring into the darkness, away from the fires, away from their comrades.

"They think of death," Kat said.

"Then we should remind them of victory."

"Victory is never further away than in the dark of night." She fell silent, and the two weaved among the fires, dropping smiles and greetings until Kat stopped next to a soldier silently staring into his fire.

He was a bit older, maybe in his middle thirties. Lines of grief were etched deeply into his face. His beard, though dark, had streaks of grey.

His expression was bleak.

Kat stood next to him for a moment before asking, "Why do you fight?"

After a long pause, the man lifted his head so the firelight illuminated his face. "I fight," he said, "for Kat." He blinked. "Not you, Your Majesty, though I fight for you as well. My daughter Kat."

Mangos sharpened his ears to listen, as did the men around him. If the answer surprised Kat, she didn't show it.

"She shared your birthday, so of course we named her after you," the man said. "You turned twelve the year she was born." He smiled, though it was clear he was looking back at better times. "To a father's eyes, she was every bit as beautiful as her namesake."

He blinked and his eyes focused on Kat's face. "I failed her, Your Majesty. I won't fail you."

Kat closed her eyes. "No," she whispered. "I never thought you would." After a second, she rested her hand on his shoulder. He bowed his head and reached up to grasp her hand.

Provisional Council, One Week Previous

Mangos could tell an outburst was coming. Sure enough, as soon as Kat stopped speaking, Trentor exploded. "Leading this army into the Loop is madness!"

Trentor might understand fighting Rhygir's mercenaries, but he didn't understand tact.

Drex, Captain of Kat's *Fedai*, raised his eyebrows at the words, his hands straying to his sword. Siln, the most senior of the Alnessi, may have frowned—it was hard to tell because of all the scars on his face—but the soft *tsk* conveyed his feelings effectively. Clearly, neither approved of Trentor's outburst.

Mangos smiled. He wasn't offended, for he, too, had a hard time remembering Kat should be given the respect of a monarch.

Only a thin wall of canvas separated them from Kat's army of slaves, refugees, and (Mangos suspected) bandits and thieves. The tent, sides glowing from the afternoon sun, felt warm, but the heat didn't excuse Trentor's lack of respect.

Undeterred, Trentor bulled on. "There is no escape from the Loop, and you'll be outnumbered. Not only that, but Rhygir's men are all experienced mercenaries. Half our men have no experience, and those who do have only experienced a massacre. They're veterans by survival, not skill. They certainly haven't tasted victory, and probably wouldn't know what to do if it came near."

"Don't demean the men, Commander," Kat said, resting her hand on the paper-strewn table in front of her. "They are survivors and better—fighters."

"Then wait and gather more men. But for the sake of your claim and your army, stay out of the Loop."

"We can't wait," Kat said. "The Bursa will prevent Bardor from sending his *Fedai* to help Rhygir, but that may change. Besides," she added, smoothing a map with her hand and placing a small stone on the corner, "we currently have food, but my money is limited, and Alness can't support an army in the field."

"The people support you," Siln pointed out.

"The food they give us leaves less for themselves. The fact is Alness can't feed itself. If we can convince the farmers to plant a crop, we may be able to get a harvest this year. That won't happen if the war drags on."

"Rhygir's bold, but he's not a fool, Your Majesty." Trentor shook his head. "He didn't move against Karn until Bardor's *Fedai* arrived. He'll do the same thing now."

Kat smiled. "Not if we bait him."

"With respect. He's the sort to set traps, not fall into them." He didn't need to say, *that's how Karn fell*.

Drex snorted. All eyes turned to the stocky *Fedai*. He shifted and glanced down. "Your pardon, Your Majesty." As an officer, he still had his tongue, something the other *Fedai* lacked.

"Speak your mind," Kat said.

Drex looked up. "You can't have it both ways," he told Trentor. "Going into the Loop is suicide, but Rhygir will not recognize that? Her Majesty goes there to draw him away from the city walls."

"Rhygir won't be able to help himself," Kat agreed.

Mangos stirred, leaning forward. For years he had watched Kat's plans as they unfolded. He had never heard them beforehand, so never heard the note of absolute confidence that hers was the higher cunning.

If Kat said Rhygir would come to battle, Mangos believed her.

"He'll think we revisit the Loop to bury Karn's army," Kat said. "And once he knows we're there, he will act to serve us as he did Karn."

Siln ran a finger down one of the many scars on his face. "Perhaps this is not the best time, Your Majesty, but Karn was not a strong leader," he said.

"And what makes a strong leader?" Mangos asked. He wondered why Siln would bring this up, just before Kat was about to divulge her plans.

"The commander must help the men find peace and provide focus for the fighting. Battle plans mean little without the men's commitment."

Ah, Mangos thought. Questions of ability. But surely Siln did not question Kat.

Kat stared at Siln for a moment and then pointedly changed the subject. "What has happened in the Loop is past. This is what we will do in the future."

Siln cleared his throat.

Kat's eyes flashed. "Very well, Commander. You won't be diverted. Say your piece."

"You've worked a miracle gathering so many, and arming, and feeding them. From nothing, you have created hope. You have even recovered your father's crown."

"But—?" Kat asked, her voice even.

"There are men here who are not Alnessi."

Kat took a deep breath. "I see." She glanced at Mangos, flicked her eyes to Drex. "It's not Drex, is it?"

Mangos tightened, not consciously, but he felt all his muscles contract a little, and he realized he was frowning. They spoke of him! "Nothing has been said to me."

"Why should the men follow you?" Trentor burst out. "You're not Alnessi!"

"I am not Alnessi, either," Drex stated, in his deep, quiet voice.

"You do not command Alnessi," Trentor said. This was not true, for Kat had placed a battalion under his command in addition to his *Fedai*.

"The men follow well enough," Mangos said. "If *you* have a problem, I'm sure we can solve it." Fists, swords, or polybolos; any would be suitable, though he didn't say such aloud.

"It's not a question of nationality," said Siln. Trentor started to protest, but Siln talked over him. "Or really of ability, for you've done well." He cleared his throat. "I'm sorry, Your Highness, but this is a concern. Drex is a trained and experienced leader. Mangos is an adventurer. Will he know how to react when the unexpected happens, and he has men under his command?"

Mangos opened his mouth but realized nothing he said would matter. The decision was not his.

"He will do well," Kat said. "A man who keeps his head on dragonback will not lose it in battle. He cannot be 'just' a soldier. He is the Mongoose," she paused and gave her words a hint of irony with a smile. "He is famed for acts of reckless bravery, and the men admire him—whether you wish to admit it or not."

"As you say." He shot a look at Trentor that seemed to say, *I raised the point. Let it rest.*

Trentor looked ready to protest, but Siln frowned, and Kat glared at him. "Your concerns have been heard. Mangos will have the right wing," she said, her voice firm. "You will be with him, Siln. Make it work."

"Yes, Your Majesty." Siln's voice was respectful, not challenging. "Once Rhygir has us trapped in the Loop, how do you propose to kill him?"

"The Loop is wide enough to draw up lines of battle," Kat said, "like this." She ran her finger across the map.

The commanders leaned forward to read the markings.

"That's madness!" burst out Trentor. Drex looked troubled but remained silent.

"Your Majesty," Siln said. "The center must be strongest, for if it breaks, the army is divided and easily defeated."

"That's the way battles are traditionally fought," Kat agreed. Her eyes flashed anger and the muscles in her jaw flexed. "But we don't want to beat Rhygir, we want to *destroy* him. He can *not* be allowed to retreat into the city.

"So," she continued, "when Rhygir attacks, the center will retreat—not break." She held up a hand to forestall Trentor's comment. "Only the center will retreat. The flanks will swing in and encircle Rhygir's army."

The men stared for a moment. Siln chuckled. "That's clever," he said.

"Here now," protested Trentor. "That might work if the center only gives way. But if it breaks entirely instead of encircling the enemy, you'll have a stronger enemy between your divided forces.

"That's why I'll command the center," Kat said. "I'll have the *Fedai* on the left with support." She nodded to Drex, who nodded back. "And, of course, on the right, Mangos and Siln."

"It's a good plan," Siln allowed, "though I have misgivings." He flashed a meaningful look at Mangos but didn't raise that point again.

"The chiefest is your insistence that Bardor will be unable to send his *Fedai* to assist Rhygir."

"I have the Bursa's word," Kat answered. "He owes me."

"He owes you a lot, including his life," Mangos said in a low voice.

"The men won't like it," Trentor said. "A few of them survived Karn's fall, and all of them know about it." He jabbed his finger at the Loop of land on the map. "That's cursed land. There's no guarantee you can defeat Rhygir anyway. And if he has five thousand *Fedai* reinforcements…"

"There have been no reports of Bardor's *Fedai* landing," Kat said. "I know Karn didn't know they had landed either. But we must seize this chance. We must trust the Bursa to keep the *Fedai* in Alomar."

"I like it," Siln said. "I was in the Loop with Karn, Your Majesty, and I'll follow you there, misgivings or no. Drex?" he asked. "What are your thoughts?"

"It's a good plan. I'd rather not fight in that trap, but the lure must be strong enough to draw Rhygir out of the city. We can't count on the Bursa forever."

"Not forever," Kat agreed. "But long enough to destroy Rhygir."

The men nodded. "I think we can count on the Bursa long enough for that," Siln said.

But so quietly that Mangos barely heard him, Trentor muttered, "Your father fell because one man failed him."

Back in the Current Time

A hunting horn blared, driving open Mangos's eyes and the sleep from his mind. An attack, and those were the inner pickets! He stumbled to his feet. The horn blared again, a short, truncated blast.

"Get up!" he shouted to the sleeping men around him. "Arm yourselves!" They weren't ready. An early attack could ruin Kat's plan.

Shouts of confusion and fear broke the morning twilight.

"Fall into your squads!" Mangos shouted. "Form ranks!"

Men rose from their rest and started to rush about. They were figures of grey in the half-light, hurrying in no specific direction, their movements marked by panic.

"Gods damn it!" snarled Siln, appearing from the confusion next to him. "This is why we had outer pickets, so we wouldn't be surprised like this!"

Mangos reached out and plucked up a man rushing past. "Form ranks!"

he bellowed, throwing the man toward the line markers. "Form ranks!" he roared again, louder.

Here and there, men ran forward, taking their positions, facing the neck of the Loop and the forest beyond, which was still dark with the shadows of night.

Mangos grabbed another man and shook him loose from his panic. "Take a moment—arm yourself. Then take your position."

Men milled by the river, trapped by their fear and the swiftly moving water. Mangos pushed amongst them, shouting orders, yelling encouragement, shoving them away from the water.

"I hate fighting before breakfast!" he yelled. "And by the gods of Eastwarn, Rhygir will regret making me do it!"

Men cast incredulous looks at him.

"He's cost me a couple hours of sleep as well!" Mangos shouted. "And I'll take that price from his hide!"

The men started moving now, and Mangos risked going to the lines. They were thin, but more men came and filled in the holes. Drex's *Fedai* held their position on the left in solid lines, armed and waiting. Men rushed to the center—whatever Kat had done there worked.

Shouting Rhygirians burst from the forest.

"Hold the lines!" *Hold the lines while the rest of the men fall in*, he pleaded silently.

More and more yelling Rhygirians followed the first. The first flowed over the rise at the neck and into the Loop proper.

The foremost Rhygirian, a tall thin man whose feet kicked up small stones as he ran, outstripped the rest. He was the tip of the spear, screaming at them, and Mangos couldn't help but watch.

The Rhygirian neared the center of the Alnessi lines. He lifted his spear as he charged. But, at the last moment, a huge, shield-bearing Alnessi stepped forward, braced his feet, and drove the shield into the Rhygirian. The Rhygirian rebounded with a crash of metal. The Alnessi roared, and the rest of the Rhygirian attack struck home.

Mangos wiped sweat from his brow. The sun crested the trees to his right, the Alnessi line held, and the Rhygirians regrouped across the neck. "They'll not retreat," he said. "And a good thing."

"Why is that?" Siln asked.

"We can't kill them if they retreat."

291

TRAPPED IN THE LOOP

Kat moved among the Alnessi, offering congratulations and thanks, words of encouragement or condolences as needed. When she reached Mangos she said, "I'm counting on you, Mangos."

"We're ready," he answered. He lowered his voice. "Can you hold the center?"

"We'll find out soon, won't we?" But she had a smile that eased his fears. "Be careful," she said and returned to the line.

The tone of the army had changed. They had survived the first onslaught. Their hatred ran cold and deep, but Mangos wanted it a roaring inferno.

He ambled forward, careful to keep his carriage relaxed. Very deliberately, he turned his back to the regrouping enemy.

"These men," he pitched his voice to carry and lifted his arm to point behind him toward the Rhygirians, "took your country. These men slew your King. These men stole your livestock and your money. They burned your homes! They," Mangos let his voice rise as he went on, "raped your wives and daughters! They killed your sons!"

He dropped his voice back down. "They're here to kill you. But!" And now he shouted, "Your Queen has given them to you instead! Soon you will not be asked to hold firm. Soon you will be asked to KILL!

"Ours is the easy task! Ours is the task for which you have prayed in the darkness of the night, for which you have lusted after each new indignity. They have seeded this ground with the bones of your kin—our task is to water it with their blood!"

The men lifted a cheer, and Mangos feared they would carry the fight to the Rhygirians. "Remember your orders, and the day shall be ours!"

"You've a knack for that," Siln said as the two looked over the army. Another roar rose, this time from the center of the line where Kat addressed the men there. "If only I hadn't seen so much death," Siln said, "I would feel better about this."

Mangos clapped him on the back. "Death's had his claws in you before, but you've always pulled free."

Siln chuckled without humor, running a finger down one of the scars on his face. "He left his marks, though."

At the neck of the Loop, Rhygir formed his troops. His silvecite armor flashed in the early morning sun. Teriz's white Kingfisher armor almost seemed a shadow as the traitor of Alness helped Rhygir prepare for another assault.

No attacking pell-mell this time. The Rhygirians still outnumbered the Alnessi; by their lines, instead of a striking like a spear, they would hit like a hammer.

Rhygir shouted, and his men moved forward. They did not yell. They came forward for the grim purpose of killing, and the Alnessi waited with the same thing in mind.

Within minutes, the armies grappled with each other. The lines held as men hacked; pushing, stabbing, slashing at any exposed weakness. The wounded fell and were trampled and, with the dead, driven into the sandy soil.

The weight of numbers began to tell. The Alnessi began to give ground.

"Hold!" Mangos bellowed. "For the love of Alness—hold!"

The men dug in; the right stopped falling back. Across the field, the left had done the same, but the center still retreated. The line began to stretch until it formed a 'U,' the men with their backs to the river.

"Hold!" Mangos shouted again.

The Rhygirians rushed the center, seeing the weakness, striving to break the line. Kat fought desperately; the men around her planted their feet and held their ground.

A horn call split the sounds of battle. Mangos's heart picked up. It called again, Kat signalling to spring the trap.

"Attack!" screamed Mangos, putting his words into action. He drove himself forward, clubbing a mercenary to the ground and thrusting his sword at the next. He didn't pause to see if the men followed; he could tell by their yells.

Like the boom of a drum, the word "KILL!" rang over the Loop. The left wing, led by Drex's *Fedai*, shattered the Rhygirians before them and swung out and around. Their chant rolled over the Loop, striking like another blow as they attacked.

"KILL!"

"Kill!" Mangos shouted, directing his men with his sword. They had momentum now. Men swarmed past, hacking and trampling the enemy, swinging wide and falling on the main body of Rhygirians from the rear.

Alnessi anger and hatred flowed like the Rhygirian's blood. Like carving meat, Mangos thought—mad butchers carving meat.

Panic rippled through Rhygir's ranks as they realized the Alnessi surrounded them. Rhygir kept pressure on the Alnessi center, but Teriz tried to turn the men, tried to face the new assault on their rear.

TRAPPED IN THE LOOP

Mangos paused to survey the field. Kat held firm in the center though Rhygir pressed hard. Mangos couldn't see Drex, but the *Fedai* waded over piles of dead and dying Rhygirians. His own men pushed forward, leaving him behind the line. Once again, he found Siln next to him.

"That's someone worth killing!" Mangos pointed his bloody sword at Teriz. The Kingsfisher towered over the men around him, a bulwark amongst the beleaguered Rhygirians. Men rallied around him, his white armor drawing them like a banner.

"Not a simple task." Siln wiped blood from his face. "There's only two men in that scrum I fear, and he's one."

No need to ask of the other—Rhygir's silvecite armor was streaked with blood, but Mangos doubted it was his. Rhygir no longer pressed the Alnessi center; he had pulled his men back a few paces and was trying desperately to organize a defense. Teriz and Rhygir knew death; they knew it approached but would not go peacefully.

Siln clapped Mangos on the back and grinned. "A far cry from earlier, eh?" Their men exulted, years of frustration being swept away in brutal joy.

"By the gods of Eastwarn, yes!"

Siln threw his head back and laughed, a mad sound. "Kill them all!" he shouted. "Today, we reclaim Alness!" The nearest men roared approval. Somebody started singing, and more voices joined in. The song spread, and Kat's men slew to the sound of the Alnessi anthem.

The encirclement grew smaller, the Rhygirians more densely packed as the Alnessi kept attacking. The Alnessi outnumbered the Rhygirians now. Kat's plan had worked exactly as she promised.

Mangos started to move along the lines, his gaze fixed on Teriz. Everything would be better if the Traitor of Alness died.

Before he could attack Teriz, a hand grabbed Mangos from behind. He spun, sword raised. An Alnessi scout let go and stumbled back, shouting words that were lost in the din of battle.

Mangos started to turn back, but the scout made to grab him again. This time, the scout pointed while he shouted. Still unable to hear, Mangos followed the man a safe distance from the fighting.

"The *Fedai* are coming!" the scout shouted.

"What?" The words made no sense.

"The *Fedai* are coming!" the scout shouted again, pointing.

The words struck him like physical blows. Impossible, yet a glance west confirmed men marching along the river. Bardor had unleashed his death in the north. Again.

"By the gods of Eastwarn…" There was nothing else to say.

The words from the council echoed in his mind, *one man failed*. Then it had been Teriz, this time the Bursa.

I shouldn't have been fighting. The scout could have found me faster; we'd have more time if I weren't fighting.

He started to work, turning men, trying to organize squads, trying desperately to pull some order from the chaos the battle had become. Eventually he came to Siln and pulled the commander back, pointing to the ranks of *Fedai* rushing to Rhygir's rescue.

"Damn the Bursa!" Siln shouted.

Mangos shouted back. "We have to save the army!" Did Kat know? It was hard to tell.

Horns rang out from the woods. If she didn't know of the *Fedai* before, she did now. Hesitation rippled through the Alnessi forces.

The surviving Rhygirians cheered, and Rhygir immediately sprang forward. The *feel* of the air changed as momentum changed sides again.

"I'll take some men and try and keep part of the neck open," Mangos said. "You pull the men behind me and out of the Loop."

"What of the rest of the army?" Siln demanded. "We can't leave them!"

Mangos shook his head. The *Fedai* had reached the Loop and started to deploy across its neck. He needed to stop them. Already Kat's left flank was trapped and Rhygir again pressed the center. "We're not! We're opening an escape for as many as can make it!"

"Then I'll hold off the *Fedai*!"

"No!" Mangos shouted. He needed to act; the men had seen the *Fedai*, and Mangos could sense their fear. He couldn't let it overwhelm them. "Get as many men out as you can! Now!" He gathered men about him as he rushed to the east end of the Loop's neck.

The battle engulfed him as he crashed into the first ranks of the *Fedai*. "Stand firm for the Queen!" he shouted. "Every minute you stand is a comrade's life saved!"

He didn't know if any heard him, he didn't know how many lived. He didn't merely yell, not words of encouragement, not taunts, just a continuous yell that seemed to come not from his lungs, but from the movement of his body.

The *Fedai* fought fiercely. The battle pressed against him, pushing him back, pinching him away from the main action. For every lunge forward, he was driven two steps back until he found himself on the schist rise. While he had been fighting, the *Fedai* pushed past him and sealed the Loop—he was outside the lines and away from the fighting.

Few Rhygirians remained, but that didn't help the Alnessi. The *Fedai* owned the Loop and needed no other help imposing their will.

Some Alnessi had given up, had thrown down their arms and pleaded for mercy, but Rhygir and his remaining men butchered them where they knelt. The *Fedai* ground forward, slowed only by the need to kill the surrendering and wounded Alnessi.

Only at the river's edge did men still fight. Some of Kat's *Fedai* had drawn back from the left flank, and they mixed with the Alnessi to form a line with their backs to the river.

Where is Kat? Mangos rose onto the balls of his feet, craning to see better. *Please let her live.*

Bodies bobbed in the shallows, and the current swept more downstream. Alnessi threw themselves into the rushing water. Rhygir stationed men along the banks to push them back into the swift current if they tried to come ashore.

"I thought the *Fedai* wouldn't come north," said a voice at Mangos's side. He turned his head to see a dozen battered and bloody men who, like himself, the battle had temporarily forgotten.

"The gods hate us," said a bearded Alnessi, his voice hollow, shocked.

"Did she escape?" asked a third. "Is the Queen safe?"

There!

Kat stood knee-deep in the river All, mostly hidden by the men around her, fighting desperately to hold what remained of her army together. "She's alive," Mangos said.

"Do we die here?" asked the bearded man, and Mangos felt a wash of pride that they would stay and fight when escape lay open.

"Make your move," Mangos muttered under his breath. He would attack opposite her, mad as it seemed, and try to break the Rhygirian lines long enough for her to escape. "Show me where."

The lines of the Alnessi broke. A great roar went up from the throats of the Rhygirians and the *Fedai* as they poured amongst the defenders, cutting them down.

"No!" cried Mangos.

The river was pink with bloody foam and black with bodies as more and more men sought to escape the slaughter on shore. Some sank, some swirled away.

"The rapids downstream will pound them to jelly," said a wiry little man. "Gods help them all."

Fedai pressed Kat. Her own *Fedai* died as Bardor's overwhelmed them, leaving her, for a moment, fighting alone. She retreated a step, her foot plunging into the deep channel of the river. She toppled backwards, vanishing into the dark water.

Mangos gasped and took an involuntary step forward. "No." He would deny it all in a single word, but it wouldn't help.

A cold feeling settled into his stomach as he turned away. "Go east," he ordered the men. "Find Siln and get away from the Loop. Get men downstream. The Queen can swim."

"You can only go into the water so many times," the bearded man said, letting his voice trail off, his implication clear.

Before you don't come out.

The Redemption of Alness

Rain dripped from the trees, cold, bitter water that ran over the rocky ground to the river All; killing water that Mangos hated, whether in rain or river. Dead men littered the riverbank to his right, dozens, hundreds, perhaps thousands. Kat's army.

Yesterday's battle had been a disaster. Since first light, he had prowled the banks, searching for Kat. She was one of many who had gone into the river, and nobody had seen her since.

Seeing a cluster of bodies, Mangos picked his way to the water's edge.

"There you are."

Mangos jumped, reaching for his sword. He relaxed as Siln approached the river, ducking under sodden branches.

"We sent what survivors we could south," Siln said. "A couple hundred is all. There are a few more wounded hidden in the woods."

"You seem to have things in hand," Mangos said, not really paying attention. He couldn't see all the bodies in the tangle so picked up a branch and prodded the mass until it broke apart. The current grabbed the bodies, pulling them into the main channel and downstream, but Mangos could tell none of them were Kat.

"We are not safe. Rhygir will hunt down the survivors."

"He has no army," Mangos said. He moved downriver, pausing to watch a body floating past from upstream.

"He has the *Fedai*."

"Yes, damn him, but he came twenty minutes from death yesterday. He needs to control the city, and the *Fedai* aren't known for their woodscraft. He'll stay close to the city for a couple days."

"You don't know he's going to sit tight," Siln protested.

"Don't you have scouts checking?" Mangos grabbed an overhanging branch and leaned over the river to get a better look at a body caught under a fallen branch. It wasn't Kat.

"A couple. We don't have enough—damn it, Mangos, you must come! For the sake of the remaining men, we must decide what to do."

"The men are few, and you can see to their needs," Mangos said. Another body floated past. "By the gods of Eastwarn," Mangos muttered, "I haven't found a live one yet."

"Mangos." Siln's voice had a note that made Mangos pause. "If Kat is dead, you *must* come."

"Very well. For a little while, then I will resume searching. Kat *can* swim."

"I know she can," Siln said. He led Mangos away from the river.

The leaves hung heavy with water, twitching under the rain, but nothing else moved. The light, filtered through grey clouds and green leaves, gave the forest a morbid pallor: whether sickly or deathly, Mangos couldn't decide.

Siln led him to a thick copse of trees. He drew aside some cut branches, revealing a guard and an opening into the interior of the copse.

It was hard to tell how many men crowded into the open area. Fifty, maybe sixty, lay wounded or exhausted. A few turned their heads to watch him; most didn't bother. Wet and muddy, they were a dispirited lot.

Trentor lay propped against a tree, his leg stretched out and swathed in bloody rags—bandages, if they could be called that. "You finally tramped in."

"You could have started without me," Mangos said. "Somebody needs to be looking for your monarch."

"We are," muttered Trentor. "*She's* dead."

"Have you seen her body?" Mangos demanded.

"No, but I saw her go into the river, and you can only go into the water so many times before you don't come out."

"She can swim, damn it!"

"Mangos," said Siln. He sounded tired and without hope. "We sent two hundred men south. There are fifty-two here. They all deserve the best decision we can make."

It was hard to argue with that; and also, what to do about Alness?

But most importantly, where was Kat, and was she all right?

"Commander," said the guard quietly. "Somebody is coming. One of ours, but somebody else is with him."

"The Queen?" Mangos asked, his hopes rising.

"No, sir, another man."

"Merchant, courtier, joker, fool," said Siln. "He must not know the battle's over."

Moments later, a scout entered the clearing. He looked around, settling his gaze on Mangos before giving his message. "This man says he's looking for the Queen." He jerked his thumb over his shoulder.

"Aren't we all," Mangos muttered.

"He says he has something for her, but he isn't carrying anything." The scout stepped aside to let the man step forward.

Mangos recognized him. "Naan," he said. He didn't know why a Pythean smith should be in Alness. They had already delivered their contract. "We've lost the armor you sent."

"And the men wearing it," Trentor muttered.

"I'd hoped to get here before the battle," Naan said. "I came as soon as I could, but the last part of the shipment wasn't finished." He looked around the clearing. "Where's Kat?"

Mangos avoided the question. "Shipment? I don't see anything."

"I hid it," Naan said with a sly smile. "I didn't want to be carrying it in case I met the wrong people."

"What if somebody finds it?"

"That won't happen," Naan said. "Although," he added, "they may chance on the mule. I better go get it."

The men were quiet as Mangos moved quickly among them. He offered a few words of encouragement, but mostly he wanted to know what he dealt with.

Damn Siln, Mangos thought. Why had he sent the able men south? Now they had no way to move the wounded. And why was he here? If he died with the wounded, who would lead the able?

Mangos summoned the scout to him. "Go fetch the rest of the men. We will *all* fall back, but we're not leaving our wounded."

He set those men who were able to fashioning crutches and litters to help the wounded travel, and as scouts returned with news, he sent them back out to keep watch on the enemy and search for other survivors.

As he sent out one such man, he said, as he had told all the others, "You must also look for the queen. She must be found."

"She is here!"

Everybody started at the deep voice. Drex strode through the opening, past the astonished guard. Three strangers followed, and then Kat.

"By the gods of Eastwarn," Mangos swore. He didn't know what else to say. He embraced her to make sure she wasn't an illusion. She held him a moment before pulling away.

"Mangos," she said, and for a moment her face lit with a warm smile, and he could hear relief in her voice.

She was alive: yes. Unscathed: no. She looked like parchment that has been wadded in a ball and then stretched flat: rumpled and smudged, though her smudges were bruises. Her hair lay in tangled heaps about her shoulders, almost as if it were as dispirited as the men about them.

But when she released him, her eyes turned hard and cold, and she looked in no way beaten.

"What happened?" he asked. "How could Bardor send his *Fedai* north?"

Kat shook her head. "Maybe the Bursa failed, maybe he never tried. It doesn't matter now." She looked at the men crowding into the clearing. "So few."

"Who are these men?" Trentor demanded.

Mangos realized three more men had followed Kat into the clearing, making six strangers. They were Hafizi, but why they would be in the rain-drenched Alnessi forest instead of their desert city, he couldn't guess.

"I found them wandering the woods," Kat said.

"A trick of Teriz," Trentor said. He pulled himself up, wincing as he moved his wounded leg. "Hafizi have no business in Alness."

That's not true, Mangos thought. *The Hafizi have always had ties with Alness.* The King's elite guard, the Kingsfishers, had been Hafizi, and other Hafizi had served in the city. But Teriz, one of the Kingsfishers, had betrayed the King. *I wonder what they want.*

The Hafizi exuded confidence, even the youngest, who could scarce grow a beard. Their wet desert robes clung to them, and Mangos wondered if the youngest had ever seen rain before.

"They are here to kill you," Trentor said.

"Their honor won't allow assassination," Mangos said.

"And the Kingsfishers are completely dependable," Trentor shot back.

"All but one," Mangos said. But one was enough. Trentor had made his point.

The eldest Hafizi spoke, his accented words firm, respectful. "It is our honor to form the Queensfishers, if the Queen will have us."

"I would not answer them earlier," Kat said.

"No!" exclaimed Trentor. "It was your father's Hafizi who betrayed us to Rhygir."

Mangos had a flash of inspiration. "This is their atonement," he said.

The Hafizi who had spoken nodded.

"Still, no," Trentor insisted.

"Only a fool turns away friends," Mangos said.

Trentor turned to Kat. "Your father believed that." He pointed at the Hafizi as he spoke. "And he was betrayed by them. You placed your faith in the Bursa, and he betrayed you." He scowled. "I have even heard more than one true-born Alnessi betrayed you in Alomar."

"Yet I have survived," Kat said, and heads around the clearing turned toward her. "I'll not quit, and I'll not die until Rhygir is dead and Alness redeemed."

She lowered her voice and addressed the Hafizi. "What is your name?"

"Elzemar, Your Majesty."

"What if I don't accept you, Elzemar?"

"We have sworn to serve you," said Elzemar. "We have no honor apart from that." He raised his head. "As it is your honor to redeem Alness with Rhygir's death."

"You cannot trust them!" Trentor said.

"According to you, I cannot trust anyone," Kat said.

"I learned something of honor in Hafiz," Mangos said. "Teriz's betrayal stains them all. What," he asked the kneeling men, "convinced you of Teriz's guilt?"

"One day while Inark sat in his darkness, he heard a voice," Elzemar said. He looked at Kat. "A voice from Alness that was supposed dead."

Mangos recalled Inark, the former Kingsfisher, in his home in Hafiz— old, blind, and crippled, lamenting his loss of honor because he could do nothing for Alness. "He recognized Kat's voice."

"He did not credit his ears," Elzemar said. "Later, we learned she was not dead. Inark said the honor of Hafiz required we provide Queensfishers." He gestured with his hand indicating, *and here we are.* "We are all kin of Inark."

"Why take a chance for six men?" Trentor asked.

"I'd take them," Mangos said.

Kat nodded. "I agree. In better times, there was an investiture ceremony. For now, I will just offer my congratulations and thanks."

All the Hafizi seemed to grow a little larger. "You give us our honor," Elzemar said. "It will make us strong in your service."

Kat nodded. "Now, let us talk of our options."

"We have no army," Siln pointed out.

"Neither does Rhygir," Kat said.

"Just five thousand *Fedai*," snarled Trentor. "Have you forgotten what they can do?"

"I'll never forget what they've done," Kat said, her eyes flashing. "But most of Rhygir's mercenaries lie dead in the Loop. That much, at least, we accomplished."

Mangos scratched his face, his mind racing. Clearly, Kat needed to neutralize the *Fedai*. He couldn't see how.

"The *Fedai* man Alness's walls," he said. What did that mean? It meant Kat wasn't strong enough to storm the city. But it also meant the *Fedai* weren't elsewhere. It made the city a shell, but one they couldn't break. And Kat didn't have enough men to beat the *Fedai*, no matter where they were.

Kat turned to Drex. "Tell them what you told me," she said.

Drex nodded. "The *Fedai* are placed under Rhygir's command. They will also obey Teriz, but no one else."

"What happens if Rhygir and Teriz are dead?" Mangos asked, beginning to see what Kat meant.

"They will return to Alomar," Drex said. "Bardor does not trust any others among the Rhygirians."

So Rhygir can't hold Alness without the *Fedai*, and the *Fedai* won't remain if Rhygir is dead, Mangos reasoned. He raised an eyebrow. "Kill Rhygir?"

"*And* Teriz," Drex emphasized.

"Of course," Mangos smiled wryly. "I'd have done that anyway."

"Of course," Kat said, a small smile on her lips.

"And how will you do that?" Trentor demanded. "We can't possibly storm the walls."

Siln sighed. "Will you shut up? Find a way to do something instead of saying what we can't."

Mangos scratched his face, trying to hide his smile. "Rhygir and Teriz will be at the palace, in the lower city." He closed his eyes, conjuring an image of the upper flats where the wall encircled the upper city, the bowl-shaped slopes of the middle city, and the broad expanse of the lower city with its waterways linking to the harbor. "The canals," he said, opening his eyes.

304

"The Main Canal runs straight from the harbor to the Grand Plaza," Kat said. "Right to the Palace's doorstep." She ran her hand through her hair. "Pass the word, I want a harbor pilot, or a sailor if we don't have a pilot. Anybody who can enter the harbor at night."

They quickly found one, a hard, grey-haired man, exhausted but recovering. "I can get us in the harbor," he said. "Not exactly a harbor pilot, but I was wharfinger for the north quay." He tapped his front teeth as he thought. "It's dark at night, the moon is waxing crescent. We'll want to go soon. Unless you want to wait a month for it to work its way back down."

"No," Kat said immediately. "Rhygir will recruit hard to replace the men he lost. Time aides him more than us." She closed her eyes and sighed. She, too, looked exhausted.

"We must move quickly to get into the harbor, anyway," Mangos said. "Tonight. Tomorrow at the latest."

Kat turned to him. "Why?"

"We can't just sail in." That seemed obvious. "I'm not Alnessi, but this is what we face." He picked up a stick and began to sketch in the dirt. "The river All flows west." He sketched it in. "The city is on the north bank. Here are the river docks, which do no good because they're outside the wall and connected by road to the river gate—manned by *Fedai*."

The others nodded.

"Here, the All empties into the bay. The city's south wall extends into the bay, cutting it in half and forming the harbor on its north side." Mangos added the wall to his map. "The river current runs like this," he drew wavy lines out to the sea, "but a flood tide runs in."

Mangos looked at the wharfinger. "Unless I miss my guess, you can float something down the river, and if you catch the rising tide *inside* the wall, ride back into the harbor itself."

"Aye, it happens," the wharfinger said. "Fallen trees mostly, but we spot 'em quickly and haul 'em out. It's right under the wall. You can't be thinking about trying to get in the city that way. You'd be spotted instantly."

"If we hurry, we can," Mangos said. "There's a couple thousand dead bodies headed toward the sea right now, and nobody on the wall will notice a few live ones amongst them." He paused to look up at the others. "We can only take the strongest men. The rest should help move the wounded to safety."

"That's a bold plan," Siln said, looking at Kat. "Do we do it?"

"Tonight," Kat said. She favored Mangos with a smile. "Well done."

"Rhygir worries me," Mangos admitted. "He has that damned silvecite armor."

"I think I can help there." Naan had returned, leading a mule. He lifted a hand in greeting. "Forgive me, Your Majesty," he said to Kat, "for overhearing Mangos's statement. You seem to have lost your armor."

Mangos cursed. He had not noticed.

"It makes poor swim clothes," Kat said.

"Then this is timely indeed." He began to untie one of the many knots holding a wooden crate to the mule's packsaddle.

Mangos went to help him. Together they carried the crate to where Kat and the others stood. Kat leaned forward in anticipation.

Naan unbuckled the strap. He paused. "I'd be lying if I said I wasn't a little proud." He lifted the top off, revealing a suit of armor.

Words failed Mangos, and he could only stare. He prided himself on knowing his steel, and while he didn't know this, it sent a shiver down his spine.

An elusive shade of red, somewhere between burgundy and blood, steeped the steel. The color went deep, deeper than the steel was thick, and, coupled with the way the light shone on the surface, seemed to twist reality.

Naan picked up the helm. "Dragon steel," he said. "Forged with dragon fire, quenched in dragon blood." He flicked the helm and it chimed like a bell.

Mangos blinked. He had never heard a helm sound like *that*.

Naan tossed the helm to Kat. It seemed to float through the air, and Kat caught it without apparent effort. "It's light," she said.

"Lighter than silvecite," Naan agreed, "and stronger."

Suddenly, Kat started to laugh. "Naan, your reputation shall exceed Marin's."

"It will. But only because you gave us the dragons and a question to answer." He smiled slyly. "With this, you can match Rhygir's armor."

The cold ate through Mangos's flesh and settled to gnaw on his bones. Experience told him he should move to try to stay warm, but he couldn't do that while pretending to be dead. He couldn't even try to shift on the log so as to ride higher in the water. Somebody might wonder why a dead body would ride a log.

He could only curse the cold and the log so small it only kept him from sinking while staying hidden under his body.

Above, torches guttered on the walls of Alness. The orange light glinted off the helms of the *Fedai* who watched him and the corpses of Kat's army float past.

The current carried him close to the bank, well within bowshot. Suddenly, he scraped over something hard and slimy—and stopped. He was stuck.

He let his arm drift under him and felt the obstacle. His numb fingers were overly sensitive, sending him more pain than information, but he recognized the rough texture of bark. He had caught on a fallen tree.

He shifted his weight, trying to roll over the tree, but his float log held him back. His sack of armor, wrapped against the water and tied to the log, didn't help. The current pushed him, the log, and the bag against the tree, and he couldn't wriggle free without making it obvious he lived.

There was movement on the bank. A small group huddled together, women, maybe? The water in his ears made it hard to hear.

Mangos cursed, quietly. They mourned the dead! One of them was pointing to him, and he could hear their cries through the water.

Why did the *Fedai* allow this? Perhaps Rhygir hadn't given precise orders, or the *Fedai* chose not to kill women. That was a small bit of humanity, but the women were drawing attention to him, and the *Fedai* watched them both.

He shifted his weight, and water surged over his head. He bit down panic as he bobbed up, still stuck. How long could he remain before Kat and the others floated too far ahead? Not knowing what became of him, they would not wait. He must get free quickly.

This is why I hate swimming, he thought.

Mangos rolled with the current, letting one arm loll while lifting his legs and pushing the tree with his other arm. The current spun him, freeing his legs and tugging at his body, which remained stuck. He was getting a lot of cursing done this night.

Suddenly, a white limb flashed in his vision as something struck him, knocking him loose. By inches, the current began to pull him free, and Mangos looked over to see what struck him.

Almost touching his head, the bloodless face of one of Kat's soldiers stared, unblinking, mouth agape. Mangos sucked in his breath in surprise, taking in a mouthful of water, and then he was free, floating away from the corpse that had knocked him loose.

"Get the men," Kat whispered as they knelt behind one of the many piles of debris where the quay hit the shore. "We've waited too long already."

Most of the men were spread the length of the quay, watching for any more that might ride the tide in while others stole skiffs.

Mangos ran, crouched over, dashing from broken crates to piles of refuse, trying to blend into anything that would hide him. He couldn't count on the darkness for concealment; the eastern sky was already turning grey.

They would attack with the men they had; they could not wait for more. He whispered, "Head to the skiffs," as he reached each man. They did, some reluctant to leave their posts, casting glances at the water hoping to pull one more comrade from the bay.

Thirty men, Mangos thought. *Thirty wet, cold men to take the city*. He thought of the women along the river and how the *Fedai* hadn't killed them. Perhaps the *Fedai* did have more humanity than the mercenaries. Perhaps they would return to Alomar if Rhygir and Teriz died. He snorted. *To hell with that. I'd give them their freedom, if they stayed and fought for Alness.* He'd have to talk to Kat about the idea.

Three skiffs remained of the dozens that had once taken cargos from the deep-water ships to the shops in the lower city. Kat stood in the first skiff, six men already at the oars. Mangos climbed in, followed by eight more men, who crouched on the broken cargo racks in the middle of the skiff.

"To the palace," Kat commanded, "and quickly."

The man in the furthest seat, who claimed the title Stroke, gave a quiet order, and the skiff leapt forward. Mangos staggered at the sudden acceleration. The other boats lagged behind, their rowers lacking experience and co-ordination.

The water of the canal was perfectly flat. Tendrils of mist rose, twisting in the pre-dawn light. Nobody spoke, except the Stroke, who used a calm, quiet voice that didn't carry beyond the gunwales.

Kat stood in the bow, her armor dull red, more like blood in the half-light. Ahead, the Palace rose, growing larger and larger as the rowers drove the skiff faster than a man could run.

"Can you find him in there?" Mangos asked.

Kat turned her head. "We won't have to," she answered. "They'll have seen us." She pointed up, and Mangos didn't doubt there were watchers on the palace roof.

"But wouldn't it be smarter to barricade themselves in the Palace until help arrives?"

"I grew up in that Palace," Kat said. "I know every corridor, every secret passage, and every refuge. It takes an army to secure that place, and Rhygir no longer has one." She turned to look ahead again. "We can hope he stays inside, but Teriz knows better and will tell him."

As they neared the Grand Plaza, they slowed and angled toward the canal wall.

"In two, hold her up," said the Stroke. Two more strokes, and the rowers squared their oars in the water. The boat's speed dropped. "Way enough."

The men docked their oars just as the skiff banged into the canal gate. "Sorry," muttered the Stroke.

Kat leapt up next to the gate. Mangos followed. The drop on the plaza side of the gate was ten feet or more, enough to show the water would be over a man's head when it was flooded.

But the plaza was not flooded, and hadn't been for some time, for the stones were still stained from the dead who had piled there. All around the outside, steps led up from the plaza to an esplanade. To their left, another set of steps led up to the great doors of the Palace.

"Karn died in this plaza," Mangos said to no one in particular.

"You," Kat pointed to two of the rowers. "Move the skiff so the others can dock." She lowered her voice, and Mangos lost the words as she walked them over the canal gate and he gathered the other men. She rejoined him as the rowers moved the skiff and took positions on each end of the gate.

The palace doors crashed open and dozens of men boiled down the steps. Mangos drew his Marin sword. "Kill them quickly." It would take time for reinforcements to arrive from the city wall, but Rhygir would not come out until he had no other choice. He had sent these men to buy time.

Mangos and Kat led the way off the canal gate and into battle.

Mangos stood panting, sweating from exertion as blood ran down his sword. Mercenaries lay sprawled across the palace steps and about the esplanade. Ten of Kat's men lay dead with them, but the way to the palace was open.

"You said you could hunt him out?" Mangos asked Kat.

There was movement in the palace doorway, and Teriz stepped out, followed by Rhygir and another swarm of men. Teriz wore his white Kingsfisher armor, and Rhygir shone; his silvecite mail a bright spot in the still, dull light.

"No need," Kat said, "here they are. Can you kill Teriz?"

"I'm looking forward to it," Mangos replied.

"We are outnumbered again, Your Majesty," Siln said.

"Just kill his men," Kat said, her gaze on Rhygir. "I'll kill Rhygir."

"I was more concerned we couldn't prevent his men from aiding him," Siln said.

"None shall interfere," Elzemar said. "We shall keep them from your back."

"That's all I ask," Kat said.

Mangos, his eyes locked on Teriz, gestured with his sword for the giant to come down to the esplanade to fight him.

"Most men are smart enough to fear me," Teriz's voice rumbled from above.

Mangos remembered Celzez, lying dead in the sand in Hafiz; Karn, his head held so he could not look away as a child was slain before him; and Jalani, as she told of the death of Prince Kalin at the fall of Alness. *I may never get a better chance to do something worthwhile*, he thought.

Teriz came down the palace steps, holding his sword before him. Most men would wield it two-handed, but Teriz swung it easily in one. The enamel had flaked off his armor in places, revealing the steel beneath. In spite of the dents and rents in his mail, Teriz moved smoothly. The armor had served him well, and he remained uninjured.

"You're not Alnessi," Teriz said as he approached. "Why do you fight?"

"I should school you?" Mangos asked, incredulous. "You, a Sandfisher and a Kingsfisher, don't know honor?"

"Honor is what my right arm can take," Teriz replied. "Blood, gold, and glory." He attacked, swinging his great blade in a short arc and recovering before Mangos could counter.

Mangos turned to keep Teriz in front of him. It brought Kat and Rhygir into view. The two sparred, their weapons flashing. Kat moved faster, Ryhgir looked stronger. Both fought with supreme skill.

Teriz attacked again; this time Mangos parried. The impact of their meeting sent shivers through his arm. Few men were stronger than Mangos, but Teriz was, and he used his strength well.

Mangos ducked away from another attack. Teriz moved quickly, but Mangos moved away, content to avoid the rush and grab another look at Kat and Rhygir.

Kat's sword clanged off Rhygir's arm, stymied by his silvecite rerebrace. She leapt back and began to probe more carefully.

Mangos swept up his sword and attacked, cutting high and stepping forward as Teriz stepped back, then cutting low on the backswing. Kat's problem, he thought, was she didn't have the strength to crack Rhygir's armor, no matter how good her sword.

Teriz attacked and turned him so he faced the city. He had no time to worry about Kat as he became engrossed in the rhythm of his own combat.

"You *dared* ruin this city," Mangos growled through gritted teeth. "You *dared* betray your people." He matched his words to his strokes, each "dare" crashing with a blow. "You *dared* wear the armor of your shame."

"Yes!" shouted Teriz, swinging a blow that sent Mangos reeling. "I dare all that." He followed with another blow and suddenly Mangos was staggering back, his arm numb and ears ringing.

Gathering himself together, Mangos parried and dodged, trying to get feeling back in his hand. He gave ground, even stepping down the first step into the plaza.

Teriz attacked with big, sweeping strokes. Mangos moved sideways, up and down the top step, making Teriz follow, seeing if the big man could keep his feet on the uneven surface.

Kat and Rhygir now fought below him, in the plaza itself. They stormed back and forth, each pouring out their energy in an attempt to break the other's defense; but their armor withstood all blows.

On the esplanade, Elzemar fought to keep his promise. He, the Queensfishers, and the rest of Kat's men held off Rhygir's mercenaries. Nobody came to aid Rhygir or Teriz, but nobody came to aid Mangos or Kat either.

Mangos sprang forward. Now he drove Teriz back, step by step along the steps. His lungs labored to keep pace with the fight, his heart pounded.

Teriz stepped forward, but Mangos did not retreat. They could only strike with short, hacking strokes. No matter how Mangos swung, Teriz parried him—and Mangos parried Teriz in turn. They relentlessly rained down blows on each other until they each fell back, gasping for air.

"Now!" screamed Kat. Mangos snapped his head around in surprise. Rhygir was on one knee, his head up, as he faced Kat. He didn't look hurt, just exhausted and weary. Kat, too, looked tired, her sword held in a low guard instead of high, and she made no move to attack.

"For the love of Alness," she shouted. "Do it now!"

The clang of steel on steel jerked Mangos's gaze to the canal gates. Two men hammered unseen gearing. Kat hadn't left them to guard the skiffs at all, Mangos realized.

The gate exploded in a torrent of brown and white froth. Water surged into the plaza, spreading out and sending spray ahead of it.

"You're mad," Mangos breathed as the water crashed over Rhygir, then Kat, and they vanished in the maelstrom.

"She'll kill them both," Teriz said.

Mangos spun and chopped. "She can swim!" he shouted, daring contradiction. He chopped again and again, beating down Teriz's defenses. "She can swim, damn you!" Though Teriz hadn't disputed it.

The water roared behind him, slapping the steps as it rose above his feet, then ebbed back, only to rise again. Cold, bitter water.

Mangos struck again as a wave slapped his back and retreated. He stepped closer, knocking Teriz's sword aside, and he knocked the Kingsfisher off his feet, head-down the steps and into the deeper water. Mangos grabbed him by the throat and held him under.

Teriz struggled, but Mangos held him, their faces a foot apart and separated by the surface of the still turbulent water. Teriz's eyes bulged as he thrashed. Mangos felt his grip slip, and he let go, counting that Teriz would try to breathe when the pressure left his throat.

Teriz rose, coughing water, his hand at his throat. He had dropped his sword. Mangos kicked him in the head, throwing him back into the water. Then Mangos reversed his hold on his sword, strode forward, and drove it through Teriz's armor with all his weight and strength. Blood welled up, obscuring Teriz as it diffused in the water.

Mangos let go of his sword. It remained upright, just the hilt sticking out of the water.

The sun burst over the palace, reflecting off the water and blinding him.

He shaded his eyes, searching for Kat among those on the esplanade. She was not there.

"Where is she?" he shouted, shifting his gaze to the water in spite of the glare. Several men ran along the edge, staring into the water, while others fought the last of the mercenaries. "Where is she?"

There, near the center of the plaza, a silver smudge in the water, entangled with a blurry red form. They struggled weakly, but it was impossible to tell who held the other back.

Mangos raced down the steps. He took a deep breath before the water closed over his head. His armor weighed him down. Swimming was out of the question, so he ran as best he could.

The dirty water stung his eyes as he fought the currents. What if Kat were swept away, how would he find her?

He leapt and barely breached the surface, grabbing a quick breath even as his armor dragged him back down.

Shafts of light illuminated the silt, but all he could see was floating garbage. No, something glimmered. He lunged—it was Rhygir, drifting along the bottom. Where was Kat?

He leapt up, his tired legs protesting. This time he barely broke the surface and sucked in more water than air, but kept looking around, praying to find her. Where was she?

There!

Her dragon steel armor like blood in the water, she moved with the currents. He rushed to her, half-swimming, half-running, and scooped her into his arms.

He churned frantically for safety, his lungs burning. Shadows passed over him, and swimmers reached down to help him, but they had no leverage, and his own protesting legs did all the work.

She did not move in his embrace.

The sun darkened as his vision narrowed. He stumbled over a step and climbed, a mad race to air before his legs and vision failed. Then he burst free, up the last few steps, and staggering on the esplanade. Men rushed to help him.

Kat's head, tucked against his chest, lolled back, and her helmet slipped off. Mangos heard, as if from far away, the sound of a bell chime.

Hands lifted her from him even as he fell to his knees and vomited dirty water across the stones. He saw nothing, though he knew his eyes were open. He heard nothing, though he strained his ears for news. He crawled in the direction he felt she must be.

Gradually, his hands appeared, and then the stones beneath them. He could hear voices, faint cries for help that grew louder as his hearing returned. He lurched to his feet and threw himself at the men crowded before him, breaking through their circle to fall again, this time at Kat's side.

She looked so small.

"Maybe..." The word meant nothing, and whoever spoke it didn't finish.

Mangos's throat constricted, and he picked up her cold hand. He held it tight, as if he could warm it. Her head was turned, and he brushed her hair back from her pale face.

"Maybe..." The word came again, and again it meant nothing, for Mangos knew nothing could be done. He regarded Kat as he never had before, for death sheds all enchantments.

He wept. Not as for a sister, or a partner, but as for a lover or a wife.

The citizens of Alness crept from their hiding places in twos and threes. They moved hesitantly, and Mangos didn't blame them. He didn't know what they should expect, either.

Though the sun was halfway up the sky, he hadn't moved. Siln had carried Kat into the palace, had taken her home, as it were; but without her, Mangos did not feel he had a home, and his mind balked at even thinking. All he could do was stare across the flooded plaza.

Somebody came up to stand beside him and rested a hand on his shoulder. He swallowed and glanced up.

"Drex is talking to the commander of the *Fedai*," Siln said. "Some may take their freedom and stay. The others will return to Alomar."

Mangos nodded.

Siln walked over to where Mangos's sword still stuck from the water and pulled it free. "This is yours," he said.

Mangos shrugged his shoulders and bobbed his head. He didn't much care. "I—she—" He shrugged his shoulders again.

"This, also, is yours," Siln said. The sun caught jewels as he held out the crown of Alness.

"That's not mine," Mangos muttered. "I don't want it."

Siln snorted gently. "What *do* you want?"

Mangos stared at the flooded plaza, not really seeing it. How could he put words to what had happened? "Time," he said. "I want time back." He tore his gaze away and looked at the crown. "I don't want that," he repeated.

"I don't think she wanted it either," Siln said. "She was happy enough to let Kel inherit before Rhygir came. But she set aside everything for her people." He looked around at the city and the people. "All that remains of her is Alness, and she's given it to you."

"A Trust," Mangos said.

"She said you understood."

Closing his eyes, Mangos nodded. He stood up, took the crown, hefted it in his hand, but didn't put it on. He climbed the steps to the palace, going home, as it were.

Mangos held the crown in his hand. The broad marble steps fell away before him, leading into the hill. The sun warmed his back; the cool air of the crypt cooled his face.

His daughter stood beside him. She did not look like her mother; rather she looked like her namesake. Perhaps something of Kat's nature had settled in the child, for she shared some of Kat's abilities as well as her name, dark hair, and green eyes.

Mangos was enormously proud.

"Are you ready?" he asked.

She smiled, an assured sixteen. "I've been planning for this a long time."

So she had, and now that she was finally of age, he would present her to the past monarchs of Alness as his heir.

"I won't be able to call you Little Kat anymore," he said. He wondered if he would ever stop though.

A long time. Mangos felt the weight of that time and saw it in the faces of the men who stood quietly beside the crypt as witnesses. In Siln, time had camouflaged his scars with wrinkles. And the Hand had been the Hand of Mangos ever since he laid the Bursa's head at the foot of Mangos's throne and said, "I could accept his betraying anyone but her."

Mangos passed his daughter the crown, as ritual demanded, and together they descended into the tomb.

Lanterns lit the long room, light shining and brass sparkling. Ten white tombs lined the walls, five on each side, each enclosed in a black iron fence. The Monarchs lay inside the tombs, their effigies lay on top. Black lines crisscrossed the nearest effigies, showing where they had been broken by looters and later repaired.

They went from tomb to tomb, Mangos introducing Little Kat to each of the Monarchs. "Your Majesty," he said, as if the King were alive, "this is Kat, daughter of Mangos and Heir to Alness." To Little Kat he said, "King Kalin laid out the canals in the lower city. He built the new palace."

After introducing the next King he said, "King Klair built the eastern watchtower."

Little Kat cleared her throat, said quietly, "Kor built the watchtower, Dad."

Mangos paused. She was right. She was always right. Klair had expanded the canals and built the library in the middle city. He smiled. Alness would be in good hands indeed.

At the next-to-last tomb, he said, "A craftsman stole King Kole's body during the confusion when Alness fell. The man hid Kole's body in a tanner's vat until it could be properly buried after the redemption. It was a very brave and dangerous thing to do."

And finally, the last tomb. "And Kat."

And Kat, he thought, feeling the ache that never truly left, and he had come to accept never would. He found he couldn't go on. There was too much to say.

If he closed his eyes, he could pretend she would wake up, that color would flood her figure and she would take a breath. If he closed his eyes, he could almost fool himself into believing it was Kat before him, not a stone effigy on a cold and lonely sarcophagus.

"You're not over her, are you, Dad?" Little Kat asked.

Mangos swallowed, not sure he trusted his voice. He spoke, and his words were hoarse. "It's hard for your mother." He shook his head, half ruefully. "All the women in my life have deserved better. Even you shouldn't have to deal with a maudlin old man today."

After a long pause, Little Kat held up the crown and ran her fingers over the two newest gems. "These are her leopard-eye emeralds, aren't they?"

Mangos smiled, remembering past adventures. "Yes, and fairly won, too."

"Will you," she hesitated. For the first time she looked unsure. "Will you introduce me?"

He put a reassuring hand on her shoulder and gave it a gentle squeeze.

"It will be my honor."

He cleared his throat. "Your Majesty, this is Kat, daughter of Mangos and Heir of Alness."

Little Kat curtsied. "Your Majesty. I hope I shall not disappoint you. I..." She faltered, looked away, her face red. Looking back she said, her words tumbling out, "I have always admired you and wish I could be like you."

They stood together until, of mutual accord, they turned and walked the length of the crypt. As they climbed the steps, Little Kat said, "We don't need to tell Mom what I said."

"Of course not."

They stopped at the top of the steps where they could see Alness spread below them. The sun sparkled on the clear waters of the canals. All that remained of Rhygir's devastation was dark streaks from fire on the palace walls, the ones that made it look like the palace wept. The streaks had faded, worn by weather; old sorrow, like the ache in Mangos's heart.

Beyond Alness lay the green hills of the headlands and the ocean. Beyond that lay the world.

"I should like to do some of the things she did," Little Kat confessed.

Mangos took back the crown as the ritual demanded. "You are not Queen yet." He pointed to the lands beyond the city. "Go have adventures like hers. Pursue without asking what you chase, and when you catch it, chase again!"

Chasing the Cat Sword

"We can't do this again," Kairi said as she watched a body floating down the river. It was one of the dead Alnessi fighters who had been floating for days, headed for the sea and eternity since the battle in the Loop. She shuddered thinking of it, but the world had changed since then.

She and Daini hid amongst the ruins of Fisher Town, across the bay from Alness. A few stubborn souls still lived here; most were dead or driven out. Like all of Alness, it had been prosperous until Rhygir's conquest. Now, half the town lay burned. Rubbish of all Alness lay strewn, broken down and washed up, on the beach. Ox yokes, fish nets, broken baskets, lobster pots—the detritus of lives destroyed all along the length of the River Al had gathered here.

People would return, though. The storm had passed, the thunder had faded.

There was a new king in Alness.

"Bastard," Daini said. She rested her foot on an overturned rowboat as she looked across at the city. Maybe she meant Mangos for taking the crown, maybe Rhygir for losing it. Maybe someone else entirely. One should never assume anything with her.

"We can't do this again," Kairi told her sister again.

Daini tore her gaze from Alness's walls. "I don't know," she said with a glint in her eye. "I can think of a few games to play. Do you think he's agreeable to playing now that the bitch is dead? But you liked him, didn't you?"

So she *had* been thinking of Mangos. And, no, Mangos would *not* be willing to play games with them now that Kat was dead. He hadn't been a fool when they met in Kalahar, only inexperienced, just like them. None of them lacked experience now, and he still wasn't a fool.

"He and that—" Daini fumed over what to call Kat and eventually didn't name her at all. "—adventure and he ends up a *king!* We adventure and we end up—" she gestured angrily, "here. I don't think anybody has lived here for years, and it *still* smells of fish."

And death, Kairi thought. *The whole country smells of death.* She liked Kat and didn't understand why Daini didn't. Perhaps Daini envied Kat's greater focus and expertise. "Kat's adventures killed her," she said.

"And ours cost you an eye," Daini retorted.

Kairi touched the patch over her left eye, and the feeling of heat and sand and a different kind of death crept out of her memory, and for a second the fear of never seeing again was raw and fresh. *It's been a year,* she reminded herself. *Anhunkten is far away. We never saw it, and I never will.*

"They're hunting mercenaries already," she said. They had cut Rhygir's emblems from their clothes, but anybody could see where they had been. "What now? We haven't accomplished anything. We go from place to place and *fail.* We didn't kill the mine worm. We didn't find Anhunktun. We were on the wrong side in Alness."

"The Alnessi were weak!" Daini snarled.

"When?" Kairi asked softly. "When they lost their city to treachery? Or when they reclaimed it from us?"

Daini snarled at her. "What do you want?"

If there was a place of peace in this world, I would go there and lay my weapons down, Kairi thought. *And if there is not, I would help make one.* And, the thought entered her mind, *If Alness can accept the Fedai that Rhygir used, perhaps they would accept us.*

They were silent, and the silence stretched out until the sound of slow-plodding hooves filled it, and a minute later a man on a horse came into sight. He led a mule with two chests lashed to a frame over its back.

"Looks like somebody's making off with plunder," Daini said, a smile spreading slowly over her face. "Stealing from a thief is hardly stealing at all."

"You think he's a thief?"

Daini shrugged. "Does it matter? Travelling alone is just saying you want to give away your goods."

The man was big—too big to intimidate. He was tall and broad and bald, with a bushy beard that covered his chin, neck, and upper chest.

"He's not looking to give away his plunder," Kairi said, warily reaching for her bow.

Just then a dog trotted out from behind the mule. It stood half as tall as the mule and must have weighed twice what Kairi did—with her full kit.

"And he's not travelling alone," she said. "He's a small crowd by himself, and that dog is a whole pack."

The man nodded to them and held up a jug of wine. "The best of

mornings to you both."

Daini made an inarticulate noise.

"No, I suppose it isn't for you," the man said. "That's what happens when you choose the wrong side of a war. Well…" He didn't seem sad for them, or offended they had fought for Rhygir. "You're better off than most of your comrades."

Kairi watched him warily. Though he had been drinking, he didn't seem drunk. Just cheerful, and maybe more talkative than he might otherwise be.

"And where are you headed?" Daini asked.

"Pytheas." He touched his forehead in gentle salute. "Naan of Pytheas, at your service."

"So what service do I want?" Daini smirked. She drew her sword and examined the blade.

The mastiff growled.

"Here now, Judge," Naan said. "She's just showing her blade for our opinion. She's not going to use it."

He's taking a lot for granted there, Kairi thought.

"Why would I want your opinion?" Daini demanded.

The man ran his hand over his bald head. "Do you *want* me to lose my temper or not?"

Daini grinned. "Either way is fine."

"Stop," Kairi said. She nocked an arrow and drew back the string a couple inches. "There's no point in fighting."

The man frowned. "Then you're pointing that bow at the wrong person, lass. She's the one sparking for a fight. Nice bow though. Wilder dragon bow."

"You know bows?"

"I know weapons."

They stood, looking at each other, a strange mixture of bemusement, resentment, and resignation. The silence drew out until Kairi wanted to shout.

Finally Daini relented and said, "All right then, tell me about my sword. Let's see if you can."

Naan said, "It's a stylish butcher's sword, a falcata. A little heavier than I'd have thought for your build, but that goes with the slash and chop style of the sword and your peculiar proclivity toward aggression. The shape is pleasing with the concave curve near the hilt and the convex curve near the tip. It's a single edge blade with a short false edge near the tip. Best for slashing, but it can thrust when needed.

"As for the weapon itself," he continued, "It's made of crucible steel known as seric steel coming from the southwest, beyond Alomar. It's good work. Given the forging and style, it's probably seventy years old, give or take a few. The wear on the brass in the grip suggests that guess is accurate."

"Huh," Daini said. "You do know your weapons. It's from Barloil."

"No, it's not. Barloil had some great smiths. Withernal forged his cursed swords there, but this one came from further inland. I hope you didn't pay for the lie of its origins."

"How do you know this?" Kairi asked.

The man touched his chest. "I am from Pytheas."

"And who's Withernal?" Kairi asked.

"My great grandfather, if you would know. He dabbled in zoomorphic blades. He died when the volcano erupted and destroyed the city."

Daini snorted and rolled her eyes. "Who cares?" she mouthed.

"What are zoomorphic blades?" Kairi asked. Daini's apathy surprised her, since her sister had an affinity for exotic steel.

"Blades imbued with the powers of an animal," the man said. "Amazing work. Not the smithing. Withernal was an adequate smith, nothing more, but as a *sorcerer*... he excelled at that."

"A blade with the power of an animal? In what way?"

Daini shook her head. "Who cares?" she mouthed again.

Kairi frowned at her sister. *Don't be rude,* she thought, but didn't say it out loud.

"He takes the primary characteristic of an animal and binds it to the steel, which infuses it to the wielder," Naan said.

Daini spun, her full attention on him. "It what?"

"Incredible idea, isn't it? You can give someone the strength of a gorilla or the speed of a cheetah. It's—"

"Why haven't I heard of these swords?" Daini interrupted eagerly. "Where are the invincible armies of elephant warriors?"

"Oh, it's fiendishly difficult to make those blades," Naan said. "Very long, very costly. They wouldn't be blades for an army. If you think a Marin blade is costly, these would far exceed them."

"I've heard of Marin blades," Daini said. "I've even heard of dragonsteel. But I've never heard of zoomorphic swords."

"They're all cursed, of course."

"Cursed?" Kairi said. "In what way?"

"Why would you curse a sword like that?" Daini demanded.

Naan shrugged. "They're not intentionally cursed, it's an unavoidable part of their creation. Too much of the animal remains. The wielder of the sword lives with the animal in their mind and it drives them insane."

Daini paced around, stopped, and stared thoughtfully into the distance. "You're telling me I could have the reflexes of a cat, and all I need to do is put up with one in my head?"

"And end up barking mad, or purring crazy if you prefer."

A slow grin spread across Daini's face. "Yeah, well, who could tell?"

Kairi's stomach turned over with an icy feeling. "What are you thinking?"

"I want one of those swords."

"Why?" she demanded, though she doubted Daini cared about why, or what anybody thought. It would be an impulse and that was good enough.

"You're the one who said we can't stay here," Daini said.

"I didn't say we should go look for a cursed sword."

"You heard mister 'I know weapons.' They're worth more than a Marin sword."

That, Kairi had to admit, was appealing. "Where are they?"

The man chuckled. "Withernal kept them all. He was going to destroy them, but did he...?" He spread his hands and shrugged. "It's hard to destroy good work. Even if it's flawed."

"Surely somebody would have discovered them if they still existed," Kairi protested.

"They're not secrets," the man said, "but Withernal wanted them to be perfect before he told anybody. I know about them because we still have the letters he wrote to Marin asking his advice. Besides, swords are rather small and Barloil was a large city."

A devious grin spread across Daini's face.

Kairi didn't like that. Still, Marin swords were supposed to be *the* most desirable weapons to collectors. But something unique, something forbidden, something *dark*, would be irresistible. They could live like queens from the proceeds of a Withernal sword. If it didn't drive them mad.

Naan cleared his throat. "If you're going to search for Withernal's forge, maybe you could see what happened to him. Marin had taken his son as an apprentice. Without a home to return to, the lad stayed in Pytheas and married. He never did return to Barloil but always wondered what happened. He had a little sister and thought his father would have found some way to save her. He always wondered why he didn't."

"It seems unlikely we could find out," Kairi said.

Naan shrugged. "It seems unlikely you'll find a sword."

That was true, Kairi acknowledged. "We *would* sell it, right?" she demanded.

Daini nodded, eyes wide and innocent. "Of course."

"Then let's go to Barloil."

The road turned at the edge of the forest. A small stone lay overturned and half-covered beside it. Kairi brushed the leaves aside and read the number. "A mile to go."

"Just beyond that village then," Daini said.

The forest gave way to homesteads surrounded by groves of olives and lemons. The land rose to a cluster of cottages. It was a village like numerous ones they had passed on their journey.

"People live here," Kairi said in surprise. "I had assumed it was like Anhunktun, or… or like Terzol is said to be. Lost and abandoned…" she trailed away as she watched a child dash from one of the cottages, closely followed by another before they both disappeared into the olive groves. "I didn't expect people to still live here."

Daini stalked forward. "They can do whatever they want as long as they haven't taken my sword."

Kairi hurried after her. "We are going to sell it, right? You aren't thinking we'll keep it?"

As the road wound through the village, the homes grew closer and closer together until each shared a wall with the next. It twisted over the crest of the ridge and turned again before the ridge dropped too sharply to build on. With nothing blocking the view, the Bay of Barl opened before them.

The water was crystalline blue, mottled with tan and white. Waves rippled over the surface, chopped by the wind when they rose too high, their white caps settling back down as they crossed the bay to where the volcano loomed, lopsided, on the opposite shore. The eruption had blown out the eastern flank. Seventy years of brush and young trees smoothed over the destruction but it would be hundreds more before it recovered completely.

The city, whether covered by lava or water, would never recover. For every building that rose from the waves, acres of water covered an unknown number of others.

Kairi and Daini made their way down, no longer noticing the village as they looked at the ruined domes of collapsed temples, the capitals of colonnaded markets, and the most striking feature, the colossal statue of a king, only his head and shoulders visible above the waves.

Bright sun sparkled off the water and small boats dotted the bay as men set or retrieved fish traps.

"What did you expect?" Kairi asked.

"Not this," Daini admitted.

They followed the road down through several switchbacks to a plaza which opened onto a small market. Beyond the market lay the docks where the warm breeze stirred white weather pennants, which Kairi assumed to mean fair skies.

Nobody paid attention until they reached the market. Sellers perked up, watching for an opening to hawk their wares.

"Fried eel?" offered the nearest vendor. "Eat it before it eats you." A row of eels hung head down from the canopy of the stall. They had spiny frills around their heads which hung open like small umbrellas. He gestured to the claypot stove behind him. Smoke rose, carrying the smell of olives, garlic, and spices.

Kairi's mouth started to water.

Daini groaned and shook her head. "Don't ever look at the merchants. That's how they catch you." She fished a coin from her pouch and tossed it to the man. "Two, and there better be change."

The man caught it. "Alnessi, eh? They don't adulterate their coin like others do. You'll get change." He gave them two parchment cones filled with chunks of breaded eel and a half-dozen mixed bronze coins as change.

"Do the eels really eat people?" Kairi asked.

"How big do you think they are?" he scoffed. "One of the old ones maybe, but not these. Enjoy in safety," he said with a derisive laugh.

"Keepsakes of sunken Barloil?" called another vendor before they had taken two steps. "All the best. Only the best."

Intrigued, Kairi wandered over.

"Don't look her in the eye," Daini said.

The keepsakes turned out to be nothing but junk. There was nothing special about the dinnerware, bits of iron tools, or warped pieces of wood. They were pitted, or split, some spotted with barnacles. There was little to look at, and none of it worthwhile.

"Only the best?" Kairi asked dryly.

"All from the sunken city," said the woman. "Wrested from the deadly grip of the sea."

Kairi picked up a ladle. It looked like any other ladle in any other city. "I hope you didn't wrestle too hard for it."

"What if I want something more—impressive—than a broken tile?" Daini flicked a shattered blue and white tile.

"The ceramicists of Barloil were renowned for their skill," said the vendor.

"Forget I asked." She turned to leave. "They weren't *that* good."

The vendor stepped forward. "What do you want?" she asked. "Maybe I can get it."

"I collect swords," Daini said. "I want one from Barloil."

"I can do that. Very expensive. *Very.* Nice blades though." She ducked behind her stall and beckoned to a boy lounging at the edge of the market. When he approached, she grabbed him and dragged him closer still. She whispered urgently. He pulled back in surprise. She dragged him closer, whispered again, and shoved him away. He ran up the ridge and disappeared amongst the houses.

The vendor smiled. "You're lucky. My cousin has a sword from before the eruption. It's his pride, but I think—if you pay enough money—maybe he would sell it."

Daini gave her a smile that didn't show her teeth.

Kairi leaned against the next stall where a woman sold wool cloth. The woman smiled something between a greeting and a smirk. Kairi shrugged, curious about this prized sword.

It didn't take long for him to return with a gangly young man holding a plain short sword. He was flushed and couldn't conceal his eagerness even as he tried to adopt an air of reluctance.

"This is Tomo," the vendor said. "Show her your sword, Tomo."

"Very rare sword," Tomo said as he laid the sword on the table in front of Daini.

The woolen vendor beside Kairi snorted. When Kairi glanced at her, she cleared her throat and looked away.

Tomo presented the sword as if it were a masterpiece. The leather wrapping on the hilt had carbonized and flaked away in places, leaving the wire wrapping hanging loose. Both the brass pommel and crosspiece showed disfiguration from heat, and the steel of the blade was discolored.

"And how much do you want for this sword?" Daini purred.

Tomo thrust out his chest. "A dozen golds!"

Daini smiled, showing her teeth like a predator. Kairi sprang forward, putting herself between her sister and Tomo. "Let it go," she said.

"Twelve golds!" Daini burst out. "For a guardsman's shortsword? There must have been *thousands* of them, and they aren't even very good. And this one—*this one* isn't even bad enough to be called bad. It's worse!"

"Let it go," Kairi soothed.

"That thing almost melted!" Daini exclaimed. "I'd bet it would break against a dry cornstalk! I'd rather fight with the ladle! For twelve golds I could buy—"

"Don't," Kairi said, not sure what Daini would buy, but sure it wasn't appropriate to say.

Daini laughed.

Tomo cringed and ducked his head. "Five golds?" he offered hopefully.

Kairi raised her eyebrows.

Daini spun and walked away. Kairi let out her breath with relief.

"Two golds?" Tomo said weakly. Kairi rolled her eyes and shook her head. "A gold?"

"Any more offers and she's likely to give you a sword in return," Kairi said. She turned to the woolen merchant. "Is there somebody we can trust to help us?"

"Try Aldo on the docks. Don't know he can help, but he won't cheat you."

"Thank you."

"Twelve golds!" Daini spat back at Tomo and his cousin as she stalked away.

Kairi kept her head down as they headed to the dock, only looking up after they left the market. Daini stopped to lean against a bollard. She looked like a wild animal pastured with the livestock.

"How disgustingly placid," she said.

Kairi nodded. "Better than Anhunktun." They had eaten raw scorpions on that adventure.

Daini curled her lip. She looked across the bay. "Now... where's Aldo?"

"Ah, Daini," Kairi said and pointed to a building with two boards nailed to the side. The top board read *Tours of Ruined Barloil* and the smaller one beneath it read *Both Land and Water, Knowledgeable Guide*, and finally, *Three Bronze coppe, Midday Meal Provided.*

"Where's the excitement in a *tour*?" Daini burst out.

A man walked down the dock toward the building. "It's a very good tour," he said. He carried an oversized bucket of water filled with eels. His narrow shoulders stooped, giving him a hollow look, but ropey muscles corded his arms and he held the bucket easily enough.

"You're the guide?" Daini demanded.

The man shrugged. "Why not? People come to see sunken Barloil. They're willing to pay for someone to tell them stories of the city and the day it died. Who am I to turn away their money?"

"What do people want to see?" Kairi asked.

"The old Regum arena, the statue of Madriman the Great—"

"I can see it from here!" Daini burst out, pointing at the statue rising from the bay.

"The view is better from my boat."

"We're looking for Aldo," Kairi said.

"He's on the tour."

After a moment's thought, she realized, "You're Aldo, aren't you?"

"At your service."

"We're looking for somebody who can guide us around the ruined city."

Aldo tapped the sign where it said *Knowledgeable Guide*. "Two silvers a day."

"It says three bronze!" Daini burst out.

"The tour is three hours." Aldo shrugged. "You want my boat all day."

"You can only do two tours a day—six bronze copee!"

"I can do three in the summer. *And* I can fit five people in my boat. That's forty-five copee a day. You're saving five copee because I don't have to provide fifteen meals."

Kairi sighed. It was hard to argue with that. The man in the market *had* said Aldo was honest. "But meals for us are included."

Aldo grinned. "Lunch and dinner. You find your own breakfast.

Kairi glanced at Daini, who glowered back. "Very well."

"Where do you want to go?" Aldo asked.

Daini exploded again. "We're not telling you!"

Surprisingly, Aldo laughed. "As long as you pay. I won't know where to go, and you won't know when we get there." He started to go into the building. "Be here tomorrow at sunrise."

"We're looking for Withernal's smithy," Kairi blurted out. Daini snorted and glared at her.

Aldo looked over his shoulder. "Why? He make something special?"

"No, just a friend of an ancestor. We thought we'd see if we could find it."

Aldo shook his head. "You don't have to tell me why, but at least put some effort into lying."

Daini ignored him. "What's that?" she asked, pointing past Kairi out to the bay.

Kairi turned to look. *If I had my other eye, I could see without turning my head,* she thought.

Across the bay, water frothed and boiled. A geyser of water shot into the air. Ten, twenty, thirty, forty feet up. A loud *FOOM!* rolled across, catching up with the sight. After thirty seconds it cut off abruptly leaving a brief cascade of rain to fall in the bay.

"What was that?" Kairi asked.

"That's Gertie," Aldo said. "She erupts every day at this time."

"Everyday? Same time?"

"Same time, every day."

"What sorcery causes that?"

"It's an effect of the volcano. There are other geysers, but none are as predictable as Gertie."

"Have they always been here?"

"No," Aldo said. "They started after the city sank. Some stop and others start whenever the volcano rumbles. Gertie started about fifty years ago and has kept time ever since. As long as we stay away near the eruption time, it's safe enough."

A chill had crept in overnight, and the morning was cold. The bay was flat with a layer of mist on the surface and pockets of steam over the fumaroles. Kairi and Daini met Aldo at the foot of the quay. He saw Kairi's bow and said, "Are you sure you want to risk getting that wet?"

"Better wet than stolen," she retorted.

Aldo shrugged. "I asked around," he said as he led them to his boat. He carried a wicker basket of food, and two thick, oddly shaped glass bowls made to fit over their eyes. A rubbery band around the edge sealed the bowl to their face and a strap held it in place. "A water mask," he explained. "It allows you to see clearly underwater.

"Nobody had heard of Withernal," he continued. "Craftsmen were usually in the north end, but I want to ask one more person. Old Jolson has been fishing the bay for sixty years. If anybody knows, he does."

He waved to an old man carrying an armful of nets at the mooring next to them. "Jolson! I have a question."

The man threw the nets into his boat. "Ask away."

"Withernal. A smith before the eruption. Where was his forge?"

"Withernal?" said the old man. "Never heard of him."

"He made cursed swords," Aldo said.

"Cursed swords?" Jolson rubbed his chin. "The kind that cursed the dog man?"

"The old man who followed Dek Tilson like a puppy?" Aldo said. "The idiot?"

"Not an idiot—cursed. My Grandpap said a sword stole his soul and even when they broke the sword he didn't get it back. Grandpap pitied him, said he sensed the eruption and ran like all the other dogs. But he was loyal, and returned the next day. But the city was destroyed and all his people were dead. He stayed around until he took to following Dek Tilson."

"That has to be one of Withernal's cursed swordsmen!" Kairi exclaimed. "What happened to him?"

"He died. Twenty years ago. Tilson too. And Tilson's wife—last year for her. They didn't have any children."

"And you thought this would help in what way?" Daini demanded.

Kairi shook her head, wishing her sister would shut up so she could think. The man had the characteristics of a dog, loyal. Loyal to Dek Tilson... But he tried to go home after the eruption... "If he wasn't following Tilson around, where would he be?"

Jolson waved toward the volcano. "By the south flow, in the old north end."

"Where the craftsmen were—and where Withernal must have had his forge."

Aldo nodded. "That makes sense. It's a hard place to search, though."

"Why is that?"

"There are some underwater vents where the water is scalding hot. The eels like it though. There's some eel fishing, but no relic diving."

Kairi remembered what the man in the market said. "That's where the old ones live, isn't it? The old eels that eat people?"

Aldo nodded. "It is."

She turned to Daini. "Why? Why do you want this? They call that man 'dog man' because of what the sword did to him, and breaking the sword didn't cure him. What does that tell you? It tells me Withernal *did* break the cursed swords. We'd be risking our lives for nothing."

"We don't know he broke them all. Maybe some remain." She lifted her eyebrows and grinned. "What else would you rather do?"

"Live to an old age," Kairi muttered.

The crystalline waters sparkled around them. Several other small boats plied the bay, nobody the least concerned with their activity. Once again Kairi felt the incongruity with their past adventures. This wasn't in the deep desert or far underground. There were no sandstorms, scorpions, or mine worms. Only the threat of death was the same.

"The city has been scavenged for years," Aldo said. "Most of what's recovered now are small, everyday items. Everyone in the village is using old dishes. Every time a tourist buys one, everybody gets a good laugh. There's so *many* of them! There's an entire city down there, after all."

"Is it even worth diving after all this time?" Kairi asked. "Surely all the great treasures have been recovered already."

"Most of the known treasures are either out of reach or recovered, yes," he said. "The Temple Treasury was recovered within weeks of the eruption. But Barloil was a large city. You can still find troves of coin if you're persistent and lucky."

"Why aren't *you* diving for treasure?" Daini demanded.

Aldo checked over his shoulder and adjusted their direction. "I do. But who wants a life picking over the dead for pennies? Some days are meant for pruning the olive trees, some for swimming in the bay. And if I should see something interesting? Well, I dive down to look."

He pointed out noteworthy ruins on the shores of the bay, as well as the tops of buildings that still rose from the waves. He kept them entertained with a steady stream of stories about old Barloil as he guided the boat to the north side of the bay. "We're passing over the Regum Arena," Aldo said, prompting them to look over the side. "It's one of the more popular ruins to view and most dangerous to dive into."

Indeed, they passed over the curved wall of the arena, so close that if they were to balance on it their heads would be above water. The seating fell away to the sand which filled the arena floor and covered the lower seats. The further wall crumbled inward. It fell on itself, covering the aisles and benches.

Of the six podiums where the combatants controlled their pieces, four remained, circling the arena as if still ready for a contest. But the Ready Room had collapsed, and the halls housing the hospitality and betting rooms were ruined. Few mullins remained in the ornate windows, and even less glass. The windows were dark holes in the crumbling facade.

Daini leaned over for a better look. "Now *there* was treasure," she said. "A fortune wagered on every game. Has it been recovered?"

"Nobody dives in the arena these days because of the eels," Aldo said.

"What? All that wealth and nobody dares retrieve it because of some slinky fish?"

"The arena was imbued with magic—exotic and unique magic that has made the eels larger than, I think, you appreciate."

"Eels? We've faced the mine worm!" She rose.

"We didn't kill the mine worm," Kairi reminded her.

"I don't see any eels here either. Forget the betting rooms, just think of the stakes in the Ready Room—and it's right there!"

"Daini, no! We're looking for Withernal's forge."

"Most of the city's greatest treasures were recovered in the first decade after the eruption," Aldo said as he started rowing again. "I've been told the volcano hadn't stopped steaming before folk were diving in the Grand Temple's Depository."

Daini slowly sat down. "I'm not afraid of eels."

They watched the city slide beneath them, looking for anything that spoke of a smithy. The ruin gave the city a superficial sameness made of fallen walls and collapsed rooves. Seaweed grew amongst the ruins, and fish swam. Sand covered much of the bay's floor, and it was impossible to tell what else it covered.

Daini began to drum her fingers on the gunwale.

The sun rose in the sky.

"Gertie will erupt soon, won't she?" Kairi asked after hours of looking.

"Soon," Aldo said. "Not far from here, but we'll be safe."

The morning dragged on.

"I don't think you should hold the sword," Kairi told Daini. Her sister was like the wind, changing directions easily, sweeping all before it.

Trying to make sense of her could drive a person mad, and Kairi feared what wielding a cursed sword would do to her.

"Afraid it will make me crazy?"

"Why take the chance?"

"I could be more of a cat than Kat! Fast, agile—"

"Insane."

"She was, wasn't she?"

"Not her! You! Those swords are cursed!"

"Only if they can get their claws into your mind."

"Daini!" Kairi said in exasperation. "You don't even know Withernal made a cat sword. If we find one, it might be attuned to naked mole-rats."

"Don't they only have one queen and they fight to determine who she'll be?"

"You're not listening!"

"I can handle a rat scurrying around in my brain," Daini said.

Kairi sighed. She'd just have to get the sword first.

Something caught her eye. She sat up and pointed. "There!" It was just a building, fifteen or twenty feet down, like so many others, but this one lacked a roof. It was just four walls surrounding a sandy floor, but in the middle, proudly sticking out of the sand, was an anvil. "That's it!"

Aldo looked over the side and nodded his approval. "A smithy for sure."

Daini stood up.

"I'll go," Kairi said. She reached for the water mask.

Daini pouted. "I have to do something. I'll go crazy sitting in the boat."

"Fine. Just let me look around." She didn't wait for an answer. She slipped over the side, fitted the mask, and dove.

The forge wasn't as empty as it first seemed. Parts of the walls were leaning, leaving dark voids underneath them. Racks had been overturned and tools peeked out of the drifting sand. The furnace had collapsed in one corner. Something that looked like bones stuck out of the pile of stones.

She swam to one of the overturned racks. Silt swirled as she tried to wrestle it from the sand. She stopped to pick up what turned out to be a hammer, the handle grown soft from long immersion. She brushed the sand from another hammer, then grabbed a pair of tongs before she pushed off to return to the surface.

She pulled herself half into the boat and dropped the tongs on the seat.

"Tongs?" Daini said. "I guess I better do this myself." She dove into the water before Kairi could answer.

"It must be difficult being her sister," Aldo said.

"It has moments." She took a deep breath and dove again.

Daini had gone to the forge and was shifting stones to see the bones better. *Whose bones are those?* Kairi wondered. *Withernal's? His daughter's? Some stranger's taking refuge during the eruption? Another smith entirely because this is the wrong forge?*

She returned to the overturned racks and shifted through the sand, finding and discarding tools but not weapons.

They both surfaced.

"Take care in the dark places," Aldo warned. "That is where the eels lurk."

Daini's retort got lost in a mouthful of seawater, but it was likely profane. She ducked back under and swam down again.

"Sorry," Kairi said before diving again.

The two scoured the smithy through several dives. The only weapons they found were in a pile of scrap metal they uncovered. There was nothing to indicate they were or had ever been anything more than normal swords, now broken and piled with old pots and bits of scrap steel.

Finally Kairi approached the anvil while Daini began to explore deeper into the shadows of the leaning wall.

Don't do that, Kairi thought. *This is exactly how trouble starts.*

She lost sight of her sister as she uncovered a long box at the base of the anvil. *What?* She brushed the sand away. The box was over three feet long and about eight inches wide. Excited, she pulled at it. It was only five inches deep and came away in a cloud of sand and silt.

Just then Daini burst out from behind the wall. She pushed up just as an eel shot out after her. The eel snaked out, more and more of it emerging. Longer and longer—the thing was four feet wide and longer and longer and longer and Kairi pushed off for the surface, still holding the box with her heart pounding.

She grabbed the gunwale and threw the box into the boat before pulling herself after it.

"I've never seen an eel that large!" Aldo screamed.

Kairi picked up her bow. "There was a time when she protected me! DAINI!" she screamed. She nocked an arrow and drew her bow. The runes on its spine flared to life.

The eel encircled Daini, preventing her from surfacing. It rushed her;

she twisted and it shot past her. Kairi drew and released.

Her arrow hit the water and veered away. It lost momentum until it stopped, hung in the water, and started to float up. She had already nocked another one and fired. The arrow struck the eel with no effect.

The eel neared the surface and Kairi discarded her bow and leapt over the side. She landed as it turned, right behind its head. Her feet slipped and she grabbed the spiny frill to stay on. The last thing she heard before the water closed over her head was Aldo's cry of surprise.

Daini was swimming frantically as the eel came back for another pass at her. Kairi yanked the spines. The eel shied violently, throwing her forward. One of the spines jabbed just below her good eye, bending against the bone and springing back. It knocked off her water mask and skipped over her eye to cut her eyebrow.

She recoiled, one hand reaching toward her eye. She slipped and grabbed the spine, pulling again as she tried to steady herself.

The eel turned toward her pull.

Sensitive spines, eh? Kairi thought. She yanked them again, and the eel turned again. *Just like the reins of a horse.* The eel turned toward Daini again and Kairi jerked again. The eel turned and rushed past Daini. It turned and she pulled again, forcing it away, giving her sister time to reach the surface.

The eel raced around, struggling to break free from the human pulling its spines. Kairi held tight even as she pulled the spines one way and the other, guiding the eel out of the forge.

Her lungs started to ache so she pulled back, forcing it up. It breached the surface with a leap and she gasped for air. *Now what?* she wondered as it dove back down.

She wrenched the eel around to check Daini. Her sister was gone, presumably into the boat. *If I let go, it'll turn on me.*

Kairi let it race, and it took her on a tour of Barloil at blazing speed. Salt water stung her eyes, and the ruins raced by, leaving impressions and little else. She forced it to stay in open water, fearing the broken buildings where it might take refuge.

She forced it up again, and it showed no signs of tiring. Her hands started to cramp, and she was afraid she'd slip off. *This is why I'm done with adventuring! Get it before it gets you? Well I got it and now what?*

Kairi forced it up again. Ahead she caught a glimpse of the patch of frothing water. *There!* She wrenched the eel around and guided it toward the froth.

She held course as it dove. A column of tiny bubbles rose. Just as they entered, the sand beneath sundered and Gertie erupted. Hot water lifted them up, past the surface, into the air. Hot air lanced into her lungs as she gasped and the water seared her skin.

Kairi's hands slipped so she threw herself as far from the eel as she could. The world spun, alternating sky and water until she plunged into the bay. A second later the eel followed and the surge of water carried her away from the geyser.

She rolled over and looked up. The geyser stopped, leaving the last water hanging in the sky before it rained down, making a rainbow as it fell.

"By the gods of Eastwarn," Kairi said in awe. "What a ride."

Kairi winced as Daini and Aldo helped her into the boat. Her hands cramped, and red blotches covered her exposed skin. Salt burned her face. She touched the cuts around her eye, and her fingers came away red.

"You IDIOT!" Kairi shouted. "Aldo told you not to poke in dark places!"

Daini grinned. "What a ride! I would have *paid* to do that!"

"No, you nearly got eaten! Look at this!" She brandished her bloody hand. "Look at this!" She waved to her bloody face. "I only have one eye left, and I nearly lost it!"

"But you—"

"Don't!" Exhaustion fought with Kairi's anger. She couldn't change her sister. It was useless to try. "Don't say 'but you didn't.' What would you have done if I had?"

"But you didn't."

"We can't keep doing this," she said. If anything, Daini was getting more reckless.

"That was unbelievable," Aldo exclaimed. "You didn't hesitate at all!"

"I didn't think at all," Kairi retorted. "Now I'm thinking I shouldn't have jumped in at all."

Aldo shaded his eyes and looked around the bay. He waved to the nearest boat, which was already rowing toward them. "We'll divide the eel with them, if they spear it and tow it back, if that's acceptable?"

The eel remained close to the surface, moving erratically.

"It's a good thing I didn't think about it," Kairi said. "Look at the size…"

"You will be well compensated," Aldo assured them.

"Speaking of compensation," she searched for the box and saw it, kicked half-under the seat. Her muscles protested as she picked it up.

"What's that?" Daini said.

"I don't know. It was in the sand by the anvil. It's the right size to hold a sword."

The box was made of fine steel. Only some encrustations and discoloration showed from its long immersion. Kairi wiped the silt from the lid, revealing a partial etching.

"*For Wither… a fine… my thanks… the best, Marin,*" she read.

"Marin!" exclaimed Daini.

"They did correspond after all, and Marin took his son as an apprentice," Kairi said.

"And Marin gave him a sword!"

"If there's anything in the box," Kairi said. She held it up. It was well-made and remained tightly closed even though it had no lock.

Aldo gave her a chisel. She scraped off the barnacles that grew where the lid met the box and used it to pry it open. A roll of parchment fell out.

Daini reached into the box, pushing Kairi aside, to seize the sword before she could properly see it. "Yes!" Daini said and brandished it before waving it around.

"Hey!" Kairi protested. "At least let us see it!"

The sword was beautiful, an ordinary, double-edged blade made extraordinary by the smith. The layers of steel made rain drops patterns down the spine of the blade. The edges shown silver in the sun so pure it could only be silvecite. A silvicite basket protected the hilt and a loop held a cat's eye emerald in the pommel that seemed alive as the light shone through it.

"Amazing!" Daini crooned as she caressed the hilt. She swung it, forcing Aldo to duck back. "The balance… the weight. All that needs to be done is to wrap the hilt. But—nothing. No strength, no speed. It's not cursed. But still, think of the treasure we can win with this!"

Kairi groaned. "We can sell—" She didn't finish. There was no point. Knowing her sister wouldn't share the blade, she picked up the parchment. She unrolled pages of small, neat writing interspersed with arcane diagrams. She didn't understand it, so slowed down, ignoring Diani's rapturous fawning over the sword. What Kairi held, she realized, was Withernal's instructions and notes to make zoomorphic blades.

The steel needed to be of sufficient purity, the craftsmanship of acceptable quality, the magic needed to be powerfully cast. The rituals were dark, filled with pain and blood for the animal. Kairi shuddered. Small wonder the swords were cursed.

She came to the last page with the final instructions. "The last thing to awaken the blade is to call it by its true name," she read. Under that, written in a sloppy, hurried script said, 'Her name is Josephine.'

Kairi read it again, out loud, "Her name is Josephine."

"Josephine?" Daini said.

Sunlight shimmered down the blade.

Daini gasped. Her expression turned to horror. "Get out... of... my head!" She waved the sword around. "I want a cat! Or a dog, or a... a dragon! Not this!" She threw it into the bilge and backed away.

"What's wrong?" Aldo asked. He inched away until he pressed against the gunwale.

Kairi rolled up the parchment and put it back in the box. She gingerly picked up the sword.

A wave of panic swept through her. *Poppa! Stop! No!* A voice shouted in her head.

She dropped it.

"What is it?" Aldo asked

Kairi ignored him. What animal thought? She reached for the sword. Stopped. Braced herself and picked it up again.

There was silence. "Hello?" She said.

You're not Poppa.

It felt like all of Kairi's insides constricted. This sounded like a child. She felt fear, but didn't think it was her own. "No, I'm not."

Where's Poppa?

"Is Withernal your Poppa?"

Aldo leaned further away. "Who are you talking to?"

Who are you?

"I'm Kairi. Who are you?"

I want my Poppa. Is the volcano done exploding?

Kairi glanced at the dormant volcano with seventy years of growth on its sides. "Yes. It's done."

Where's Poppa? He said I'd be safe from the fire, but then he hurt me. I don't like it when he hurts me.

Is this who I think it is? Kairi wondered.

Who is that? The voice asked.

You can hear my thoughts? Kairi thought in alarm.

I don't know! I feel strange. Where am I?

Kairi felt the voice sniffle. "Josephine?"

What?

"What do you know about zoomorphic blades?"

I don't know what you mean.

Kairi closed her eyes. "I think we have a lot to talk about."

K airi shook her head. "We're not going to sell it."

"It's a Marin sword *and* a zoomorphic blade," Daini said. "We can name our price."

"It's a *child*," Kairi said. "You were the one who didn't want to sell any sword we found."

"Because it's supposed to make me fast! What will this one do? Make me take afternoon naps?"

Kairi glanced at the sword resting across her lap. Jo, as she was called, was resting. Maybe asleep? Who could tell with a sword? "It was the only way Withernal could save his daughter."

Daini scoffed.

Kairi carefully lifted Jo and laid her in her box next to the parchment. "I'm going to Pytheas. Naan might be able to figure out what this means for her."

Daini curled her lip. "She can't be restored. Her body's long gone, burned, rotted, or eaten by fishes—"

"Stop," Kairi said. "I know she can't go back, but having another person in your head is nothing like having an animal. At the least, Withernal's descendents deserve to know what happened to their great aunt."

"Who is only four."

"Who has been four for seventy years."

"The road to Pytheas goes through Alness," Daini said.

Kairi smiled wryly. "I'll stop in to see Mangos. We can trade stories."

Daini rolled her eyes. "I'll come by some day to say 'hi' to your children."

Strangely, it felt like a relief. She had been afraid Daini would try to force them to stay together. But Daini was content to let Kairi take Jo north by herself. Kairi didn't know where Daini would go, it didn't matter. She didn't know what the future held for herself either. It was ironic, and a relief, that in spite of having a bow and now a sword, her days of reckless adventuring were over.

At the Gaming Table

I'm thrilled by the opportunity to present some ideas for bringing the adventures of Mongoose and Meerkat to the gaming table! I love taking short fiction, like the kinds included in Appendix N, and figuring out ways of adapting it into gameable content. I'm of the belief that a great story can be quickly and easily adapted to an adventure with just a few stat-blocks and notes. Those who have followed the Cirsova blog over the years have seen a few "proof of concept" examples, such as the one-off I ran based on Basil Wells' Raiders of the Second Moon or the Edgar Rice Burroughs' Pellucidar hexcrawl.

So, the contents of this section will not be anything like typical published adventures, modules, setting supplements, etc. These are guidelines and suggestions to help get you started if you were considering running an adventure based on, or inspired by, Mongoose and Meerkat. We hope you have some fun with these, and we hope that you enjoy Mongoose and Meerkat enough to want to bring them to your table!

P. Alexander, Ed., 2020

The Battlefield of Keres

The Battlefield of Keres is more than just a location; described as 50 miles across, it's an entire region that you can drop in your game world, offering tons of opportunities for an adventuring party to explore. Using 6-mile wilderness hexes, the battlefield comprises up to 52 hexes!

The main geographic boundaries of the region include the Karris Mountains to the north and the Balmis Swamp to the south.

The Duke had his command fortress on the western edge of Keres.

Duke's Command Fortress:

The Command fortress is a large stone structure that straddles a highway leading into the region of the battlefield. This would be a great place to drop a one-page dungeon.

There are few notable features on the surface ruins, however there are places where horses could be stabled, goods stored, and prisoners or travelers held. The ruins are littered with a mix of contemporary trash left by treasure-hunters and the detritus of the ages.

Graffiti on the walls, including "Madness saved me" written above manacles in a room that was once a holding cell.

More notable is the doggerel written by the main gate:

"Should you venture past this gate,
Gird your weapon and hope forsake.
For Keres demands blood and gore,
And death shall feed it evermore."

On the hills near the fortress, adventurers can find 1d4 ruined polyboloses [ballistae], once used to cover the skies from attacks by flying monsters. There's a 50% chance that with some tinkering and the right parts, they could be made operational again. Parts salvaged from others could be used to make repairs to another; if at least 2 are still present on the site, someone with some engineering skills could probably get one operational.

Cost: 75 GP, Encumbrance: 6,000 [500 towed], AC: 4/6, HP 9, Full Crew: 4, Range: 100/200/300, Damage d10+6, Rate: 1-per-2, Ammo Cost/Wk: 2,000.

Hooks

There are plenty of reasons why adventurers would want to explore the Battlefield of Keres. While it may have been picked over by looters over the ages, there are still plenty of notable treasures to find.

Kat mentions Karl, an antiquities fence, who might be looking for particular treasures.

Of course, the party could also end up looking for an item on a bet, like Mangos, and be in a race with other treasure hunting parties to find it first. Treasure hunters/rivals such as Thierry will form parties comprised primarily of Fighters and Thieves, however there is a chance that they may also include Magic Users looking for artifacts or even Clerics hoping to put some of the dead to rest.

[Some excavation may be required in some cases, though there are still artifacts which may be found at surface-level. This region is a great place to drop small one-page dungeons to represent small redoubts, fortifications, and sally-points from the time of the battle. The best treasures will likely be found where the fighting was the fiercest, and therefore the anomalies and 'haunts' the thickest and most dangerous!]

Treasures

Myriad treasures can still be found on the battlefield, including:

Gorman's Helm: +1 to the Morale of any NPCs under the command of the wearer. Additionally, +1 to any reaction rolls.

Gorman's helm is guarded by a very powerful demon that is disguised as an imp. The demon will only attack those trying to retrieve the helm.

AC: 0, HD: 12+4, Move: 120'(40'), Attacks: 2 Fists/1 Breath, Damage: 2d4/2d4/*, Save As: F12, Morale:10, Alignment: Chaotic

*:Demon's breath attack deals its current HP in fire damage. Save vs. Breath for ½ damage. Remember to roll for items!

Alazar's Crystal of Sight: Up to three times per day, the user may see any place or object that they wish to observe. Images will last up to one turn. Magic Users and Elves may use Alazar's Crystal of Sight like a normal Crystal Ball. Unlike Crystal Balls, Alazar's Crystal of Sight may be used by any class, provided the user makes a successful Save vs. Magic. Non magic user/elf characters who fail this save take one point of damage in the form of a severe headache. This failed attempt counts against the three daily uses.

Encounters and Exploring the Battlefield

Not only is the Battlefield of Keres very big, it is VERY haunted! Traveling quickly across the region, adventurers are certain to have at minimum one encounter per 6-mile hex, most likely (80%) a magical anomaly. For groups more thoroughly exploring the battlefield on a hex-by-hex basis, it's recommended to subdivide the hex into 1-mile hexes, with a 1-in-6 chance of an encounter per mile.

1: Bandits/Rival Treasure Hunters
2: Wights*
3: Wraiths*
4: Skeletons*
5: Herd Animals
6: Bears
7: Large Cats
8: Mule
9: Snake, Viper
10: Snake, Rattler
11: Wolves
12: Dire Wolves
13: Adventurers/Travelers
14: Demon**
15-20: Magical Anomalies***

*:Encounters with undead haunts will typically indicate a region of the battlefield where fighting was fierce. In these areas, just below the surface, digging will probably turn up innumerable skeletons along with mundane artifacts that soldiers would have had. Wraiths might indicate the presence of sorcerers who died in battle, increasing the chance of a party scavenging a magical item.

**: Demons were summoned to fight in the battle; some have become trapped, and tied to the land. Some guard treasures, while others may have been summoned to defend choke-points, defiles, river-crossings, etc. While many of these demons will be held by their commands [eg., a demon summoned to prevent crossing a bridge will kill anyone trying to cross the bridge], they may not go out of their way to pursue or harass adventurers who leave them alone. Some might try to bargain to gain their release from the battlefield, however, as likely as not, demons may wish to kill adventurers simply to alleviate their boredom.

***: See section on magical anomalies.

Magical Anomalies

Countless spells were cast during the battle, and that magical energy still permeates the land, often augmented by the deaths of many powerful magic users, the presence of demons, and magical artifacts littering the battlefield.

Some anomalies, such as the firenado that Kat and Mangos encounter, may be visible and ever-present as a reminder of the many spells that were cast. Others are like landmines, waiting to go off.

Casting Detect Magic will reveal that there are anomalies everywhere! The entire battlefield will radiate an aura of magic, making it difficult to spot distinct anomalies [50% chance, modified +5% for Wisdom bonus].

Determine the nature of an anomaly as follows:

First, roll % to determine the spell level
1-50 chance 1st level Magic User Spell
51-80 chance 2nd level Magic User Spell
81-99 chance 3rd level Magic User Spell
00: Roll 1d6+1 to determine level Magic User Spell

Then, roll on the spell chart for the level to determine the effect. Treat the caster-level as MU 6.

Many anomalies will produce ongoing phenomena; eg. a fireball manifests as a perpetual firenado, light/darkness will appear as globes of light/shadow, etc. Others will act like traps, sprung by those close enough to trigger them; Detect Magic will cause elves and magic items the party possesses to glow, Wizard Lock would place a magic lock on all of the party's boxes and latched items, Read Magic would cause a Magic User's scrolls to spontaneous cast at random, etc.

Brandy & Dye

Brandy & Dye is a much smaller-scale adventure than the Battlefield of Keres, but it's still ripe for adaptation!

AT THE GAMING TABLE

The recommended approach would be to draw a series of circles to represent the holmens with lines connecting them to represent the bridges. Make sure that at least a couple of the holmens are connected to the edges of the valley! Also, make note of where the ice sheet and Devil's Arse are located, in case anyone wants to try Mangos's gambit of creating an avalanche.

The adventure hook would be more or less the job that Kat and Mangos are hired for: the dyers are at odds with the distillers over use of the holmens to collect the resources necessary for their trades, poop and berries respectively.

The "Royal Reward" is, of course, the royal dye made from the guano of the Minix bird. 1 bottle is worth 1000 gp.

Adventurers will have opportunities to negotiate and fight in order to resolve the situation.

The first group of distillers consists of Lijas and two companions. Lijas has a crossbow, while the others have a club and a spear.

The distillers and dyers are all Normal Men, however they tend to be hardy due to their trade, with higher than average HP and better than normal Morale:

AC: 9, HP 4 (1d4+1), Move 120'(40'), Attacks 1, Damage: By Weapon, No. Appearing: 2d4-1, Save As: F1, Morale: 8

The men on the holmens are gathered in groups of 2-3, with between 0-2 groups per holmen. They are armed with spears, clubs, and bows.

The rope bridges that connect the holmens are very dangerous. Falling from a bridge would be certain death.

Anyone can try to shake groups and individuals off the bridge. Individuals standing on the bridge may make a strength check at +2 to hold on. Individuals moving across the bridge while it is shaken must make a dex check to grab hold of the bridge while keeping their footing THEN a strength check to hold on. Treat workers as having Strength and Dexterity of 12. The person attempting to shake the bridge must also make a strength check at +4 to not fall while shaking the bridge. It's risky for ANYONE on the bridge! Shaking the bridge takes one full round to build enough swing momentum to force saving throws, but once the bridge is swinging, the person can continue to swing the bridge for as long as they're able to hold on.

Additionally, you can cut the ropes on any bridge, taking one full round per rope. This, of course, will risk any rewards for dealing with the situation, as it's VERY difficult to repair the bridges.

Sword of the Mongoose

Again, this story is much smaller scale than Battlefield of Keres, or even Brand & Dye, but it offers an excellent adventure hook: a necromancer is hanging out at an inn, using rumors of treasure to lure adventurers to their death and into his service as undead.

Not long after adventurers set forth in search of the Marin Sword, rival adventurers will be in pursuit as well. Use your discretion in creating rival parties, but they will primarily consist of Fighters, and Thieves, though Normal Men and youths may also set forth in search of treasure.

Marin Sword

While Marin Swords are non-magical, they are master works and nearly as valuable as +1 swords. Treat as +1 and silver; can hit etherial undead, vampires, and werewolves, etc.

Jalani and Celzez

Jalani and Celzez are refugees-turned-merchants, having appropriated a cart of wares. They have very little coin on them, however if adventurers wish to purchase mundane non-weapon items from them, they may so at book-price.

Revenants

These zombie-like undead are under the control of Isak Yan; they will not

349

attack unless provoked, but rather will try to funnel adventurers to Isak Yan's tower.

AC:8, HD 3+1, Move: 90'(30'), Attacks: 1, Damage: 1d8 or by Weapon, No. Appearing: 2-8, Save As: F2, Morale: 12, Alignment: Chaotic.

Isak Yan

Isak Yan is a necromancer posing as a merchant, using stories of the Marin sword to lure adventurers into his trap, where he will perform hideous necromantic experiments on them [and probably turn them into revenants!]. He is a 5th Level Magic User, and knows the following spells: *Charm Person, Dark, Protection from Good, Continual Dark, Locate Object.*

AC:9, HP: 11, Move: 120'(40'), Attacks 1: Damage: 1d4+1*, Alignment: Chaotic

Isak Yan possesses a magic black dagger. The dagger is +1. Individuals killed by the dagger may be brought back as revenants. Additionally, the dagger has a single charge shattering spell that will destroy any one weapon [only magic weapons are allowed a saving throw]; upon using the shattering spell, however, the dagger will also be destroyed.

The Valley of Terzol

The hook here would be the same as, or similar to, what brings Kat and Mangos to Terzol: Andor the merchant [or a similar fellow] has some treasure he wishes to retrieve from the ruins of Terzol—and possesses a "receipt" for goods yet uncollected after all this time! He claims to be an adventure himself and is willing to hire the party as escorts to retrieve the treasure, for which he will pay well.

The jungles are dense and treacherous, filled with snakes, biting fish, crocodiles, and even Terzoli remnants!

Venomous Snakes

AC: 6, HD: 2*, Move: 90'(30'), Attacks: 1 Bite, Damage: 1d4 + poison, No. Appearing: 1-8, Save As: F1, Morale: 7, Alignment: Neutral

Non-Venomous (Constrictor Snakes)

AC: 6, HD 3*, Move: 90'(30'), Attacks: 1 Bite / 1 Squeeze, Damage: 1d4/2d8, No Appearing: 1-3, Save As: F3, Morale: 8, Alignment: Neutral

Biting Fish

These will attack anyone foolish enough to get into any of the rivers and streams of the Terzoli jungles, sometimes even leaping out of the water to attack adventurers crossing bridges.

AC: 2 (very small), HP: 1, Move 160'(50') (swimming), Attacks: 1 Bite, Damage: 1 per round*, No. Appearing: 8d8

Fish that bite will latch on and continue to do damage each round they remain attached to their victim. Attempts to knock off biting fish are against AC 9.

Crocodiles

Crocodiles in the Terzoli jungles come in two sizes:

Normal: AC: 5, HD: 2, Move: 90'(30'), Attacks: 1 Bite, Damage: 1d8. No. Appearing: 1d8, Save As: F1, Morale: 7, Alignment: Neutral

Large: AC: 3, HD: 6, Move: 90'(30'), Attacks: 1 Bite, Damage: 2d8, No. Appearing: 1d4, Save As: F3, Morale: 7, Alignment: Neutral

Terzoli Remnants

The Terzoli jungles are still inhabited by the descendants of the people who once inhabited the mighty cities of Terzol, though they live in a regressed and decadent state of savagery. These people live in the some of the stone ruins in the jungle on the outskirts of the larger ruined cities in Terzol. Some may wear random pieces of ancient Terzoli armor as symbols of status, but are typically equipped only with primitive weapons, particularly favoring blow guns.

Large groups of Terzoli (10+) will be accompanied by a leader wearing bits of ancient Terzoli armor. Very large groups of Terzoli (30+) may be accompanied by a War Chief wearing a piecemeal suit of Terzoli armor, possibly with a metal Terzoli weapon, and one leader for every 20 warriors.

Warriors:
AC: 8, HD: 1+1, Move: 120'(40'), Attacks: 1, Damage: By Weapon, No. Appearing:4-32 (40-320), Save As: F1, Morale: 8, Alignment: Neutral

Leader:
AC: 7, HD: 2+2, Move 120'(40'), Attacks: 1, Damage: By Weapon, Save As: F2, Morale: 9, Alignment: Neutral

War Chief:
AC: 5, HD 4+2, Move 90'(30'), Attacks: 1, Damage: By Weapon, Save As: F5, Morale 10, Alignment: Neutral

Terzoli Remnants primarily fight with spears (1d6), and blowguns (1d2 + poison). War Chiefs may have Terzoli swords or axes (1d8).
Between one War Chief and one Leader or 6 Leaders, one could assemble a "full" set of ancient Terzoli armor that would be AC 4 [equivalent of Plate -1]. While not particularly good for protection, certain antiquarians would pay 10x book price for a set.

The Hand of Bursa

Your contract has stolen from the Bursa, a powerful crime lord, and while the Bursa and his underlings may not care about the specifics of what was stolen, Andor must be killed as a matter of principle. The Hand of the Bursa is an expertly trained assassin, and will kill Andor (or whomever hired the party) at any opportunity. This is an easy task as Andor has the stats of a Normal Man. The Hand only cares about the job and will not bother the party beyond killing their mark. However, if players choose to fight the Hand, they will face:

AC:4, HD:5**, Move:120'(40'), Attacks: 1, Damage: 1d6 or By Weapon*, Save As: T5, Morale 10, Alignment: Chaotic, Treasure Type: U + V

*The Hand of the Bursa has the Thief class's special attack when striking unnoticed, granting him +4 to hit and doubling the amount of damage

352

rolled. Additionally, the Hand has the skills of a 6th level Thief.

One additional assassin with stats the same as The Hand but with 4 Hit Dice rather than 5 will appear for every 3 party members (not counting non-levelled NPCs). Despite having Morale of 10, the Hand and any assassins are only here to kill Andor and retreat if it looks like the party stands a reasonable chance against them.

Giant Snake

Hidden in recesses within the ruins of the Terzoli cities are enormous snakes…

AC: 6, HD 6+2*, Move: 90'(30'), Attacks: 1 bite/1 squeeze, Damage: 2d4, 2d8, Save As: F4, Morale: 8, Alignment: Neutral

The Burning Fish

Don't get us wrong, we LOVE The Burning Fish, but it's much more of a "cozy" story, a mystery for the players to work out, than a proper TTRPG "adventure". So while we think it's a fine story to run at your table, you don't need us to give you any stats to do so. All you need is the story itself!

The Golden Pearl

Marumbi

Marumbi has monopolized Killanei's Elibli fruit for many years. The fruit has made him incredibly hearty for his age, and at 80 years old, he is still a strong fighter. While he is cunning enough to keep his fellow islanders from ever gaining any advantage, he's a disagreeable brute who mostly gets by on intimidation.

Fighter 4, STR: 15, Wis: 13, Con: 18, Dex: 13, Int: 8, Cha: 7
HP: 30, AC 8, Move 120'(40'), Attacks 1, Damage (by weapon, spear: 1d6+1, knife: 1d4+1), Alignment: Chaotic

Golden Pearl

While not especially rare around the one particular island where they are found, Golden Pearls occur no more frequently than regular pearls and so take a good deal of work to acquire. [Any 10 x 10 square of oyster bed has a 5% chance of having a pearl oyster; one bushel bucket of oysters harvested has a 1% chance of containing a Golden Pearl if the bed is not being systematically cleared.] It is even more difficult to hold onto a Golden Pearl, since the natives of the island will almost certainly poison anyone who finds one, forcing them to use it.

When swallowed, a Golden Pearl will completely negate any mundane poison. If a character affected by a magical poison swallows a Golden Pearl, they automatically succeed at the saving throw vs. poison.

Giant Pearls

Certain giant oysters are far more likely to contain Golden Pearls. If a 10x10 square of oysterbed has a pearl oyster, there is a 10% chance that pearl is inside a giant oyster. These oysters will always have either a giant pearl (75% chance) or multiple smaller pearls (25% 1d6).

Giant Pearls are priceless treasures. A small shaving from a Giant Pearl has the same effect as a regular Golden Pearl. Additionally, any poisons coming into contact with the pearl will be completely neutralized.

Killanei

Killanei is dryad-like tree spirit who appears as a woman with large eyes, long hair, and wearing a leaf-green dress with yellow-orange flowers. She is bound to her island grotto and cannot leave. The locals attempt to win her favor so that she will grant them an Elibli fruit, only one of which grows a year and, even then, only when Killanei wills it.

AC 5, HD 2**, Move 120'(40'), Save As: E4, Morale 6, Treasure: Special, Int 14, Alignment: Neutral

Elibli fruit

The Elibli fruit which Killanei grants as a boon to one individual who finds her favor must be consumed immediately as it cannot survive a trip off the island. The cumulative effects of consuming Elibli fruit can be tremendous.

Consuming an Elibli fruit has the following effects:

-All hit points restored

-All poisons, diseases, and non-magical status ailments cured

-Constitution raised by 1/10 of one point

-Character suffers no adverse affects of aging for one year

The Battle in the Loop

Kat's Forces

While Mangos was spending his wealth on wine, women, and fancy antique weaponry, Kat was investing her treasure with the intention of raising and equipping an army.

The core of this force are the handful of elite *Fedai* and heavy spearmen who act as the center. The rest of her forces consists of the Alnessi remnants. Though loyal, and often veterans, their ranks have been thinned heavily by attrition and lack of supplies. While unable to withstand a prolonged pitched battle, these troops are integral in closing the noose around Rhygir's advancing forces.

Fedai: 50

AC: 3 [plate], HD: 1+1, Move: 6", Attacks: 1(Pike, Short Sword), Damage: 1d6, Morale: 10

Footmen, Pike: 1000

AC: 4 [Splint[1]], HD: 1, Move: 6", Attacks: 1 (Pike, Short Sword), Damage: 1d6, Morale: 8

Footmen, Heavy: 2000

AC: 4 [Chain + Shield], HD: 1, Move: 9", Attacks: 1 (Spear, Short Sword), Damage: 1d6, Morale: 8

Footmen, Light: 1000

AC: 6 [ring + shield[2]], HD: 1, Move: 9", Attacks: 1 (Javelin/Short Sword/Hand Axe), Damage: 1d6, Morale: 7

---

[1] *Optionally treat as Plate -1 if using AC 9 base*

[2] *Optionally treat as Leather + Shield if using AC 9 base*

Rabble: 500
AC: 8 [leather[3]], HD: 1, Move: 12", Attacks: 1 (sling, Club, Improvised 2-Handed), Damage: 1d4/1d6, Morale: 6

Kat

Kat's Dragon steel armor is ultralight plate of exquisite quality. While it grants Armor Bonus equivalent to Plate +2, Kat's movement is 9" as though she were wearing Leather armor. Due to its lightness and flexibility, her dragon steel armor allows Kat her full Dexterity bonus to AC and is not subject to class armor restrictions, however she may not use her Thief skills or backstab while wearing it. Kat has the skills of an 8th level Thief. Kat has a magical limiter placed on her CHA stat (14); treat as CHA 17 with the limiter removed; treat as CHA 18 for Alnessi troop morale rolls.

AC: -2 [Plate +2 + Shield + Dex(2)], HP: 22, Move: 9", Attacks: 1, Damage: 1d8

Mangos

Mangos has matured significantly during his years adventuring with Kat, though soldiering is very new to him. He is very strong and swift, but his skills as a swashbuckler may not translate to fighting on the line. He'll give it his all for Kat and Alness, however. Mangos has the skills of an 8th Level Fighting Man and wields a Marin sword of exception quality (+1).

AC: 2 [Chain + Shield + Dex(1)], HP: 53, Move: 9", Attacks: 1, Damage: 1d8+3

Rhygir's Forces:

Alness, having been thoroughly sacked, provides no domain income beyond what is able to sustain Rhygir's remaining occupying troops.[4] Due to lack of forage, Rhygir is unable to field any mounted troops, however, Rhygir's forces significantly outnumber Kat's. Rhygir's troops are invigorated by the victories over Karn's rebels, but they have grown fat

---

[3] *Optionally treat as Leather -1 if using AC 9 base*
[4] *Rhygir holds onto tremendous amounts of looted wealth (Type H), however, no new wealth (or much food, for that matter) is being generated by the city-state.*

and restive after three years of occupation and despoiling Alness.

Footmen, Heavy: 4000
AC: 4 [Chain + Shield], HD: 1, Move: 9", Attacks: 1 (Spear, Short Sword), Damage: 1d6, Morale: 8

Footmen, Light: 2500
AC: 6 [ring + shield[5]], HD: 1, Move: 9", Attacks: 1 (Javelin/Short Sword/Hand Axe), Damage: 1d6, Morale: 7

Rhygir

Rhygir is a fierce and brutal warrior. He has led his mercenaries to victory over the royal Alnessi forces and spent the last few years resting on his laurels, brutalizing the occupied city and squashing any resistance. Rhygir is an exceptionally strong and hardy 9th Level Fighting Man. He goes into battle with heavy armor. Though most of the horses have been slaughtered for food, as the warlord of the north, Rhygir still maintains a personal mount that he may use in combat. He will use dirty tactics at any opportunity in hand-to-hand. His armor is of masterwork quality silvecite plate (+2). Due to its lightness, silvecite plate only reduces movement to 9" rather than the 6" of normal plate.

AC:0, HP: 49, Move: 9", Attacks: 1, Damage: 1d8+2, Alignment: Chaotic

Teriz

Teriz was once one of the Kingsfishers, the elite royal Alnessi guard, before he betrayed the king to Rhygir. Teriz is a very large, strong, and hardy 8th Level Fighting Man who now serves as Rhygir's second in command. His white Kingsfisher armor counts as exceptional Splint +2 or Plate +1.

AC:1, HP: 52, Move 6", Attacks 1, Damage: 1d8+2, Alignment: Chaotic

Bardor's Fedai

Bardor's *Fedai* are a wildcard. In Trapped in the Loop, they are able to completely turn the tide of battle, allowing Rhygir to snatch victory from

---

[5] *Optionally treat as Leather + Shield if using AC 9 base*

the jaws of defeat. On their own, they could likely defeat either or both forces.

Fedai: 5000
AC: 3 [plate], HD: 1+1, Move: 6", Attacks: 1(Spear, Short Sword), Damage: 1d6, Morale: 9

Just Another Crappy Story That Kills Everybody In It

I'm not the hero of the story; I don't have the attributes. I'm not a nobleman's son or a street urchin. Fortune hasn't blessed me with some hidden talent or made me the subject of an ancient prophecy. I'm a guardsman.

You know the guardsmen. We're the nameless space-fillers the bad guy kills to demonstrate how nasty and dangerous he is. Our entrails figure more prominently than we do.

I work in the Fictionverse. That's the grey area between what the author imagines and what the reader reads. It's where scenes are staged and tested. In what is, for us, real life.

"Left some," said the scene manager as she looked over the throne room, comparing it to her checklist.

Bob inched to his right.

"Your other left," I whispered.

There is no good story if you're a guardsman, and this was worse than most. The script was amateurish; the story wasn't finished; most of the scenes weren't even finished. That meant once we started, anything could happen.

If I was to guess, I'd say the author was young, early teens, maybe. What existed of the story was full of old tropes clumsily assembled into the barest frame of a plot—a plot that threatened to fall apart at any twist.

Unfinished scenes, young author—just the recipe for things going in unexpected directions and very bad endings. Trust me, nobody wants to die in a stupid story.

The manager stood in the side doorway holding her arm up. "Scene starts in three, two, one." She dropped her arm and stepped out of sight.

"Go!"

The hero walked in the main doors. Oh yeah, young author. This hero was a paragon. Muscular, square-jawed—half how the author saw himself, half how he wanted to be. The Point-of-View camera rode on his shoulder, turning with every motion of his head. He focused on the king, then quickly scanned his daughters before making his bow.

"Ogling the girls," Bob muttered.

"Shut up," I whispered. "You'll intrude on the story."

Bob rolled his eyes. "Writers group will edit it out."

"Like you want that," I said. Writers groups are dodgy things sometimes, and you don't want their attention. There are stories of entire supporting casts ending up with handlebar mustaches and violet leotards because some writers group thought it gave "deeper nuances in the psychedelic troposphere."

"What do I care? I'll probably die in scene six. You'll have another Bob for re-writes." But he shut up as the hero started to speak.

"I am York, oh wise King," said the hero. "I've come to lift the curse from your daughters."

I lost the king's answer in the swarm of narrative buzz that drowned out the dialogue. A glimpse of movement by the eldest princess caught my attention. The POV camera now sat on her shoulder, pointing right at York.

Not cool. POV shifts jar everybody. Scenes are a lot more stressful when you don't know where the camera is. You can't do the little things to help the scene along, like move a fallen dagger a few inches closer to the struggling hero so he can reach it when he stretches. You just can't let that get seen through POV.

I straightened up a little now that I was in the visual background. The narrative buzz faded, and each person got to say what they wanted: the curse lifted, the curse lifted, the curse lifted. All very correct. Nobody asked me, but I would have told them I wanted to survive the story and all its rewrites. If they pushed, I might have said I wanted a bit of the happily ever after—not a lot, I'm not the hero, but enough to not be drawn out of the pool of featureless background characters until I die a pointless death in some hack's trunk story.

"That's a wrap," the manager called as a serving girl led York to his chambers to wash before dinner. Actually, she was a fairy disguised as a serving girl who would reward his virtue with tips about the princesses' curse, but it's all the same in this scene.

"King," the scene manager said, pointing to him. "Banquet hall in half an hour. Princesses—be ready to enter fashionably late. Crowd in the seats. I'll need two guards." She gave us a meaningful look.

"I am not testing the food," Bob muttered.

"The scene's a little sketchy, but I don't think you'll need to." She consulted her clipboard. "If the author writes it in though…" She didn't finish. She didn't need to. The writer's word is law, no matter how stupid or impossible. If the author writes that you'll belch polka-dotted canaries, get ready to have your tonsils tickled.

We both nodded. We knew the score.

"Hold on a moment," she said before we could leave. We waited as the crowd moved off set to where craft service was topping off the buffet. When they were out of earshot, she said, "I'm going to need your best work on this story."

"That bad?" I asked.

"Worse. The writer is basically letting the scenes run wild. We could lose York in scene five, seven, nine, ten, twelve…" She trailed off, leaving me wondering if she were exaggerating.

Still, losing the main character left us with, well, a Failed Story. That creates a black hole in the Fictionverse that sucks in all the characters and sets the story used or might have used. A Failed Story creates everything the story lacks *and destroys it*. It's the most fantastically spiteful, wasteful thing in the Fictionverse.

A shiver ran down my spine. It's one thing to die in a story; it's another to let the story kill everything it touches.

Meetings and dinners (and what is dinner but a meeting with food?) make bad scenes. Everybody is sitting around; there isn't any action. You almost *have* to poison somebody to make it interesting.

"I am not testing the food," Bob repeated as we took our places at the door.

"If the author were that dramatic, he would have written it in clearly," I said.

"Okay, you test York's wine."

The thought made me distinctly uneasy.

"Ready in five," the scene manager called. The king sat in his seat at the high table. York sat at his right. The four chairs to the king's left were empty.

The rest of the court sat at the lower tables. Fresh rushes had been strewn on the floor, and the room smelled of roast pig and fresh bread.

"Make it look good," I told Bob. "We're not just guarding York, we're guarding everybody."

"And go," the manager called.

"My thanks, your majesty," said York, "For your hospitality."

Where was the POV camera? Nowhere near York or the king.

Just as the king answered, the door to the royal wing opened, and the princesses filed out. York stood and bowed as they sat, in unison, in their own chairs.

"Booooo-ring," Bob whispered.

"And how will you free us from our curse?" the eldest princess asked once everybody was seated again. The crowd stilled, leaning forward to hear York's answer.

I panicked. York had no set dialogue, he had to make something up on the spot. The author hadn't even disclosed what the curse was. Did they turn into swans? Dance with demon princes? Spend the royal fortune on chainmail lingerie? What could he possibly say?

"In the forest is a ruined castle," York said. "In the courtyard is a well of cool water. Through long years of ruin, the well has gathered moonlight, mingling it with the sorrowful water. By taking water from the well and drinking it in the presence of the princesses, I will be able to discern the nature of their curse."

Nice!

"I see you are, Sir, something of a sorcerer," said the king.

"An old story of the wood folk, Your Majesty." He smiled at the eldest princess, "But one that may be helpful."

Just outside the door, I saw the fairy serving girl watching the scene. I knew where the idea had come from.

I tried to watch the rest of the scene, I really did. But watching people eat... eh. I resolved to go back to the script to see if the fairy girl had been named and how she was described.

She obviously had fairy blood, and I wondered if the author used the word "elfin" to describe her. Authors often use that word even though it doesn't really describe anything. And were her lavender eyes part of the script or a nice coincidence?

When the scene ended, I walked over and introduced myself. "I'm one of the guards," which, of course, she knew.

"No name?" she asked.

"We're pretty much all Bob. You?"

She shook her head.

"You gave York a great line there," I said. "How'd you manage to write that into the story?"

"Backwriting," she answered.

"What's that?"

"It's when a character takes the scene the author starts, but by carefully introducing new elements, we change or create the story.

"Authors are sometimes surprised by their characters seeming to take a life of their own," she went on. "That's what's really happening. But it has to be subtle, and it has to be good, and it has to be consistent with the character as the author sees them. If Backwriting is done wrong, the author gets disgusted and throws away the entire scene. That leaves a hole in the story and increases the chances of a Failed Story."

Risky. But she had managed it. I smiled my appreciation. "You sure solved the problem."

"I only postponed it. I didn't insert how the princesses are cursed; that would have been too blatant. Really, I just bought us time." She sighed. "This is a really bad story to have been drawn into."

"It's not going to be a pro sale, that's for sure."

Before I could say anything more the scene manager shouted, "I need a Bob!"

"That would be me," I said with a sigh. I couldn't leave York's safety to the other Bob. "I'll talk to you later."

"I'd like that," she said.

"A new scene just appeared," the manager said, checking her clipboard.

"A trip to the forest," I guessed. "And I'm going to protect him from wolves."

"Yes and no," she said. "It's a trip to the forest, but only York is mentioned."

"Oh my god, is the author *trying* to kill his main character?" I ran my fingers through my hair as I tried to think. Maybe we could use Backwriting again. "Okay, how about we act out a little scene where the eldest princess tells me to follow York and keep him safe, but not let him see me?"

She nodded her head, thinking. "That might work. The forest scene is pretty loose, you'd have plenty of latitude to act outside POV and still have it explainable."

"We'd need to keep the princess scene short, but since she's already had the POV camera, it shouldn't jar the author too much," I said.

"Unlike the rest of us," the manager said with a frown. "God, I hate the way he jumps POV. But," she went on more positively, "you're right. We do it well, and the author won't even notice. We do it badly... maybe he'll think of it as an idea he didn't use."

"That's just crazy talk," said the eldest princess when I told her the idea. "We can't really be that desperate." She looked enchanting (of course), but there was doubt and fear in her expression.

Just then, two men in FDS (Fiction Delivery Service) uniforms approached. "Is the scene manager around?" the elder of the two asked. "I got a delivery of wolves. Understand you need 'em right away."

"Wolves?" said the eldest princess in a small voice. "How many?"

"Eight. Had nine, but one's a little gimpy. Giving it the day off."

She grabbed my arm and pulled me back toward the sets. "Where do you want to have the scene? In the banquet hall, or maybe I seek you out as you're going off duty?"

Long story short, and shorter is better, in a very dramatic scene, York managed to reach the ruined castle, find the well, and return with the water. The baying of wolves heightened tension, the embers of a woodsman's fire allowed him to make a torch, and he managed to fight off three attacking grey wolves.

The fire was a good idea, thank you very much. It solved a lot of problems, and any questions about the woodsman could be answered in rewrites. No reader would be able to tell more wolves had bayed than attacked, and I could hide the bites on my hands and back with gloves and a cloak.

But what would happen when York drank the water and knew the princesses' curse? I really hoped the author would just withhold the information. We could finish this as a trunk story, and at least it wouldn't Fail.

"Who cast this curse, anyway?" Bob (the other Bob) asked as the crowd gathered in the main hall again. York waited outside for the scene to start, but we had a couple minutes as everybody found their place.

"Maybe we'll find out when we find out what it is," the fairy serving girl said with a shrug.

"Catering is serving roast boar after the scene," I said. "You want to get some?"

She smiled. "As long as we don't have to patch the plot, I'd love to."

"Where do you stand?" I asked, meaning for the scene.

"I'm not mentioned, so I have some discretion. Do you mind if I stay over here?"

"Best view in the house," I said.

Once the manager gave the "Go," I gave York a nod of recognition as he entered the hall. "You'll have to help him figure out how to break the curse," I whispered to the fairy serving girl. "That's how these stories work."

"I know," she whispered back. "Any suggestions?"

I didn't answer, for the king stood up and took York's hand.

"I see you were successful," he said.

"Yes, your majesty," York replied. "This drink will reveal your daughters' curse." A breath of wind stirred the rushes as he unscrewed the top of his flask and held it up.

A silver mist swirled out of the flask. A low moan rode the wind and was echoed by the fearful crowd. In unison, the princesses turned their heads away.

Without flinching, York swallowed the water. He shivered, nearly a convulsion, and staggered. The flask fell from his hand and clattered on the floor. I started toward him, but the fairy serving girl grabbed my arm. York braced himself, and though he swayed, he didn't fall.

He stared at the princesses for a long minute while the crowd held its breath. Finally, he blinked and looked around.

"Well, man, what did you see?" asked the king. The princesses turned back.

"On the youngest's seventeenth birthday, blight shall fall upon all your daughters. They shall neither laugh nor sing. Their sleep shall be tormented, and they shall in turn torment all around them. Nothing shall cheer them ever again."

That would be Friday. Two days from now.

The king's face turned red. "Who is responsible for this curse?"

"Gerard VanDelfin."

JUST ANOTHER CRAPPY STORY...

An inquiring whisper raced around the room, sounding like a parliament of owls. "Who?" "Who?" "Who?" Nobody could place the name.

The king's woodsman snapped his fingers in inspiration. "That old poacher? He's been hung these last sixteen years!"

"I remember now," said one of the ladies-in-waiting. "Wasn't there a rumor he had fairy blood?"

I turned to the fairy serving girl. She had gone white. "My half-brother," she whispered.

"Can you break the curse?" the king asked York.

"I—," his voice faltered. "I don't know. But," and now he sounded determined, "if I can't, I'll die trying."

"He can die at the end," Bob said. He, the fairy serving girl, and I stayed near the doors to the banquet hall while the rest of the cast gathered around the scene manager, trying to read her clipboard over her shoulder. "Tragedies aren't Failed Stories. Better him than me."

"Unless it's not at the end of the story," the fairy serving girl said. "If he dies too early, the story could stumble forward two or three more scenes until it implodes. Killing the hero has to be done *right*."

She let out her breath in an exasperated sigh. "I have never worked on a story with so many revisions between revisions," she said. "It's like he's writing it as we go. I had no idea I had a half-brother who was hung for poaching!"

"There's one in every family," I said. "I don't hold it against you."

"My half-sister was hung for poaching," Bob said.

The fairy serving girl blinked as though trying to wrap her mind around this. Evidently she failed because she said, "I hope the author's writing right now, because I have no idea how York can break that curse."

"There's hope, though," I said. "That was a pretty good twist. Maybe the writer won't need our help."

"Here we go, people!" called the scene manager. "Next scene is here! York and Bob and," she looked around until noticing the fairy serving girl next to me, "the fairy serving girl out by the Hanging Tree in the forest. The one with the ring of stones beneath it."

The cast burst out talking, none of the words distinct as they jumbled together.

"Okay, okay!" the scene manager shouted above the noise. "Yes, there

366

are continuity problems! No, I don't know how those three characters ended up together in the scene! But it's not fatal. In fact, there's a lot to like in that setting, and extensive re-writes can fill in the gaps. Except for those three, I suggest you enjoy the fantastic meal catering has set up on the castle green."

She didn't say, but I think everybody's mind added, *Because it may be your last.*

I'd never actually seen the Hanging Oak before. The scene manager was right, there was a lot to like about it. The oak was ancient; it had long outlived its seedlings and its seedlings' seedlings. Nothing grew under its expansive branches. You could hang a dozen men and have room for a dozen more.

It was full of dark shadows and strange rustlings. When my feet stirred the humus, it released a sweet, musty smell that reminded me of an open grave. Ropes hung down here and there, grey with age, the ends frayed— stems of long fallen fruit.

Beneath the oak, leaves clogged the fairy circle. Brown and withered, their season had passed, yet they clung to the quartz-flecked stones as if some of their magic would grant new life.

"Do you really use this circle?" I asked the fairy serving girl.

"Didn't you read the backstory?"

I admitted I hadn't. I usually just skim the story to see if I die, and I'd read this story even less closely when it was clear I wouldn't get an answer.

"Then, no," she said. "I'm more of a sunny meadow/mountain stream kind of fairy."

"How about you, York?" I asked. "You have experience with this?"

He gave me a look I can't describe, and he better not use it in a scene because I'm pretty sure the author couldn't describe it either. "I'm a scrivener's son. I'd rather write the hero's lines than say them."

"Take five," the scene manager called as we moved to take our places.

"Five? We haven't even started," York said.

"She's hoping for a last-minute revision," the fairy serving girl said. "Like a successful conclusion to the scene."

"I wouldn't mind knowing I'll survive," I said. I was the only Bob around and, as such, didn't fancy my chances.

We were about to commune with Gerard's spirit, and he had cursed four little girls with a lifetime of unhappiness. He seemed exactly like the sort of character who would make the story Fail if given half a chance.

We waited as the scene manager flipped pages, growing more frustrated until she finally said, "All right, let's get started."

York and the fairy serving girl entered the circle. I stood outside guarding while they lit a fire. This part was easy, and their lines weren't hard.

York sprinkled some dirt from the Potter's Field around the fire while the fairy serving girl sang a summoning charm. An angry moan stirred the rope dangling next to me.

We really need another Bob in this scene, I thought.

The base of the fire turned red. The red ran up the flames and swirled up into the night on a cloud of sparks. Green followed red, and blue followed green. Violet so dark it was almost black followed blue, and then Gerard stood in the fire, facing away from me.

I could see the sparks rising through him.

"Gerard," the fairy serving girl said.

"Fairy serving girl," he said.

The bastard! It's one thing for the author to call a character "the third guard on the right" or "fairy serving girl" but the characters can't. He's her brother and *should* have used her name. The story clunks when he doesn't.

Gerard turned to me, a smirk on his damned face. "Disposable Bob."

A ripple raced from the furthest edges of the plot through the story to converge on Gerard. It was the opposite of a stone hitting the water. The story had started to Fail.

"Gerard," York commanded. "Attend to me."

Gerard's nature forced him to turn.

"How will your curse be visited on the princesses?" York asked.

"Would that be the curse of awkward teenage boyfriends? Looking at you, I think it already came true."

The fabric of the story shivered again.

"Or," Gerard continued, "is it the curse of 8:00 am Monday morning chemistry labs?"

A larger ripple ran through the story. Anachronisms in dialogue can ruin a story on their own.

"So fresh from Hell, I'm surprised you jest," said York.

Gerard shrugged, "What is Hell but a rust belt city with falling tax revenue, aging infrastructure, and a declining job market?"

This time I felt the ripple in my bones. A second, smaller ripple followed it. There was no doubt Gerard wanted the story to Fail and that he enjoyed taunting us.

York tried to backhand Gerard; his hand passed right through. Gerard laughed.

"He's toying with us," the fairy serving girl whispered. "These little 'wrongs' against the story add up."

"Nothing you can do affects me," Gerard told York.

"Is that true?" I whispered to the fairy serving girl.

"Sort of," she whispered back. "He can affect the things involved in his death, and they can affect him. That's why we could summon him here at the Hanging Oak. As for the rest? He's beyond things of this world, yes."

"We need to do *something*." I quietly drew my sword.

Gerard saw me and laughed. "Even cold steel will pass through me."

Give me a sign, I thought at York. He was the hero, he needed to at least *look* like the idea was his.

Puzzled, York gave me a confused little shrug.

Close enough! I stretched up to grab the rope next to me and reached as high as I could to cut the longest length I could.

"What are you doing?" Gerard demanded.

I dropped my sword and in a flash had the rope around his neck. It didn't pass through.

"This is the rope that hung you," I said as I jerked him back. "It knows how to bite your neck." He made little strangling sounds. Very gratifying.

I lowered my voice so only he could hear. "York is going to ask you some questions, and you're going to answer him. If you try to sabotage the story, I'll make sure there isn't enough of your soul left to summon again. Then we'll take our chances with the curse."

He gurgled at me, and I jerked him silent. "I don't care if the author didn't write the dialogue. Make something up—but it better be good." I nodded to York.

"How will your curse strike?" he asked.

"Make it good," I reminded him as I loosened the rope enough for Gerard to speak.

"It will strike on many clawed feet," he gasped.

I tightened the rope, not enough to choke him, but enough to let him know I found his answer wanting.

"True!" he croaked. "It's true! A monster will visit each of the princesses and consume their happiness."

A monster that eats happiness? What sort of demented idea is that?

"This creature," York said, "when will it strike?"

"Early. It's been waiting."

"For what?" the fairy serving girl asked.

Oh, good God. Did we really need to know that? She was getting too drawn into the scene. Still, that was probably a good thing, it meant the story was stabilizing.

"For the youngest to reach her majority. Children's happiness is too sweet," Gerard said. Dumb answer—I twisted the rope. "Too unpredictable," he amended hastily. "It might grow back, you never know."

I let that one slide. It was at least arguable.

"And how do you kill this beast?" York asked.

"You can't kill it. It is born from pain and suffering. It feeds on only joy." I started to tighten the rope, but he rolled his eyes backed and whispered, "I'll play your game for my soul's sake, but I won't write you an easy fight."

"I lose nothing by destroying you," I reminded him.

"Except the reader's respect, and you still can't kill the monster."

I gave him a vindictive little shake. "Fine. Ask your sister to send you back. And her name better be as pretty as she is."

He didn't even struggle. "Evangeline, send me back."

The fairy serving girl started. A smile dawned on her face as she raised her hands and sang what sounded like her summoning charm backwards. A pair of flaming hands appeared from the embers, grabbed Gerard's ankles, and yanked him into the earth.

The POV camera winked out, and York sighed. "That could have gone better."

"I have a name," Evangeline said with a happy smile.

The scene manager stepped out of the forest and met us with a tired look. "There's good news and bad news," she said. "The good news is the story hasn't Failed yet. The bad news is Gerard damaged the overall arc. It's become fragile and anything less than a happy ending might finish it off."

The scene manager addressed the cast in the castle courtyard. York, Bob, Evangeline, and I stood in the back of the crowd. Evie hadn't gotten over her name. At least somebody was smiling.

"Penultimate scene," the stage manager said. "Big fight. Bobs will die."

"Did she say 'Bobs,' as in more than one?" Bob asked.

"Listen, please," she said before anyone could reply. "We're not out of the woods, so I need everybody's best efforts. It looks like the monster is overwritten by, well, by quite a bit. It won't be easy to kill."

"But we will kill it, right?" York asked.

"That's the hope." Maybe Gerard's information was unreliable.

"Can't this author write one complete scene?" complained the king. "Just one? This story should never have made it to the Fictionverse."

"But it did, and here we are, so places everyone," said the scene manager.

Another half-dozen Bobs joined us as we filed into the castle, all of us kitted out with chainmail and short swords.

"I hear there's a new zombie book being written in Nebraska," said one of the new Bobs. I couldn't tell if this were optimism or fatalism. The Fictionverse isn't above raiding its own graveyards for mindless dead, so technically being killed might not be the end of you.

But, really, it was.

"I do not like the look of this," Bob (the first Bob) muttered. And he shouldn't. More Bobs don't increase your chances of living; it only increases the number of dead guardsmen.

We put the princesses into their chamber. Evie stayed with them. All the Bobs took up position outside the door while York started the scene off-camera.

I took a minute to shake the other guards' hands. According to the script, we all stood at attention until the monster crept in and attacked. Only then could we fight, and the sounds of conflict would alert York.

And that's where the script ended.

We took our positons and waited. And waited. I had no idea where the POV camera was, nor did I know how long the phrase, "and the night dragged on" lasted.

Sometime later, there came the click-click-click of many claws on stone and the smell of wild animals. Nobody moved, nobody looked.

"It's behind me, isn't it?" whispered one of the Bobs.

What can you say? It's in the script.

There was a pause, the sound of sniffing, and a horrible scream. Finally, we could move.

The beast was—well—it was some idiot's *pet* dolled up with fangs and long claws. It was a five-year-old's idea to use their golden retriever as some terrible monster. Glowing eyes, huge claws, spiked tail, and fuzzy, floppy ears—it had them all.

It attacked the next Bob, biting at his side and tearing. Blood and chain links sprayed up, slowing down to catch the torchlight so they glistened and sparkled—graceful and elegant.

The POV camera zipped in, slowed, and orbited the cascade of blood and metal.

This isn't a movie, I thought, caught in dramatic slow motion. *The author can't even write a decent scene, and he's already fantasizing about how it will look on video.* Chainmail doesn't even come apart like that.

Thankfully, time sped back up, and Bob could fulfill the destiny of a Bob without a twenty-minute scream. The links went clink, Bob went thud, and the hallway degenerated into confusion.

York leapt into the fray, chopping at the beast. His sword bounced off. He grabbed a torch and thrust it into the creature's mouth. It bit off the end and spat it out.

The beast slashed one of the Bobs with its tail, leaving long, smoking gashes across his face. It shook off another Bob that tried to tackle it and shredded the man with its claws.

I poked at it, trying to find a soft spot; although it looked adorable in a terrifying sort of way, it didn't have any.

It lifted its head and saw York standing in front of the princesses' door. Ignoring the attacks of the Bobs, it leapt. York fell back against the door, trying to keep it away from him. Its teeth got closer and closer.

I barreled into it, knocking it away. The door opened, York fell into the room, and the door slammed shut.

I got back up and faced the beast. Maybe York and Evie could come up with something. All I could do was buy time and die like a Bob.

The door opened, a hand grabbed the back of my collar and dragged me into the room. The door slammed again.

"There's no way I'm leaving you to face that thing," Evie said.

Could she do that? The POV camera was up in the rafters, and she obviously could because the story hadn't imploded.

The door shuddered as the beast hit it. One of the panels cracked.

"Maybe you should let it curse us," the eldest princess said. "Better that than..."

York dying? But them being cursed was an unhappy ending, and according to the scene manager, the story would Fail.

"No," York said. "We can't do that." He hefted his utterly useless sword.

"You're a scrivener's son," I whispered. "Backwrite!"

He blinked as if he hadn't thought of it. The beast hit the door again, and splinters flew. "What if the author rejects it?"

"This author isn't in a position to reject any help he gets!"

York swallowed and nodded. "What shall I do?"

"Gerard said it eats only joy, feed it something else!"

"What?"

The POV camera started to come down from the ceiling. "Think of something," I whispered just before it settled on his shoulder. He was the hero; it was his show now.

The beast hit the door again.

York turned to Evie. "Draw the sorrow out of this room into a ball."

She looked aghast. "I'm not sure I can."

"If the beast can draw out happiness, you can draw out sorrow," York said.

The beast hit the door again. The crack in the panel widened enough to see the glow from its eyes.

Evie gave a little 'well, it can't hurt' shrug and began an elaborate chant/dance routine so ridiculous I had to smile in spite of the impending death breaking down the door.

A dark fog gathered in her hand, and my spirits lifted further. It was working! She passed the ball to York, who couldn't suppress a smile of his own. He faced the door.

This time the panel burst when the beast hit it. The beast thrust its mouth into the room, snarling and snapping. York slammed the ball of sorrow between its teeth. I leapt forward to seize its muzzle and hold it closed.

It tore itself free, but not before swallowing the sorrow. It backed up, shaking its head, whimpering. Tail curled underneath it, it turned, unsteadily, and vanished down the hallway.

"It won't be back," York said. "That left a bad taste in its mouth."

"And cut!" called the scene manager.

Everybody burst out in relieved laughter. We had done it. Only one scene left, and that was a short one.

"Into the throne room," she said. "Let's wrap this up before any more revisions land."

The princesses hiked up their dresses and ran. Shouts summoned the rest of the cast, and excited, relieved people filled the hall. The king took his throne, York stood before him, the princesses smiled to show there was no curse.

A narrative buzz filled the room, but nobody minded. The story was finally coming to a successful close.

"Hold it! We have revisions!" the scene manager shouted. Everybody froze. I felt a knot of ice water in my stomach. She held her clipboard up to catch the torchlight.

"And with no more sorrow," she read, "they had no choice but to live happily ever after; after York and his bride, the happiest of them all were Evangeline and Robert." She looked up. "Robert? Who's Robert?"

"That would be me," I said with sudden realization. As Evie and I took each other's hands, I added, "You know, the story was a little rough, but there might be hope for the author."

Made in the USA
Monee, IL
31 March 2025

14745032R10217